RENNO—The great Senecan Sachem now a warrior in full manhood, never will he fight more bravely and win more scalps, but he is destined for a life-and-death battle against a dark force—born of evil and harbinger of death.

BETH—Fiery-haired and passionate, she will be called to foresake her heritage for her heart and face the ultimate test of her courage in Renno's arms.

HODANO—Twisted in spirit and flesh, this shaman with a serpent's tongue allied himself with darkness and vowed to destroy one man: the White Indian.

BILLY THE PEQUOT—Stouthearted and intrepid, the sea called him to the whale-road and to Renno's side through the storms of nature and man.

COLONEL BURNHOUSE—Ambitious and arrogant, he admired Renno's prowess in battle, but underestimated the value of honor and an Indian's sacred word.

TOSHABE—Regal and solitary, Renno's widowed mother must hel............................. even as she faces

D0013035

The White Indian Series
Ask your bookseller for the books you have missed.

The White Indian Series
Book XV

SPIRIT KNIFE

Donald Clayton Porter

Created by the producers of
**Wagons West, Children of the
Lion, Stagecoach,** and
Winning the West.

Book Creations Inc., Canaan, NY · Lyle Kenyon Engel, Founder

BANTAM BOOKS
TORONTO · NEW YORK · LONDON · SYDNEY · AUCKLAND

SPIRIT KNIFE

*A Bantam Book / published by arrangement with
Book Creations, Inc.*

PRINTING HISTORY

Bantam edition / February 1988

*Produced by Book Creations, Inc.
Founder: Lyle Kenyon Engel.*

ISBN 0-553-27161-X

Published simultaneously in the United States and Canada

Bantam Books are published by Bantam Books, a division of Bantam Doubleday
Dell Publishing Group, Inc. Its trademark, consisting of the words "Bantam
Books" and the portrayal of a rooster, is Registered in U.S. Patent and
Trademark Office and in other countries. Marca Registrada. Bantam Books,
666 Fifth Avenue, New York, New York 10103.

PRINTED IN THE UNITED STATES OF AMERICA

0 9 8 7 6 5 4 3 2 1

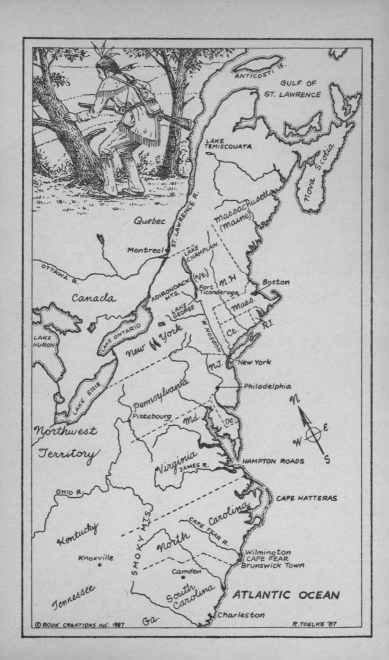

ANTICOSTI IS.
GULF OF ST. LAWRENCE
LAKE TEMISCOUATA
Nova Scotia
Quebec
ST. LAWRENCE R.
Montreal
LAKE CHAMPLAIN
Massachusetts (Maine)
OTTAWA R.
Canada
ADIRONDACK MTS.
(Vt.)
Fort Ticonderoga
N.H.
Boston
LAKE GEORGE
Mass.
LAKE ONTARIO
New York
HUDSON R.
Ct.
R.I.
LAKE HURON
LAKE ERIE
N.J.
New York
Northwest Territory
Pennsylvania
Pittsburg
Philadelphia
Md.
De.
OHIO R.
Virginia
JAMES R.
HAMPTON ROADS
CAPE HATTERAS
North Carolina
CAPE FEAR R.
Kentucky
Knoxville
SMOKY MTS.
North
Camden
Wilmington
CAPE FEAR
Brunswick Town
Tennessee
South Carolina
ATLANTIC OCEAN
Ga.
Charleston
© BOOK CREATIONS INC. 1987
R. TOELKE '87

N E W S

Prologue

~~~~~~

The dark magic is strong in the time of cold, for it is then that the evil one holds sway, stilling the earth itself with his iron chill. It is then that the force of life is weakest and most fragile.

In that time of cold when darkness predominates, when evil resounds in the night on the voices of wolves and even the evergreens moan, their limbs creaking under their burden of snow, a fire burned low in a round-topped Seneca-style longhouse in the depths of a forest, where the rays of the weak winter sun could not penetrate.

On stakes around the longhouse stark white skulls gleamed—the skull of a wolverine at the entrance, then the skulls of deer, a wolf, and, in direct contradiction to every belief of the Seneca, the skull of a man.

From within, unheard save by one chilled and hungry owl, came a scream of ultimate pain. The owl, startled, hooted once and, stirring a flurry of dry snow, took wing.

A voice chanted in a low, guttural growl, rose into louder malevolent tones, and ended with a shrill falsetto shriek.

Inside the longhouse dry wood was added to the fire. As the flames leaped high, there came another scream of agony from the young man who was tied to a strong stake. He was being burned to death. The one who had captured this lone hunter for his own dark magic purposes was greatly displeased by the young man's refusal to accept his fate with dignity.

In the shadows cast by the flickering fire, the shaman's face could not be seen, for it was hidden under a mask fashioned from wolverine fur. Even though it was cold in the longhouse, he wore only the mask and a breechclout. His torso gleamed with strange, ugly markings in vivid colors. His voice growled in a chant, and his one good eye seemed to see through the roof of the longhouse and into the dark heavens as he called upon the forces of evil.

Soon it would be time. He danced stiffly around the dying man, his own spirit reaching out to absorb the tortured spirit of his victim.

The shaman's voice was now a sharp rasping sound. He sprinkled dark powders in a circle, enclosing the two spirits . . . with something else inside the circle. He could feel the victim's powers fading and poised himself to seize them. Then, with one final scream, the young warrior died and there was a convulsive leap by the open-mouthed masked figure, then stillness.

The shaman was saddened—not because of the final result but because, in this time when all was in a state of change, the warrior had died so badly. In the past a captured warrior would have stoically endured his pain in this ultimate test of courage. Now courage was dead; the white man already ruled vast areas and, the shaman knew, would rule even more.

For many reasons the shaman, born Seneca, claimed no kinship with that tribe or with any man, for he had linked himself with the forces spoken about only in whispers and always with dread. Outcast for his horribly scarred face, he had found his place by advancing when most men fled, seeking the link that would, he hoped, be completed that night.

He danced with the strength of two spirits in the blackness, the force of the dead man in him. He halted to push back the wolverine mask, revealing a face of horror and a dead, white, staring eye.

"It is time, great one," he whispered.

He had prepared the special block of wood, had polished it with fire, and had smoothed it lovingly. The knife had been honed to a razor's sharpness.

He lifted the wooden block, extended his red tongue to lie atop the block, and then, by feel, positioned the sharp blade and with one quick motion sliced his tongue down the middle. His face did not move. There was not so much as a sigh of pain. Drops of blood flowed to sizzle in the fire, and the smoke that rose reeked of something not human.

The rest was delicate. He used thread made of gut and a needle made by the white man to stitch the sliced tongue and slow the flow of blood. Still there was no show of pain or weakness. He cast a contemptuous glance at the slumped, blackened corpse of the warrior.

He could not understand his own words, but he knew his thoughts. *Now, great spirit of darkness, I speak with your tongue. Now I praise you with two tongues, the tongue of the serpent.*

He sat gazing into the dying embers, letting his spirit continue to devour the spirit of the dead one, to merge with it absolutely. His one eye seemed to glaze. His body stiffened, and he suddenly felt an unnatural chill. His skin crawled in waves.

He was rewarded! He heard no words nor, at that time, did he fully understand. He saw events of the past sweep by, then a hint of future greatness. His heart soared! He saw himself, exalted and honored, before sachems . . . and then a terrible anger overcame him, for he saw his greatness threatened. He intensified his concentration, swallowed the blood seeping from his split tongue, and cried out, begging for clarification, for a warning of the obstacles to his future ambitions.

For a moment he saw them clearly: a tall warrior, dressed as a Seneca but with blue eyes and a pale, sun-browned face. At his side was a woman.

The shaman cried out, a roar of protest, and the vision faded, but the pale face would remain etched in his memory. Although he knew somehow that it would be a long time before the confrontation came, he promised himself and his guiding spirits that he would be ready.

In time the tongue would heal. In time he would forget the woman's face, for it had not been clear to him. But he would not forget the blue eyes and the pale, white skin of the warrior. The face would become the symbol of his hatred for everything that had happened to him.

Chapter I

Ah-wen-ga was dead. The spirit of death had called her name softly, but still it was heard over the gusting sighs of a frigid northwest wind and the gritty pepperings of sleet. There at her side in the lodge of her second husband, Loramas, grand sachem of the Cherokee, were two generations of her issue. She died peacefully, after having allowed herself one last look and lingering caress of her great-grandson, Little Hawk.

Toshabe, Ah-wen-ga's daughter-in-law, began the ritual Seneca chant for the dead. Her voice was low, throaty, and mournful. In her maturity Toshabe was a striking woman. Her French and Erie blood had combined in her the best features of both races. The tears that crept to wet her long, black eyelashes heightened the intensity of her large eyes, and the grief—for herself and her own loss, not for Ah-wen-ga—made her face all the more beautiful. Her

5

long black hair, still showing the youthful gleam of health, hung in long braids, and as she knelt by Ah-wen-ga's side, holding the frail old hand from which she had felt the vitality of life slip away, she reached out with her other arm to draw the boy Little Hawk close to her side. Then she looked up at her two strong sons, for tradition dictated that Renno, the eldest, sachem and heir to the customs and responsibilities of a long line of Seneca sachems, speak.

Renno, too, grieved for himself and his loss. He joined his mother in the chant for the departed. The ancient words that offered him comfort spoke of the journey now being undertaken by the spirit of his grandmother. He sang and thought in the Seneca language, a language quite difficult to translate into English. He was joined in the chant by his brother, El-i-chi, and his sister, Ena. Now Ah-wen-ga was traveling toward the West, the Place across the River, and he could imagine the reception she would receive on the other side.

It was a roll call of honor. Waiting for Ah-wen-ga would be Renno's grandfather, beloved first husband of the departed Ah-wen-ga, Ja-gonh of the blue eyes and blond hair, tall and distinguished. At Ja-gonh's side would be standing Ghonkaba, father of Renno, husband of Toshabe, he who had seen the future, who had broken away from the League of the Iroquois and his own tribe to ally himself with the colonists in the War for Independence. And in a place of honor, ready to welcome Ah-wen-ga to the West, would be the great Renno himself, the original white Indian—with his wife, the pale and beautiful Betsy, to his right, and his foster father, old Ghonka to his left, burly, square-shouldered, the complete measure of a Seneca warrior, with Ena, his wife, at his side.

Yes, she would be welcomed, his grandmother, and he did not grieve for her death, for she had lived a long and fruitful life and had mothered great leaders and warriors. She had earned her rest.

As he sang the mournful farewell, another level of his mind was composing an epitaph for her.

He could remember Ah-wen-ga as a younger woman, beautiful, with enormous dark eyes and lush figure. She had aged so gracefully, her hair taking on only a hint of gray, and she had retained her physical vigor to the end, when the winter fever took her and not even her strong spirit could continue the fight to live. He could remember her seated beside a campfire, telling him and others the tales of past glory, the great war, the courageous feats of Ja-gonh and Ghonkaba; how she was captured by the French when she was young, to become a mistress of their king; how Ja-gonh left the forests of his native land to venture to France to rescue her.

"You lived long and well, Grandmother," Renno said aloud.

The chanting voices became quieter as the sachem spoke. "May your journey to the West be swift and pleasant, and there may you give our respects to our ancestors. You loved and were loved, Grandmother, and your memory will inspire, lead, and guide us with the wisdom you have always displayed."

Old Loramas lifted one wrinkled hand and wiped his eyes. A sob escaped him, but there was no reproach in the minds of the two brothers, Renno and El-i-chi, nor in that of Loramas's grandson, Rusog, husband of Ena. When Loramas lifted his head and chanted a farewell to his wife in a high, strained voice, all were respectfully silent.

Outside, the wind was dying, the sleet turning to freezing rain. Ena stepped forward and scooped Little Hawk, Renno's son, into her arms. "Time for you to be in bed," she said.

"Me go West, with Grandmother Ah-wen-ga," Little Hawk piped very seriously.

"There will be a time for that, my young chief," Ena said, trying to hold back her tears. "The manitous will come for you, too, in your time, after you have fulfilled your destiny."

Now El-i-chi's voice joined that of Loramas in mourning. The sturdy young warrior's face showed the strain of recent months. *He has not yet recovered from Holani's death*, Renno was thinking as he looked at his brother.

Indeed, death had been a frequent visitor among the women of Renno's family: First El-i-chi's wife, the spirited Chickasaw girl Holani, had been killed in the dry plains in the far west—so distant from the Cherokee lands in the shadows of the blue, smoky mountains that they had been forced to bury her body in a long-dead city of the Pueblo Indians. Then death had called for Renno's wife, Emily, and he had not even been with her to sing her spirit into the white man's heaven. And now Ah-wen-ga.

So they stood, two strong young Seneca warriors, the tall sachem and his brother, equally bereaved, their stoic faces hiding the agony within their hearts, to sing the spirit of still another beloved woman to the West.

Now the women came to prepare the body and gently shooed the men from the lodge and into the icy morning. A brilliant sun burst from the smoky hills to the east and made a glistening, diamond-bright fairyland of the Cherokee-Seneca village, with its mixture of traditional lodges and newfangled log huts that many were building, complete with fireplaces so that the still, knife-sharp air was scented with the pleasant aroma of burning wood.

With a clasp of arms, the brothers parted, Renno making his way over the ice-filmed ground to his lodge. He never entered the lodge without seeing a faint, flickering presence, the image of Emily, so pale, so beautiful, her corn-silk hair lifted high to reveal the delicate curve of neck that was so dear to him. But now the lodge was empty save for spirits, and as he stirred the embers of his fire and added dry kindling, he allowed himself one deep moan of loss, a sound for all the dead.

They came from afar to honor Ah-wen-ga. Cherokee warriors who had fought under Renno's command in the joint Cherokee-Seneca efforts to safeguard their hunting

grounds paid the Seneca sachem honor and in gruff, stoic
voices offered their sympathies and their joy that a good
woman was now with her loved ones in the West.

Acting as both sachem and medicine man, Renno
participated, making the ceremony a joint one, since
Loramas was Cherokee, whereas Ah-wen-ga had been a
Seneca.

She was buried in sacred ground on a January day
when the ice had melted from the straining limbs of the
trees and a pleasant hint of warmth had moved in behind
the storm. But the thaw was fleeting, and village life
returned to its winter norm: young hunters brought back
freshly slain deer for roasting, and axes rang as woodpiles
were replenished. There would be more cold before it was
time to celebrate the new beginning.

Loramas came to Renno's lodge, walking in the brittle, feeble way of the very old. "I am thankful that you are
well," Renno said in greeting, offering a skin-covered seat
near the fire. Loramas, without removing his buffalo robe—it
seemed that even pure fire could not warm his aging
blood—sat with a sigh and was silent for a long time.

When Loramas spoke, his voice quavered. Renno was
a bit startled, for he had not previously noted that Loramas
was so feeble. "I will join Ah-wen-ga soon in the West."

"As the manitous will it," Renno replied gently. "But we
have need of your wisdom for a while longer, great Chief."

"No, no," Loramas said impatiently. "All things change.
Now the responsibility lies with the young and the strong—
with you and with my blood grandson Rusog, who still is
without a son."

Renno nodded. It was one of his sorrows, and a much
greater sorrow for his sister and her husband, Rusog, that
Ena was still childless.

"One was missing," old Loramas remarked.

"Yes," Renno said, nodding again, feeling a jolt of
longing, for Loramas spoke of Renno's infant daughter,

Renna. After Renna's birth Emily had died from childbed fever. The tiny girl was with her white grandparents, Roy and Nora Johnson, in Knoxville, where Renno had, in his sorrow, agreed to let her stay rather than risk a winter journey to the Indian village.

"In the last hours," Loramas said, "Ah-wen-ga spoke often of the infant."

Renno waited.

"She wished the best of two worlds for the child," Loramas continued. "She wished that the child know and honor the traditions of the Seneca, while also being educated in the ways of the white man."

"So," Renno said, simply acknowledging the statement without commitment, for he experienced considerable mental torment about his daughter.

"She spoke, toward the end, of other things," Loramas said. "She spoke of the homeland of the Seneca."

Renno rose, for that subject was always disturbing to him.

"The manitous of your people will guide you, my son, and yet it is my wish that our peoples remain as one, that you will think of these hills as your own, as well as Cherokee. I will not ask you to make that decision now, but I will pray that it is the will of the spirits for you to continue to be brother to Rusog and that Seneca and Cherokee remain one."

That, however, was the main cause of Renno's concern: whether or not to stay in the pleasant Cherokee lands and allow the smaller tribe of Seneca to become gradually integrated with the more numerous Cherokee. In spite of his white blood, Renno was not just Seneca; he was fiercely Seneca, in the tradition of his all-white great-grandfather, for whom he was named. He was constantly asking himself what the original Renno would do in this position. True, Seneca and Cherokee had common fathers, far back in the dim reaches of the past, but with

Ah-wen-ga's death came the realization that an era was ending. Ah-wen-ga had been one of the last who remembered the Seneca lands of the North, one of the few survivors of the southward trek.

"Loramas, I am half-sick with thought," Renno admitted.

The old man nodded, lifted himself laboriously, paused in the doorway to look back over his shoulder, and then was gone.

The lodge seemed to close in on Renno. He paced the narrow confines, saw the bed he had shared with Emily, the crib where Little Hawk had played, the fine cooking utensils Emily had used so well to prepare foods that were a delicious mixture of traditional Indian and white recipes. He saw the books she had brought into the lodge. And then the walls seemed to contract, and he had to breathe deeply to get enough air into his lungs. He abruptly stopped pacing and with sudden resolution began to prepare himself with weapons and warm clothing.

He thought once more of Emily as he left the lodge, remembering her fond smile and gentle acceptance of his periodic need to be alone in the forest. He stopped first at Ena and Rusog's lodge, where Little Hawk was watching Ena grind corn. Renno greeted his son with Seneca formality, using his full name, Os-sweh-ga-da-ga-ah Ne-wa-ah, his hand uplifted.

Little Hawk's eyes brightened, and he leaped to his feet to seize his bow, made specially for the little boy. *"Ge-yase naogeh,"* he said.

"One day," Renno said approvingly. "One day you will shoot your deer."

Little Hawk drew the bow and stalked the lodge, looking for deer.

"The food will be ready soon," Ena said. She saw that her brother was outfitted for the forest, and she recognized the pain in his eyes. There were prescribed ways for a warrior to show grief, but a Seneca sachem could not mourn indefinitely. Her heart went out to him, but she knew that he would not appreciate it if she voiced her sympathy. "El-i-chi left for the hunt alone," she said. "I sense that my other brother will also be leaving."

"The boy . . ." Renno said.

A stick arrow clanked against Ena's cookpot and bounced away. "Hold, warrior," Ena said with a fond smile. "The deer that stews in the pot has already been slain." She smiled up at Renno. "I will tend him."

A wall of dark clouds low in the northwest spoke of another weather change as Renno left the village at a warrior's trot, eager to put the sounds of the settlement behind him. He traveled toward the roiling, low clouds, finding that his lungs labored at first, but he soon settled into the rhythm, feeling the good, pure stretch of muscle, the youthful vigor of his body, and the increasing pounding of his heart. When he reached his pace, his heart slowed and the ground seemed to speed by of its own accord under triple-layered moccasins, fashioned for warmth and dryness.

He blanked his mind of all concerns, savoring the sweetness of being alone in the wilderness. He heard the quick scurrying of a surprised squirrel, saw the flowing grace of a fleeing red fox, and noted a solitary crow flying high, headed, as he was headed, toward the northwest.

He increased his pace, and the chill air seemed to knife cleanly into his lungs. Running had always been a catharsis for him, and he needed release from his sorrow and concerns. He ran lightly, silently, and now the distance between him and the village would have been measured in miles. He traveled to bypass Cherokee homesteads, splashing now through shallow creeks.

That night he slept, warm and snug, wrapped in a great bear-hide robe. His fire faded to embers as an early-morning snow fell in big, white, drifting flakes from a dark-gray sky that lowered to close everything in semigloom. He hunted and killed late in the day, passing up the opportunity to slay a deer, since so much of it would have gone to waste. Instead he chose a fat winter rabbit for his roasting fire. During the second night the snow came quietly, softly. He had to push himself up and shake the white covering from the bearskin when he awoke.

Although his swift pace had carried him far, he felt not alone but secure in the cold, snow-dimmed forest. He set his course toward a distant ridge, moving silently through four inches of snow. In the shelter of the ridge he gathered pine boughs for a bed, dry wood for his fire, and made his camp beneath a sheltering overhang of rock. The snow gradually obliterated his tracks. A pair of fat, sassy rabbits—not seeing him sitting motionless, wrapped in the great bearskin—frisked in the new snow. When the female spotted him, she froze, then gazed at him with huge, frightened eyes, her nose twitching. But Renno simply laughed softly and said, "Play, Sister, for I will not eat you this day."

Now, as the thicker snow made a solid blanket to hide him and absorb sound, he felt free to grieve, and grieve he did with a soft chant of loss and sadness. He felt neither hunger nor thirst. He did not sleep during that long night of mourning, and with the dawn he purged his mind of sadness and looked out on a bright new world of gleaming white, with sparkling snow crystals reflecting such dazzling points of light that he experienced one lingering moment of sheer pain, remembering how Emily had so loved freshly fallen snow.

He raised his face to the clean, blue sky. "I await," he whispered. "Guide me, spirits of my ancestors. Teach me, manitous."

Nothing stirred—not bird, not animal, not even the wind. A laden pine bough bent one more fraction of an inch, and a fall of packed snow plopped into the ground cover. Then the silence returned.

He reviewed the recent past and puzzled, once more, over the spirit message he had received after Emily's death, when he had been told in a vision: "She was of us and yet not of us, else she would still be with us." Nor could he be sure of the meaning of another spirit message: "The flame-haired one is the future."

By closing his eyes he could see the face of the Englishwoman Beth Huntington, with whom—in company with her brother and the others—he had made a long journey to the mountain of gold, beyond the Rio Grande, and back. It had been so soon after Emily's death, he could not believe that Beth was intended to be a permanent part of his future. Her role in his life was now surely over, for she had gone back to England with her brother and the Spanish woman who had become William Huntington's wife.

Indeed, he did not wish to know the future. Oh, he would have been pleased if some spirit message had reassured him that his son, Little Hawk, would one day be sachem, and that his daughter, Renna, would have a full and rewarding life, but he did not care to know what lay ahead for himself. He prayed to the manitous only for guidance, as to the proper course of action for the sake of his people.

The day passed in bright, sweet beauty, and with the night came a new and fiercer storm. Never had Renno seen such a storm. Howling winds drove snowflakes to sting his face, even far back under the rocky overhang. The winds heaped drifts high, and the new fall added to the snow already on the ground until any attempt to move would have had to be made through a knee-deep covering. The severity of the storm, the wildness of the winds, and the cold all expressed Renno's state of mind, and through a long night he continued to pray and fast. The dim light of dawn made only a token difference between night and the storm. He was startled to see and hear the flap of wings over the howl of wind. Suddenly a flash of darkness that was a young hawk landed near Renno's spitting, dancing fire. The bird's wings looked odd, and Renno realized that the hawk had lost feathers to the strong winds. The hawk's hard, clear eyes examined him, and the bird opened its cruel beak to utter one harsh cry before folding its wings to sit staring at Renno.

"Welcome, Brother," Renno said, for the hawk and the bear were the two most powerful totems of his clan. Many times in the past the appearance of a hawk had indicated that a vision was forthcoming, but now nothing happened as the storm reached a peak of fury and the young hawk shivered and became weaker and weaker before Renno's eyes.

"My brother needs food," Renno said, but he knew that it was useless to go out into the blizzard. He bundled himself into the robe, after building up the fire to provide warmth for the very ill-looking hawk, and saw the hawk's fierce, bright eyes gradually film over.

The white Indian dozed. He was brought into instant alertness by a sound half-heard, something from his sleep. Motionless, head cocked, he waited for the sound to repeat itself. It came, so faint as to be almost indistinguishable from the howl of the storm. But it was a cry, a cry for help in Seneca. Renno rose, plunged into the snow only to sink to his knees, and pushed his way against a wind so strong, he had to lean against it to make forward progress. He did not hear the cry for help again, and the blizzard limited his visibility to a few feet. The dense pine forest added to the gloom, so he almost missed seeing the source of the call for aid. A grandfather pine, hoary with age and with a trunk so large that he would not have been able to span it with his arms, had lost its battle against the elements and had crashed downward into the snow. Renno

thought about climbing atop the fallen trunk to use its
height for better visibility, but then as he stood there,
snow stinging his eyes, he saw a glint of color, a movement. The tree had pinned someone underneath it.

Renno leaped forward, only to sink into the drifted
snow, and felt the chill to midthigh. Then he was digging
furiously into the snow and managed to uncover a man's
head, then shoulders. The man's face was painted in a
manner that Renno had never seen, but the pattern was
nonetheless familiar to him. The poor fellow was Seneca.
Renno's heart beat faster as he determined that the stranger
was breathing but unconscious. He dug frantically and saw
that the man's legs were pinned under the tree. Snow,
compacted under him, resisted Renno's bare hands. He
reached for a dead, low limb protruding from the pine,
broke it away, tested it for strength, and then began to use
it as an implement to dig into the compacted snow.

It took over an hour to free the man's legs. Renno,
panting from his concentrated effort, carefully drew the
legs from under the huge, fallen tree and examined them.
One was broken badly—the white bone protruding and
blood already freezing on the torn buckskins. The skins he
wore were not the skins of animals taken in the Cherokee
lands. The stranger felt cold to the touch, so Renno reasoned that it was more important to warm him than to be
concerned with his broken leg. He lifted the man gingerly, to find that he was of less than medium weight—a
thin, rather small man, perhaps young and not yet fully
developed.

The trek through the deep snow had tired Renno, but
he moved resolutely, for the wind was dying, the day was
ending, and the air was growing colder.

The hawk perked up as Renno carried the wounded
man into the cavelike overhang. "Another wounded one,
Brother," Renno said. He eased the stranger down beside
the fire onto his own sleep skins, covered him with the

bear robe, and began massaging the man's hands and face. After some time color began to return to the stranger's face and he was breathing more evenly. Renno knew that he would need food when he recovered, and Renno himself was hungry. With one last look at the stranger, he took his Spanish stiletto and the strong English longbow that had been a gift from William Huntington and ventured out.

The snow had stopped, although low clouds still scudded swiftly overhead. The wind had died to a chill breeze from the northwest. The deep snow was unmarked by the spoor of game, and soon the night would make it impossible to hunt. The manitous were with him, however, for he heard a scrambling sound in a clump of snow-covered bushes and, when he moved closer to investigate, saw two rabbits dash out, having difficult going in the deep snow. He threw his bow over his shoulder, having no need for it. Wallowing in the deep snow, he gave chase, and within a few yards and after several attempts to dodge him, a warm, frightened animal was in his hands.

"I honor your life, Brother, as you give life to others," he said.

As he walked back toward the overhang, passing on the other side of the fallen tree from which he had rescued the Seneca, he saw the object that was going to be instrumental in another great change in his life. It was the color of the object that caught his eye in the twilight. Only the tip was exposed, but it was bright red and stood out against the whiteness of the snow. When he reached for the object, he knew at once that the injured man had been carrying a Seneca messenger stick, a notice to all tribes that he was on a peaceful and important mission. Renno tucked the stick into his sash. He had one more thing to accomplish before going back to the fire. With his stiletto— that masterpiece of workmanship taken long ago, it seemed, from a dead invader of Cherokee lands—he cut suitable splints for the man's leg.

Again beside the fire the white Indian quickly dressed the rabbit, scooped out its still-warm entrails, and tossed them, along with the head, to the hawk. The bird cried out harshly and began to tear at the warm offering with its beak. The cleaned carcass of the little animal was soon suspended on a roasting stick over the fire, and Renno busied himself with setting the Seneca's broken leg. The man started to rouse as Renno moved the leg to find a better fit for the broken bones, but then he moaned and once more fell unconscious. When the splinting was finished, the torn flesh covered by a crude bandage of cloth torn from his own clothing, Renno tried once more to rouse the messenger by massage. Failing, he tested the rabbit for doneness, found it to be just right, and ripping off a haunch, ate as he mused over the turn of events. He had received no message from the spirits . . . or had he? Was the appearance of the hawk at the height of the storm a sign? Was the messenger himself a sign?

He checked on the unconscious Seneca several times during the night, and the man seemed to be resting peacefully. The hawk also looked much better, and twice when Renno awoke to stoke the fire with branches, the bird roused itself to stare at him, eyes gleaming fiercely in the firelight.

Renno awoke with first light. There was a brightness to the morning that indicated a lack of cloud cover. The bird was arching its wings, as if testing their worthiness after having lost so many feathers. The hawk hopped to the top of the snowdrift that almost blocked the overhang, twisted its head to look at Renno with one bright eye, and with a cry, leaped into the air. Renno stepped into the cold, brittle morning and watched the hawk above him, wings beating to gain height. The bird circled, cried harshly, then zoomed down, wings outspread, to fly with strong, beating wings toward the north. Twice more the hawk came back to circle, cry out, swoop down, and then fly straight and true toward the north.

Renno went back to check on the messenger, who was breathing strongly but still could not be roused. Renno ventured into the forest and with his stiletto and tomahawk cut the raw materials to fashion a travois back at the overhang. He placed the Seneca messenger on that conveyance, lifted it by its handles, and, with two strong poles making deep tracks in the snow, leaned forward, struggling through deep snow, setting his course for home.

The messenger, jolted into awareness of pain by the movement, began groaning as midday approached. An hour or so later he spoke, and Renno set the travois down and squatted beside the messenger.

"You are among friends," the white Indian said. "You are injured but not too badly."

"Ghonkaba," the messenger whispered weakly. "You wear the paint of the Seneca. I must reach Ghonkaba."

"Ghonkaba, my father, is dead," Renno replied. "I am Renno. Your messenger stick is safe with me."

"Renno?" the messenger echoed. "The white warrior? But he is dead."

It was obvious to Renno that the messenger was hovering between awareness and blackness. "Talk no more," he advised. "Soon we will be in my village, where you will become strong again."

"Ghonkaba of the Seneca," the messenger gasped, then passed out as Renno lifted the travois poles again.

In open areas the wind had blown the snow so that it was possible to make good time; in other areas Renno had to struggle through deep drifts. He traveled on as darkness came, having the light of a half-moon to aid him. He slept for a few hours after the moon set, and was moving again with the first light. Once or twice the messenger regained consciousness, but he was delirious with fever so his words were disjointed. He spoke of a woman, of his mother, and of his home in the North, but he could not answer Renno's questions. The white Indian began to fear that the messenger would die before delivering the message intended for Ghonkaba.

He pushed himself hard during the day and into the night, and as the pale moon sank he was near enough to his village to recognize his surroundings and to travel in the darkness of the early morning hours. As false dawn came, he smelled the fires of the village, and with the rising sun he entered the outskirts, hissing to quiet barking dogs and deeply inhaling the good, fresh aroma of breakfast corn and stew.

He took the messenger directly to his mother's lodge, for she was, with the single exception of old Casno the medicine man, the best healer of his people. Toshabe was warming her morning meal.

"I thank you that you have returned, my son," she said, then, without further words, assisted Renno in removing the messenger from the travois and carrying him inside to a warm bed.

"I will get Casno," Renno said. Toshabe nodded as she began to unwrap the bandage to look at the messenger's leg.

Casno had been long awake, for he was afflicted with that disease of old men, the inability to sleep through all the long hours of winter darkness. He struggled into his robes, took up his pouch of medicines, and walked with Renno to Toshabe's lodge, where he joined her in bending over the messenger's bed.

"Eat, Renno," Toshabe told her son, "and then rest. His spirit hovers between his body and the West."

He left the messenger in the capable hands of the old man and his mother, helped himself to Toshabe's generous pot of hominy and venison stew, and ate with a hunger that made each taste sheer pleasure. Then he went to stand beside the two healers.

"He has a message for Ghonkaba," Renno said.

Toshabe looked up for a moment.

"I must know the message," he continued.

"If the manitous will that he lives, you will," Casno said with a grunt of effort as he lifted the messenger's leg to reset it. The bones jerked into place with an audible grinding sound. The messenger did not react.

Renno was so exhausted he did not even bother to build a fire in his lodge. He fell into his bed, nestled down among the warm furs and hides, and was asleep within seconds. He was awakened six hours later by a small boy bouncing onto his stomach and yelling his name. The sight of his son's face was tonic. He pulled the boy down among the coverings, tickled him until Little Hawk yelped in pleasure, and then grinned up at Ena, who apologized for being unable to keep the child away any longer.

"The messenger is still unconscious," she added, "but he has had periods of near awareness, in which he asked for Ghonkaba. Our mother says that he will live but may not be able to make sense for another day and night."

"So," Renno said, getting out of bed.

"There is food," Ena told him.

"I could eat the haunch of a very large buck all by myself," Renno said.

"Me eat whole deer," announced Little Hawk.

"You are not yet a warrior," Renno teased. "For you, you may only gnaw the bones."

"Me chief," Little Hawk said, crossing his arms and trying to look stern.

"Not yet." Ena laughed, picking the boy up by the seat of his buckskin trousers.

It was pleasant to take a meal with Ena and Rusog. The great chief of the Cherokee was Renno's brother-by-marriage, but he was more like a blood brother. As he ate he listened to Renno's description of finding the Seneca messenger in the great storm. Little Hawk wanted to know more about the hawk, his namesake, who had shared Renno's fire. They indulged the small boy and let him be the center of attention until Ena dragged him away to prepare him for bed.

"El-i-chi has not returned?" Renno asked Rusog.

"He sent back two freshly killed bucks with a hunting party. They encountered him to the west. Far," Rusog said.

"To the west?" Renno asked, his face not showing his concern. To the west were the Chickasaw. Farther west, much farther, were the Spanish, who had killed El-i-chi's wife, Holani.

"Perhaps he won't attack the whole Chickasaw nation alone," Rusog said dryly. Renno chuckled. "He will come back," Rusog added, and brought out a pipe. The aromatic tobacco smell soon filled the lodge.

Ena returned and reported that despite his protests, Little Hawk had fallen asleep immediately. She busied herself cleaning up the remains of the meal, then settled down beside Rusog and took the pipe from his hands to puff deeply. Renno, who did not smoke for pleasure, waved off Rusog's offer to share.

"Young hunters saw a pair of wolves on the eastern ridge," Ena said from behind a cloud of smoke.

"So near?" Renno asked.

"The old ones say wolves howling by day indicate change," Rusog remarked.

"The only thing that does not change is change," Renno said.

"With the new beginning," Ena said, "I will travel to Knoxville and get Renna."

"We will speak of it," Renno replied.

"My brother," Rusog said, looking serious, "Ena and

I have spoken of this. You have no wife. We have no children."

"Yes," Renno said.

"I will be the mother they have lost, my brother," Ena offered.

Renno laughed. "And will you teach my daughter to be willful, stubborn, and to fight as a man, as you do?"

Ena tossed her head. "Rusog does not complain."

Rusog chuckled. "Once I said, 'Ena, stay here and make me a new shirt,' and she said, 'I will chew the deer hide for a new shirt at night, when there is no hunting to be done.'"

"My daughter will be a gentlewoman," Renno declared, winking at Rusog, "and will not run wild in the wilderness doing man's work."

Ena, knowing that she was being teased, flashed a smile. "She has our father's blood, Brother. I think she will choose for herself."

"You are probably right," Renno said drowsily. He was, for the moment, at peace.

Chapter II

In Toshabe's lodge, made cozy by a blazing fire, Renno stood beside wise old Casno. With the morning, the Seneca messenger had opened his eyes and tried to pull himself off the bed, and Toshabe had summoned her son immediately. It was a Seneca affair and, according to the weakly spoken words of the messenger, a matter for the sachem.

"My brother," Renno said, "you have been told that my father, Ghonkaba, has traveled to the Place across the River. I am Renno, sachem. My mother, Toshabe, and Casno, our medicine man, have tended you in illness. We thank the manitous that you live, and await your message."

"Greetings to our southern brothers from the sachem Cornplanter," the messenger began, his voice gaining strength as he spoke.

The message was long, requiring much explanation, and Renno listened closely, his concern growing as the messenger spoke. The crucial point was that the Seneca sachem Cornplanter wanted to council with the chief of that segment of the tribe that had fought on the side of the colonists and later departed from their ancestral hunting grounds to join the Cherokee in the lands west of the Smoky Mountains.

His mission completed, the exhausted messenger slept while Renno, thinking moodily, was silent, as were Casno and Toshabe. It was Toshabe who spoke first. "They chose their path," she said with an edge to her words. "They chose to fight against the colonists on the side of the British, and when your father questioned their wisdom, he was cast out."

"The Seneca are not our enemies but our people," Renno reminded her. Ghonkaba had been banished with honor, but it was a bitter memory nonetheless.

"I can see, then, that you have made your decision," Toshabe said. She sighed wearily. "Go, then. Ena and I will tend Little Hawk."

Renno turned away, sorrowfully thinking that he would be away from his son for months . . . thinking, too, of his infant daughter. "And Renna?"

"That is your decision to make," Toshabe answered.

Old Casno grunted, his preface to speaking. Renno waited. "The infant has known only the close confines and the warmth of a white-man's cabin. It would not be wise to bring her here at the height of winter."

"Is she, then, to be white and weak and helpless in the life that the manitous have given us?" Toshabe asked.

"She will have your teaching," Renno said firmly.

"The spirits of our ancestors would allow nothing less," Toshabe shot back, turning away to tuck the coverings around the sleeping Seneca messenger's neck.

Communications between the Seneca village and the outlying white settlements around Knoxville were not, to say the least, swift. Upon his return from the far west,

Renno had found correspondence and pamphlets, some months old, and even in his grief he had taken the time to read the latest letter from his old friend, George Washington.

The white Indian was not ignorant of the fragile condition of the new union of American states, but because of the message from Cornplanter, he felt that he should gather more information before going into council with the northern Seneca. A detour through Knoxville would serve two purposes: He would be able to discuss events with his father-by-marriage, Roy Johnson, and he would see Renna.

He traveled light, scorning a horse. Soon, with his farewell to his son still fresh in his mind, he held his infant daughter in his arms and saw a resemblance to Emily in the tiny face and sparse, light hair. On the first evening, after a fine meal, he and Roy sat before the fireplace in Roy's tiny study and Renno spoke of the Seneca stranger.

According to the messenger, things were not good in the homeland of the Seneca. Before the coming of the white man, the Seneca, along with the other members of the League of the Ho-de-no-sau-nee—the five tribes—had ruled vast stretches of land and had achieved a lasting peace among themselves. But now, according to the messenger, the league was being punished for having fought on the side of the British. Their power had been eroded and was now broken. The once-firm union of the tribes was weak, with wholesale desertions of tribal units. Many members of the Five Nations—the Cayuga, the Onondaga, the Mohawk, the Oneida, and even the Seneca—had left their traditional homelands to accept land grants in Canada from the British.

Roy Johnson, head of the area's militia and active in regional politics, dug out an old account of the treaty of Fort Stanwix, forced upon the league in 1784. That treaty had taken vast areas of land from the league nations on the excuse that those lands had been seized from other Indian tribes through the once-superior strength of the league.

"Your Seneca," Johnson told Renno, after reading for a few minutes, "seem to have been confined to a much smaller area of land in central New York State."

"The messenger spoke of great discontent," Renno said, "especially among the young warriors."

"My friend," Johnson said, "there is great discontent everywhere in what British newspapers call the 'Disunited States.' "

"Yes," Renno agreed, "General Washington spoke of just that in his last letter to me."

Roy Johnson could not stifle a sudden chuckle. Renno looked at him questioningly, and Johnson laughed aloud.

"Sorry, Son." Johnson chuckled again. "I was just thinking: Here we sit, a backwoodsman and an Indian dressed in buckskins. Forgive me for saying this, but you carry with you the scent of the wilderness. Yet in your pocket is a letter from George Washington, and in your head is enough knowledge to keep you in a conversation with the best of those muckleheads who came up with those bloody Articles of Confederation that leave all thirteen so-called states to do as they damn well please and the devil take the hindmost."

Renno, affecting a British accent, a parody of his friend William Huntington, said, "My dear sir, I do indeed see the incongruity."

Johnson roared and slapped his knees. Still laughing, he rose to jerk down a jug from the mantle and offered it to Renno. When Renno politely refused, Johnson tipped the jug and gulped mountain corn whiskey—frontier fire—and wiped his mouth with the back of his hand.

"Yep," he said, seating himself. "We're all in one helluva fix. This is supposed to be a nation, and it was for a while, while we were fighting. We pulled together then because the people who controlled the flow of money, trade, and power in the colonies knew they'd be tried and hanged as traitors if the British won. But now it's every man for himself."

"General Washington says that the nation won't last unless a strong central government is established," Renno remarked.

"Well, those who hold the power in the various states will be reluctant to give it up," Johnson said. "It'll take some kind of outside threat." He chuckled again. "Not that there are not outside threats now, for God's sake. The British, the French, and the Spanish would like nothing better than to see the thirteen states divide into two or three pea-poppin' little countries that they could bully individually—the British, especially, don't like the idea of a unified country of almost four million people here in the New World. They'd like to divide and conquer."

Renno nodded his agreement. "Even though we supposedly won the war, the British still have an army in North America—at Fort Niagara, among other places. They continually urge the Seneca and the other northern Indian nations to cause trouble for the United States. That is Cornplanter's concern and why he has called for a council with my people."

"How do you know this Cornplanter doesn't want to convince you to go to war against the white settlers here in the South?" Johnson asked.

Renno shrugged. "I have only the words of the messenger. He relayed Cornplanter's hope that the word of Seneca who fought on the side of the Americans would be heard by the restless ones in the North. Cornplanter seeks an alternative for the Seneca other than fighting the Americans or leaving their homelands."

Johnson took another pull from the jug before responding. "Even if all Indians were united, they couldn't stand against the floor of white advancement. The Indian's only choice is to integrate, to become a part of this nation, Renno."

"Right here in our own little family we have the problem in miniature," Renno said. "Renna."

"Yep."

Renno outwaited Johnson.

"Now your son, Little Hawk," Johnson said, "he's going to be like you—living as an Indian, but white in blood and with a knowledge of white ways. Both Nora and I hope that you'll allow him to spend some time with us so that he'll know the world of his white grandparents better." Johnson paused. "And we pray that you'll allow us to rear Renna."

Renno looked at the flickering fire. "Renna, too, must know the ways of the Seneca."

"Sure, sure," Johnson said quickly. "She can spend the summers with you, maybe. She can learn a lot from your wise, old ones. Your mother. And Ena can teach her to be independent. A bit of spunk is good in a woman."

"There is time to speak of that," Renno said.

"We've come to love that tiny girl," Johnson admitted, a bit uneasy about making such a confession.

"I know," Renno said. "She is of you, as well as of me."

In silence each man mused his own thoughts as a lonesome wind whined around the log cabin. When Johnson spoke, his voice was low. "You're traveling into territory that will be strange to you, Renno. And from what we hear, a man could get killed up in the northwest territories. Settlement is sparse, but a Miami chief named Little Turtle is reportedly trying to form an alliance of all the tribes north of the Ohio to keep white men out of the territory. I guess I don't have to tell you to be careful."

"I have much to return to here," Renno assured his father-by-marriage.

Indeed, during the initial stage of his journey, as he passed isolated white homesteads, Renno's thoughts were focused on what he was leaving behind. The wilderness around him was unfamiliar. He set his direction by the sun during the day, or by the great bear in the sky after dark. Now running, now walking, the long, long miles passed under his feet, and he was in an area of forested rocky hills several days after having last held his daughter in Knoxville. The hunting was easy and water plentiful. Winter was withholding her last assaults. The moderate weather was fine for travel.

Thinking of his own personal losses—and of his two motherless children—made him doubt the wisdom of traveling into situations that were potentially dangerous. Doubt was a new emotion for him, for in the past he had always acted with assurance, a sureness of mind brought about by guidance from the spirits that were so much a part of his life. He knew that a man without a goal is often indecisive and that even momentary indecision in times of crisis can be fatal.

Still, what could he, one man, do to affect the fate of the new American nation? How could he—a stranger, a Seneca who belonged to a group that had, in the past, gone its separate way—convince the northern Seneca that their best hope lay with the United States and with gradually adapting to the white man's way of living?

As he trod the rotted leaves of the past autumn, he appealed to the manitous for guidance, but there was no sign until midday, when he trotted easily down a long slope into a deep, wild valley where a stream cut its boisterous way through beds of rocks. He heard the harsh hunting cry of a hawk and looked up to see the bird soaring toward the north. Ahead of Renno was a sheer cliff on the steep side of the valley, a glinting, dark wall of stone that took on the distinctive coloration of flint as he approached. The hawk dived from far up, falling like a stone down the face of the cliff and, with one cry, soaring again.

A clear picture came into Renno's mind of a fire . . . a camp . . . a spot under the towering flint cliffs. But it was only midday, and he could add miles to his journey before resting.

He could not explain to himself why, but with the sun at the zenith he stopped, built his fire, bundled into his robe, then gazed at the azure sky, seeking a sign. But not even the hawk appeared.

Into the night he sat motionless. The only sound was that of the rushing stream fifty yards from his dying fire. The lights in the sky—a sliver of a moon and the stars—were cold, hard glints of ice fire. His body, kept motionless so long, seemed to have left him, and there were only his questioning mind, his doubt, and his prayers for guidance. Then he saw a broad-shouldered apparition, burly and strong, the face glowing with the war paint of the Seneca.

"Father of all, great Ghonka," Renno whispered, and bowed his head, for he recognized the dimly glowing face.

The manitou, the spirit of the great sachem who had adopted the original Renno, lifted one arm, his puma robe falling to his waist to reveal the powerful thick chest, also touched with the war colors of the Seneca. One finger pointed up to a spot on the flint cliff behind Renno. With a crackling sound and a burning odor, a white-hot lance of fire shot from the spirit's extended finger. Renno gasped as the lance of fire sprayed sparks, sizzled, and burned a pattern into an area of smoothly weathered flint. Then something fell, landing just behind Renno. Reluctant to take his eyes off the manitou, the white Indian reached behind him, felt heat, and lifted the object.

It was quite hot to his hand, but Renno did not flinch as he seized it and drew it in front of him. In the glow of light from the embers of the fire, he saw that it was a flint knife. He hefted it, stabbed into the darkness, and grunted his approval. It was perfectly balanced, and the haft of it fitted his hand well. His fingers tingled as if the knife gave off a power of its own.

The spirit spoke in a voice that was deep, calm, and very human. "Once the hard stone was all we had. We had no iron, no fine Spanish steel as in your stiletto, no longbow such as that by your side. Remember."

"I hear, great Ghonka," Renno said.

"Where the rains fell and where the sun shone, all was ours," the spirit said, in a voice of sadness. "But all things change."

"Instruct me, Father," Renno whispered.

"For a great warrior, a fine weapon. You are young, but in you resides the wisdom of those who came before you," the manitou replied as the flint knife seemed to glow in Renno's hand. "Let it be your companion. Paint your face with the markings of the Seneca messenger and carry a messenger stick. Woe be to any who dares dispute your peaceable passage."

"I am content, Father," Renno said, no longer feeling doubt. He bowed his head.

"Beware of the one who speaks with the tongue of the serpent," the manitou added, and in one blink of Renno's eyes, Ghonka was gone.

With a shout of triumph, Renno sprang to his feet, brandishing the spirit knife. His wild war whoop echoed and reechoed in the valley. He stood there in the blackness of the night, a warrior in full manhood, tall and fair, his arms and legs powerful, his broad, well-muscled chest expanding with the sweet, cool night air.

And now the hawk soared with him, pointing the way . . . northward, ever northward. He was in his element in the virgin wilderness, sleeping by night and moving with the first light, often eating as he traveled. His ground-eating pace brought him into the land of the Shawnee, where he did not pause but showed his messenger stick to the sentries of the villages and was greeted as he moved past, his legs pumping, his face to the north.

He measured the days and then the weeks with notches on the messenger stick. Winter was still his constant companion, and he had traveled far enough north by now to feel a difference in the chill of the nights. He realized that he had taken the wilderness path as a personal preference, for he could have traveled eastward from Knoxville, and then northward through Virginia, where there were roads. Even if the common joke about roads in the United States were partially true—that the few roads were not passable in winter, not even jackass-able—he could have ridden or been a passenger on mail coaches. But he was Seneca, a man of the wilderness, and each day he saw new sights, indulging his desire to know what lay just over the next rise.

To get his bearings, he greeted an old Shawnee warrior near a village. He was west of his ideal route, and ahead lay the lands of the Miami, where, the old Shawnee said, a traveler, even a peaceful one, should tread with great care. He altered his route toward the northeast, the old Erie hunting grounds his goal.

Some days later he made a cold camp, sleeping without fire, and steeled himself against the severe cold. He was awakened by something and became fully alert, weapons in hand. He realized that an odor, not a sound, had broken his sleep—a faint tinge of smoke in the air. It was not the clean, good smell of dry wood burning; instead a hint of foulness drifted to him. At first light he was moving forward cautiously, and two hours later he saw the source of the smoke: a log cabin had been burned.

The manmade things inside the cabin had added rankness to the smoke, for the stench was much in the air as the embers of the cabin smoldered. From a place of concealment Renno studied the scene carefully. A bloody, huddled lump near the burned cabin drew him forward for a closer look. It was probably the scalped body of a white man. The unmistakable stench of burned flesh came from three unidentifiable heaps among the charred chaos of what had been a family home.

Renno shook his head sadly. Clearly there was no peace in this land.

Now his camp was cold each night, and he ate from his emergency rations of pemmican. Two days after passing the burned homestead, he hid in a thick stand of evergreens to watch a war party of ten move quietly and purposefully toward the east. He waited for the war party to be well distant—and to be sure that no other followed— then ran lightly until, in the late afternoon, he heard the talk of message drums. The distant booming came from the west, then from the east and ahead of him. The white Indian slowed his pace and moved with great caution, for though he could not interpret the drums' messages, it was quite likely that his progress toward the northeast had been observed.

That suspicion was confirmed when, as he moved through deep forest along a game trail, he heard the soft call of an owl from the front, to be answered by a similar call from behind him. He checked the readiness of his weapons, eased the English longbow into position for instant action, checked the primings of the fine brace of pistols given to him by William Huntington, then clasped the spirit knife. Regardless of the weather, the delicately carved knife seemed always warm to his touch and thus comforting.

He had not long to wait. They stood blocking the pathway, as it widened into a glade—four of them, warriors in paint, and to his interest he recognized the markings of not just one tribe but of Mohawk, Erie, and Miami.

Flint knife grasped in one hand, the message stick raised in the other, he said, "I am Renno, messenger to Cornplanter of the Seneca."

The Miami tall warrior spoke arrogantly. "I see only a cowardly Seneca *je-yeh*," he said, spitting out the Seneca word for dog.

Having sensed danger for hours, all his senses alert, Renno's reaction was instantaneous. In one motion he sheathed the flint knife, dropped the messenger stick, and drew his bow. One arrow, powered by the strength of the English longbow, ended the insults of the Miami warrior forever, and two others followed so swiftly that there was scarcely time for the Erie to yell out in surprise. And then, even as Renno was putting distance between himself and the warriors he had sensed closing in on him from the rear, his hands were busy. The fourth warrior who had blocked his way, the Erie, loosed his own tomahawk, which spun away harmlessly as one of Renno's arrows lodged in his throat, penetrating the spinal column to bring instant death. Two more, attacking from the rear, met arrows as they leaped into the glade, one aiming a musket, the other with tomahawk raised high.

Six of the enemy were down. Spirit knife in his left hand, tomahawk in his right, Renno met the charge of the remaining two with the fighting cry of an angry hawk. The spirit knife found a pathway to death between a Miami warrior's ribs, and with one swing of his tomahawk, Renno came near decapitating the last, another Miami.

The entire deadly drama had been played out in less than a minute. The forest was quiet now, save for the distant pulsing of a drum from the south. His fighting blood surging, Renno threw his head back and once more sounded the scream of an attacking hawk. As if in confirmation, the fighting roar of a bear answered him from the thickets along the river that lay ahead of him.

He did not question his quick victory against such

overwhelming odds. The manitous had been with him. The warriors from three tribes had violated a sacred trust in threatening a messenger painted for peaceful passage.

He used his stiletto in quick, harsh slashes, not concerned with neatness, took the scalps of all the fallen warriors, and with a grim face tied them to his messenger stick. Renno rarely did anything without purpose. He had no need for coup or for the eight scalps that would rot and stink before he reached Seneca lands. But by tying eight scalps to his messenger pole, he was offering the ultimate insult to the dead and impugning the honor of any who condoned their actions. For eight to be killed by one, and for that one to be a messenger on a mission of peace, was to say that the dead had been inept warriors, no more dangerous than ancient, toothless women.

By the increased signs of travel on the trails, he knew that he was nearing a settlement or an encampment. He trotted on, not worrying about concealing his presence. The talking drums sounded as he moved. Perhaps those who dwelt here could not fight, but they seemed quite competent in keeping track of his progress. He came to the river and trotted past a group of women drawing water. They gasped and pointed in astonishment to the eight bloody scalps flapping from his messenger stick.

Just up the river was a village, crowded along the water under bare-limbed hardwood trees. Renno ran directly into the village, past barking dogs and shouting children, past women who paused to gawk and a few warriors who stared at him incredulously. It was an Erie village. Renno saw the way to the central square, slowed his run, walked tall and proud to stand before the medicine lodge, planted his messenger stick in the ground, crossed his arms, and waited.

The women and children congregated behind him, whispering and giggling. A few warriors stood silently, eyeing him defiantly. Soon the door to the large medicine lodge opened, and a tall Miami with the trappings of a great chief stooped to exit through the doorway without bumping his feather-crested head. He halted facing Renno at a distance of about six paces.

"What is the meaning of this?" the tall Miami chief demanded, pointing toward the messenger stick with its dripping scalps.

"Is it the custom of the men of this land to violate the safe passage of one with a message stick?" Renno asked.

"Who has done this thing?" the Miami chief wanted to know.

"Their tongues did not live long enough to speak names," Renno answered.

A warrior took a step forward, but the Miami chief halted him with a swift wave of his hand. "Speak, then, messenger."

"My words are for Cornplanter, of the Seneca."

"You are far afield."

"I had thought to be in the land of the Erie, my brothers by ancient treaty and by the Iroquois League," Renno said. "Perhaps I am mistaken, since a Miami chief speaks for my Erie brothers."

There was a sullen silence until an old Erie warrior, scarred and decorated with the totems of many battles, emerged from the lodge behind the Miami chief.

"We are all brothers," the old man said. "All who have hunted this land and who have common ancestors." He indicated the chief with a sweep of his arm. "Little Turtle, of the Miami, is our brother. You, Seneca, you are our brother."

Renno nodded. "And these?" He pointed to the eight scalps.

"Our young men," the old Erie said sadly, "are confused and angry. They tend to look upon any incursion of our lands as a threat. But, Seneca, you are welcome. Our

warriors will escort you northward into the land of the
Seneca."

"I have come this far without escort," Renno informed him.

"Good," the old Erie said, looking startled. "You will
eat."

Leaving the messenger stick with its bloody decoration standing upright in front of the medicine lodge, Renno
entered. Older men, obviously senior warriors and sub-
chiefs, joined the old Erie and the Miami Little Turtle.
Women brought fresh roasted meat, delicious fish stew,
and dried fruits, with cold water to drink.

"You travel from the south?" Little Turtle asked after
a suitable period of silence was allowed to give Renno
time to take the edge off his hunger.

"From far south, the land of the Cherokee. I am
Renno."

The old Erie chief, who had seemed to be half-dozing,
jerked his head up and leaned forward, his dim old eyes
examining Renno closely. "There was a great war chief
called Renno, of the Seneca."

"My ancestor," Renno replied.

"You, then, are of those Seneca who fought with our
enemies in the white man's war," Little Turtle challenged.

"My father chose to fight with the Americans," Renno
responded.

"And now?" Little Turtle asked.

"I fight only against those who threaten me and mine,"
Renno said, finishing a bowl of stew and putting the bowl
beside him on the floor.

"Then you will fight with us against those who invade
our hunting grounds," Little Turtle said.

"It is true," the old Erie said. "I, Standing Beaver,
will speak."

The old man stood. "You have called the Erie your
brothers, Seneca, for you know little of history—how the

Iroquois League came against the Erie and made him Iroquois. Those who refused were exiled. But that is past. The present is this: these lands are coveted by the whites. This is the time when Indian must stand by Indian, regardless of tribe. The whites at whose side you fought will overrun you next, Seneca, there in the South."

Standing Beaver seated himself with great care for his old bones.

"Only children and old women will stay out of this fight," Little Turtle declared.

Renno showed no emotion at the implied insult.

"It is clear that these lands are coveted by the whites," Little Turtle continued with great feeling. "I know it, Standing Beaver knows it, all know it who can see the sun when there are no clouds. I have come here from Miami hunting grounds to the west to unite all Indian peoples against this final act of greed by the white man. As you traveled northward did you not see the proof of their intentions to drive all of us from our ancestral hunting grounds?"

"I saw dead and burned white women and children," Renno said. "That is not the way to a lasting settlement with the white man."

"What you saw you saw," Little Turtle said offhandedly. "How you saw it is in your eyes. Had I seen this, I would have said, 'So, other invaders of our lands are dead.' " He stood, and Renno realized that rather than for his benefit, the chief's oratory was more for the others. "They come in a devouring flood, and they take all. They kill all the beaver and all the game animals, while the Indian starves or moves farther into the wilderness. Our brother, Cornplanter of the Seneca, knows this, and it was for this reason that he sent a messenger to the south to seek council with our southern brothers."

Renno had never known an Indian who could lie well to another Indian. Lying was against the basic code by which all Indians lived and was excusable only when speaking to an enemy or to a white man. Neither Little Turtle's words, his eyes, nor his posture gave credence to his claim that Cornplanter the Seneca wanted war with the United States.

"All will join with the Miami! All—the Seneca, the Mohawk, the Onondaga, the Oneida, the Cayuga—all the scattered, small tribes who have already suffered from the white man's greed." He faced Renno. "Go to council with the Seneca. Tell them that they must join us. Tell them that to be neutral in this war will mean the end of them as a nation, that they will be reduced to living in the white man's backyard, begging for the scraps that he throws out to his dogs. Tell them that if they do not join us, it will be the end of the Seneca as a people."

Little Turtle stepped closer and glared down at Renno. "Tell them that only small children and old women will not join this fight."

Twice now the Miami had thrown the insult at Renno. Renno clamped his teeth tightly to resist the impulse to let the spirit knife taste the Miami's blood. It was for the Seneca that he remained silent. Now that he knew the potential for war on the northwestern frontier north of the Ohio, his duty was to his own people and the people of his ancestors, whose chief had asked his council.

There was a sense of danger in the silence—a sullen, brooding warning. Renno knew that he might very well die here in this village where Erie, Miami, and others heeded the war talk of Little Turtle. He could, of course, kill a few before he himself was killed, but he would nonetheless be dead, and Little Hawk and Renna would be fatherless as well as motherless. His counsel for sanity would never be heard by the northern Seneca, and that was of great importance.

So it was that the proud white Indian swallowed the Miami war chief's arrogance and insults. In the interest of self-control, Renno concentrated his thoughts on his worthy friend, Se-quo-i of the Cherokee, who had put aside the weapons of war to work in precious metals and fashion things of beauty while he experimented with ways to adapt the white man's magic—reading and writing—to the language of his people.

Slowly Renno rose. He faced Little Turtle and spoke softly in a low voice. "The eight who questioned my right to free passage today do not doubt my courage, nor do they call me child or woman."

He held the silence for a long, long time, his eyes boring into Little Turtle's. Then he spoke, turning toward the senior warriors and the old Erie chief. "My first duty, since I carry the messenger stick, is to complete my mission, to council with Cornplanter. Little Turtle tells us that Cornplanter favors war. So. Too long have the different factions of the Seneca been separated by great distances and by incompatible loyalties."

Even that much, he knew, was dangerous—if Little Turtle had not lied about Cornplanter's sympathies concerning a new war against the whites, Renno had just said that he would side with Cornplanter.

"I thank you, Standing Beaver, for your hospitality," Renno said.

"Go in peace, Seneca," Standing Beaver said.

As it happened, Little Turtle's true colors were made clear to Renno when, no more than a mile from Standing Beaver's village, he climbed a tall tree and looked back at his trail to see a party of some twenty warriors leave the village in haste and run northward along the route Renno had taken.

He climbed down from the tree, rid the messenger stick of scalps by scraping them off against a tree, then turned to the southeast, slipping through the forest as quietly as a spirit. He had killed eight and knew he could kill half of twenty, but instead he ran, against the urgings of his pride, for the sake of others. He ran to the south, following the course of a small stream, and as night fell he turned directly eastward, for he was a marked man and knew that Little Turtle would go to extremes to prevent him from counseling with the Seneca chiefs. Such a council would no doubt unite the Seneca and ally them with the Cherokee on the side of peace and cooperation with the United States.

His line of travel was now directly eastward, toward the lands of the white man in the state of Pennsylvania.

Chapter III

The early literature of the North American continent abounds in the accounts of exploratory travelers. Beginning with de Soto's excursions in the Southeast, chroniclers wrote of the unique characteristics of the vast new land, its varied animal life, and its native peoples. Had Renno been accompanied by a scribe, the sheer extent of his travels would have earned him a place in history.

Although he was still in his twenties, Renno had seen more of the United States than perhaps any other man living. He had seen the beauty of his native land from the northern lakes of the ancient Seneca homeland where he had been born, to the swamps of Florida peopled by the renegade Seminole. He had traveled by foot and by coach and by horse through most of the thirteen states, and only recently he had made the epic journey to the lands beyond the Rio Grande in the dry mountains far to the southwest.

His solo journey from the Cherokee nation northward into the lands once ruled by the Erie was an awe-inspiring saga unto itself, but that did not occur to Renno. He was a man of the wilderness. With the most basic tools he could provide the necessities of life—food, warmth, water, and shelter—not only for himself but for a family. His superbly healthy body had traversed hundreds of miles without strain, and although he had a mission, he took joy in being alone, seeing, experiencing, and claiming new ground. Even now he was filled with ecstacy as he came to the impressive river that was only slightly less amazing than the Mississippi at Chickasaw Bluffs.

The winter crossing of the great Ohio River left him undaunted. Spring had not come to those northern latitudes, and the challenge was met by the simple expedient of quietly borrowing a canoe and rowing across the icy waters.

Although his excellent memory for places made him familiar with some parts of Pennsylvania, the western areas of the state were unfamiliar to him. He knew that he had left the true frontier behind when he began to skirt white homesteads and then, on the approach to the thriving town of Pittsbourgh—or Pittsburgh as some were beginning to spell it—he began to get curious stares. Hostile Indians had long been driven out of Pennsylvania. Some Indians had adapted to white ways. It was unusual to see an Indian, especially one with pale skin, light-brown hair, and blue eyes, dressed in the buckskins and robes of the aborigines and armed with a variety of weapons.

Renno's correct and unaccented English caused further puzzlement as he inquired for the newspaper office, for he had come into the city for news, having been secluded from all sources of information for over two months.

His arrival in the cluttered outer office of the newspaper caused quite a stir, and soon he was surrounded by several curious men vying to question him about his appearance, his travels, and his reasons for being in Pittsbourgh. When

Renno said that he had just traveled through the north-western territory, a balding, pipe-smoking man in shapeless, soiled woolens silenced the other men with a raised hand.

"Young man," he said, "I am Elmer Culpepper, editor of this thing we loosely call a newspaper. Have you indeed been among the Miami?"

Renno nodded.

"Did you see any preparations for war?" Culpepper asked.

"The Miami chief Little Turtle calls for war," Renno said.

For several minutes he answered Culpepper's questions, while two reporters jotted down his words. He mentioned nothing of his intentions to go north to Seneca lands, and when Culpepper's questions slowed, he asked questions of his own, listening to the editor's answers with great interest.

Culpepper believed that the efforts of George Washington and others to strengthen the Articles of Confederation and form a strong central government would reach fruition in May, when a congregation of leaders would begin in Philadelphia.

"Jefferson of Virginia has called the convention an assembly of demigods," Culpepper said, laughing, "since so many important men will be there." He paused, and a serious expression settled around his eyes. "Only time will tell if they can show demigodlike wisdom."

"Washington will be there?" Renno asked.

"Of course. They wouldn't be able to draw enough of a crowd to watch a cockfight without the old man," Culpepper replied.

Culpepper, who knew nothing about the situation among the tribes of the League of the Ho-de-no-sau-nee, told Renno that there was great pressure to begin settlement of the lands north of the Ohio.

"Haven't the Americans taken enough of the Indians' lands?" Renno asked.

Culpepper spread his hands. "The march of history, my friend, will not be slowed."

"Tell those who go into the northwest to go in strength, then," Renno said, "and to expect blood."

Culpepper, a widower, insisted that Renno lodge with him. They dined in a tavern near the newspaper office, where Renno, to Culpepper's amusement, attracted no little attention. In Culpepper's home—there was a nice view of the Monongahela River from the front stoop—the talk continued, with Culpepper becoming increasingly impressed by Renno's grasp of the situation facing the United States and the Indians. Having determined that Culpepper was a sensible man without prejudice—in fact he was sometimes almost sympathetic to the Indians' problem—Renno confided in him, telling him of his mission to the Seneca.

"Well, young fellow," Culpepper said, "you've bitten off quite a chaw. You'll be going in there, one man, without much influence. It might be better if you'd contact the Indian affairs people. That way someone who could halfway speak for the United States would go along with you."

Renno made no comment then, but later, stretched out on a bed for the first time in a couple of months, he lay awake for long hours considering his problem. In his experience agents to the Indians represented their own interests without regard for those of the Indians, so Culpepper's suggestion to take some Pennsylvania government official with him was not worth considering. Certainly a Pennsylvania agent would not be able to speak for the United States. It was also becoming clear to Renno that the Americans' attitude toward those Indians who had fought against them was more important in the long run than what was happening in the unsettled areas north of the Ohio.

He did not have unlimited time, but he had time. Events tended to take form slowly in winter. With the new beginning, communications would become easier among those to the west who wanted to fight and those whom they were trying to persuade to join them. But even if Little Turtle made contact with the Iroquois League, there would be no swift decisions, for such weighty matters would dictate many councils.

Over a breakfast of salty fish and hard bread, Renno told Culpepper, "I have decided to go to Philadelphia to talk with General Washington."

"I'll be glad to give you a letter of introduction, for what it's worth," Culpepper offered. "I myself haven't met the general, but the press carries some weight. It might be hard for you to get to see him. He'll be busy."

"He will see me," Renno assured the editor.

"Well . . ." Culpepper muttered doubtfully. Then he smiled. "If I may make a suggestion, Renno, I think you'll find travel through the civilized parts of the state a bit more comfortable if you, uh, dress a bit more in conformity with such areas."

"Yes, thank you," Renno said. "Perhaps you can recommend a good place to purchase suitable clothing."

"Well, there are places, but prices are sky high. Maybe we can find something cast-off, cheap."

Renno drew from an inner place in his buckskins a deerskin pouch and produced several gold coins, the good gold of the Apache, minted in Charlotte. "Will this be enough?"

"Lord God," Culpepper gasped. "In these days of paper money that's almost enough to buy the store."

Renno left Pittsbourgh by coach, dressed in woolens but hatless, his long hair gathered behind. His longbow and tomahawk were carefully wrapped as baggage. Concealed on his person were his stiletto and the spirit knife, the latter always emanating warmth. In his belt he carried the two matched pistols, for it was not at all unusual for a gentleman to carry arms. Indeed, his fellow passengers who noticed the weapons were grateful for the presence of so assured a young man who was well armed against any incident on the little-traveled roads.

There were times, especially as the road wound its way through the mountains, that Renno could have made better time afoot, but he had committed himself to this so-called civilized way of travel, so he stayed with the coach lines, spending the nights at inns and often sleeping on the floor since it was the custom for several men to share a bed.

Spring announced its appearance as he traveled through the well-kept farmlands of the Dutch country, with April rains churning the roads into quagmires. The men aboard had to dismount often and push the coach out of deep mud.

He arrived in Philadelphia toward the last of April. His gold was welcomed by an innkeeper. He slept, ate well, had the mud and dust of travel cleaned from his belongings and his clothing, then inquired of the inn-keeper, early on a lovely spring morning, as to the meeting place of the delegates to the Constitutional Convention.

"Well, the big shindig hasn't started yet," the ruddy innkeeper said, "but some of them have arrived. General Washington and most of the Virginia delegation are here."

Having been told where the Virginia delegation were staying, Renno went out into the teeming streets. Only a few minutes of walking convinced him of the desirability of living in the wilderness, but soon he was entering the lodgings where Washington had temporarily taken up residence.

The general was seated in a wing chair in a nicely decorated salon. Following the sound of Washington's strong voice, Renno stepped through an open door where several well-dressed gentlemen were seated, listening respect-fully. Renno recognized only one, the aging Benjamin Franklin of Pennsylvania. The white Indian halted quietly inside the door, but the movement caught George Washington's eye, and he paused midsentence, gazing at Renno with his piercing eyes for a moment before a smile split his face.

"Is it you?" Washington asked, springing to his feet with a vigor belying his years. "Yes, by glory, it is!" He advanced, hand outthrust.

Puzzled by the warmth of Washington's greeting, the other men looked on.

"My friend, it must be a matter of importance to take you so far from your home," Washington replied. "But we are happily met, for I have only recently received a message that concerns you."

"I do have matters that I would like to discuss with you, General," Renno said, taking Washington's hand in a quick, firm grasp.

"Of course," Washington replied. "First, however, introductions are in order." He put his hand on Renno's shoulder. "This young man Renno," he announced, "is the finest scout and the finest fighting man who ever served with me. I count him as a friend. And these gentlemen are the Honorable James Madison, Governor Edmund Randolph, Mr. George Mason, and I think you may have recognized our ancient philosopher and diplomat, Benjamin Franklin."

One by one Renno shook hands with men who had already shaped the destiny of a nation. The formalities concluded, Washington said, "If the matters you would like to discuss are personal, Renno, we can adjourn to another room. If they concern the welfare of the United States, these gentlemen should hear them."

"I have come from the northwest territories, General," Renno said.

"Good. We need some solid intelligence about what's going on out there," Washington said. "Have a chair, my friend."

James Madison leaned forward with interest as Renno

told of his encounter with the war chief Little Turtle, his own mission to the Seneca, and his impression of the attitude of the Indians in the northwest territories.

Franklin asked penetrating questions and nodded in satisfaction as Renno answered clearly and concisely. "Damned British," Franklin growled. "Still trying to serve up trouble, as if we didn't already have enough of our own."

Finally Renno said, "And so, General, I have come to Philadelphia to inquire about the intentions of the United States concerning the Iroquois League, specifically the Seneca."

"I assure you, Renno," Washington said, "that our greatest hope is to make peace with the Iroquois League; in fact, to have all Indians become valued and honest citizens of the United States."

Madison, embarrassed by that, cleared his throat. "I don't think that's what this young man wanted to hear, General."

"On the contrary, sir," Renno disagreed. "General Washington's hope is shared by me."

"Renno's people fought at my side," Washington said. "His father—and the son after him—believed that the Indian's best hope was somehow to become integrated with the United States."

"There are problems, of course," Franklin said.

"Yes," Renno admitted. "But among the Cherokee there has already been some adaptation: there is more farming, and more houses now replace the traditional lodges. I do feel that complete adaptation is far in the future for some tribes or only a forlorn hope among the Indians of the Northwest—in spite of men of goodwill such as the Seneca Cornplanter."

There was a spirited discussion, with Renno answering questions and doing a lot of listening. He knew that to a certain extent the fate of his people rested with men

such as these in the salon. Of course, a part of him was
infuriated to think that such men would expect the Indian
to change his traditional way of life and give up the hunting grounds, which the white men considered an uneco-
nomical and wasteful use of large tracts of land. But Renno
knew that the tide of history was on the side of the white
men and he would always be caught between two forces.

It was Washington who ended the discussion, which
had begun to stray far afield from the Indian problems.

"Renno, I have had a message that concerns you, so if
you'll dine with me in my suite . . ."

Both men ate heartily. Washington had been suffi-
ciently exposed to Indian customs to know to delay discussion of anything beyond the goodness of the food being
consumed until hunger had been satisfied. He leaned
back, sighed, and patted his stomach.

"I have had a communication from a certain English
lady," he began.

"Beth?" Renno asked, surprised.

"Indeed," Washington said. "I will admit that I was
quite startled by your sudden appearance. But coinci-
dence though it may be, I'm infernally glad you showed
up, for I was at wit's end trying to find a way to get your
message to the North Carolina frontier." He smiled.
"Enough rambling. Miss Huntington is in trouble, and she
asks your help."

Renno felt inner tension immediately. "But she's in
England!"

"Not so." Washington rose, found a letter atop a
bureau, and handed it to Renno. "Here, read it for yourself. She's in this country. In North Carolina, in fact.
Wilmington, where Cornwallis wintered before the battle
of Yorktowne."

Renno scanned the letter quickly:

. . . You see, for reasons that I will not detail here, I did not return to England with my brother and his bride but decided to make my own way in this new country, which I have come to love. But now I find that a woman alone is easy prey, indeed. I urge you, General Washington, to get this appeal for assistance to Renno by any means possible.

"Not much detail," Washington commented when Renno looked up, indecision on his face. "But the woman is in trouble."

"I have my mission. . . ." Renno said.

"At the risk of becoming personal, my friend," Washington said, "it is my guess that this Englishwoman means something to you."

"We became good friends during our journey to the western lands," Renno replied, "and I would help, but—"

"Son," Washington said as gently as a gruff old soldier could manage, "the situation in the Northwest has been simmering for a long time now. The British have never stopped harassing us on the frontiers. That's not going to change overnight. Nor do I think that Cornplanter and the other Iroquois League chiefs will make any hasty decisions."

"What would you suggest I do?" Renno asked.

"Go to your friend. A man's lucky if he has two good friends in a lifetime, and most have only one. I myself will see that Cornplanter gets the message that you'll come to him before the snow falls again. Plans are already under way to handle any trouble that Little Turtle might stir up. After you've assisted Mistress Huntington, come back and we'll try once more to straighten out the affairs of our beleaguered country."

Renno was silent, but a phrase kept ringing in his mind, a message from the manitous. It had come to him before he had ever seen Beth: *The flame-haired one is the future.*

"I will go," Renno declared.

"Good, good," Washington said. "Before you leave, I'll introduce you to William Blount, one of the North Carolina delegates to the convention. He can probably give you some inkling of what Beth Huntington has been doing in Wilmington."

William Blount knew Wilmington well. He told Renno that it was a small port on the Cape Fear River in southeastern North Carolina. Wilmington had begun to come into its own in recent years, only after Brunswick Towne, an older port nearer the mouth of the river, was burned by the British at the beginning of the war.

"Beth Huntington," Blount said. "Yes, of course. She's that red-haired Englishwoman who raised the ire of every lady in Wilmington by competing openly in a man's field. Came to town with gold, spent a lot of it in buying property and opening up a trading company. Had a couple of ships." The North Carolinan delegate shook his head. "Fool woman, she was. Should have known that a woman couldn't make it in such a business, especially with the confounded British acting the way they are."

Renno had to smile. It sounded just like Beth—headstrong, much like Ena.

"I'll be glad to do anything I can to help you, young man," Blount offered. "This much I can do for sure." He went to his desk and penned a letter of introduction to one Nathan Ridley.

"Ridley came to Wilmington just after the war," Blount explained. "Saw that it was an up-and-coming town, so he opened a shipping business—branch of a business in Norfolk, I believe."

The name had seemed very familiar to Renno, and with the mention of Norfolk, it came to him that he and Nathan might be distantly related, for Betsy Ridley, his great-grandmother and wife of the original Renno, had been a Ridley from Virginia.

Now Renno was eager to be under way. He hoped that Beth's problems were not too serious and wondered how she would look after the long months that had passed since he had last seen her in Charlotte.

Renno went to pay his respects to Washington. When he told the general that Beth had gone into the shipping business, the general rubbed his chin thoughtfully.

"Then we can guess at some of her problems," he said. "Most probably she is suffering with the rest of us, with threats to her shipping coming from the Spanish to the south and from the British to the north. The British are trying to strangle us from the sea by not permitting vessels to trade with ports in Canada or the West Indies. But British goods still come into *our* ports. In fact, that's one of our problems; we're spending too much money on imports and not allowed free trade for our own domestic products. If your Mistress Huntington is caught up in that, well . . ."

Although Renno was not an expert on international trade, he felt that more than business problems had engendered Beth's plea for help. He made his farewell to Washington and, acting on the general's advice, made the trip from Philadelphia to New York by horseback, for he would be able to reach North Carolina faster by sea than by land.

New York City, the site of bitter battles and British repression during the war and the victim of disastrous fires in 1775 and 1778, had become a bustling, growing city. Once again Renno walked among milling, noisy crowds and was reminded of the peace of his own lands. In the early morning hours he made his way to the harbor, where luck was with him, for a coastal sloop was in the final stages of loading for stops in Norfolk, Wilmington, and Charleston. Renno, paying for a berth with his dwindling supply of gold, watched as lines were cast off and the ship began to move toward the sea. Before night closed in, he got his first look at the seemingly boundless ocean from the deck of a small ship where constant motion seemed to be the only rule.

Although he did not experience seasickness, Renno found that travel by sea was monotonous. The sounds were the same: the flap of sail, the rush of wind, the wet, sloshing sound of waves, and bawled orders of officers to the crew. The good weather held as the ship entered Hampton Roads and offloaded its consigned cargo at Norfolk, but they put to sea with lowering skies, sailing into a howling storm.

Renno stood on the deck, braced against the mad lurchings of the ship, marveling at the intensity of the weather. He had, of course, experienced storms in the wilderness, but there it was possible to find shelter. Here on the open sea there was no place to hide. At first the ship seemed to be helpless before the fury, but as Renno watched the skilled crew handle reduced sails, he realized that the vessel was still under control. He respected more and more those men who had chosen the sea as a livelihood.

The sloop beat its way southward past the cape of great storms and, with the weather on the mend, rounded Cape Fear and sailed the broad, dark river. They had taken on a pilot at a small village near the river's mouth, and he led them safely down the gradually narrowing waterway until the eternal green depths of a pine forest were close on the western bank.

The town of Wilmington perched on a high cliff overlooking the river, slanting downward to the north and the harbor-associated establishments along the waterfront. Two ships were dockside, and men were busy transferring cargo. A fine pair of bays pranced along the water street pulling a shining surrey. Renno was ready to disembark the minute the sloop was drawn along the wharf. He waved to the captain, shouldered the pack containing his longbow and tomahawk, checked to see if his stiletto and the spirit knife were safely in place, stepped onto the solid planking of the wharf, and drew a long breath of relief.

He did not have far to look for his destination. He saw a garish wooden sign, the name Ridley outlined in red, and walked to the entrance. Inside, amid a helter-skelter assortment of pitch barrels, coils of line, and other marine items, he saw a young man sitting behind a littered desk.

"Yes, sir?" the young man said, as Renno stood before him.

"Nathan Ridley?"

"No, sir. You'll find Mr. Ridley in back." He lowered his eyes to his work while Renno walked to a closed door, opened it, and peered into a large warehouse. A white man and two blacks were halfway down an aisle.

"Nathan Ridley?" Renno called.

"Here, sir!" the white man called back. He gave a quick series of orders to his men about how he wanted certain merchandise shifted; then rubbing his hands together to dislodge soil, he came toward Renno, head cocked in question. He wore well-made, tightly fitting knee breeches, a long-sleeved shirt slightly soiled by his work, and plain hose and buckled shoes. His brown hair was sleeked back into a tie at his neck. He seemed to Renno to be quite young, and there was a friendly smile on his face as he approached, his hand outstretched. He halted at a few paces, one eyebrow raised.

"I know you," he stated.

"I think not," Renno said, "but members of our families have known each other in the past."

Renno, even when dressed as a white man, made a striking appearance. His clothing fit well, but his well-developed torso and powerful legs made it seem that his garments were just a bit too small. His sun-browned darkness made a striking contrast to his penetrating blue eyes.

Ridley came and took Renno's hand.

Renno, intent on examining this man who was perhaps a distant cousin, was silent for a moment, and Ridley disengaged the handshake, his eyes falling on Renno's tomahawk in his belt.

"Well, now," Ridley said, reaching for the weapon to find that his wrist was suddenly caught in a grip of steel. "Sorry," he apologized, moving back. "It's just that I haven't seen one of those weapons in a while."

Renno released Ridley's wrist, flicked the tomahawk from his belt, and extended it haft first.

Ridley examined the fine workmanship. "This is Seneca."

"Yes," Renno said.

"Can you use it?"

Renno took the tomahawk and, with a flip of his arm, sent it whirling, embedding its head in a timber twenty feet away.

Ridley grinned. "Am I right in thinking that I am in the presence of a long-lost cousin? Would one member of that family you mentioned have been Betsy Ridley of Virginia, who married a white Seneca Indian?"

Renno nodded solemnly. "I am named for the white Indian she married. I am Renno."

Ridley was delighted. He pumped Renno's hand again and bade him welcome. He was full of questions. He made several suggestions almost in the same breath, the gist of which was that Renno was to be his guest. Then he laughed. "Listen to me run on," he said. "How can I be of help, Cousin? What business brings you to us?"

"I seek the Englishwoman Beth Huntington," Renno answered.

"Ah," Ridley said, his smile fading. "A friend?"

"A friend," Renno confirmed. "Is she well?"

"I suppose so. Don't see much of her."

"It is my pleasure to meet you, my cousin," Renno

said, "and I hope that you will find time for us to get better acquainted, but my first business is with Beth Huntington."

"I understand. Her place is just up the wharf to the north. Can't miss it. Join us for dinner tonight. The family will be very interested to hear about the Seneca side of our ancestry."

"Would you hold that invitation open for the time being?" Renno asked.

"Of course. I understand," Ridley said. "And if there's anything I can do—"

"Do you know of any trouble that Mistress Huntington has encountered?" Renno asked.

"Matter of fact, yes. Seems she's lost a ship. If you need me, you'll find me here in this fine place from light to dark."

Renno walked north, still carrying his bundle, until he saw a sign: *HUNTINGTON—SHIP'S CHANDLER— SHIPPING*. A rusty cowbell attached to the door rang as he entered. A solidly built older man, white hair nothing more than a fringe around his bald pate, looked up from a rocking chair.

"If it's supplies you're after," he said, "you've come to the wrong place." The accent was stuffily English. Renno felt a tinge of nostalgia, for the old man sounded like William.

"I would like to speak with Beth Huntington," Renno said.

"Who would?" the old man demanded arrogantly.

"My name is Renno."

"By Jove!" the old man exclaimed, lunging heavily to his feet. "You're that wild Indian I've heard so much about!" He waddled forward on stiff legs. "My pleasure, sir," he crowed, reaching out his hand. "And my thanks to you for helping my son and daughter retrieve my gold." Then, before Renno could answer: "Although, sir, it seems to me that you could have retrieved a bit more of it. At least enough to go around."

Renno laughed. He could see a definite resemblance to William in the timeworn face and, more vaguely, to Beth. "I take it, sir," he said formally, "that I address Lord Beaumont?"

"Indeed not," the old man said. "Lord Beaumont is in his rightful place at the ancestral hall in stuffy old England." He winked. "In this new country to which my willful daughter has lured me, I am plain Cedric Huntington."

"And your daughter?" Renno asked.

"You've only just missed her. She took passage on a schooner, northward bound, just days past."

Perhaps, Renno thought, he had passed close by the ship carrying Beth during the storm.

"Spunky wench, my Beth." The old man chortled. "I wanted to go, but she told me I was getting too heavy in the stern to do much running about."

Renno was feeling frustrated. First he had abandoned his mission to the northern Seneca, and now he had missed Beth entirely. Sensing that Cedric Huntington would be a proud man, Renno did not tell him that Beth had sent a message asking for help.

"May I ask Beth's destination?"

"Quebec," Huntington answered. He peered doubt-fully at Renno for a few seconds. "Look here, I know all about that letter that she sent to you through General Washington." The old man frowned, turned, lowered him-self wearily into the chair. "Have a seat," he invited, "and I'll tell you what has happened since you last saw Beth."

The story came slowly, with many detours, in the manner of old men. Renno listened patiently, putting it all together in his mind. For whatever reason—and Renno suspected that he knew the reason—Beth had decided not to go back to England, choosing instead to take a small share of the gold and establish a business in the United States.

William, meanwhile, had taken his Spanish bride back to England, where the Apache gold ransomed the ancestral holdings by paying off his father's gambling debts. Renno guessed that the old man had felt a bit shamed because his children were forced to bail him out of debt and, seeing William well settled with a new wife and then children, had felt bored with England and decided to join his willful Beth in Wilmington.

Beth had used her gold to purchase the establishment on the Wilmington waterfront and two ships, a fine four-masted schooner capable of sailing any ocean in the world and a sloop for the coastal trade.

"It was our intention," Huntington continued, "to use my doubtful influence in an effort to overcome the British prohibition against American trade with the West Indies and the Canadian ports." He grinned ruefully. "It seemed a good idea at the time. If successful, this trade would have made a fortune for the firm of Huntington, as well as benefiting the port of Wilmington, the state of North Carolina, and the United States as a whole."

But the reality did not proceed according to plan: first, seamen and local residents and officials resented the fact that Beth was trying to run a man's business. Next, their initial attempt to break the British blockade by sending the schooner to Canada had brought disaster. Although Huntington, through his contacts, had been assured that a cargo of rice and indigo would be welcomed in Canada, the four-masted schooner had disappeared. Months later word came through Huntington's sources that the vessel had been seized in Canada by military officials. The firm, having now only the small coastal sloop, suffered a devastating financial setback. Beth had contacted Renno in hopes that he could use his good offices with George Washington—and through Washington, the American government—to pressure the British in Canada to return her ship and pay for the cargo.

"But you know Beth," Cedric Huntington said, sighing. "She didn't know whether or not the letter had reached you. She couldn't wait. Nothing would do but that she take ship for Quebec to visit the British military governor there and convince him that since she is a British subject he should return our ship."

Although it was warm and springlike, Renno felt a cold chill, and without his willing it, his right hand sought the warm haft of the spirit knife.

Chapter IV

Although Renno had never traveled as far north as Canada, he had heard from his father about those northern lands and the past involvement of his ancestors in battles at Quebec against the British. It was difficult to envision Beth in the same city that had once been attacked by his great-grandfather Renno and the great Ghonka. Upon hearing from Cedric Huntington's lips the one word, Quebec, Renno's initial reaction had been a chill of foreboding. As the spirit powers of the flint knife warmed his hand, he knew in that split second that he, too, would go to Quebec.

Renno would not have been able to explain why he was so compelled to find Beth. He might have said that the feeling of foreboding was a message from the manitous who so often guided his actions. He would have denied that anything other than friendship for Beth influenced him, for he still mourned for Emily. Beth had traveled at his side and had fought with more skill than many men; thus she was a companion in arms, and any person who had Renno for a friend had a friend indeed.

Renno felt that Beth's father could not give him the information he would need about getting into Canada by sea because the old man was new in the United States. He also felt that he could not afford to take time to travel the hundreds of miles by land.

Although Huntington expressed his pride in Beth's spunk and courage, he was obviously concerned. Renno told him that something would be done and not to worry. His way of action clear to him, the white Indian asked for a place to change clothing. Directed to a small storeroom, he removed the white man's clothing he had worn since leaving Pittsbourgh, donning his own clothing and feeling greatly relieved and much more comfortable.

When he came back into the office, Huntington blurted, "I say!" and came to his feet. "Quite impressive."

"I'll be back," Renno told the old man.

Arrayed and decorated as a Seneca warrior, all his weapons displayed now, he earned a few curious gawks as he walked, straight and tall, to Nate Ridley's firm. The young clerk in the front office leaped to his feet and, for a moment, looked as if he might try to escape out the window.

Renno held up one hand, winked, and said, "Masquerade party."

The young man looked around nervously. "Oh, it's you," he said, and blew out a deep breath.

Nate Ridley chose that moment to come into the room, halted in midstride, then laughed. "Cousin, you look quite fearsome. No, let me amend that. You look quite capable." He examined Renno. "The man my great-great-aunt Betsy married must have looked much like this."

"It is possible, since there is a resemblance among the men in my family," Renno agreed. "My ancestor would have carried neither modern pistols nor an English longbow."

Nate was admiring Renno's facial paint. "I'll wager no one in Wilmington has ever seen war paint."

"This is not war paint," Renno said. "I am painted for council and peace."

"I'm pleased to hear that," the young clerk chimed in.

"You must come home with me so that my son, James, can meet you," Ridley urged. "He's wild about tales of the frontier and absolutely enthralled by what few stories I know about Aunt Betsy and her Renno."

Renno nodded.

"Let's be off, then," Ridley said, but their departure was delayed as the outer door burst open. A figure almost as imposing as that of Renno charged in, seeming to explode into the room with an energy expressed by a short, thick body with powerful legs. Dark skin proclaimed that the new-comer was Indian, but unlike any Renno had ever seen.

"This," Nate Ridley said, "is Billy the Pequot."

"Seneca?" the Pequot asked, examining Renno with bold, black eyes.

Billy the Pequot was not overdressed. His sole apparel was a sturdy but faded pair of wide-legged seaman's breeches, short enough to expose his thick, strong ankles and bare feet. Billy's black hair was pulled to a peak and secured at the very top of his head with a band, forming a crest that fell to hang down his neck. More spectacularly, all of his exposed, thick, only lightly haired chest was decorated with vivid tattoos. The motif of the decoration was definitely salty, with the main picture showing a short, strong figure in the prow of a whaleboat, harpoon raised and aiming toward a blowing whale.

"Seneca," Renno confirmed, extending his arm, Indian fashion, to be clasped by the shorter man. "I have heard of the Pequot tribe," Renno said, not adding that he had thought that the Pequot, one of the first groups to come in contact with the European invasion of North America, were no longer in existence.

"Then you are one of the few," Billy said, in English ringing with the sharp accent of the Northerner. "There aren't many of us left."

"Your land?" Renno asked.

The Pequot grimaced. "Long Island. We not only had to survive the English but the Dutch before them."

"Billy is a shipwrecked whaler," Nate explained. "He's been waiting for a ship north."

Renno considered himself to be a good judge of men, and he had liked this short, energetic, somewhat cocky Indian immediately. "I, too, need to find a ship going north," he said.

"Good, we will look together," the Pequot declared. "I long to feel the deck of a good ship under my feet again, to have the harpoon in my hands."

"Billy, the *Estelle* hasn't made harbor yet. We expect her any day," Nate said. Then, thinking how much his boy would enjoy visiting with two Indians of such different cultures, he continued, "Renno is joining my family for dinner. Please come along with us."

"My pleasure," Billy said.

Peggy Ridley, Nate's wife, was putting the finishing touches on the meal, working over a huge, black, iron stove in the kitchen of the Ridley house, which sat on the Front Street bluff overlooking Cape Fear. She was not expecting Nate until dark, so she was surprised to hear the front door open while the sun was still over the western horizon.

"Is that you, Nate?" she called, wiping her hands on her apron and starting out of the kitchen to halt in midstride as she came face to face with two apparitions in her own dining room. A small squeal of surprise escaped from her before Nate, laughing, stepped out from behind Billy the Pequot's broad bulk.

"What on earth?" Peggy gasped.

"You know Billy," Nate said, now chuckling. "And

this is our cousin, Renno of the Seneca, great-grandson of my aunt Betsy."

"Gentlemen," Peggy said, blushing, "forgive me. It's just that—"

"It's not war paint," Nate added.

"Thank goodness for that," Peggy said. She was a fair woman, well formed, dark of hair, and her face had a rosy glow from working over the heated cookstove.

Although he was taking pleasure in Nate's amusement, Renno knew that they had played a cruel trick by startling Peggy. He said softly, "Please forgive us, Mrs. Ridley. Cousin Nate thought that your son might be interested to see me in Seneca dress. I'm so sorry if we've frightened you." Then he bowed.

The contrast in the cultured voice and his appearance left Peggy completely nonplussed. She wiped her hands on the apron, smiled at Renno, and said, "I'm sure James will be pleased." She turned to Nate. "Did you invite these gentlemen for dinner? There's plenty." She smiled again at Renno. "I'm eager to hear more about Nate's aunt. She's a legend in the Ridley family."

James Ridley, aged seven, was enthralled to have both Renno and Billy at table. Eyes wide as Peggy and Nate coaxed Renno into telling tales of the frontier and of the original Renno and Betsy, the child totally neglected his dinner.

It was a pleasant meal. Renno noted genuine affection between Nate and his wife in the way they glanced at each other and the love in her voice when Peggy asked if Nate wanted another serving. Although there was no physical resemblance between Peggy and his own fair-haired Emily, Peggy's gentleness was a bittersweet reminder to him of what he had lost. While Billy the Pequot spoke of his love for the sea, for the adventure of chasing the great whales, and for subduing such huge creatures with his harpoon—"setting the iron"—Renno withdrew into himself and questioned the wisdom of his being so far from his home and the children Emily had given him.

"All right, James," Peggy was saying, "that's enough excitement for the night. Time for bed."

"Please, Mother," James begged, but a stern look from Nate sent him, head bowed, away from the table.

Not long after, Nate led the men to a covered veranda overlooking the river at the foot of the bluff. Across the river the low, flat marshes extended toward a distant tree line, and Renno could almost feel the distances . . . could almost smell the far frontier . . . the dense, private forests of the Cherokee lands.

"Well, Cousin," Nate said, leaning back, putting his feet up on a low stone wall, "so you want to go north. I take it that your mission has something to do with Beth Huntington."

"She and her brother traveled far and fought well with me," Renno replied.

The evening was pleasantly cool. The spring flowers, azaleas, lilies, and flowering trees, perfumed the twilight. From across the river came the mournful call of a whippoorwill.

"It is my understanding," Nate said, "that she went to Quebec."

"So I am told," Renno said.

"That was very unwise," Nate continued, and Billy nodded in agreement. Renno waited in silence, for it was obvious that Nate had more to say. "There is no great fondness for the British here, so the lady, as you might guess, was not well received. Cornwallis didn't win many friends during his occupation of Wilmington, and many of our citizens came here from Brunswick Towne after the British burned it."

"How well did you know her?" Renno asked.

"It was inevitable that we run into each other, being in the same business," Nate answered. "I found her to be very beautiful, quite pleasant, and a fierce competitor. She came to me, asking how best to get to Canada, and I advised her to abandon the idea. She said that there was no danger, that her father had, through correspondence, arranged a meeting with an important government official."

"Did she mention his name?" Renno asked.

"No," Nate said, "but my guess is that he is an important military man, since most of Canada is administered by military governors."

"Why would the British seize the Huntington ship after having assured Cedric Huntington that she would be welcomed in a Canadian port?"

Nate shrugged. "Maybe the ship was seized by someone other than the person with whom Huntington was negotiating. Or some person in local power might have seen a chance to make an immediate profit by seizing it—and with impunity. After all, the ship belonged to a British renegade who had deserted her own country to live in the United States. Even if it had been a United States ship, the government is in no position to retaliate. All that anyone could do would be to lodge a protest through diplomatic channels."

Billy the Pequot had been silent until that time. "The Huntington ship is not the only one that has been seized, or stopped and searched, by the British."

Nate grunted. "That's true. I don't think many people know it, but there's a crisis building up. Conditions for British seamen on British ships are abominable. Given the chance, many jump ship in American ports. They find life easier on American ships, but the British don't like losing their seamen. That may have something to do with the Huntington ship being seized, because several British seamen were working on her. The Brits consider such men to be deserters, and they feel within their rights to stop an American ship and seize any such so-called deserters."

"What is the best way for me to get to Canada by sea?" Renno asked.

"I'll tell you, Cousin, what I told Beth: forget it. No American ship will take you. You'll have to ship to the islands, then take a British ship."

"That would be very time consuming," Renno objected.

"There is a way," Billy the Pequot ventured, and Renno looked at him expectantly. "The Huntington sloop is now being loaded wth pitch and salt for the voyage to Boston."

"But you'd risk losing the Huntingtons' last ship if you take her into Canada," Nate protested.

Billy stared at the evening star, hanging low to the south. "I am only a harpooner," he confessed, "but had I lost a great schooner and my daughter, I would willingly risk losing a small sloop."

"I will speak with Cedric Huntington," Renno decided, agreeing with Billy's rationale.

"I'll be traveling on the sloop," Billy said. "I will teach you how to set iron during the trip."

Beth's father showed no hesitation at all when Renno told him of his proposal. "I'll be eternally grateful," he said. "I've cursed myself endlessly for letting her go, my friend."

The Huntington sloop was dismayingly small. With Billy at his side, Renno stood dockside and watched as stevedores loaded the last kegs of salt.

"Don't let her looks fool you," Billy warned. "She's a good ship and can take anything the sea throws against her."

"And yet there is doubt in your voice, my friend," Renno said.

"Not because of the ship," he said, and pointed toward the small seaman who was coiling line on the bow of the sloop. "That one is a British deserter. How many others are aboard?"

"We'll have to talk with the captain," Renno said.

He led the way to the gangplank, waited until burly stevedores had cleared, and walked onto the deck of the ship.

"There," Billy said, pointing. A tall, slim man in dark breeches and coat, his gray hair gathered at the nape of his neck under a tricornered hat, was yelling obscenities at a group of men lashing casks to the deck.

"Captain O'Brien?" Renno inquired when the dark-clad man was silent for a moment.

O'Brien swiveled. His face was pocked, and his large nose showed large pores and an unhealthy tinge of red. "What in thunderation hell are you?" he demanded.

Renno silently handed him Cedric Huntington's letter. The captain opened the letter, muttering, and glanced at it. Then his gray, bloodshot eyes glared balefully at Renno. Although it was early morning, Renno caught the stench of rum on his breath.

"We'll see about this!" O'Brien yelled, turning almost to run off the ship, disappearing into Huntington's office.

Renno noted that Billy was examining the ship, but the white Indian was not able to draw any conclusions from the Pequot's impassive face. To Renno's eye the ship seemed sound if a bit untidy. The seamen appeared much like the ship's crew on the voyage to North Carolina from New York City. They seemed efficient as they prepared the ship for sailing.

A large bearded man in the faded dress of a ship's officer saw Billy and came lumbering toward where the two Indians stood. He had been at the stern, overseeing the stowing of cargo.

"Well, harpooner," the large man said with a wry grin, "this ain't exactly your sort of ship."

"It is better than walking or swimming," Billy replied affably.

The large man was examining Renno with a critical eye. Billy gave Renno a wink and said, "Mr. Tarpley, I'll have you meet the owner's agent aboard, Mr. Renno."

Tarpley blinked and rubbed his bearded chin before speaking. "Well, blimey," he said, "so that's what sent the cap'n running. The owner's agent, you say?" He stuck out a hand. "Sir, I am Moses Tarpley, first mate of this tub."

Renno said nothing. Tarpley was big and rough looking. His speech branded him as a long-time man of the sea. He cocked his head and squinted one eye. "May I ask, sir, if there was something else that disturbed the cap'n other than having an owner's representative dressed up like a wild Indian?"

"Perhaps he didn't like his orders," Renno suggested.

"Be those orders a secret, sir?" Tarpley inquired.

"They are intended for the crew," Renno said.

"I see. It's like that, is it?" Tarpley rubbed his beard again. "I think those orders cover more than a trip to Boston Harbor and back."

"We will deliver our cargo in Boston and then sail northward into Canadian waters," Renno explained.

"Hell's bells," Tarpley said with a wide grin. "I'll bet ole— I'll bet the cap'n needed a change of britches after that. Canada, you say?"

"There are British sailors on your crew," Renno stated.

The first mate's grin faded. "Yes, sir," he admitted. "And I think I get your point right off. They's four of the limeys, sir."

"I will speak with the captain about them," Renno said. "In your opinion, can those men be replaced quickly?"

"That depends on how much bonus money you're willing to pay," Tarpley said frankly.

Renno saw Captain O'Brien come storming across the wharf. "Thank you, Mr. Tarpley," he said. The first mate gave an informal salute and went back toward the stern of the ship. O'Brien half ran up the gangplank and, puffing from his exertion, swept by Renno and Billy, trailing a gruff order to follow him. Renno motioned Billy to stay on deck and followed the captain to O'Brien's quarters in time to see O'Brien take a quick pull at a silver flask before returning it to his jacket pocket.

"I don't like this," O'Brien muttered. "I don't like it at all. We might as well get one thing straight. On this ship I am the captain and—"

"That is as it should be," Renno interrupted, his voice cold. "I take it that you have no objection to your orders from the owner, Captain."

"I have a damn lot of objections," O'Brien complained. "We've lost one ship to the British. Damned foolishness to lose another."

"Captain," Renno said evenly, "I don't think it's too late to replace you."

O'Brien's face went red. "The devil!" he shouted. "This is my ship, and where she goes I will go, and you'll not have to question my courage."

"Good," Renno said. "You have four British seamen aboard. Send them ashore at once and have them replaced if you can't get by without them."

O'Brien sputtered for a moment, then calmed. "Yes, that makes sense. Where we're going it wouldn't do to have limey deserters aboard. I'll see to that at once."

"While this vessel is on the sea," Renno stated, "you are captain as long as you control the ship, the men on her, and your thirst for rum."

O'Brien's face flooded with color again, but he was silent.

Renno stared into the captain's bloodshot eyes. "I'm sure you have your work, Captain, if we're to get under way on time." He turned without waiting for an answer and found Billy on deck. The Pequot showed him to the cabin they were to share.

"It's a good enough crew," Billy said as Renno stood inside the small cabin and examined the two bunks. "Not the best. Not the worst. But I wouldn't want to have to depend on them in a fight."

"If there is a fight," Renno told him, "I will have already lost."

Renno stood on the bow of the little ship as she made her way down Cape Fear on a falling tide. Moses Tarpley was maneuvering the ship and giving the orders. Captain O'Brien was apparently in his cabin. Tarpley, remembering Renno having said that the question of taking the ship into Canadian waters was to be put to the crew, had offered to have the men assembled on deck, but Renno had declined, telling Tarpley that there would be time for that in Boston.

Once again Renno watched the deeply forested western bank of Cape Fear slide slowly by. And then there was the open sea and night, and when he went into the cabin, Billy the Pequot was already asleep. A spring northeaster met them head-on as the ship put out farther to sea to skirt offshore from Cape Hatteras.

Renno, uncomfortable in the closed cabin, spent most of his time on deck in spite of the dampness, the wind, and the chill. He had gone there on the morning after the ship had run into the storm, leaving Billy asleep. Overhead the sails strained, and the ship was rolling in a quartering sea with a motion even more violent than Renno had experienced on his one previous ocean trip. He had to cling to rigging to keep his footing, and white water cascaded over the deck repeatedly. He was considering going below when he saw Billy emerge from the hatchway and, hanging onto rigging and the rail, make his way to stand beside Renno, wiping windblown water from his face.

"The captain must think he's in a race!" Billy shouted to be heard over the storm. "If he's not careful, he's going to rip the sticks right out of her."

Renno wasn't sure what Billy meant, but he knew that things did not feel right.

"He's carrying too much sail," Billy yelled. "If the winds get any higher, the strain will be too much for the masts."

The deck watch was huddled in various places of shelter. The storm moaned and crashed around them.

"Look, there's Tarpley," Billy said, punching Renno's arm to get his attention.

Bent over against the wind, the first mate made his way to the wheelhouse. He was inside only a few minutes before he came out, his arm around Captain O'Brien. The captain was unsteady on his feet. Tarpley escorted the captain to his cabin and reappeared, bawling orders that could be heard even over the howling of the wind. Seamen left their shelter and swarmed up the rigging, and within minutes great sheets of canvas had been lowered and furled and the ship's frantic motion had eased.

The storm blew itself out before another dawn, and the ship plowed northward through calming seas. Now it was pleasant to be on deck. Renno stood near the bow, watching the waves and the flight of sea gulls following the ship in hope of a tasty tidbit. As Billy had said, she was a good ship. Beth had named it *Apache*. That name had given Renno pause when he first saw the ship, and when he had found out that the four-master that had been seized in Canada was called *Seneca Warrior*, he had been given more food for thought, and it all pertained to the relationship between him and Beth.

It had never made sense for her to have stayed in the United States. True, she had been impressed by the vastness and the beauty of the country, but she had not chosen to stay in that wilderness. She had settled in a small port city in North Carolina. Why?

Renno remembered that during that long and dangerous trip to Devil's Mountain, he had spent much time with Beth, first to learn Spanish, and later for the pleasure of her company. Nothing improper had ever passed between them, but nonetheless Ena had expressed concern. Upon their return, when he discovered that Emily had died in his absence, Beth had been sympathetic, but as befit a friend. There had never been any indication that Ena's fears of Beth falling in love with Renno had cause. Beth had always been a model of propriety, except, perhaps—and he had to smile at that memory—when she had been frightened by a concert of coyotes while taking a bath in a river and, in her fear, had run naked into his arms.

And yet she had stayed—and named her largest ship the *Seneca Warrior*, for him. Had she stayed in the United States to be within reach of Renno? Had she chosen to go into business in Wilmington to give him time to get over his grief at Emily's death? And what were his own feelings?

The flame-haired one is the future.

He was a young man, and a young man needed a wife. But there was another spirit message that haunted him: *She was of us and yet not of us, else she would still be with us.* He had never been sure of the meaning of that, but it was clear to him that the message had referred to the fact that Emily was a white woman, not an Indian, not *of us*.

He admired Beth greatly. She was a beautiful woman and a fighter. Yet she was white and, moreover, English. To think of her living the life of a Seneca . . . no. Her part in his future could not be as his wife. In some other way she had something to do with the welfare of the Seneca people, and it was yet his to understand. He knew only

that he would find her and bring her home, with or
without her ships. For a moment that was enough.

From behind him a commotion on the deck broke
into his reverie. He turned to watch. A whistle piped a
call, and the crew began to assemble. Billy the Pequot
came forward to explain that the bosun's pipe call had
been an order for the crew to fall out and witness
punishment.

A burly sailor was lashed to a mast, and a bosun's
mate ripped away his shirt and began to lay on a cat-o'-
nine-tails. Renno, accustomed to death and blood, felt
his stomach lurch as the man's pale back began to show
ugly, raw, open cuts. Blood streamed down while the
bosun's mate counted to ten and halted. Captain O'Brien
had come back from his cabin and stood, hands behind his
back. He stepped toward the man lashed to the mast.

"Will you talk now, blast you?" O'Brien demanded.

"I told you, Cap'n, I don't know," the man sobbed.

"Lay on ten more," the captain ordered.

Moses Tarpley stepped up and had a whispered con-
sultation with the captain while the crew muttered among
themselves.

"Do you know the reason for this?" Renno asked
Billy, who shrugged. Renno walked toward the group of
men in time to hear O'Brien curse the first mate and see
him give Tarpley a vicious shove. Tarpley regained his
balance, and the captain turned to the bosun's mate with
the lash.

"Do as ordered!" O'Brien shouted.

"That's enough, Cap'n," shouted a seaman from the
massed crew. "We say that's enough."

O'Brien's hand went to a pistol in his belt. "Hold
your tongue!" he roared.

"We won't stand by and see you bare the bones of
one of our mates," the spokesman warned.

"You'll take a ball in the face, then," O'Brien threatened, drawing his pistol. The crew started to surge forward, and Moses Tarpley leaped to O'Brien's side, a pistol in hand.

Renno, not knowing why the lashed seaman was being punished but seeing that a mutiny was in the making, made his choice quickly. He leaped forward, ran to stand beside Tarpley, tomahawk in one hand, the spirit knife in the other. He was immediately joined by Billy the Pequot, who brandished a wicked-looking hunting knife.

"Ease off, men," Tarpley shouted. "You might take all of us, but a lot of you will die first."

It was Renno's cold, blue eyes and the weapons in both his hands that were most instrumental in stopping the forward surge of the crew.

"Mr. Tarpley," the crew's spokesman said, "Jones, there, didn't do nothing."

"There will be no more punishment for the moment," Tarpley said.

"You disobey my orders?" O'Brien screamed, turning his pistol on Tarpley. "I said that this man, this thief, will receive ten more lashes."

"Cap'n," Tarpley said pleadingly, "he's had enough."

"I'll show you," O'Brien shouted, swinging the pistol at Tarpley, lunging forward to reach out just as the ship made one of its regular leaps over a wave. Tarpley jumped aside to avoid the blow aimed for his head, and the captain staggered forward, stumbled, and toppled headfirst over the rail and into the ocean.

Renno and Billy had been left standing alone.

"Let's take 'em," the spokesman shouted, edging forward.

"You will be the first to die," Renno vowed coldly, moving to meet the sailor.

The seaman stopped.

Moses Tarpley had recovered, and ran to stand before Renno. "There'll be no killing on this ship. We have a man overboard. Bosun, get your men into position and prepare to come about. Prepare to lower the longboat."

"Let him drown and good riddance," someone shouted.

"You have three choices," Tarpley said. "Obey orders, disobey orders and face a trial in Boston for mutiny, or do your worst now."

For a moment the issue was in doubt. Then the bosun's mate who had whipped the man still tied to the mast took out his knife, slashed the man's bonds, turned, and shouted, "Prepare to come about. Boat crew at the ready."

There was another momentary pause, and then the crew began to obey orders.

They searched the waters without success until darkness came. Billy the Pequot showed his mastery of small boats by going with the party in the longboat. Renno found Moses Tarpley in the wheelhouse.

"Near thing, that," Tarpley said. "I told him to ease off. I told him, and I told him. But with the rum—"

"Why was that man punished?" Renno asked.

"The cap'n accused him of stealing a demijohn of rum out of his cabin, sir," Tarpley replied.

"Apparently you don't think he did," Renno said.

"Hard to tell, sir. Sailors are sailors and like their rum, but the cap'n—"

"Can you control the crew?"

"They're good men, sir," Tarpley said, nodding. "Treat 'em with the respect due a hardworking sailor, and they'll do their jobs."

"Tell them that, Captain Tarpley," Renno said.

Tarpley looked at Renno and grinned. "Well, I guess you have the authority to make it official like that. I'd be acting captain, at any rate, until we make port."

"Captain, I will need a crew on which I can depend when we sail from Boston Harbor. If you can bring these men into shape, fine. If not, we'll replace them in Boston."

"Give 'em a chance, sir. Let me work with them for a couple of days, talk to them."

Renno nodded. He was turning to leave the wheel-house when the bosun came in, giving that informal salute. "Mr. Tarpley, there's a sail coming up astern."

Tarpley told the man at the wheel to hold the ship steady, then grabbed a telescope and ran to the stern, Renno with him.

"She's a four-master," Tarpley said. "She's big and she's fast." He lowered the telescope. "May be just a merchantman, big schooner."

"And if not?" Renno asked.

"Man-o'-war," Tarpley responded grimly. "And since we ain't got many of those, if that's what she is, chances are she's British."

Tarpley called the bosun. "All sails," he ordered. Then, to Renno, "We can't outrun her if she's really after us, but we can delay the inevitable."

With all sails set, the *Apache* leaped through the seas. Behind her the British sails grew larger until Tarpley could see her clearly. "She's a man-o'-war, all right. The *Assiduous*. She's got good legs and enough canvas to cover Manhattan Island. I won't even tell you how many guns she's got. She's the one been stopping and boarding ships traveling out of American ports."

"Her intentions?" Renno asked.

Tarpley shrugged. "Maybe she'll just check our crew for deserters. Maybe she's shorthanded and wants a few of our own crew to fill in. At any rate, all we can do now is wait."

Renno did not have to ask Tarpley why a fight was not one of the options. The *Apache* was a small merchantman, and she carried four small guns, four pounders—guns that had not been fired, according to a crew member he had questioned, as long as that man had been aboard. In the captain's locker—Renno had made it his business to find out after the near mutiny—were four muskets and six pistols, plus a few rusting cutlasses.

By midafternoon the English warship was near enough that Renno could see many men on her decks. He prepared his weapons. He had a quiver of good steel-tipped arrows for his English longbow, plus two pistols, a tomahawk, the stiletto, and the spirit knife.

Billy the Pequot was honing the blade of a cutlass with a stone. "Well," he said calmly, "we can't outrun her and we can't fight her, but I'll see myself deep-sixed before I get impressed aboard her."

Chapter V

It was planting time. Toshabe, who had learned about growing things after coming to the land of the Cherokee, had always enjoyed that time of year. Her garden plot was next to that of her daughter, Ena. Thus it was that both women were lucky enough—or unlucky enough, depending on their degree of patience—to have Little Hawk as a helper. The progress of planting was sometimes slowed by the necessity of keeping the active boy from running through already planted rows, or of inspecting some trophy of the hunt, such as a small lizard.

Months had passed since Renno's departure. There had been no word from him. El-i-chi, however, had returned in due time from his own grief-induced seclusion in the snowy wilderness, and it seemed that Toshabe's younger son had become somewhat adjusted to his loss. He was still moody, though, and there were times when he would not appear in Toshabe's lodge for a meal for days, only to come back into the village from the hunt laden with fresh meat.

Toshabe would have been hard put to say which of her children gave her more pride. She was still a young-looking woman, belying the fact that she had three off-spring who were accomplished adults. Her eldest, Ena, was in her late twenties, having been born when Toshabe was still a slim girl. There had been times when she had had her doubts about Ena, the beautiful warrior maid, and Ena's childlessness was a continual sorrow. Now, how-ever, seeing her daughter so proud, so well formed, playing at being the good Cherokee wife, amused her. But Ena's good-wife act went only so far, and she was soon bored with the planting of peas, beans, potatoes, corn, pump-kins, melons, and cabbage. She had recruited three ado-lescent Cherokee girls to help on the second day with planting, and now Ena was acting as supervisor. She had offered to have the girls help Toshabe with her planting, but Toshabe enjoyed the smell and feel of the earth.

The sun was warm, the breezes gentle. Little Hawk had built a pen for captured lizards and was, for the moment, occupied. Toshabe, at the far end of the plot from where Ena was directing the work of her helpers, heard a noise and looked up to see a face she knew well, a fourteen-year-old Seneca girl called Ah-wa-o, the rose. She was a quiet girl, strongly built, with doe eyes and a lovely petal-fresh face that honored her namesake.

"Honorable Mother," Ah-wa-o said, "my father, Ha-ace, has sent me to help you with your planting."

"That is a friendly gesture," Toshabe said, bending quickly to hide the fact that her face began to burn at the mention of the warrior. Recovering, she stood and smiled at Ah-wa-o. "But you have your own planting to do, Ah-wa-o. Tell the panther, your father, that I thank him."

"My planting is all done, honorable mother," Ah-wa-o said. "It would give me pleasure to help you."

"Well, come then, child," Toshabe invited. "The maize is next."

It was not the first time that Ha-ace had extended goodwill toward her. For some months now, after a suitable period of mourning following the death of his wife, the senior warrior had been seeking Toshabe out, bringing to her during the winter the choice cuts of a newly slain deer and sending Ah-wa-o to her lodge with pails of fresh water.

Ha-ace was a man in his prime, a good example of the Seneca warrior, a man who had followed Ghonkaba faithfully and had fought with him during the white man's war. Although he had never aspired to leadership, Ha-ace had been one of the more dependable warriors during the long trek to the south, and he had given his allegiance to Renno for the fighting that had ensued in the new homeland of the Seneca.

Ena, seeing that her mother now had a helper, walked to stand nearby. She was smiling widely. "Hello, Ah-wa-o," she said so sweetly and so archly that Toshabe felt her face burning again. She had not asked for the attention of Ha-ace, a man five years her junior.

"And how is your father?" Ena inquired sweetly.

"He is well," Ah-wa-o said, unaware that Ena was gently needling her mother by speaking to her in this manner.

"It is good of Ha-ace to send you to help," Ena continued, her voice dripping honey. "I'm sure that my mother will repay him, when the new crops are ripe, by cooking him a fine meal."

"Ena," Toshabe said, "I'm sure you have work to do elsewhere."

Ena smothered a giggle and turned away. Toshabe glared after her, then seeing Ah-wa-o's puzzled expression, she smiled. "Perhaps I *will* cook you and your father a fine meal."

The work was finished early. Ah-wa-o had been a great help, and as Toshabe stood and stretched the tired muscles in her back, she had to admit that she was grateful after all. "Come," she said, "we will bathe in the stream."

Ah-wa-o smiled gladly. She chattered happily as they walked toward the stream, found a secluded place, and washed the sweat and soil from their bodies, unashamedly naked. They rinsed their clothing, too, for these would dry quickly in the warm air and sunshine.

The woman and girl climbed onto the mossy bank. Toshabe's figure was mature. And while it was true that she was no longer a slim girl, she made an impressive picture as she stood on the bank of the creek, shaking the water from her dress. A beam of sun coming through the trees highlighted her well-formed breasts.

When Ah-wa-o giggled, Toshabe looked up at the young girl, and Ah-wa-o pointed across the stream, hiding herself behind her own dress, to where Ha-ace stood tall, arms crossed, his face impassive, his chest bared to the spring warmth, his legs extending like strong pillars from below his loincloth.

Toshabe flushed and held her doeskin dress in front of her. "This is a place for women," she said sternly.

"Forgive me, Toshabe," Ha-ace replied. "I had no intention to intrude upon your privacy."

"Go, then," Toshabe said.

A smile spread on Ha-ace's handsome face. "And yet, I am glad I did," he admitted. Then he was gone, having faded quickly into the forest.

The warm flush of her face spread throughout her entire body. Although the Seneca did not subscribe to puritanical beliefs about the evil of nudity, there were standards of modesty, and they had been breached by Ha-ace.

And yet, she was thinking, he had smiled with pleasure. He had seen her naked and had been pleased. She slipped the dress over her head, and Ah-wa-o, still giggling, helped her pull the wet garment down.

"My father likes you," Ah-wa-o said.

Toshabe, experiencing sensations she had thought dead

with Ghonkaba, was a little confused. Into her thoughts came, in a rush, Ena's teasings, thoughts of Renno, so far away, and of El-i-chi. Then she drew herself up, shoulders back, head high.

"Ah-wa-o," she said, "we will not wait for the new crops for me to cook a meal for you and your father. Ask Ha-ace to join me in my lodge for the evening meal."

The village was small. More than one pair of eyes saw the tall warrior and the pretty girl striding toward Toshabe's lodge and entering. Two who saw were El-i-chi and the old shaman, Casno. Casno said nothing, but he noted that El-i-chi followed the progress of the pair until they disappeared into his mother's home, and that there was a cold expression on El-i-chi's face.

Above all else, El-i-chi wished that he had gone north with Renno. For months now he had fretted and had tried to still his restlessness with hunting or running and tramping aimlessly in the wilderness. The wound in his heart caused by Holani's death was no longer raw and open, but it still ached, especially in the night. To find peace of mind he had sought out Casno. El-i-chi could never believe that harm would befall Renno, but he was wise enough to know that his brother, whom he admired above all men, was in harm's way on his mission. But he was the brother of the sachem, and should the worst happen—the manitous forbid—it would be up to El-i-chi to provide leadership for the southern Seneca. With this realization came another: he knew little about the tribe's customs and history.

Old Casno's joints were stiffening more with each passing year, and there were times when he felt that it would be a great blessing for the manitous to escort him to the West, where he would once again walk without pain and gladly greet those who had gone before him. He had been more than pleased to teach El-i-chi about Seneca traditions. Although El-i-chi was quite young, in his early twenties, Casno had long felt that it was time for the young man to become more involved in tribal matters.

Casno knew that El-i-chi was made of good stuff, with the blood of Renno, Ja-gonh, and Ghonkaba in his veins. Even though he had previously been interested only in counting coup, fighting, and the loss of the wild Chickasaw girl, El-i-chi proved to be a good pupil, absorbing and memorizing the legends, sacred chants, and ways of the Seneca. He was such a good pupil that Casno began to have higher ambitions for him, and to the old man's pleasure, El-i-chi had shown interest when Casno suggested that perhaps the young man would become his apprentice, with the goal of becoming the tribe's medicine man upon Casno's call to the West. However, El-i-chi had not agreed immediately.

"I am a war chief," El-i-chi said doubtfully.

"A great one," Casno agreed. "Were I young and in battle, I would be proud to follow you or to have you at my side. I, too, have taken scalps. A medicine man can wear two hats, one for peace, one for war."

With that El-i-chi was satisfied, and now his brain was beginning to be stuffed with the lore of the medicine man, the recipes for healing potions, and the chants of healing, cursing the enemy, or simply imploring the manitous.

He found that the intense study—for Casno wanted to waste no time, feeling that his call from the spirits could come on any day—kept him from remembering the blood on Holani's face when he held her there in the far desert and saw that life had left her. But now he had a new distraction.

"My mother entertains," he said some minutes after he had seen Ha-ace and his daughter enter Toshabe's lodge.

"I had thought you noticed," Casno said slyly.

El-i-chi looked at Casno questioningly.

"She is a healthy woman, still young," Casno reminded him.

"But—"

"Ha-ace is a strong warrior, a good hunter."

"He is not Ghonkaba," El-i-chi said.

"No one can be Ghonkaba," Casno agreed. He rubbed an aching elbow. "She is a widow. Ha-ace has lost his wife."

El-i-chi did not like it. He wished that Renno would return so that they could discuss this new thing. He left Casno at the old man's lodge and trotted down the slope to the Cherokee village, there to be greeted by a flying small boy who launched himself at his uncle as El-i-chi came in the door of Rusog's lodge.

Ena and Rusog were quite lenient with Little Hawk, since the couple was childless. It was not Ena's fault, nor could Rusog be blamed, for their often fiery relationship was at its best in the privacy of their lodge. Rusog, of course, wanted a son, but his love for Ena was such that he did not mourn their lack of offspring.

So it was that Little Hawk was the undisputed master of that particular Cherokee lodge and was indulged in all things reasonable. Neither of his guardians would permit him to be destructive or disrespectful.

Since it was Uncle El-i-chi who was having meat with them, Little Hawk was allowed to eat with the adults. He bragged proudly to El-i-chi that he had taken three prisoners that day.

"Good, good," El-i-chi said. "Did you make them slaves, or did you take their scalps?"

"No scalp lizards," Little Hawk said seriously, and El-i-chi had to hide his mouth behind the drumstick of a nicely roasted turkey to keep from laughing.

The meal finished, Little Hawk wanted El-i-chi to tell the story about the search for the Apache gold. "I have told you that story many times," El-i-chi said.

"Tell again," Little Hawk begged, and then he went to sleep almost immediately in El-i-chi's lap as the story unfolded. El-i-chi fell silent, and Ena carried the boy to bed, covered him, then came back to sit looking across the fire at her brother.

"Something troubles you," she said. "Is it concern for our brother?"

"I would that I were with him," El-i-chi admitted, "but Renno is Renno."

"Yes," Rusog said. "We need not fear for Renno."

Ena, being a woman and the eldest sibling in the family, remembered times when she had tended El-i-chi, as El-i-chi often tended Little Hawk. "I will speak plain," she said.

"Doesn't she always?" El-i-chi asked, with a nod of amusement to Rusog.

"I am pleased that you study with Casno," Ena said. "It is fitting. One brother the sachem, the other brother the shaman."

El-i-chi nodded.

"And yet you are troubled. Don't deny it," she said. "True, you have lost a wife. I had come to love her, too, El-i-chi, and I mourn her, but the spirits will preserve her so that you will meet by and by."

El-i-chi looked away. The death of Holani was still a painful subject for him.

"So," Ena said. "You are a man, and you are young. You are Seneca, and there are nubile Seneca girls." She waved off a disgusted look from El-i-chi. "Forgive me, my husband," she said to Rusog, "but I think this must be said. Too long have the men in this family sought wives outside the tribe. True, the laws of kinship prevent you from selecting girls who are second or third cousins, but there are others, pretty too. A Seneca medicine man needs a Seneca wife."

"You speak truth," El-i-chi said. "When I am ready—"

"It is time for you to be ready," Ena broke in. "A man should not live alone."

El-i-chi, uncomfortable with the subject, started to rise. Ena reached over and put her hand on his arm. "But still that is not what is troubling you."

"You have the insight of a manitou," El-i-chi complained half-seriously. "You tell me."

"I think it is because the warrior, Ha-ace, pays court to our mother," Ena suggested, watching for the reaction. She smiled grimly when El-i-chi's face went stiff. "Ah."

"It is not fitting," El-i-chi protested.

Ena laughed and took El-i-chi's wrist. "I think it is wonderful. Mother has been long alone. She has paid tribute to the memory of our father for long enough. She has slept in a cold bed long enough."

El-i-chi jerked his arm away from Ena's hand and leaped to his feet.

"Listen, Brother," Ena said seriously, "do nothing to prevent this match if it is indeed the choice of our mother and Ha-ace. Give her the chance of having someone to lean on as she grows older."

"She has me," El-i-chi pointed out. "And Renno."

"But can you warm her bed?"

El-i-chi spat to show his disgust, then left the lodge.

When he was gone, Ena sighed. "What we need is a medium-sized war to occupy that one's mind."

"You favor Ha-ace's courtship, then, so much?" Rusog asked.

"I do," she answered emphatically. "My mother's beauty matches that of most women half her age."

"True." Rusog stretched lazily. "Indeed, were I unmarried, I might myself be having a meal in Toshabe's lodge."

With a hiss, Ena threw herself on him, bearing him down. "I am more than enough woman for you."

"Perhaps that is true," Rusog said, his hands finding

the sweet handles of her hips, his mouth touching her face. "Let us see. But if you don't be less noisy, you will awaken the boy."

Thoughts of love were far from the mind of Cornplanter, sachem of the Seneca. The new beginning had come, and the land, wet from a winter of snow, was drying now that the warm breezes were blowing. Cornplanter resided in a typical Seneca village that occupied a clearing in the virgin forest. To that village had come a messenger from George Washington, whom Cornplanter knew well, having fought against Washington's forces during the white man's war and having sat in council with him to agree to the treaty that, said many, had ended the greatness of the Seneca. The first messenger had said that Renno would come before the fall of the next snows. The second, Striking Snake, a war chief of the Cayuga, was another matter.

He sat now across the medicine lodge from Cornplanter, face painted for war. The formalities had been respectfully completed, the pipe had been passed, and Cornplanter held it in his hand.

Cornplanter, like the sachem from the south whom he had never met, had so much white blood that his face was the chiseled, fine, strong-nosed visage of his white ancestors. Under heavy, curved eyebrows, his deep-set eyes were dark and piercing as they stared at the Cayuga across from him.

Around him were the elders of the Seneca, mostly men who had fought in both the French and Indian wars, when the League of the Ho-de-no-sau-nee had turned the balance of power toward the English settlers, and in the great white man's war. They, too, waited to hear the words of the Cayuga war chief.

"Great chiefs," Striking Snake said after a long, dramatic pause, "I bring you greetings from our brothers to the west and from our British allies in Canada. And I speak for our brothers the Miami, and for their great chief, Little Turtle."

Cornplanter remained impassive.

"Long before the white man came to America," Striking Snake went on, "the wise leaders of the Seneca, the Cayuga, the Onondaga, the Oneida, and the Mohawk knew that it was wrong and wasteful for brother to fight brother. The great peace was declared." That was another way of referring to the League of the Ho-de-no-sau-nee. "For three hundred years we lived in peace and plenty in our land. Our warriors hunted deer, duck, turkey, and pigeons. They fished and trapped the beaver to clothe our young. Our longhouses were home to our people from the land of the deep snows in the north, around the great lakes of clean water, and into the hills of the south. Our messengers carried wampum to far places, and our peoples were great."

An old man grunted in approval. Cornplanter kept his impassive expression.

"Orenda, the powerful spirit who related all of us, made us part of nature. The master of life was kind to us, and our women grew food in plenty. The great tree of the sisterhood of all tribes, which was shown to our ancestor Degandawida by the manitous, grew tall, and an eagle perched at its top to keep lookout for our enemies."

Striking Snake paused to look around. In spite of his unappealing sharp face and eyes that seemed unable to look into the eyes of another man, he was an accomplished orator. He knew he had the attention of the leaders of the Seneca.

"Before the coming of the white man, we hunted lands that are now the state of New York, the state of Pennsylvania, and the lands of the Ohio, and many tribes paid tribute to us and looked to us for their protection. And how is it now?" Striking Snake asked.

An old man spat disgustedly. Others grunted.

"Now the white man tells us that we must confine our hunting to a pitifully small piece of land. No longer can our young warriors advance themselves by wandering. No longer can our hunters follow the deer where the deer takes them."

"It is true," someone muttered.

"Now the white man extends his claim into the hunting grounds of others," Striking Snake said, "and there are those who will fight. I have told my friend Little Turtle of the Miami, who now fights, that all the men of the League of the Ho-de-no-sau-nee, all the brave warriors of the Seneca, have not died in the wars of the white man. I have told Little Turtle that we will stand at his side and, while driving the white man from the northwest territories, gain for ourselves new lands that are as rich in game and sweet water as those that have been wrested from us." He looked around, challenge in his eyes. "Have I lied to my friend Little Turtle?"

Cornplanter knew that the Cayuga was not finished. He made no sound.

"Moreover, while we gain lands in the northwest, we also gain lands in the north, across the lakes, in payment for our victory, because the British in Canada, who will fight at our side, have promised us large tracts of land in Canada."

Striking Snake swept his shifting eyes down the line of senior warriors of the Seneca. "I have spoken," he said.

"Once before we trusted the promises of the British," said an old man who had fought against the colonists in the great white man's war. "We fought, and our young men died, and the British went away, leaving us at the mercy of our enemy."

"This defeat rankles in the heart of the British," Striking Snake answered. "They would remedy it."

"Many of our young warriors have already taken their families into Canada," said another of the Seneca.

"Where they have lands extensive beyond belief," said Striking Snake.

"To fight once more against the United States would mean breaking a solemn treaty, agreed to by our sachems," a younger man pointed out.

"Has the white man never broken a promise?" Striking Snake asked quickly, and there was a snort of derision from several men.

"The Seneca are divided. Those who fought with the United States live to the south," Cornplanter said, thinking that it was now time for him to speak. "Would you have us divided once again, for there are those who have had enough fighting."

"Has Cornplanter lost his will to fight?" Striking Snake needled.

The sachem drew himself up and looked at the Cayuga coldly. "You come to us with a messenger stick," he said, and that was enough to let the Cayuga know that had it not been so, Cornplanter would have repaid the insult.

"The sachem of the Seneca to the south will counsel me," Cornplanter said. "He who has already joined the United States, who has fought on their side, will give us his thoughts. I am interested to know how the United States treats its allies, to see if their treatment matches that which we received from the British . . . desertion."

Striking Snake felt quick anger. In so many words Cornplanter had kept the Seneca uncommitted. Striking Snake had not been with Little Turtle when Renno, the Seneca sachem, had traveled through the northwest territories. If he had been, he would have killed the Seneca and taken his scalp.

"We will speak of this later," Cornplanter declared, indicating that the council was over.

There was nothing Striking Snake could do. His own people, the Cayuga, had also delayed making their decision, and the others of the once-powerful league were

even more indecisive. Hatred gnawed at his stomach even
as he took one last meal with the Seneca before leaving.
He himself would kill white men. They had taken all that
was dear to him—his home, his father, his brothers, and
lastly his wife and young son. His mission in life was to kill
white men, and any who were not with him were against
him. He would tell the British not to count on the loyalty
of the league and that fire and death would have to be
rained on those who stood with the whites of the United
States.

A puff of smoke exploded from a cannon port on the
starboard side of the British man-of-war *Assiduous*. Renno
saw it, knew what it meant, and braced himself as the
sound of the cannon's roar came to him. The ball made a
rushing sound through the air and splashed into the water
a hundred feet in front of *Apache*'s prow.

"Strike sails, Bosun," Moses Tarpley ordered. "Prepare to accept a boarding party."

Billy the Pequot stood at Renno's side as the *Apache*
slowed then wallowed in the waves. A longboat was lowered from the *Assiduous*, then two more. Oars worked in
unison, and soon the longboats were alongside the *Apache*,
and British sailors, armed to the teeth, clambered aboard,
taking a defensive position with swords at the ready.

"Captain coming aboard," said one of the British sailors, and all sprang to attention.

First, a plumed hat showed above the gunwale, then
a stern, young, arrogant face. The captain's eyes raked the
deck, lingered for a moment on Renno, and then the
officer was leaping lithely onto the deck to stand with his
hands on his hips. "And who is in command of this vessel?" he demanded.

Moses Tarpley stepped forward. "Captain Tarpley, at
your service, sir."

"Muster your crew, Master Tarpley," the Englishman ordered imperiously.

Tarpley knew better than to argue. He gave orders, pipes blew, and those crew members not on deck came on the run.

"Take a few men below to be sure we're honored by the presence of all," the British captain said to one of his officers.

Renno had seen the type before. He guessed the Britisher to be a second or third son of a peer, without an inheritance of his own, trying to make a place for himself with the Royal Navy. The white Indian had fought against such men and had found some of them to be worthy foes, if a bit weakened by their own high opinions of themselves. He stood ready to sell his life dearly, but for the moment he was silent.

"No one below, sir," was the report as the search party came back on deck.

"I am Horatio Jaynes, captain of His Majesty's ship *Assiduous*," the arrogant Britisher said. "I have reason to think that deserters from His Majesty's service are aboard this vessel." He walked, making his heels sound on the deck, to peer into the face of a crewman. "Speak to me," he ordered.

"What do you want me to say, sir?" the crewman asked nervously.

"Listen closely, all of you," Jaynes said, raising his voice. "I want to know your names, your ages, the names of your families, the places where you live."

Jaynes had found that the quickest way to detect a deserter was by hearing him speak, for the Americans, as they were beginning to call themselves, perverted the English language abominably.

One by one he stared into the faces of the crew and listened carefully as each man talked. When he came to Billy the Pequot—whose hand was on his cutlass—he lifted a handkerchief, sniffed, and moved on to look into the pale blue eyes of Renno. Renno's cold gaze caused him to step back a half pace.

"Ah," Jaynes said. "A blue-eyed Indian?"

Renno had seen Tarpley and the crew of the *Apache* humiliated by this strutting peacock in his fancy uniform. He spoke with his English accent.

"There are no British deserters on this ship," he reported.

Jaynes's jaw dropped. He glanced behind him, then back to Renno. "An interesting manner of speech, my Indian friend."

In French Renno declared, "Nor are there any deserters from the French navy."

"You interest me," Jaynes said.

"And you, me," Renno said, switching to English and the rough frontier accent, "for my knife longs to gut you."

Jaynes blinked and looked down at a quick movement to see the flint knife an inch from his waistcoat.

"Take me this one," he ordered, not taking his eyes off Renno.

"If one man moves," Renno hissed, "you will be the first to die."

Jaynes pursed his lips. "By the Almighty, I think you mean it. Who in Hades are you?"

"I am Renno, of the Seneca."

"Indeed?" Jaynes asked, stepping back again, looking at Renno from head to foot. "I have heard of you."

"There are no deserters on this ship," Renno repeated.

"It was my understanding, Renno of the Seneca, that you were to counsel Cornplanter."

Renno hid his surprise well.

"Is this true?" Jaynes asked.

Renno had been regretting his rashness, but now he realized that his defiance had brought him a valuable piece of information. So the British were interested in the outcome of his meeting with Cornplanter. "It is true."

"And so you sail to the north," Jaynes said. He turned away. "Prepare the boats," he ordered. He took two steps, his hands locked behind his back, then faced Tarpley. "My apologies, Captain," he said. "I trust there will be no hard feelings. Apparently you honor the agreements between our two countries, for there are indeed no British deserters aboard."

The British sailors were climbing down into the rowboats. Jaynes stood at the rail, hand on chin, musing. Then he looked at Renno. "Sachem, a word with you?"

Renno joined Jaynes by the rail, where the Britisher spoke softly. "To speed your mission I offer you a berth with us. We can put you in Boston Harbor far ahead of this sloop."

Renno had been doing some quick thinking. He could only guess that Jaynes had learned of him in Canada. What he could not answer was why the British were so eager for him to meet with Cornplanter. Had the northern Seneca sachem already committed himself to the British? Certainly the British could have no hope that Renno would ally himself with them, unless they were hoping that Cornplanter, greatest sachem of the main portion of the Seneca tribe, could influence him.

"Captain, I thank you for your concern," he said. "I find the *Apache* to be swift enough for my purposes."

"Well, then," Jaynes said, turning and disappearing over the gunwale. Two of the longboats were already moving toward the *Assiduous*. Jaynes's boat quickly followed.

"What was that all about?" Billy the Pequot asked, coming to stand beside Renno as Tarpley shouted orders behind them and the *Apache*'s crew began to scurry up the rigging to hoist sails. "That pretty man knew you."

"He knew *of* me," Renno said.

"What's this about a council with Cornplanter?" Billy pressed.

"My friend, there is a long story to tell. And since you plan to leave us and go back to your whaling when we reach Boston, there is no need for you to know," Renno said.

Billy gazed into the sky, watching the flight of a gull for a moment. "About that," he said. "This is not the time of year for the whalers. I can get a ship at any time. And although I have sailed the far northern waters, I have never been to Canada."

Renno nodded. "There will be danger."

The Pequot shrugged. "There is danger everywhere. A waterspout can come up from a clear sky and swallow a ship, men and all."

Renno had come to respect the strong, squat Pequot. Billy would be a good man to have at his side.

"If you feel the urge to see Canada so strongly," he said with a smile, "come with me to our cabin, and I will tell you that long story."

Boston Harbor was crowded. British merchantmen were there, along with many American ships. The *Apache* had to wait for wharfage, and while she was anchored in the harbor, Renno asked Captain Tarpley to muster the men.

"The *Apache* will not sail south just yet," he told them. "She sails to the north, into Canadian waters. I am going into Canada to find Beth Huntington and the *Seneca Warrior*. The *Apache* will be under the command of Captain Tarpley. Any man who accompanies us will be paid a bonus of one golden English guinea upon our return to Wilmington. Any who choose to stay here in Boston will be paid wages for the voyage here. I will give you time to consider this matter. Please give your decisions to Captain Tarpley."

Renno went to his cabin and waited. Within a quarter hour there was a knock on the door, and Billy the Pequot, followed by Tarpley, entered.

"Only one man wants off," Billy said, showing his strong, white teeth in a grin.

"Well, you've got your crew," Tarpley said happily, "and a captain who is not quite sure he's got good sense."

"Good," Renno said.

Tarpley was looking at him oddly.

"Is there a problem?" Renno asked.

"Where the hell did you learn French?" Tarpley asked.

"My grandmother once spent time in France," Renno explained, "and my mother is half-French, half-Erie."

Tarpley rolled his eyes. "And that tea-sipping limey talk. Next thing I know, you'll be telling me you're the long-lost son of old King George hisself."

Chapter VI

Billy came aboard the *Apache* as she was preparing to cast off from Boston. The Pequot carried some of the most deadly and effective-looking weapons Renno had ever seen.

"Tools of the trade," Billy said in answer to Renno's questioning look and handed one to the white Indian.

Renno hefted the lance with a five-foot oaken shaft tipped by a steel spear that had a wicked, very sharp cutting head. "For throwing?" he asked.

"For close-in work," the Pequot replied. He brandished a shorter device, a harpoon, with a heavier shaft and a shorter steel extension that was tipped by a swiveling head. This would penetrate flesh and then swivel to form a wide implantation when reverse force was applied, to prevent its being pulled out easily.

Now Renno hefted a harpoon. It had respectable weight.

"A bit of nostalgia, Billy?" Moses Tarpley asked, walking up to see the lance and the three harpoons. "I hardly think we'll be after whales."

"We might find other uses for them," Billy suggested.

Renno himself had added a good musket to his arsenal. He had spent some time with Tarpley while the cargo was being unloaded, studying charts of the approaches to the St. Lawrence River and Quebec. As a young man Tarpley had sailed to the ports of Canada's maritime provinces before the war.

"We should be able to get well into the Gulf of St. Lawrence," Tarpley told Renno, "barring bad luck like running into the *Assiduous*. But if there's any traffic at all on the St. Lawrence after we round the Gaspé peninsula and head southwest, we'll be seen."

"Perhaps this will help," Renno said, producing a large, ship's-sized Union Jack.

"At a distance, maybe," Tarpley said.

The ship got under way without ceremony. Soon the cool waters of the Atlantic were all they could see, with Nova Scotia to the northeast. Tarpley took the *Apache* well offshore, and it seemed to Renno, who still was not fully adjusted to life aboard ship, to be a long, long time before the sloop came to a northerly course. The fair weather held, to the amazement of the sailors, who always expected rough weather that far north, and then *Apache*'s bow pointed westerly. Tarpley showed Renno their progress daily as they passed the Magdalen Islands to their port and then caught sight of Anticosti Island on the starboard.

Renno could not see much difference when Tarpley told him that they were now entering the impressive St. Lawrence, for land lay below the horizon. Two days later land could be seen on both sides, although still distant. As the waterway that gave settlers access to the Canadian interior began to narrow, Tarpley maintained a full alert for other vessels, but luck was with them.

Then, on a glowering, low-skied morning, Renno was

summoned to the wheelhouse, where Tarpley paced nervously. The captain pointed ahead to an island in the middle of the river. "There are several of those," he said, "which restrict us to a narrow passage, and then Quebec."

"And?" Renno asked.

"And you think we're just going to sail into Quebec harbor in broad daylight?" Tarpley asked incredulously.

"Yes," Renno answered.

Tarpley rolled his eyes and gave orders that required some fine seamanship. When the wind died to nothing, sailors in the longboat towed the *Apache* to round the last island that blocked their view of the fortress city. Seeing how the British stronghold was situated, Renno gained even greater respect for his ancestors who had participated in attacks on that seemingly impregnable site. But then his eyes were searching the harbor, where tall ships were at anchor.

"There!" Billy said, pointing. "The *Seneca Warrior*."

Renno saw tall masts and a sleek, beautiful hull. The ship that Beth had named for him was very impressive. She lay on her anchor line as if resting, and he saw no activity on her deck. He changed into clean buckskins and painted his face for council.

Moses Tarpley had been studying the ships at anchor through his telescope. "Renno," he said when the white Indian appeared at his side, "if you have any idea of trying to pass us off as a British coaster, forget it." He pointed and handed the telescope to Renno. There, at dockside, was the *Assiduous*.

"I think we've got someone's attention," Billy said, as two launches put out and began to make way toward the *Apache* as she drifted slowly.

Renno stood impassively, arms crossed, all weapons in place, as the boats neared and a uniformed official stood in the bow of the lead launch and yelled, "Ahoy! What ship?"

Renno nodded to Tarpley.

"The sloop *Apache*, out of Boston!" Tarpley yelled back.

There were armed men in the boats.

"Stand by to be boarded," the British official shouted as the launch drew alongside. Armed men scrambled aboard, their muskets pointed at the crew members on deck.

The official struggled over the gunwale, puffing a bit.

"Captain Moses Tarpley at your service, sir," Tarpley said with a salute.

"State your business, Captain," the official commanded.

"Passenger service, sir," Tarpley said. "We have brought Renno, sachem of the Seneca, for a meeting with the military governor of Quebec."

"Your cargo?" the official asked, for he would share in the profits from seizing this intruder.

"In ballast, sir," Tarpley said. "Our sole purpose is to deliver the sachem."

A look of disappointment settled over the official's face. "Are you the chief?"

Renno nodded. His weapons were prominent.

"I see," the official said. "You will remain here, under guard. I'll get word to the governor."

"You will escort this ship to anchorage, and then you will take me to the governor," Renno commanded, his blue eyes piercing those of the official.

"I say!" the official exploded, but his bluster soon faded. The military governor, Colonel Caleb Burnhouse, had been having many councils with Indians of late, and Burnhouse was not a man to cross lightly.

"You are expected?" the official asked Renno.

Renno nodded curtly.

The official considered the situation, still regretting that *Apache* was not another of those hopeful but foolish American ships that sought to do trade with ports where entry was forbidden. "We will tow you to your anchorage," he said at last.

"So far so good," Moses Tarpley said as the British boats, oars cutting deeply, towed the *Apache* to a spot not far from the *Seneca Warrior*. The anchor went down with a clank of chains.

Renno told Tarpley and Billy to wait for him. "If you don't hear from me in twenty-four hours, see what you can do about getting out of here."

"I'm ready to get out right now," Tarpley admitted.

Renno boarded the launch, and the rowers took him swiftly to the docks. The British official escorted Renno to a small building where a red-coated British soldier stood guard, and soon Renno, escorted by two redcoats, was walking through the streets of the town toward the government house.

Colonel Caleb Burnhouse sat in his office with his boots propped on the edge of a scarred desk that had survived a voyage from England and more than one war. He did not move when a knock came on his door and a young lieutenant entered, saluted, and said, "Sir, there is an Indian here who claims to be chief of the Seneca nation."

Burnhouse let his feet drop heavily, his heels thudding onto the floor. "His name?" He could not believe that Cornplanter would have come to Canada. He had been courting that gentleman through emissaries for over a year, and from all reports, in spite of Cornplanter's white blood, he was as unreadable and as indecisive as any full-blooded Indian with whom Burnhouse had ever dealt.

"Renno, sir," the lieutenant said.

"Renno?" Burnhouse mused for a moment. "Have him wait. Tell him I'm busy. Then get Captain Jaynes in here."

Captain Horatio Jaynes was already in government house, chatting with Burnhouse's staff officers. He was in the colonel's office within minutes, tall, as arrogant as ever, and impeccably dressed. His shore-dress uniform was resplendent with medals and gold tassels.

"There is an Indian here who claims to be Renno, sachem of the Seneca," Burnhouse said.

"Interesting," Jaynes said, taking a silver snuffbox from a waistcoat pocket and sniffing daintily. He had reported his encounter at sea with the *Apache*.

"It is obvious that he was not going to parley with Cornplanter, as he told you, if he is indeed here," Burnhouse remarked.

"Obviously," Jaynes agreed. "Where is this beggar? I'll have a peek at him."

Jaynes, in concealment, saw Renno standing with his arms crossed, fully armed, in a reception room. Jaynes walked back into Burnhouse's office. "It is he," he confirmed. "Why would he lie to me? If he intended coming here all along, why wouldn't he say so?"

Burnhouse looked out his window toward the harbor for a moment. "Indians lie as a way of life."

"Shall I confront him?" Jaynes asked.

"No, no. I'll see him alone." As Jaynes turned to go, Burnhouse said, "You haven't forgotten dinner? We haven't had much chance, as yet, to discuss conditions at home."

"No, no. It will be my pleasure, sir," Jaynes replied.

Burnhouse did not call his aide immediately. He put his feet back up on the desk and mused. He was a man of forty-five years, delicate-looking at first glance until one noticed that his nose was strong, his eyes hard. His lean form was deceptive, for he had marched his miles and had fought his share of battles.

As he wondered about the meaning of this sudden and unannounced appearance of a so-called Seneca sachem, he wished for the man who was his primary liaison with the various Indian tribes, the Cayuga Striking Snake. But the Snake was not yet back from his most recent journey into the lands of the old Iroquois League.

The colonel finally decided that he could manage without Striking Snake. He was experienced dealing with the Indians; before and during the war he had worked with the Choctaw in the south, trying to win their sympathies for the British cause in the conflict that was obviously coming. And for the past few years he had come to know the intransigence and duplicity of the half-dozen northern tribes that had fought with the British during the war.

His mind was not yet clear on just what tack he would take with this uninvited visitor. He knew only what Jaynes and Striking Snake had told him about Renno: that this chief was from beyond the Smoky Mountains of North Carolina, where a branch of the Seneca had migrated after fighting with the rebels. Burnhouse did not see how a small tribe of Indians so far south could help the British cause, unless this Renno had influence with the league. The league, if provisioned and armed from Canada, could cause a lot of trouble for the damned rebels in the border areas.

Caleb Burnhouse had never accepted defeat. The rotters in London and the king himself had not known enough about the war or the importance of the vast lands of America to understand what they were losing when they signed the treaty ending it. The desertion of the Loyalists in America rankled him almost as much as the defeat of proud British armies by ragtag farmers. He had been with Cornwallis at Yorktown, witnessing the surrender with a burning shame that had never given him any peace since. And he had other reasons to be a bitter man. Others had suffered from the war, but few had been robbed of so much as Caleb Burnhouse.

The Burnhouse Plantation, near Camden, South Carolina, had been one of the showplaces of the entire continent. That magnificent house where he had grown up, from which he had marched off to war with his regiment to face that drunken backwoodsman Francis Marion, had been burned to the ground by rebels. His mother and father had died there while the continuing battle of Camden raged around them. Even the fine horses died in the burning stables, and meanwhile one of Francis Marion's foragers was raping and mutilating Burnhouse's sister.

Burnhouse rarely saw his sister, whom he had managed to find and bring to a small holding in Nova Scotia, the remaining property of the once rich and proud Burnhouse family. She still woke up screaming in the night, even after all these years, and her scarred face was an unpleasant reminder to him of the losses he had sustained.

Burnhouse was a man who had not forgiven anyone— not the rebels, not the Loyalists who fled, not the government in England that had so pusillanimously surrendered a great nation to a handful of poorly armed men. His two remaining goals in life were revenge and recovery of at least portions of that lost empire.

His attitude toward Indians was much the same as it had been toward the black slaves who had flocked to the British armies in South Carolina. All the dark races were savage subspecies and therefore expendable, as had been the Indian allies in the northern areas. Burnhouse, although he had left South Carolina to join Cornwallis's army before the evacuation at Charleston, would have agreed with those men of the British army who left hundreds of their black allies to starve or die of disease on an island off the South Carolina coast, even though promises had been made to take the loyal blacks to England. But since these promises had been made to near animals, they were thus breakable.

Perhaps, he thought, his lanky legs outthrust, his feet on the desk, some use could be made of this Seneca sachem. He called his aide and in a couple of minutes was looking up at a man who was not quite like his expectations. He saw a young, self-assured white man in Seneca dress, who met his eyes without blinking until Burnhouse rose without offering his hand.

"We welcome you to Quebec, Sachem," Burnhouse said. "Will you sit? We have much to discuss, I suspect. But first some refreshment. Tea? Brandy?" He did not want to get the beggar drunk, but if he was indeed an Indian, his tongue might be loosened a bit by a couple of judicious ounces of good brandy.

"You are Colonel Caleb Burnhouse, military governor of the province of Quebec?" Renno asked, ignoring the offer of refreshments.

"I am," Burnhouse responded. "And you are Renno, a sachem of the Seneca."

Renno nodded. This one, he knew, was a man. The scar that just showed at Burnhouse's collar told Renno that the colonel was not a garrison soldier. His bearing and casual alertness told Renno that this was a formidable military man.

"Please sit," Burnhouse said. Renno sat on a hard, wooden chair and continued to assess his opponent. "You are welcome, of course. His Majesty's government is always interested in the welfare of our Indian allies and friends."

"I speak for the southern Seneca," Renno said, and waited for Burnhouse's reaction.

The colonel said, "Ah," in a way that gave away nothing. Then, "I know a bit about you, not much. You fought with the rebels."

Renno nodded. He was fully capable of matching Burnhouse's ease of language, but he had found that sometimes it paid to act the stoic, impassive Indian word miser. In an effort to get an Indian talking, white men often chattered on, revealing information and making points that would have been made better at a later time.

"And has your alliance with the Americans profited you, Sachem?" Burnhouse asked. "We had incomplete reports some time ago of a small war involving Spanish forces on the Tennessee River frontier. Did you fight side by side with your American friends again?"

"With our brothers the Cherokee," Renno said.

"Ah," Burnhouse said, nodding. "There was no help from the so-called United States?" He tried his own waiting game, lost, then said, "Perhaps you are ready to speak of the purpose of your visit here?"

"It is said that you give large tracts of land to those who fought with you," Renno said.

"Yes, indeed." Burnhouse felt that he was getting the picture. "But you have hunting grounds to the south."

"More and more whites cross the mountains," Renno explained.

Burnhouse was intrigued. He envisioned Indians savaging the frontier of the United States from the great lakes to the far south. "It is said that you seek to parley with Cornplanter."

Renno nodded. "First I speak with you."

"Yes, very wise," Burnhouse agreed. "Perhaps we can help in the reunion of the separate elements of your tribe."

"I have talked with the whites of the United States," Renno said. "They offer small reservations for the league. They have taken much land as punishment because the league fought with the redcoats. I know their minds. Now I would know yours."

Burnhouse was pleased. The man was shopping for the best offer. "There are vast lands in Canada. The problem of getting your people here—"

"Can be solved."

Burnhouse's previous dealings with various Indian chiefs had taken much time and patience. He did not want to try to rush this young sachem into a discussion of a possible role for his tribe in his own plans.

"Sachem," he said, "I'm sure you would welcome a rest after your journey. It is late in the day. I would be pleased to have you as my guest for the evening meal. And I would like to have you meet, on a more friendly basis, the ship's captain you encountered at sea, Horatio Jaynes. Over good food we can speak further of our mutual interests."

Renno nodded.

"Excellent," Burnhouse said. "I'll have one of my men escort you to my quarters and give you a chance to rest." He almost said, "and freshen yourself," but decided that that might be an undiplomatic remark to make to an Indian.

Renno rose when the young lieutenant came back into Burnhouse's office, acknowledged Burnhouse's introduction of the young man, and walked at the lieutenant's side to a sturdy but unimpressive two-story house not far from Burnhouse's office. He noted grimly that he was not to be bedded down in the house proper, but in what must have been either slave or servants' quarters in back. He assured the young lieutenant that he would be content, and the officer left him to examine quickly a suite of small rooms furnished with worn but serviceable furniture.

The first thing he did was to check for a route of departure, should that become necessary. There was no activity around the colonel's quarters as Renno went out a back door into a fenced enclosure. Beyond the stone fence, easily climbed since it was no more than five feet high, was an area of less impressive housing, then the waterfront.

The house that served Burnhouse as quarters was built in the British colonial style over an English basement. Smoke came from one chimney, but Renno detected no movement in the house except in the kitchen area of the basement, from which issued a male and female voice in idle conversation. The second story of the house showed a few windows at the back. To the front was the narrow street along which the British officer had escorted him. Escape, if it became necessary, would be best accomplished toward the harbor.

He had completed his scouting of the area and was

ready to go back to the quarters assigned to him when he
heard a noise, froze for a moment, and then looked up
toward the second story of the house. He saw through
distorting glass a gleam of red, a pale face. His heart
thudded. The window opened, and through iron bars he
could see clearly that Beth Huntington was waving at him,
one finger to her lips to tell him to be silent.

After a quick check, he leaped up, seized the roof of
the back stoop, pulled himself up, and using a drain pipe,
climbed to the first-story roof, which extended out just
enough to allow him to stand. Hugging the wall, he inched
his way toward Beth's window.

"Renno!" she whispered excitedly as he reached the
window, his head just high enough to look into the room.
He hissed for silence and reached for the iron bars to
steady himself.

"How many in the house?" he asked.

"Three servants, one soldier outside my door," she
whispered back.

"We will wait," he said. "Have they mistreated you?"
He had not intended to ask that question, but it flew out
of him, and he realized, with a small shock, that his first
thoughts had been centered not on his pleasure in seeing
her but on what might have happened to her at the hands
of the hard-eyed British colonel.

"Aside from seizing my ship and keeping me a virtual
prisoner, no," she told him.

"I am here," Renno said, beginning to move away.
Beth made a gesture for him to stay, but he merely
nodded and whispered, "I am having the evening meal
with the colonel."

"I eat at his table," she said.

"Then you don't know me," he said, and was gone,
dropping lightly to the ground, looking around to make
certain that he was still unobserved, and going to his
room.

Words kept ringing in his head: *The flame-haired one is the future*.

Now, at least, he knew where she was, and freedom in the form of the *Apache* was in the harbor. It was a long way up the ever-widening St. Lawrence to safety, however, and there was the other matter of Beth's ship the *Seneca Warrior*. He did not have a large enough force to fight his way out of the heart of a strong British garrison, and in the sloop *Apache* he could not be sure of evading pursuit.

A good soldier never passes up a chance to eat, sleep, or relieve himself. Renno slept, curled onto a couch with his weapons at his side. He was awakened by a knock, and when he opened the door, a house servant in livery said, "Dinner is to be served in a few minutes." The man waited while Renno stepped back to get his longbow and quiver, then led him through the back entrance and up a long hall. Renno heard Beth's voice before he entered an expansive dining room to see her standing, wineglass in hand, before a large fireplace in which a fire had been kindled to chase the evening chill. Burnhouse stood near her, and Renno quickly recognized the captain of the *Assiduous* standing to one side.

"Ah, there you are," Burnhouse said. "Now that we are all here, let us be seated."

Jaynes took Beth's arm delicately, escorted her to sit at Burnhouse's right, then took the end of the table opposite Burnhouse. That left Renno to sit at Burnhouse's left. The table was large enough to seat at least ten people. Renno looked across at Beth. She had her flame-colored hair raised high and arranged in an intricate style. She wore a green velvet gown with a string of pearls at her neck, glowing against her soft skin. Renno noted with some amusement that he had not been introduced to Beth.

"So, Sachem," Jaynes said, "we meet again under different circumstances."

Renno nodded. He hoped that the elegant Jaynes would not prove to be a troublesome complication.

"Our host didn't see fit to introduce us," Beth said coldly, playing her part well.

"Forgive me," Burnhouse apologized. "My dear Mistress Huntington, our guest is Renno, a chief of the Seneca."

The introduction was hardly formal, but Renno nodded at Beth impassively and turned his head to watch the servant enter with the first course, a tasty fish chowder done in the French manner.

"I trust that you will treat this guest better than you've treated me," Beth said to Burnhouse as he lifted a spoon. "Or, Chief Renno, have they kidnapped you too?"

"Sachem," Burnhouse said quickly, "you'll please excuse Mistress Huntington. I have had some difficulty in explaining to her that any attempt to break the British blockade against American ships by trading at British ports is tantamount to treason."

"And I," Beth said archly, looking at Renno but addressing Burnhouse, "have had some difficulty convincing Colonel Burnhouse that the Huntington name goes centuries back into British history and that my ship is a British ship, not American."

"Our women," Renno said, deliberately speaking around a mouthful of the chowder, "give us no trouble."

Beth flushed and looked away. Jaynes laughed. Renno noted that Beth's petulant complaints had not upset Burnhouse—that, indeed, there was a look of desire in his expression when he let his eyes rest on her.

"Please don't try to give our new ally a false impression of our British hospitality, my dear," Burnhouse said. "Have we not made you quite comfortable here?"

"Oh, quite comfortable," Beth agreed. "I am grateful to you, Colonel. I'm even grateful for the guard you set outside my door. However, I do think that in the interest of kindness to your men, you should make the guards' tour of duty shorter. The poor fellow who sits there at night almost always falls asleep from the tedium."

She was, Renno knew, giving *him* a piece of information.

"I have offered to make your stay even more comfortable," Burnhouse said suggestively, and Beth cast a quick glance at Renno out of the corners of her eyes. "But enough of this." He lifted his glass. "A toast to the brave and noble Seneca. May our friendship grow."

Renno touched his lips to the wine in his glass. He had never acquired a taste for alcohol. He had seen what overconsumption of alcohol could do to a man, and he saw no reason to put into his body something so potentially harmful.

"Chief," Jaynes said, "if you had told me that your destination was Quebec instead of the Seneca reservation for council with Cornplanter, I could have brought you here several days sooner."

"That is true," Renno replied, looking up to see a servant place steaming roasted beef on his plate.

"Yes, it is, isn't it," Jaynes said, a hint of displeasure in his voice.

"Perhaps the sachem saw no reason to entrust such delicate information to the first passing stranger," Burnhouse said.

"That is true," Renno agreed.

Beth, watching Renno in his lo-the-stoic-Indian act, almost laughed.

"The sachem is considering joining us," Burnhouse said.

Renno felt a cold chill. The very fact that Burnhouse was willing to make such a statement in front of Beth indicated that he had no intention of releasing her.

"Is that so desirable?" Jaynes asked skeptically.

"Quite desirable," Burnhouse replied. "The League of the Iroquois can put thousands of warriors in the field."

"Warriors?" Jaynes sneered. "Half-naked savages with stone axes?"

Burnhouse's cold eyes caused Jaynes to flinch. "Those half-naked savages, Captain Jaynes, ravaged the frontier during two wars. Their actions tied up rebel troops that otherwise would have been standing against our armies."

"Give me one brigade of redcoats," Jaynes said, "or even of Hessians."

"*Captain* Jaynes," Burnhouse said, his voice cold, deadly.

"Sorry," Jaynes said, flashing his teeth at Renno in an insincere smile. "No offense meant, old man."

"Captain Jaynes," Beth spoke up, smiling sweetly, "have you ever faced an Indian warrior in combat?"

"There are few Indians at sea," Jaynes declared. "Their canoes tend to sink, you know, in anything other than a quiet ripple."

"Perhaps it would be educational for you to face an Indian warrior," Beth suggested. "A test of arms?"

"Splendid idea," Jaynes responded, wiping his lips neatly on a linen napkin. "What say you, Chief? A friendly bout, just for the sport of it?"

"I do not fight for sport," Renno said.

"Ah, I thought not," Jaynes replied. He sipped at his wine and then continued. "Is it true that all Indians are deathly afraid of the long knives, of the saber, the sword, the foil?"

Renno was coldly silent.

"Actually, I would pit the newest recruit in a British regiment armed with a saber against any Indian," Jaynes said.

Renno chewed thoughtfully, let the silence linger. Then he looked at Burnhouse and said, "I can see, Colonel, why you need help, with men like this in your force."

Burnhouse laughed deeply. Jaynes flushed and pushed back his chair. "You have just declined a friendly challenge," he said. "Another insult and the challenge will not be friendly."

"As you like," Renno agreed, pushing back his chair and standing tall. "Your choice of weapons, sir?"

Jaynes stood, his face still flushed with anger. "Foils, of course."

"Now Jaynes, is that fair?" Burnhouse asked.

"I will not do more than pink the chief," Jaynes promised. "It is merely an object lesson, if you please."

"Your pleasure," Renno said, striding to the mantel, reaching up for one of the crossed foils hanging there. He waited until Jaynes had taken the other foil and stood flat-footed, motionless, the awkwardly held foil straight out in front of him.

"So, Chief," Jaynes said, now posing fashionably, one hand on hip, knees bent. "Here comes your first lesson in the use of the long knife." He lunged, as pretty as an illustration in a book of fencing instructions. With smooth motion, Renno flowed into a defensive pose and parried the thrust easily.

"Not my first lesson," Renno corrected, moving with the swiftness of a cat to rip three small rents in the front of Jaynes's jacket just over his heart.

Jaynes danced back, startled. As he looked down, his face grew quite serious. He moved forward, only to yelp in surprise as Renno's foil slid down his blade, contacted the grip, and with a twist loosed the foil from Jaynes's hand to send it spinning to clatter on the floor. Jaynes gaped in astonishment, and with lightning swiftness Renno's foil flicked the buttons off Jaynes's waistcoat one at a time, then flashed downward to sever the tie to his breeches. With a cry of dismay Jaynes caught the falling breeches, and showing his linen, his face flooded with surprise, shame, and embarrassment. He turned his back to Renno to hide himself from the eyes of the woman at the table. Renno slapped the captain's exposed backside twice with his foil, causing Jaynes to leap in surprise. The captain whirled, tugging at his clothing, his eyes burning with rage.

"Perhaps just a little sport," Renno said mockingly, aping Jaynes's prissy accent. He turned away and hung the foil back over the mantel, then seated himself. Jaynes, sputtering, whirled and stomped out of the room.

"Impressive is not a strong enough word," Burnhouse said. "May I ask where on earth you learned to fence?"

"On the frontier," Renno replied.

"Very odd . . ." Burnhouse said.

Renno smiled. "A British officer taught me when I was young. He said that he needed the practice against someone young and agile." He had not lied, for his fencing mentor, George Washington, had been, at least technically, a British officer at the time he first put a foil in the young boy's hand.

"I'm afraid you may have made an enemy in old Jaynes," Burnhouse said, "but no matter. He'll be at sea when you lead your Seneca to join us, my friend."

"We must talk of that," Renno said.

"Right-o," Burnhouse answered. "Will you excuse us, my dear?"

With one backward look at Renno, Beth retired, and he saw the swirl of her green skirts as she started up the stairs. Burnhouse poured himself brandy and lit a pipe.

"There is fine land north of the lakes, west of Niagara," Renno began.

"I'm afraid that's committed," Burnhouse said, "but farther to the west . . ."

Renno stated his needs for his tribe in square miles. There was some careful bargaining on Burnhouse's part, but then agreement.

"And now your part, my friend," Burnhouse said.

"I will go now to council with Cornplanter," Renno said. "I will tell him that our relationship with the United

States has not been equally rewarded, that our young warriors have died for promises that were not kept." It was true that he had been taught that to lie was a withering of the spirit of manhood, but that rule was not meant to be applied when talking with an enemy. "Cornplanter may or may not join us, but many of his young warriors will, as will warriors from the other tribes. That done, I will travel to the south, to prepare my people for the journey to the north. We will enter through Miami lands, where, no doubt, the war will already be under way."

Burnhouse leaped to his feet and extended his hand to Renno. "We will give you all the help you need."

"New muskets. Much powder and shot. Food. Warm blankets and cooking utensils."

"Done," Burnhouse promised. "May I offer advice about how to reach Cornplanter's Seneca lands in New York State from here?"

"Yes. I am far from home," Renno said, although he could picture the geography of the entire region in his mind.

"It will be simpler for you to go by boat up the St. Lawrence to Montreal, then take water transport across Lake Ontario. It will cut the time of your journey by many weeks."

"I accept your counsel," Renno said.

Chapter VII

Burnhouse escorted Renno across the open space between the main house and the servants' quarters. The colonel moved well, lightly and silently, and when a small noise came from the darkness, he and Renno both noted it. It was clear to the white Indian that the British soldier had had some wilderness experience.

"Good night, then," Burnhouse said at the door. "Tomorrow we will speak of transportation for you."

Renno did not bother to light an oil lamp. He lay down on the bed, covering himself, and was asleep almost immediately, although he had mentally prepared himself to awaken soon. His weapons were close at hand. When he awoke and checked the progress of a half-moon, he knew the time to within a quarter hour and felt the quiet that comes after midnight. He had not undressed and was alert immediately, so no time was lost. He checked for activity around the colonel's house, but all was dark, silent. He eased into the night, moving like a shadow across the courtyard. He had taken note that the massive oak front door of the colonel's house had impressive locks.

He flowed down steps to the entrance to the kitchen below ground level. That sturdy door was almost directly below the window of the room where Beth was being held. He did not know where Burnhouse's bedroom was located . . . possibly across the hallway from Beth's room, at the front of the house. He had already noted that the other rooms in the servants' quarters were occupied, with the sound of snoring coming from one, and assumed that all three house servants slept there, away from the house proper. That being the case, it would be unlikely for the kitchen door to be barred from the inside. He tested the door. There was minute movement allowed by the bolt of its keyed lock. One of the servants would have the large key in his possession in order to enter the house early in the morning.

The door opened inward, so that the bolt and its recess in the doorjamb were protected. Renno used the Spanish stiletto, thin and sharp, and quickly began cutting away the wood. The yowl of a prowling house cat made Renno momentarily tense, but then he was back at his work. It took almost a half hour for him to cut away enough of the protective moldings to feel the stiletto contacting the metal of the bolt, and another few minutes to get a hold strong enough to push the bolt back. He waited then, listening for any sound.

In the courtyard the cat yowled again and was answered by the low, eerie challenge of a tomcat. Renno waited. For minutes the two cats exchanged a wild serenade of challenge, then with piercing screeches, they clashed. Suddenly something moved past the alcove where Renno crouched—two tomcats entangled in a battle that would have little effect on the world but was deadly serious for them, an airborne ball of fur seeming not to touch the ground as it shot past.

The danger was that the cat fight had awakened the colonel or Beth's guard.

One cat disengaged, gave a final yowl, and vaulted over the fence around the courtyard. The silence of the night was now unbroken. Renno waited patiently for five more minutes, then entered the kitchen and closed the door behind him. He could feel heat radiating from the fireplace and saw a glow of banked embers. The house creaked once and he tensed, but it was simply the thermal contraction of timbers in the floor of the lower rooms, the ceiling of the English basement.

His eyes adjusted slowly to the darkness. He could make out the shape of a table and the darker spot that was the basement stairs leading upward into the dining room. He crept up the stairs on silent, moccasined feet. The door to the dining room was not locked. The light of the half-moon made it possible for Renno to pick his way around the table to the hallway, and then he paused at the foot of the stairs to the second floor, for there was a dim glow of light coming from the upper hall.

He went up the wooden stairs slowly and with great care, to lessen the danger of a creaking riser, pausing now and then to listen, like a mountain lion stalking a wary deer. As he neared the top he heard the soft buzzing breathing of a sleeping man. There was a braided oval rug on the upper landing. He paused there and peered carefully around the corner and into the hallway. The red-coated guard, uniform loosened for comfort, his musket leaning against the wall, slumped in a chair, legs stretched out, arms hanging at his side. He seemed to be sleeping soundly. He was on the near side of the door to Beth's room, and the door was about fifteen feet from the landing. Three other doors, two on the side opposite Beth's room, opened to the hallway.

Renno stood, tested the floor with each step lest a board creak, and padded quietly forward, inching his way until, with a leap, he landed without sound and struck the

guard with the flat side of his tomahawk on the left temple—
not striking to kill, although with such a blow, there was a
fine line between rendering a man unconscious for a long
time and crushing the skull at one of its thinnest points.
The sound of the blow seemed overly loud. Was there a
crunch of breaking bone? He was not sure. He lifted his
tomahawk for instant throwing, then faced the hallway and
its three other doors. The colonel could emerge from any
one of the doors, a pistol in hand.

He held his readiness for perhaps a full minute, but
there were only the sounds of a house at night—a sigh of
wind, the creak of a timber contracting as it chilled with the
cool Canadian night. The key was in the lock of Beth's door.
He turned it slowly. The lock bolt creaked as it slid back,
and then he was easing the door open. Beth's scent filled
his nostrils: the woman, her perfume. He closed the door behind him. He could hear her breathing deeply and evenly
in sleep. He padded to the side of a large, four-poster bed.
Her hair was loose, spreading over the pillow, seeming to
drink in the pale light of the moon through the window. He
belted his tomahawk and eased one hand behind her head
before suddenly clamping the other over her mouth.

She jerked into wakefulness, her eyes flying open,
her throat contracting in a scream smothered by his hand.
"Quiet, Beth," he whispered, his lips close to her ear.
Her hair smelled of some scent, a clean, heady fragrance.
Her body relaxed from its sudden tenseness. He removed
his hand, and she put her arms up and seized him, drawing herself to him.

"Thank God," she whispered.

"Let's go," he said, but he was reluctant to leave her
embrace, knowing with his entire being the womanly softness of her, with nothing separating them but a blanket
and her nightgown. He loosed her hold, and she threw
back the blanket. He saw the pale gleam of her beauty.

"Dress for ease of movement," he instructed her. She
went to a wardrobe and made small noises that tensed

Renno. He knew that he could kill more guards and even the colonel, but to do so would add risk, and now his main goal was not to kill the enemy but to get Beth and her ships safely away.

Beth dressed in wide-legged sailor's breeches, a shirt and jacket. "I found these more practical for shipboard living," she explained as she lifted her hair, tied it, and hid it under a knitted seaman's cap.

Renno opened the door quietly. The guard was slumped in his chair, but he was sleeping the long sleep now. The house creaked. The oil lantern cast its yellowish glow. Renno guided Beth ahead of him down the hall, breathing easier when they had negotiated the stairs and were on the ground floor. He was guiding Beth toward the dining room, headed for the kitchen. She halted, and he pushed into her, wondering at how he could still be so aware of the closeness of her when they were in danger.

"Renno," she whispered, her lips near his ear, her breath warm on his face, "in the study. An oilskin pouch. The colonel's papers."

"There is no time," he said.

"In that pouch you will find proof that he conspires with certain Indian tribes to make war against the United States."

She pulled away before he could stop her and was moving silently in the darkness. He stood guard, watching the front door and the stairs. She was back in a few moments. The oilskin pouch, with a strap for carrying, was around her neck, hanging under one arm. He led her through the dining room, down the steps into the basement kitchen, and then they were in the cool night air.

He boosted Beth to the top of the stone fence, aware once more of her warmth and softness. He vaulted up and lowered her to the alley on the other side of the wall and then, her hand in his, they ran lightly toward the harbor.

Now came the most dangerous moment. Troops were quartered in houses and warehouses along the waterfront.

There would be watches aboard the ships in the harbor. He said a short word of thanks to the manitous when the half-moon ducked behind a cloud and gave them the security of darkness as he led Beth onto the decks and began his search for a suitable boat. He found it quickly—a small dory with oars lying in it. He helped Beth down into the boat, climbed in after her, cut the tie with his knife, and pushed the boat away from the piling to which it had been secured. He sat at the back of the dory and maneuvered it with one oar, as if it were a canoe. That made for slow, awkward going, for the dory did not have the lightness and agility of a canoe, but it prevented the clatter of wood on wood and the squeak of an oarlock.

The moon came out from behind the cloud and gave a dim light. His only choice was to go forward. He felt better as he passed close in the shadow of a large British merchantman and saw no activity or hint of a watchman on her decks. Then he was in more open waters, the nearest anchored ship a hundred yards away. He could see the distinctive shape of the *Apache* ahead. Time was all important because there would be only a couple of hours of darkness before the early dawn of a Canadian summer day. He put the oars in the oarlocks and leaned to his work, and the dory now sped over the water.

The *Apache* was dark. He came at her from the stern and pulled the dory alongside. "Hold the dory in position," he told Beth, helping her to sit between the oarlocks. He leaped high. The dory rocked under him, making considerable noise of sloshing water. He seized the rail of the *Apache* and drew himself up, to feel a sharp prick on his chest as something pressed there.

"Hold," he said, for he recognized the squat, powerful form of Billy the Pequot. The object at his chest was Billy's lance.

"I almost skewered you," Billy said.

"Lower a ladder for the woman and secure the dory," Renno ordered.

Renno saw Billy begin to lower a rope ladder, then he raced to the captain's cabin, entered, and shook Tarpley by the shoulder. "We go," he whispered.

"Damn," Tarpley growled.

Beth was standing on deck. Billy was waking the crew, cautioning each man to silence. The ship began to come to life. The longboat was lowered, oars dipped into the dark water, and she moved. The anchor winch creaked dismayingly, but there was no reaction from the other ships. They were, after all, in secure harbor. They had no reason to be alert.

Moses Tarpley found Renno standing watch, his eyes scanning the wharves for any movement. "The *Assiduous* hauled out of here early in the evening," Tarpley told him, "downriver toward the sea."

Renno nodded.

"I see you've got what you came for," Tarpley said.

"Not quite," Renno said.

Slowly, laboriously, the *Apache* made her way out of the harbor. When she was far enough away to be hidden by the night from the shore, Renno watched as sailors went aloft and unfurled sail. There was a favoring breeze, light but steady. Tarpley called in the longboat that had been towing *Apache* with her oars.

Beth had left Renno's side to go into the captain's cabin, where she opened the oilskin pouch she had taken from Burnhouse's study. There were military documents dealing with troop supplies and transactions for purchase of food from local suppliers. Just as she began to wonder if she had wasted effort in stealing the pouch, she came to a series of copies of correspondence between the military governor and officials in London. She read rapidly, stowed the papers back inside the pouch, and went on deck.

Renno was standing beside Billy, who was steering the *Apache*.

"I've been looking over Burnhouse's papers," Beth said. "I can give you the numbers on British troops in the province of Quebec, their state of readiness, and their armaments."

"Good," Renno approved. "Such information will be of interest to General Washington."

"There was something else," Beth said.

Renno just looked at her without asking.

"We can also show that Burnhouse has approval and financial backing from London to incite trouble among certain Indian tribes. There's proof that London has advanced sums in gold to buy arms for Indians, both in Canada and in the northwest territories. The Miami are mentioned specifically, and in one letter Burnhouse states his confidence that the League of the Iroquois will go to war again."

"This should clear up any doubt about who is stirring up the trouble north of the Ohio," Renno said.

"There's also an interesting letter from a British minister, outlining the British intention to foment the differences among certain groups of states, or individual states. He actually used the phrase 'divide and conquer.' "

"This, too, will have influence at the Constitutional Convention," Renno said. "But we've got to get it to the delegates first." He turned to the captain. "If we should split the crew from the *Apache*, would we have enough men to sail both the sloop and the *Warrior* to Boston Harbor?"

Tarpley rubbed his chin. "It could be done. We don't have the *Seneca Warrior*, though. If we had her in our hands, the biggest problem would be navigation. I'm the only one qualified to get a ship out of the Gulf of St. Lawrence without running into a British island, and then to navigate open ocean to Boston. We couldn't count on keeping the ships near enough to each other for one to follow the other. There would be a hundred ways of losing sight, and then the one without the navigator aboard might get into trouble."

"I can take the *Apache* to Boston," the Pequot offered.

"Can you now?" Tarpley asked. "And where did you learn navigation?"

"Time can hang heavy on a whaler," Billy explained. "Men get bored. I spent my time picking the brains of a friendly first mate who later got his own ship. He was amused that a Pequot wanted to learn how to use a sextant."

"Well," Tarpley said, "they're your ships, Mistress Huntington. The final decision is yours. Me, I think I'd settle for getting the *Apache* out."

"But I'm greedy," Beth said, grinning, "especially about what belongs to me."

"Captain, decide whom you want from *Apache*'s men to staff the *Seneca Warrior*," Renno said. "We'll get her for you. When you see me flash a lantern, bring your men aboard."

"Have you considered that the *Assiduous* might not have gone far in the night?" Tarpley asked. "She could be anchored up ahead, waiting for light to navigate the river."

"When we have *Seneca Warrior*, *Apache* will lead. If we run into trouble, you will surrender the *Seneca Warrior*. The woman will be with you."

"I will not," Beth protested. "I will be with you here on *Apache*."

Renno was silent for a moment, then nodded assent. Beth would face danger either way. If *Apache* encountered the *Assiduous* and tried to run or put up a fight, the danger was death. If the *Warrior* had to surrender and Beth were aboard, she would be taken back to Burnhouse. He checked his weapons, then went to the rail. "Watch for my signal," he said.

Billy the Pequot came to his side. "Two men will have a better chance."

"It is not your fight," Renno reminded him.

"Unless I choose it to be," Billy said flatly. "We go."

They took the dory, Billy at the oars, propelling the small boat swiftly back toward the harbor, winding their way around anchored ships. There was an anchor light burning forward on *Seneca Warrior*, so they approached her from the stern. Billy held the dory in place while Renno climbed up the *Warrior*'s side and peered over the gunwale. He saw no one but reasoned that any guards would be lax, perhaps even sleeping. He reached down, after Billy had tied the dory, and helped the Pequot up. He motioned that he would take the port side. Billy disappeared into the darkness, a wicked knife in his hand, and Renno started forward.

The only man on deck was a redcoat. He was not asleep but leaned against the wheelhouse, smoking a pipe. It was the smell of tobacco that drew Renno quietly to him, and it was the spirit knife that sliced, sending a gush of blood, breaking the night with an eerie gurgling sound. Renno eased the body down, then ran forward to check the bow. He found Billy on the starboard side, waiting outside the hatch leading into the wheelhouse. Renno darted in. The house was empty, as were the officers' quarters, save for the captain's cabin, where a sleeping redcoat died without awakening.

A quick search below showed that the *Warrior* had been freshly provisioned, as if for a voyage.

"They were getting her ready," Billy commented when they had completed their search. "She's got all her water kegs full. Salted meat. Potatoes. Probably going to take her to the islands or England and put her to work under new ownership."

Renno ran back topside. There was, he knew, no more than an hour before dawn. He found a signal lantern and swung it in the direction of the *Apache*. It seemed to take a long, long time before he saw the shape of a longboat emerging from the darkness. A rope ladder awaited. Tarpley was the first on deck. As the handpicked crew came scrambling up, grunting with effort, he began to whisper orders, and soon men were scaling the tall riggings of the ship and had the anchor winch protesting.

When, at last, *Seneca Warrior* began to move, urged onward by men rowing in the longboat and by a smidgen of sail seeking the slight, steady breeze, Renno saw that there was activity beginning on the waterfront. Lanterns were being lit, and the ring of metal falling on metal came across the quiet waters. But now the graceful tall ship had steerage way, and the longboat was being drawn alongside to be hoisted aboard. Ahead there was a mass of darker substance, the first downriver island.

"There's *Apache*," Moses Tarpley told him.

"Take no chances with your life," Renno ordered. "Nor with the lives of the crew."

"Well, they'll fight before chancing being impressed into the English navy," Tarpley said.

Renno and Billy took the dory and rowed toward the *Apache*. It took some doing, for she was moving downriver slowly under sail. When they were aboard, Billy went forward to take command of the ship. Beth, her hair loose and windblown, was in the captain's cabin. She leaped to her feet when Renno came in. Her eyes flashed with excitement.

"We're going to do it, aren't we? We're going to get away with both *Apache* and the *Warrior*."

"If that is the will of the manitous," Renno said.

Although she was dressed as a man, the seaman's clothing did not hide the fact that this flame-haired one was very much a woman. Her full breasts, unfettered, mounded under the rough shirt. Her hips flared, filling the seaman's breeches as no man could.

"The *Assiduous* is somewhere ahead," Renno warned.

"That hateful man." Then Beth brightened. "But you humiliated him, Renno. His only thought will be to get far away from anyone who saw it or will hear about it. He's making for the open sea as fast as his sails will carry him."

Suddenly Beth's eyes lost their excitement, her lids lowered slightly, and she half turned her face away. "I knew I'd see you again, but I had hoped it would be under more pleasant circumstances."

Renno could find no words.

"I had no right to ask you, to send for you," she said.

"You had the right of a friend," Renno soothed.

She smiled. "Yes, thank you. Perhaps sometime I will have the pleasure of repaying you."

"Let's not consider that until we know what you would owe." Renno found it easy to smile in this woman's company. "So far you have two empty ships, both of them at risk."

"And my freedom," she reminded him.

His smile faded. "The crew of the *Seneca Warrior*?"

"Impressed. Taken by British men-of-war. I suspect some are aboard *Assiduous*." She seated herself. There was so much to talk about, so many experiences to be compared. Much had happened to her since she had last seen Renno in Charlotte. And yet she was content just to sit and relax and look at him. There was a smear of blood, not his own, on his right arm, but she was not squeamish in the least about it. Nor, now that she was with him, was she concerned about the danger ahead. He was Renno. She had seen him defeat a tremendous force of heavily armed Spanish soldiers, had followed him across half a huge continent, had killed at his side.

"You're tired," she said. She looked at the broad, comfortable captain's bed and flushed furiously at her own thoughts. To break the embarrassing silence, she asked, "Do you like the name of the schooner?"

"I am honored," Renno said. "Now sleep."

"I can't."

"It will be light soon. I'll awaken you then."

"Yes, well," she said. "I am a bit tired."

Already it was growing light in the east. The river islands were behind them, the river was widening, and the *Apache* scooted along under a full complement of sail. Billy, as acting captain, seemed to be in his element.

"Always thought I knew as much as most of the skippers I've sailed under," he said when Renno entered the wheelhouse. "No sign of traffic." Meaning, no sign of the warship *Assiduous*. "Cookie's down below. There'll be hot food soon."

"It will be welcomed," Renno said.

In the full light of day he could see the *Warrior* gliding along a mile behind them, under light sail. The river ahead was empty.

"It seems too easy, somehow," Billy mused. Hours had passed without incident, and the breeze had freshened, putting a roil of foam in front of the *Apache's* speeding prow.

Renno had been thinking the same thing, but he did not add his concern to Billy's worries. When the mess call came, he went to Beth's cabin, roused her, and had food delivered there. She did quick, graceful things with her hair, piling it high atop her head, and began to eat hungrily. Her excitement was gone. She seemed oddly subdued. Renno ate in silence, watching her with pleasure.

Finished, she wiped her mouth on the sleeve of her shirt—there were no napkins. "They laughed at me in Wilmington," she said. "I suppose they were right."

"You tried. There can be no failure, no success, unless one tries."

"They said a woman couldn't run a shipping business, and they were right."

"What do you hear from William?" Renno asked, wanting to change the subject.

"Oh, he and Estrela are foolishly happy. A baby is due soon. Your children?"

Renno felt a weight of guilt. "Little Hawk is with Ena and Rusog. Renna is with her grandparents in Knoxville."

"Little Hawk is such a fine little boy," she said.

"Why didn't you go back to England?" Renno asked, a hint of harshness in his voice.

Her eyes widened. "Did you want me to?"

He considered his answer, knowing confusion. "It is your rightful place."

"No," she said. "It's William's rightful place, and he will be a great lord Beaumont. My place?" She turned away. "I don't know."

There was a long silence. At last she turned to face him. "We were always honest with each other, weren't we?"

"Yes."

"I will be honest now. I did not go back to England for many reasons: One, I truly felt that I had no place there anymore. My only choices would have been spinster-hood—to be an imposition on my brother and Estrela for the rest of my life—or marriage to someone I didn't love. I felt at home in the wilderness, Renno. Oh, there was danger and often discomfort, but by God, I was alive. And I had friends, truer friends than I could ever have in England. Ena and Rusog, El-i-chi. You."

"The wilderness is not the place for a white woman," Renno said.

"No? Why was I so happy there, then? Why do I think of nothing but those vast, clear skies, the unlimited, unbelievable distances, the beauty of waking to a chill, frosty morning with the smell of freshly killed game roasting?"

Renno had no answer.

"You're thinking of your wife, aren't you?" Beth asked softly. "She was white, and the wilderness killed her. . . ."

"She was born to the frontier," Renno said.

"She died of childbed fever," Beth said. "It was not the wilderness that killed her, but the ancient malady that kills in every country, in rural areas and in cities."

She rose, put her hands on his shoulders as he stood. "You can't blame yourself for her death, Renno. Nor can you blame the wilderness."

His eyes seemed to fall forever into the green depths of hers.

"I stayed because I wanted to see you again, Renno," Beth whispered. "I won't throw myself at you. I wouldn't speak about it before, even if I had had the courage, because your wife had so recently died and I could see how deeply you had loved her. I cried for your pain. I wanted so much to hold you, to comfort you, but I couldn't. But I knew that time would heal you. I'll be honest: I stayed because Little Hawk and Renna need a mother, and you need a wife." She laughed. "Listen to me. What a shameless hussy. I think I've just proposed to you."

He put his arms around her and pulled her to him so forcefully that the breath was driven from her lungs. His lips were hot on hers, and she felt the swift, happy tears come.

"I knew it, I knew it," she whispered when he broke the kiss and, still holding her tightly, looked into her face. She was remembering how sweetly El-i-chi and Holani had loved each other, and how they had become man and wife in a simple, wholesome way, merely pledging themselves to each other. They had been as married as any couple who had ever had the benefit of a wedding in a huge, English cathedral, with officiating priest or ministers and with a few pieces of paper. The nearness of the bed sent a tingling awareness in her as he kissed her again, and she let herself sink into his body. She stiffened as he pulled away and laughed heartily, throwing back his head.

"What?" she gasped.

He had trouble stopping his laughter. "I was just remembering that night when the coyotes howled and you ran to me—"

"Wicked man," she accused with a smile.

His face sobered, and a look of deep, deep yearning was in his eyes. She lifted her lips, surrendering.

"Not now," he whispered, gently pushing her away.

She took his hand.

"We will speak of this when there is no danger," he promised.

She felt her heart sink, but she smiled. "As you say."

The two ships sailed on under fair skies and a warm sun, the *Warrior* having to shorten sail to keep from overtaking the slower *Apache*. Beth stood by Renno's side at the bow, seeing only empty water ahead as the day grew old and the sun was far down in the west. The Pequot came forward to join them.

"So far so good," Billy said.

"Perhaps I've found a new captain for the *Apache*," Beth told him with a smile.

Billy grinned. "Tempting, miss, but she's hardly fitted for my chosen profession."

The river had widened during the day, and the far banks were now low on the horizon. Renno was beginning to hope that Beth had been right, that the *Assiduous* had made all speed for the open sea. There would be a better chance of avoiding her there.

The cook did himself proud with the evening meal, with salt venison, potatoes swimming in gravy, and fresh vegetables. Renno asked Billy to join him and Beth in the captain's cabin, knowing that to be alone with Beth would be too tremendous a temptation. He was reluctant, not to commit himself but to ask her to make a commitment while he had so many things left undone. He knew that he would have to leave her in Boston, for he still had to see Cornplanter and the other chiefs of the old League of the Iroquois.

Now, in the twilight that deepened with each heaving swell of the river, the three of them stood on deck again, peering into the growing darkness.

"I'd feel more comfortable if we could anchor for the night," Billy said.

"You're doing just fine," Renno assured him. "The river is wide."

"And the shores often rocky," Billy responded. "I will slow her. I wouldn't be surprised if the wind drops off. We've been very lucky so far."

Sometimes touching her, Renno could feel Beth's warmth and softness at his side as she swayed with the ship's motion. His thoughts were on her, and he was jarred into self-condemnation when Billy hissed and pointed ahead, then ran back to relay orders in a quiet voice. Renno knew that he should have seen it first—a light, then more lights. The *Apache* was slowing, and on her stern a crewman was sending a signal to the *Seneca Warrior* to slow.

Now it was evident that a great ship lay ahead, broadside to them in the center of the river.

"That's *Assiduous*, all right," Billy said, having come back to the bow. "Damn and thunderation."

"We can sneak past her," Beth said. "The river is wide here."

"We might," Billy agreed, "by hugging the far shore. But the *Warrior* draws more water. She's tall. Her sails would stand out against the sky."

The *Apache* was drifting silently. Behind her the *Seneca Warrior* had slowed but was gaining even as her sails went down. Soon both ships were motionless and silent. The breeze sighed mournfully through the rigging of the *Apache*, as if bewailing her furled sails. And into that silence came a sound unlike any that Renno had ever heard. It started low, then surged into a high, haunting wail that was oddly near-melodic.

"What on earth?" Beth asked.

Billy shushed her, then looked out over the wide dark river as the sound came again from nearer at hand. Beth reached for Renno's hand and squeezed it hard, for she, too, was hearing those bizarre, beautiful sounds for the first time.

"It is the singing of the great blue whales," Billy informed them. "There are at least two of them."

"Whales?" Beth asked, with both skepticism and relief. "For a moment I thought it was the angel of death."

"They are very far from their usual hunting grounds," Billy said. "Strange."

With a hissing roar, a great whale surfaced, blowing air from its massive lungs to make a white spume of water from its blowhole. Billy spoke in the guttural tongue of the Pequot, then turned, flashing his strong white teeth. "I was just saying hello to my big brother of the sea."

The whale dived and lashed the water with its great flukes, only to surface a couple of minutes later on the other side of the *Apache*.

"He knows that we are not hunting for him," Billy said.

As interesting as the whale was, Renno returned his attention to the threatening situation. The lights of the *Assiduous* were perhaps three miles away. But as he gazed at her, a great form rose between him and the British ship, and once again he saw a whale blow.

"Another!" Billy shouted excitedly. "And another!" he added as a whale surfaced still farther away in the direction of the *Assiduous*. "Renno, are you a gambler? Have you ever cast the dice with much at stake, praying to the spirits for a winning combination?"

Renno, deep in thought but without a plan to get past the blocking warship, turned his head toward Billy, wondering why the Pequot had asked such a question.

"Blue whales *never* come into such restricted waters," he said. "It is like intervention by— What do the Seneca call the spirits?"

"Manitous," Beth answered.

"Intervention by the manitous," Billy said, "and yet the action will have to be ours. Shall we cast the dice, Renno?"

Renno listened incredulously as Billy outlined a wild scheme.

"It's a risk," Billy warned when he was finished.

Renno, a man of the wilderness, was out of his element on the water. The plan had daring and would require luck, skill, and courage. And it was, he felt, preferable to doing nothing, because the only way he could think of to avoid the *Assiduous* was to put the entire party ashore and make his way back to Maine by land. His grandmother had often told the tale of the original Renno's epic run from Nova Scotia to Maine under heavy pressure of time. Renno had no doubt that he could make his way back to the United States by land, but to have a woman and two dozen sailors with him would make the feat difficult. Moreover, such a solution would cost Beth her two ships.

"Thank the manitous that I was not born a Pequot and thus crazy," Renno said with a laugh. "Let us cast the dice."

While the dory was lowered into the water, Billy made his preparations. He had loaded huge coils of line into the small boat and then had climbed in gingerly, carrying his harpoons. Renno pushed the dory away from the *Apache*, and it was soon lost to view in the darkness from the bow where Beth stood.

Three times, as Billy rowed carefully so that there

was no noise as the oars dipped, great whales surfaced so
near the boat that Renno felt he had only to reach out to
touch them.

At a distance of about a hundred yards from the
Assiduous Billy stopped rowing and, with his mouth close
to Renno's ear, whispered, "You know I'd do it myself,
but I'm a true sailor, and sailors don't swim well at all."

Renno removed his clothing, felt more naked for lack
of weapons than for lack of clothes, and lowered himself—
after Billy had looped the end of a line around his waist—
into the water, sucking in his breath at the chill. He began
swimming carefully, taking precautions that his hands and
feet did not break water and make noise. The line was
paid out behind him by the Pequot and after a while
became so heavy that he had to use all his swimming skill
to maintain a forward motion. He could hear the creaking
of the *Assiduous* as she swung on her anchor line to a
shifting breeze, drifting her stern nearer.

Since the *Assiduous* was a ship of the line, it was
almost certain that there was a watch, so he could not
count on the British lookout to be sleeping. He swam the
last few yards until he was in the deep shadow of the ship,
breathing slowly and carefully through his mouth to prevent even the noise of panting.

The white Indian followed instructions and located
the great log that was the shaft of the ship's rudder.
Barnacles had grown there, and he accidentally cut himself, the saltwater beginning to sting immediately. He
clasped the rudder log, wrapping his arm around it, heed-
less of barnacle cuts, and began to loosen the rope. The
pull on the line was great, so he would have to hold it
tightly when he loosed it from his waist to prevent its
sodden weight from pulling it out of his hands.

A bell clanged on board, and he froze. He waited for
long minutes, but there was no alarm. He did not know
that the bell signified the hour of one in the morning.

He tugged on the heavy line, trying to thrust the end of it around the rudder log to his other hand. The rope slipped, causing his heart to leap, for he had almost lost it, and that would have required swimming all the way back to the dory. With one straining movement he reached the end of the rope, pulled it around the rudder log, and then tied it securely. The line was now firmly attached to the rudder of the *Assiduous* just above the spot where the great blade of the rudder flared out. With a deep breath he pushed off, swam underwater until he was well away from the ship, and then surfaced. Nearby he heard a roiling of water and looked up to see the white spume of a blowing whale. In the darkness he could not see the dory at all.

Chapter VIII

El-i-chi had had enough of horses. He could understand the need for horses by the Comanche, Apache, and other western Indians who were forced to travel great distances. There were extensive plains of grass for feeding the animals, and the nomadic life of the western Indians made the horse invaluable. In the forests, however, a horse was a liability; a warrior moving on foot could outpace a man on horseback because the horse had to take so much time picking a path through the undergrowth.

El-i-chi had kept the horses brought back from the journey west, and although he had supplemented their food with some grain during the winter, the economy of the Seneca did not provide grains for horse feed. The animals came into the time of new growth with their ribs showing gauntly, but the new, sweet grass soon fattened them. El-i-chi announced that he would take the horses into Knoxville, to sell them for whatever the traffic would bear. He did not say that he was also feeling a bit brain-bloated from all the lore and knowledge that old Casno had been forcing on him, but a vacation from learning, he secretly felt, would be welcomed. Add to those two motivations the natural urge to be on the move in the pleasant days of late spring, and the trip to Knoxville became inevitable.

El-i-chi had at first intended to take only a couple of young warriors to help handle the horses, but he found that there were some interested volunteers. The first was his sister. When he mentioned his plans during a meal in Ena and Rusog's lodge, he saw a thoughtful look come over Ena's face.

"I will go with you," she declared.

Rusog, who had ceased to be surprised by his wife, went on eating.

"Me go too," Little Hawk announced. "Ride horse."

"You're a little short in the tail feathers for that," El-i-chi said, grinning at his nephew.

"The boy will go," Ena decided.

"Hold," El-i-chi said, raising a hand.

"He will be no trouble to you," Ena promised. "I will take care of him."

"But—" El-i-chi protested, then laughed, looking at Rusog. "I'm sure she must have a good reason."

"We have talked of a journey to Knoxville," Rusog confirmed.

El-i-chi chewed a roasted chicken breast and waited for further information. He was finding the chicken, obtained from a Cherokee who was raising chickens white-man style, to be bland, for his palate was used to the taste of wild game.

"It is time Renna came to her own people," Ena said grimly, for she was fully aware that she would meet resistance to that idea from Nora Johnson.

"That is for her father to say," El-i-chi said.

"Those are his stated wishes," Ena told him.

"And you, Rusog?" El-i-chi asked.

"I have been to Knoxville," Rusog said.

El-i-chi did not comment. He knew that Rusog still had no love for the white man.

El-i-chi's next volunteer was even more of a surprise.

"I will go with you to Knoxville," his mother said the next morning.

"It is not a long trip, Mother," El-i-chi said, "but we will be riding, and it will be tiring for you."

Toshabe smiled. "I could keep up with you walking or running. I'm sure I can manage to keep up with you on the back of a great horse."

El-i-chi said no more. He already had a woman and a small boy for the trip. Another woman would be no additional burden.

"You go to Knoxville," said the panther, Ha-ace, coming to the pasture where El-i-chi was inspecting the horses. "You will need someone to help you with the animals."

This El-i-chi did not like, for he was still disturbed by the panther's attentions to his mother. But Ha-ace had fought at his side and was a respected senior warrior. To refuse would have insulted Ha-ace's honor, and that was not to be done lightly.

When the journey finally got under way, El-i-chi looked over his companions with a jaundiced eye. He felt that he was leading a migration, like the Comanche following the buffalo, because now the party included two women, a small boy, and a fourteen-year-old girl, for, as Toshabe said, "Ah-wa-o has not seen Knoxville."

Ah-wa-o took to riding as if born to it. Ha-ace had some difficulty until he got the hang of it, and Toshabe rode with determination, reins held stiffly before her, legs tensed against the sides of the horse. She complained only to Ah-wa-o on the second night, saying, "What evil spirit gave us the horse?" She was rubbing her backside tenderly, an expression of disgust on her face.

"Honorable Mother," Ah-wa-o said, "the secret is to

become one with the animal, not to fight his motion, but to move with it. Take a deep seat."

A *deep seat*, Toshabe thought as she lowered her very disturbed backside onto the back of the horse next morning. "Words without meaning," she said to herself. She tried, however, by relaxing and letting herself sink down. The bony back of the horse caused her to wince, so she kept trying different positions, all in vain. She did not, of course, let anyone, especially Ha-ace, see her discomfort.

"You ride well, Toshabe," Ha-ace complimented, pulling his horse up to walk beside hers.

"It is nothing," she replied, wincing inwardly as the backbone of the horse seemed intent on breaking her own bones.

"Notice my daughter," Ha-ace said.

"She rides well."

She noticed that Ah-wa-o's back was straight, her legs relaxed. She tried to imitate the girl. *Well*, she told herself, *she does not have the weight or the width that I have.* But suddenly something seemed to change. She was still sore, but she no longer had to fight the motion of the horse. It was almost as if she had lowered her body somewhat, to, as Ah-wa-o had suggested, take a deep seat.

"Actually," she marveled, "there's nothing to it."

Ha-ace was gazing at her striking profile with much pleasure. At first he had felt that he had set his sights too high, that the widow of the great Ghonkaba was beyond him. But of late he felt that he had been getting certain signals of approval from this captivating woman who had been in his eyes for months.

"Toshabe," he ventured, his heart in his mouth, "there, just to the southwest, is a small valley. A stream cascades down into it, and the water is cool and inviting in the summer. There is game, and it is seldom that anyone goes there."

"It sounds beautiful," Toshabe said, casting a glance at him, wondering if he was just making conversation.

Ha-ace swallowed. "It is a place for two," he said.

"So," she said, inwardly ordering herself not to blush.

"A place for a man and wife to become acquainted," Ha-ace continued, his voice so soft that Toshabe hardly heard him.

Toshabe saw the stricken look on Ha-ace's face and knew immediately what his words had cost him. This warrior had established himself as one of the tribe's best hunters. He had taken his scalps in war and had been trusted by both her dead husband and her sons. Even though she knew that it would cause a shock for El-i-chi, and perhaps even an adjustment for Renno, she had made up her mind. Now she sensed that unless she spoke, even to an indirect proposal, it would be a long time before this brave warrior—who would have unhesitatingly ridden, yelling a war cry, into the teeth of a heavily superior number of foes—would have the courage to speak more directly.

"I would see this place," she accepted.

Ha-ace's face was impassive, but he was trembling inside. Had she understood his implied meaning? He forced the words. "With me."

"With you," she confirmed, reaching out to put her hand on his arm.

"You please me," he said simply. Then he kicked his horse into a gallop and went dashing forward, to pass El-i-chi and Ena, whooping as he rode. Toshabe shook her head and laughed. All men were such little boys at heart.

El-i-chi picked a campsite near Knoxville. With the morning, he and Ha-ace began to move the horses. He did not ask Ena to help, knowing that she had other plans.

Ena, Toshabe, and Ah-wa-o walked into the settlement after enjoying a leisurely breakfast. Ah-wa-o was all eyes, for she had never seen so many white people, wheeled vehicles, and log and plank buildings. At first the girl was so interested in gathering new sights and new impressions that she did not notice that she and the other two women were the object of much curiosity.

"Why do they stare at us?" she asked finally, looking up at Toshabe.

"The white man is not known for his courtesy," Toshabe explained, taking Ah-wa-o's hand.

Roy Johnson was enjoying the early-morning air on his front porch, a ceramic mug of coffee in hand, leaning back against the log wall of his house in a straight-backed chair. He saw three Indian women coming, walking with that proud, free posture he had come to admire, and mused, at first, that they made a striking picture. Then he recognized Ena and Toshabe. He let the chair crash down onto all four legs and stepped off the porch.

"Toshabe! Ena! We are honored," he said. "Come in, come in."

Johnson's eyes were shifting from mother to daughter. There was a family resemblance, and to his amazement, it seemed that Toshabe could pass as Ena's sister. Incredible, he thought, how some Indian women seemed not to age at all, in spite of living with the elements.

"You'll want to see that granddaughter of ours," Roy said, taking Toshabe's arm and guiding her up the steps. "Nora, look who's here," he called as he opened the door.

Nora Johnson was cleaning up from breakfast. Renna was in a crib in the kitchen, doing the thing babies do best—sleeping. Nora's face showed quick panic when she saw Toshabe and Ena, but she recovered quickly and came forward to greet them. There was a moment for the introduction of Ah-wa-o, who spoke only the most basic English, and then Toshabe was leaning over the crib, her dark eyes intent, noting that Renna seemed to combine the best features of both Renno and Emily.

"What brings you to town?" Nora asked.

Toshabe looked quickly at Ena and spoke. "El-i-chi sells horses."

"The Spanish horses?" Johnson asked. Without waiting for an answer, he turned toward the door. "I had my eyes on a couple of those."

"They have been reserved for you, as a gift from Renno," Ena assured him. "El-i-chi will bring them when he has found a place for the others."

"Renno is back, then?" Nora asked, her heart heavy, for she had dreaded the day when Renno would come for his child.

"No," Ena answered.

"He's been gone a long time. . . ." Nora said.

"The journey to the old Seneca homelands is a long one," Toshabe reminded her.

"Where are your manners, Nora?" Johnson asked teasingly. "Ena, Toshabe, Ah-wa-o, please have a seat. There are bacon and biscuits still warm from breakfast."

"We have eaten," Ena said.

Toshabe took a chair in the kitchen, pulled it to Renna's crib, and sat studying the sleeping face of the child.

"Soon she will be walking," Toshabe said.

Nora came to stand beside Toshabe's chair. A smile made Nora's thin face seem quite pretty. "She tries to crawl now."

This woman loves the child, Toshabe was thinking. *Renna is all she has of her dead daughter.*

Renna chose that moment to begin to stir, squirming, then opening her eyes. Toshabe could see their blue color. *But*, she thought, *she is of Renno, as well.*

Renna's chubby hands began to make frantic motions in the air. "She wants to be held," Nora said. "Toshabe?"

Toshabe lifted the infant. She was big for just over six months of age, a solid little mass of baby. The blue eyes sought Toshabe's face, and something that could have been called a smile moved her lips.

"She's hungry," Nora said. "I have her food prepared." She bustled in the kitchen for a few minutes. Then the two grandmothers coaxed the baby to take mashed vegetables from a small spoon before giving Renna milk.

Ena watched, her face impassive. Johnson, eager to

see his horses, had excused himself and left. Toshabe put Renna on her shoulder and, with a few pats on the back, encouraged an outrageous belch. Ah-wa-o giggled.

Ena felt that it was time to speak. "We have come for the child," she said flatly.

Nora's face was stricken. "But Renno is not here."

"He will return soon," Ena said. "His daughter should be there to greet him."

Nora had steeled herself to resist even Renno, for she had been sure that Renno would come. They had made a tentative agreement to have Renna spend time in the Seneca camp, but she was so young, and she felt that Ena and Toshabe had no right. It was Renno's place to come for his daughter.

"He may be dead," she said, her voice a bit belligerent. "You haven't heard from him. He's been gone for months. Renna is his child, not yours."

"We obey the wishes of Renno," Ena answered.

"You can't have her," Nora said, clutching Renna to her breast. "She's only a baby, and unused to the hardships of living in the wilderness. You cannot have her."

Ena's impassive face turned to Toshabe. She had not anticipated this. In her life the father's will was paramount. "You defy the wishes of the child's father?" she asked, her voice carrying a quality that gave warning to Toshabe, who stood quickly.

"We will have no bad blood between us," Toshabe said firmly, her eyes on Ena. "We will leave Renna with her grandmother until Renno returns."

Ena's first impulse was to take the child, but she bowed to Toshabe's wisdom. True, it would not be good to fight over the child. Without another word she stalked from the house.

"Toshabe . . ." Nora pleaded.

"Renno will come," Toshabe said. She rose. Ah-wa-o, who had not understood all that had been said, rose with her.

"Toshabe, please understand," Nora begged. "I don't want hard feelings between us, either, but—"

Toshabe touched Nora's arm. "We will work it out," she consoled. "When Renno returns, he will want the child with him."

El-i-chi had had no problem selling the horses. He took some payment in gold and some in credit with Knoxville merchants. Others could come, pack the supplies purchased by the credit, and bring them back to the village. His work was done. He presented two fine horses to Roy Johnson, with Renno's compliments, and was pleased by Johnson's obvious gratitude. He accompanied Roy back to the Johnson house to be told that the women had departed. He visited with Nora and played with his niece, then walked with Ha-ace back to the camp, to find Ena and Toshabe preparing for the trek home.

"The child?" he asked.

"The woman refused us," Ena said. "Perhaps we should simply go and take Renna."

"We have already discussed that," Toshabe said in a tone that invited no argument. "We will discuss it further when Renno returns."

El-i-chi felt a great urge to turn his feet northward, to go far and find his brother.

"We will go home," Toshabe said. "My garden will be in need of weeding."

Toshabe enjoyed the trip back toward the village much more than she had the trip to Knoxville riding that bony horse. It had been a long time since she had covered such distances walking, and her legs liked the freedom. Her muscles, tightened by the riding, now eased themselves. To be a part of the wilderness, to travel through it so quietly that their passage would not have been audible to anyone a hundred feet away, roused memories for her. And she had something else to please her, for now Ha-ace walked with her, often taking her hand, oblivious to El-i-chi's disapproving looks.

At approximately the halfway point Ha-ace said, "Here, should that be our desire, we will leave this path and go to the south to the small valley where the water is clear and cool."

It was Toshabe who made the announcement. A cheery fire burned, and the small group had just finished a fine meal of roasted venison. "Ha-ace and I will be one," she said without preamble. "I will share his lodge from this day."

Ena grinned. El-i-chi leaped to his feet and moved quickly away into the darkness.

Toshabe squeezed Ha-ace's hand, rose, and followed El-i-chi into the night. She found him standing stiffly beside the small stream near their campsite and deliberately walked noisily so that he would be aware of her approach. He glanced at her, his mouth a tight line, then looked away into the darkness.

"When Ghonkaba was murdered, I grieved," she reminded him, "just as you grieved for Holani."

El-i-chi was sternly silent.

"My lodge has been empty too long," Toshabe continued, "and yet I know your thoughts."

"But you are—" El-i-chi blurted, then halted himself.

"Old?" She laughed. "How old was Ah-wen-ga when she became one with Loramas? We are much alike, we women and you men. We are not naturally creatures of solitude. Our bodies long for a touch, for the warmth of another. The manitous made us that way. Someday you will know that longing—even if your heart at this moment says no—and you will take another, even while honoring the memory of Holani."

She put her hand gently on El-i-chi's arm. "Be pleased for me, my son, that I have found a man who wants me. He will not fill Ghonkaba's place, but he fills my heart, and I would have your blessings, not your anger."

"Wait and get Renno's thoughts. He is sachem."

"I believe that he will approve," Toshabe said simply, "for he, too, knows the sadness of an empty lodge. I will have a new young daughter who is fond of me. I will teach her, and she will fill my old age with pleasure. Would you deny me this?"

El-i-chi turned, looked down at Toshabe's face, and saw that there were tears on her cheeks. He put his arms on her shoulders. "I know the emptiness."

El-i-chi's thoughts were chaotic. She was his mother, she had always been there when he needed comfort, and it was true that she was not an old woman. He thought about what his reply might be if *he* were sachem. If Toshabe were another woman of the tribe and not his mother, he would bless her union with Ha-ace, a worthy warrior, for a woman needed a man to hunt for her, to protect her. While it was true Toshabe had two sons and a daughter whose husband paid honor to her, Renno was gone long, and both Rusog and El-i-chi would be in the forefront to face any danger that threatened the allied tribes. Looking at the problem from the viewpoint of one who would become chief shaman, possibly sachem, the answer was clear.

And, in that moment, El-i-chi took one last step toward his full maturity. "I have been thinking as a child," he apologized gently. "A child jealous of the affections of his mother." He took her arm and led her back toward the fire. Ha-ace looked up as they came into the glow of the flames.

"I will speak," El-i-chi said.

Ena tensed herself, then relaxed and felt a flow of pride as El-i-chi spoke.

"My brother, Ha-ace," El-i-chi began, "in the fight against the Spanish and the Chickasaw, you were often at my side, and I saw you take many scalps. There is no man I would rather have at my side in a fight, and no man I would rather have as a member of my family."

· Toshabe beamed. Ha-ace leaped to his feet and clasped El-i-chi's arm. Toshabe came to stand by Ha-ace's side, and the look of love and pride on her face made Ena want to sing and weep at the same time.

El-i-chi grinned at Ena. "My sister, we will have a new little sister. Now we will have someone to carry our water and gather our wood."

"Oh, yes," Ah-wa-o said, thus, with her eagerness, negating El-i-chi's teasing. Ena laughed. "And I will help both Toshabe and Ena with the gardening."

El-i-chi, with a wry grin, admitted defeat and sat down. When he awoke with the dawn, Toshabe and Ha-ace were gone. He made the remainder of the trip home with his elder sister, who had always been able to tease him with impunity, and a new little sister who, it seemed, was learning fast.

In a time of plenty there was little need for the long hunt. He was at Casno's mercy again and so spent many a warm, summer day listening to the patient old man and his sometimes esoteric teachings. His heart, however, was far to the north, his very being seeming to cry out for action, for movement.

Renno oriented himself by looking back at the *Assiduous* and then at the stars. Without the weight of the long line now attaching the British ship to the dory, he could move easily in the water and soon saw the low, dark spot that was the dory. Billy hoisted him into the boat, to prevent any noise, his short, thick body not showing the strain of lifting Renno's weight.

Billy sat still at the oars while Renno used his hands to brush away water from his skin and then donned his clothing. Finally Billy heard what he was listening for— the plaintive song of the blue whale—and as a whale surfaced and blew, he began to row quietly toward the great beast. Now there were three whales ahead of them, and Billy was watching the coil of line become smaller as it was drawn off the dory. He motioned to Renno to trade places with him. Then, with Renno at the oars, he began to thread a line to his harpoon.

"Come alongside that one," Billy said, pointing to the largest of the whales, whose broad back seemed to be motionless. Renno leaned into the oars and felt the boat rock slightly as Billy stood. They were within mere yards of the whale.

"Easy, my brother," Billy whispered, talking to the whale. "It is not the hunt. Easy, for we need your assistance."

With hand motions Billy had Renno move the dory in until Renno was sure that it was going to collide with the whale's back. The eerie singing had reached a crescendo, with several whales joining in to produce the music. Billy said, "Back oars."

Renno stopped the dory, and before he could speak, Billy leaped, landed on the whale's back, and in the same motion drove the iron deep. "Forgive me, my brother," Renno heard him say, "for the pain I give you."

A spurt of foam and air came from the whale's blow hole, and his huge flukes lashed the water behind them. Billy leaped again toward the boat, his feet slipping on the whale's back, and he half fell into the dory, setting it to rocking wildly. But that was mild compared with what happened next: the whale churned the water into a white foam, lifting the small boat high as the beast's back came under it, and it seemed to Renno that they flew for a distance before the dory hit the water again with a loud smack of sound and a tremendous splash.

The line was whipping off the coil at a speed that caused it to smoke against the damp gunwale of the dory, and then the entire coil was gone and the dory was clear, no longer attached to the line that extended from the harpoon in the whale's back directly to the rudder log of the *Assiduous*. Renno rowed clear of the foam and disturbance left by the sounding whale while Billy looked back at the black bulk of the *Assiduous*.

"About now . . ." Billy guessed, and as he spoke there was a great crash of breaking timbers from the *Assiduous*. Something was being towed through the water at a fast rate of speed, making toward the dory. As it passed, Billy was able to see that the great strength of the whale's body had ripped the entire rudder off the British warship.

"She still has her guns," Billy warned, "but she cannot steer, except roughly, with her sails."

Renno was rowing strongly out of harm's way, and half an hour later he pulled the dory alongside the *Apache*, where Beth was waiting.

"We heard a crash," she said, "and we feared—"

It was no time for talk. The short northern night would be ending soon. "We will send the *Warrior* past her before they can reorganize," Renno said.

Billy operated the signal lamp. *Apache*'s crew were ready to raise sail. The *Seneca Warrior*, seen dimly, was a ghost in white as her sails were set and the breeze gave her headway.

"They will be too busy trying to figure out what happened to notice her," Renno told Beth as they stood together on the deck and watched the *Warrior* move toward the northern shore, putting the maximum distance between her and the *Assiduous*'s still-dangerous guns. "We'll let her get well past before we move."

"For what it's worth," Billy said, "our guns are ready."

"I hope we will not have to use them," Renno replied.

"If we do, we'll have a slight advantage. *Assiduous* will be a sitting duck, while we'll be moving, and they'll have to maneuver the ship into firing position with longboats to get a line of shot on us," Billy told him.

Slowly, very slowly, the *Seneca Warrior* was reaching for the north shore and seaward. She was visible to Renno because he knew where to look. And then she was out of sight in the darkness. They waited, Beth clinging to Renno's hand and scarcely breathing.

"It's going to be light in an hour," Billy warned. "It's now or never for us."

With relayed, whispered orders, the *Apache* began to move, not following the path taken by the larger ship, and soon they were hugging the southern shore. Billy had chosen to go to the south, rather than to the north of the *Assiduous*, because the shoreline was wooded there and the *Apache*, with her old, darkened sails, would blend into the shadows of the trees. Moreover, because of the *Apache*'s shallow draft, she would be able to move quite near the rocks.

To the east there was a hint of light. They were coming directly opposite the *Assiduous*. The warship was a blaze of light now, and shouted orders came faintly to them across the water.

"We're going to make it!" Beth said, just as a flash of fire hid the dark bulk of the warship. The flash was followed by the boom of naval cannon.

"Get down!" Billy shouted. It seemed to take an age, and then the water erupted around the *Apache* as the British shot rained down.

"Gunners, fire at will!" the Pequot roared, and the *Apache*'s small guns on the port side boomed. But another salvo from the warship put shot into the *Apache*'s rigging. The mainmast took a direct hit and, with sails and rigging tangling and ripping, crashed down onto the deck.

"We hit her!" came a shout from the *Apache*'s gunners, and when Renno looked, he saw that the foremast of the *Assiduous* was down. Meanwhile, the *Apache*'s forward momentum was carrying her past the warship.

"If we can make it for just another mile . . ." Billy said.

But it was not to be. The *Assiduous*'s guns roared, and this time shot crashed into the timbered sides of the sloop.

The *Apache*'s small guns scored another hit on the Britisher's rigging, and the crashing of fallen timbers could be heard.

A seaman came scrambling up from below. "Cap'n," he gasped, "that last salvo holed us. We're taking in water fast, and both guns are out of action. Four men are dead."

"Just another mile," Billy pleaded, but then the rest of the *Apache*'s standing rigging came toppling down in a great roar of sound and the sloop was slowing, to become dead in the water, the sea pouring in through her hull.

"We cannot save her," Billy said sadly.

"Get the men into the boats," Renno ordered. "Row for the sea."

The orders were issued. Fortunately they had moved away from the *Assiduous*'s deadly broadside range. Renno saw British longboats in the water around the *Assiduous*. "They're trying to move her broadside to us again," he warned.

The *Apache* crew were scrambling into the boats. Renno, Billy, and Beth were the last on deck. The Pequot motioned to Renno and Beth to begin the climb down the now tilting side of the listing sloop to the longboat. Renno took Beth's arm to guide her.

"Renno," she gasped, "the documents. We must not leave them behind."

The *Apache* felt the fury of more shot as Beth jerked away and ran on the slanting deck toward the cabin.

"Leave them!" Renno yelled after her.

"We're going down fast," Billy reported.

"Go with the men," Renno ordered. "Leave the dory."

"As captain I will be the last to leave," Billy decided.

Renno did not have time to argue. He could feel the *Apache* dying under him. He had never been on a sinking ship before, but something told him that time was short, that soon the ship would take her last plunge. He seized Billy from behind, and as easily as Billy had lifted him into the dory, he lifted Billy over the side and dropped him. Billy hit the water with a great splash, came up sputtering, and was hauled into the boat by several men. Renno turned and fought his way toward the cabin on the wet, slippery deck and gained the hatch just as a new salvo slashed into the stricken sloop. He heard a crash from below and dived down the hatchway to see the cabin in chaos, water flooding in through a new rent in the hull. Ceiling timbers had collapsed, and under a jumble of shattered wood and fallen items, Renno saw a glint of flame-colored hair. He fought his way up the slanting deck and began to rip away tangled bedding and debris.

"I'm all right," Beth said, her eyes very wide. "I don't think I'm hurt, but I can't move."

A large deck support had pinned her down. Luckily, she had fallen onto a mattress tossed off the bunk and thus was cushioned, but the weight of the beam lay directly across her thighs. Renno heaved at the beam until his muscles strained, but he could not move it. Water continued to pour into the cabin, and from somewhere there came a great groaning of timbers and then a shattering crack. The *Apache* was mortally wounded, and those sounds were her death agony.

Once more Renno strained at the beam without moving it, then began to attack the surrounding debris, heaving, tossing aside bits and pieces until he had exposed the mattress that cushioned Beth. Beth's head was pointing down the sloping deck, and the list became more pronounced by the minute. Already water lapped at her hair, wetting the back of her head.

He saw that the fallen beam was embedded in the wall of the cabin and that the jagged end had punched a hole in the cabin deck. He would not be able to move it.

"Renno?" Beth asked, her eyes even wider.

No time for talk. He searched for a solution, knowing that he had only minutes, possibly seconds.

The flame-haired one is the future.

The white Indian felt a warmth at his belt, seized it, and felt the haft of the spirit knife. He knew that he had one slim chance of getting her free before the *Apache* sank below the dark waters. Overhead a salvo from the *Assiduous* smashed wood, and he could smell smoke. He began to rip at the sodden, tough mattress covering, ripping and yanking away bits of the covering and the almost solid cotton packing. The water came to Beth's ears, so that she had to lift her head uncomfortably.

"Renno, leave me," she begged. "There is no need for both of us—"

"Hush," he said, ripping and slashing at the mattress and its stuffing with the spirit knife.

A cannonball smashed into the side of the hull, sending a shower of flying debris into the cabin. Renno felt a sharp sting on his cheek but ignored it.

"I can move my right leg," Beth said.

He pulled out a sodden mass of cotton, and she said, "I can move them both now."

The *Apache* mourned her own death with a cracking of timbers, the groan of things shifting, and then a crashing as she tilted more. Through the rent in the hull Renno could see the dim light of morning. He moved, slid his hands under Beth's arms, and put all his strength into pulling. She screamed as pain hit her legs, and then Renno fell backward as her legs came free. He saw blood on her thighs, and then he was lifting her toward the great rent in the hull.

"Grab the broken timbers," he shouted. "Pull yourself through."

Water roared into the rent as the *Apache* rolled onto her side. He pushed Beth the rest of the way out, grabbed and held as the sea rushed in to fill the cabin. He felt the sloop sliding down, down. Water rushed over him, almost tearing the longbow from his back, preventing him from pulling himself out the rent in the hull. Suddenly, the cabin filled with water, it seemed more calm. Renno heaved himself up and out, feeling a jagged piece of wood slice into his calf.

He was in the water. The sinking ship seemed to be reluctant to give him up. There was a forceful suction that pulled him down, down, to follow the ship, as he kicked his legs and fought toward the surface with his arms and legs.

His lungs convulsed, demanding air. His limbs worked strongly, his body fighting for life, and then he was moving upward, free of the downward suction. He could see dim light but so far above that it seemed he would not make it.

He burst into the air, sucking great lungfuls, then swiveled his head.

The manitous were still with him. He saw Beth swimming toward him, calling his name. He breathed deeply and took his bearings. The *Assiduous* was far away. He could not see the boats from the *Apache*. The southern shore was about two hundred yards distant. He pointed, nodded, and Beth nodded back as they began to swim side by side. She still clutched the oilskin pouch that contained Colonel Burnhouse's papers.

Chapter IX

Captain Horatio Jaynes was spoiling for a fight. His officers and crew, fearing his temper, were treading lightly as the crippled *Assiduous* put back into Quebec harbor for repairs. Jaynes stormed off the ship and stomped into the government house, cursing a clerk who told him that the governor was busy. He pushed his way past, bursting into Burnhouse's office, where the military governor was talking with a sharp-faced Indian. Jaynes had had his fill of Indians. He had not actually seen the Seneca during the set-to on the St. Lawrence, but he suspected that the Seneca had had a hand in this second humiliation.

"Please send this aborigine out," he demanded, standing with his legs apart, his hands behind his back.

"Don't be an ass, Jaynes," Burnhouse said. He was in no mood to have this supercilious fellow on his hands again, having thought himself well rid of him, with the

Assiduous back at sea. "This man is a respected ally. He is Striking Snake of the Cayuga, and he's going to be of more assistance to the crown than a naval officer who apparently can't hold his own with a gentleman's weapon."

Jaynes's face flushed. He was on the verge of issuing a challenge, but Burnhouse's next words cooled him slightly.

"I trust, Jaynes, that you're here to report that you stopped the two American ships that were stolen out of the harbor last night."

Now Jaynes's face burned red for a reason other than anger. "They managed to disable *Assiduous*," he muttered, his voice so low that Burnhouse had to lean forward to hear.

"Damn," Burnhouse said, "can I trust my ears?"

"By stealth and treachery," Jaynes sputtered, "they ripped the rudder off my ship, leaving me helpless to maneuver. We did, however, sink the sloop."

"Ah," Burnhouse said, smiling. "How many of her crew did you take?"

Jaynes swallowed. "We were helpless to move," he repeated. "The crew got past us in boats. But they can be overtaken easily once I've done some quick repairs on *Assiduous*."

"So," Striking Snake said, "the Seneca has bested both of you."

"I don't have to take this from a savage!" Jaynes shouted.

"Shut up, you fool!" Burnhouse shouted back, rising.

"Sir!" Jaynes protested.

"Clerk!" Burnhouse roared, and his aide came rushing in. "Send orders to the harbor. I want every available ship to move immediately, to look for ship's boats between Quebec and the sea. Tell them to scout both shores to be sure that they didn't land and abandon their boats."

"Colonel," Striking Snake said, "if men went ashore, they would be led by this Renno, this Seneca. If they are to be caught, it will not be by your redcoat soldiers. Another Indian will have to find sign. If the good captain will be kind enough to show us on his charts where he sank the sloop, I would like to conduct the search myself, starting there."

"Good," Burnhouse agreed. "Thank you, Striking Snake. However, I would prefer that you not become involved in a lengthy chase, for I need you here. There have been some complications, and we need to move forward with our plans as rapidly as possible." He was not going to admit before Jaynes that he had been robbed of documents that could alert the United States to his plans.

With a marked chart in hand, Striking Snake boarded a small British naval vessel. It was not until the next morning that he was taken to the shore near where the sloop had sunk. He began to check the rocky shoreline carefully and was rewarded when he saw a hint of brown stain on a rock. *Blood*, he told himself. Not all of the sloop's passengers had managed to leave her in her boats.

He had great difficulty in finding the trail that had been taken away from the shore, but a hundred yards into the forest he found a spot where the detritus of the forest floor had been carefully rearranged to conceal evidence that someone had rested there. Then, after making a long casting semicircle, he found tracks. He returned to the shore. Colonel Burnhouse was just coming in to where the boat crew awaited Striking Snake.

"Two landed here, after swimming," Striking Snake said. "One or both were bleeding. One is a man skilled in the wilderness. The other is smaller—a child or a woman."

"A woman," Burnhouse decided, his eyes narrowing. "It is unlikely that there would have been a child on board."

Striking Snake shrugged.

"Can you follow them?" Burnhouse asked.

The sharp-featured Cayuga nodded. "With one or both losing blood, they will not be moving at their best speed."

"Take as many men with you as you need. If the man is the Seneca, bring me his scalp. If you find Mistress Huntington, a red-haired woman, I want her back unharmed."

Striking Snake nodded. "Give me four men with frontier experience, if possible. We will move fast."

Horatio Jaynes, pacing the quay as a new rudder was installed on his *Assiduous*, wanted revenge for his humiliations. He had had orders from Burnhouse to capture the *Seneca Warrior* and return the valuable ship to Quebec, but actually, he intended to get within fifty yards of the *Seneca Warrior*—after firing warning shots across her bow—and then blast the unarmed ship with all aboard her to kingdom come, with a full broadside to her guts.

Although Beth swam by Renno's side to the shore, when she tried to stand, she almost fell, favoring her left leg, where her breeches were torn and blooded. With the morning light Renno knew that it was necessary to get off the shore and out of sight, so he swept her into his arms and started for the tree line, only to feel severe pain in his own left leg. He glanced down to see blood dripping all the way down his calf, leaving stains on the rocks of the shore. Nothing could be done about that at the moment. He had to get out of sight before the advancing dawn made them visible to search parties.

He continued into the trees until he found a leafy opening, put Beth down, loosened her belt, began to ease the breeches down over her thighs. Although she blushed, she made no protest, for she felt aching pain in both legs, especially her left. Her plain white pantaloons, only lightly ruffled, were torn also, and Renno eased them up to expose a shallow gash laterally across the left thigh.

"Is it bad?" Beth asked.

"It is not deep," he said. He pushed the pantaloons up to expose her upper thighs. "You are badly bruised on both legs."

"I believe it," she said.

"Rest," he said. He felt the pain in his calf as he rose.

Beth saw the blood. "You're hurt too."

"Rest," Renno repeated.

He had to travel for some few hundred yards before he found the plant he was looking for, alongside a small stream that emptied into the St. Lawrence. He went back to Beth with his hands full of the broad green leaves. He noted with approval that she had removed her chemise in his absence and was busily tearing it into lengths. Pulling her pantaloons up, Renno applied the leaves to her shallow wound and bound it with strips of her chemise. Then and only then did he look closely at his own wound. He saw that it was going to be a painful one, jagged, varying in depth. He remembered the blow to his calf as he left the sinking ship through her torn side. He must have brushed against a splinter of jagged wood.

"Let me," Beth said, moving to sit beside him. "Lie on your stomach." He lay down.

"Pull the gash together as best you can," he said. "Layer the leaves, then tie it tightly."

"You're still bleeding."

"Not badly," he reassured her. His face did not change expression when she put pressure on the cut, bandaging it tightly. Afterward he checked the bandage; since blood was not soaking through, he nodded in satisfaction.

"Now that I know I'm not severely crippled," she said, attempting a smile, "I think I might be able to walk."

"Rest," he said. He had to give his own wound time to stop bleeding.

"We're a long way from home, Renno," Beth said.

"Yes, but not too far."

"The men on the boats—"

"Perhaps the *Seneca Warrior* waited for them," he said.

"I pray so. I hate to think of them in a British prison or impressed into the British navy."

Renno made no comment. The fate of all were in the

hands of the manitous. One of Beth's ships was lost. If it was the will of the manitous, the other would escape. The men who had been aboard the *Apache* were in the hands of Billy the Pequot, who knew the water.

It was the need for water that persuaded Renno it was time to move. He had wanted to rest for as long a time as possible, fearing that his wound would be opened with the effort of walking, and if so, he would not be able to carry Beth far. He stood and tested his leg. There was pain, but the bleeding did not start again. He helped Beth to her feet. She tested her legs gingerly and made a wry face.

"The bruised muscles will be sore," he said. "Walking will help loosen them." He took her arm and, favoring his left leg, led her toward the south.

Beth laughed. "A fine pair we are," she said. "Only one good leg between us."

"A day, two days, you'll feel better," he assured her.

They wasted no more energy in talk. It was challenge enough to keep moving. They paused at the stream, drank deeply, and refreshed themselves by washing arms and faces; then they pressed on.

"Do you know where we are?" Beth asked when Renno called a rest and they sank down on a bed of moss near another small stream.

"*Apache* went down near the village of Three Pistols," Renno said.

"That tells me a whole lot," Beth teased.

Renno had studied the charts and maps aboard the *Apache* well. "If we travel due south, in about seventy-five to a hundred miles we will come to the border of Maine."

"So near?" she asked, her hope soaring.

Renno nodded. He did not tell her that reaching the Maine border was going to be difficult, that once they had crossed into Maine there would be rough, mountainous terrain, and that northern Maine was so thinly settled, they might have to walk another two hundred miles to find people. But they would take one problem at a time; now the challenge was to put miles behind them and to cover their tracks in case they had been seen on shore.

They did not put many miles behind them that first day, and after falling into the black, deep sleep of exhaustion, Beth had great difficulty getting to her feet, for the bruises were now livid, her frontal thigh muscles swollen and extremely painful when moved. Renno's wound had scabbed overnight, but it still looked angry. He had to walk carefully, not flexing the calf muscles, and the small wound on his right cheek was beginning to be very sore. Beth noticed him repeatedly touching the wound as they struggled along, so she pulled him to a halt and peered closely at his cheek. "Hold still," she ordered, and used her fingernails to extract a wooden splinter from the wound. Blood and pus erupted, and she told him to remain still while she squeezed to get all corruption out of the hole left by the splinter, lest the wound become infected.

Renno knew that the area south of the St. Lawrence was thinly populated, but he remained alert for a chance encounter with a backwoods trapper or an Indian. Only a few painful miles were behind them when twilight came. He risked a fire and roasted a large snowshoe rabbit. His leg was badly swollen and felt hot to the touch, so he cleaned it thoroughly in a stream and applied a fresh leaf poultice. There was, thank the manitous, no sign of infection. Beth's gash was much improved.

"I'll have a fine scar," Beth said. "Thankfully, it will be where no one can see it." She flushed, realizing that she was discussing her upper *limb*, that she was leaning against a tree with her breeches down to her knees and her undergarment exposed. Renno, from a culture not so modest, didn't even seem to notice her exposed skin.

Not that her upper thighs were things of beauty.

They were still swollen and displayed a range of color from dark blue to purple and tints of angry red.

Renno finished tying the bandage, rose, limped to the fire, and picked up the skin of the rabbit he had killed. It had been laying flat, near the fire. As he turned back, Beth was pulling up her breeches slowly and painfully.

"No," he said.

She looked at him questioningly. He sat down beside her, his injured leg extended, the warm rabbit skin at his side. He began to push her pantaloons up, and she caught his hand instinctively. He looked into her eyes and smiled. She removed her hands from his, and he exposed her bruised thighs and, gathering the warm pockets of fat from the rabbit pelt, began to massage her bruises gently.

She moaned, for there was a pleasure mixed with the pain. His hands seemed so smooth, his fingers so gentle.

She chortled, and he raised his eyebrows in question.

"I was thinking of how awful I'm going to smell in the heat of the day tomorrow."

"Does this hurt?" he asked, his hands moving upward to the upper limit of her bruises, to the well-shaped, quite womanly upper thigh.

"*Ummm.*"

"It will help loosen the muscles."

She laughed again. In spite of the soreness, in spite of the pain, it *was* loosening something, something deep inside her.

"Now we will get a good night's sleep," Renno said.

He slept on the opposite side of the fire. He had built a nest of leaves for her, and she slept soundly until, with the morning stars bright, she awoke shivering. Thinking to put more wood on the fire, she sat up. Renno's sudden reaction startled her, for he was instantly on his feet, crouching, tomahawk in hand.

"I'm cold," she whispered. "That's all."

He lowered his tomahawk and came to her, eased her

down into the nest of leaves, and lay at her back, curling himself around her, his arm around her waist. Her eyes were wide open for a while, and then she slept. When she awoke, Renno was not beside her. She opened her eyes, started to call his name, then saw him, crouched, the English longbow in hand, at the edge of the little glade where they had made camp. When he heard her movement, he turned his head and motioned her to be silent.

A noise had awakened him just after dawn. When the noise was repeated, he was already alert, weapons at the ready. At first he had thought that it was a prowling animal, but now he knew different, for he had detected two different sources of sound—one at his front, the other back along their path of travel. At least two men were approaching stealthily. He motioned Beth to come to him, and she crawled across the little glade, past the ashes and embers of the fire.

"There," he mouthed, indicating a position behind a large tree. When she was in place, he handed her his pistols, which he had cleaned as best he could, drying them from their dunking and doing his best to dry the fuses. His powder had been protected by the powder horn.

Now he waited, blending into the lush growth of the forest, and he could hear the approach of at least two men, booted. He was sure no Indian would make so much noise. Soon they would be near. He had an arrow nocked and another between his teeth for instant use. He caught a flash of movement, saw a stray beam from the rising sun glint on metal. Tensed, ready, he moved instantly when Beth hissed, "Behind you."

He whirled, and the movement saved his life as an arrow sang past his ear and embedded its head in a tree. His own arrow was following a likely course, although he saw only a hint of darkness among the leaves.

"Get him!" a man yelled in English, and Renno faced

his front again, arrow readied, to see two British soldiers rushing toward him, sprinting through the trees. He loosed his arrow as a musket blasted, the ball cutting leaves quite near his face. One soldier went down with an arrow in his heart, and the second was charging, yelling, his bayonet at the ready. Calmly Renno drew an arrow from his quiver, and the deadly shaft thudded into the charging man's chest.

A pistol blasted behind him as two muskets also joined the echoing sounds. The white Indian rolled to his side, hearing balls pass where he had been, coming to his knees to loose an arrow before he realized that the man was already falling, Beth's pistol ball in his chest. Another redcoat was rushing toward him, his bayonet fixed, the blade pointed at Renno's heart. Renno rolled and came to his feet with the spirit knife in his hand. As the redcoat tried to change direction, Renno slashed quickly to see a spurt of red, hot blood from the redcoat's throat even as he fell.

Beth was kneeling, looking around with very wide eyes, her second pistol at the ready. Renno nocked an arrow. There was an eerie silence. He felt fresh blood oozing from his wound as he ran, ignoring the pain, to the spot from which an arrow had been shot at him. He saw disturbed leaves, a drop of blood, and a few paces into the trees found his arrow, the tip bloody. He knew that it had not been a serious wound, for as he followed the tracks, he saw only one more drop of blood.

The arrow had glanced off a tree, losing some of its momentum, to pierce the fleshy upper right arm of Striking Snake, but not to the point where the arrow's barbs were embedded. Striking Snake had angrily jerked the arrow out and flung it away, while moving backward quickly into the shelter of the trees. Then he had moved forward toward the sounds of fighting to see the four redcoats lying dead, the victims of a single man. Striking Snake spat and considered his situation. He had been traveling lightly and moving fast ahead of the slower redcoats when he caught up with Renno and Beth. He had only his bow and arrows and his tomahawk. The white woman had an unfired pistol, and Renno, he admitted, was formidable. He had not committed himself to the British cause to be a single-combat hero against such a man. He had asked Burnhouse for men, and he had gotten four who had died like boys, unable to kill one single enemy. He slung his bow over his shoulders and began to run lightly toward the north. This Renno, he told himself, would die in a most uncomfortable way, at some later date.

"You're bleeding again," Beth said.

"We will take one musket, powder and shot, and two jackets for the night chill," Renno said, motioning toward the dead men. "I will look for their packs and food supply."

"I can't—" Beth said, then closed her mouth. Fighting down her rising gorge, she moved to the side of one of the fallen soldiers, the one who had pumped much blood from his severed jugular. She went quickly to another, less messy one. She retrieved powder and shot and the fallen musket, then had to roll the man over to take his jacket. She had a second jacket when Renno returned with a British field pack slung over one arm. Beth expected Renno to scalp the fallen enemy, but instead he gathered the jackets, tied them to the pack, took the musket in hand, and set out with Beth at their slow, still painful pace. They paused three hours later at a deadfall, where clear rainwater, which had collected in a hole left by an uprooted tree, made decent drinking. They munched on good British field biscuits and jerky.

"The man who used the bow?" Beth asked. "Will he be following us?"

"He moved north at a fast pace, faster than I could move."

"He'll bring others," she quavered.

"Perhaps not. We will put more distance between us and the St. Lawrence." He had been musing over the situation since the attack. Somehow Burnhouse knew it was he and Beth moving toward the south; he would not have sent men after two crew members. And Burnhouse would be fully aware of the proximity of the Maine border. Men—Indians—moving faster than he and Beth could move with their injuries could overtake them or even outdistance them and lie in wait. Indians friendly to the British lived around a large lake that lay just to the east of a direct line of travel to Maine, and Burnhouse, if he were persistent, could send out dozens of Indians who were familiar with the land.

Beth repacked his reopened wound and had to use the same bandage after washing it as best she could. When she was finished, he stood, helped her to her feet, and turned directly west.

"West?" Beth questioned.

He nodded.

"So you do think they *will* send others after us."

"It is a possibility we must guard against," he replied calmly.

"But that will take us back to the river," she said.

He stooped and drew a rough map in the earth after clearing away leaves. "Soon we will turn toward the southwest and enter New York State along the river that flows from Lake Champlain."

"It's so far," she groaned.

He smiled at her. "You are a woman who said she loved the wilderness."

She laughed. "As the proverb says, I am snared with the words of my mouth. I'm not sure I love *that* much wilderness, but then we don't have any choice, do we?"

After three days of walking, during which her soreness eased a bit during the day and returned with a vengeance at night, they traveled due west. At the end of the third day Renno killed a yearling buck, dressed out a haunch, and began looking for a suitable place to rest. He found it in a little wooded valley—a cozy, shallow cave, hidden by the rise above it and the forest in front of it. He and Beth spent the remaining hours of daylight gathering deadwood. Renno built a fire at the mouth of the cave, and they soon smelled the delicious aromas of venison as it roasted. For water they had two British canteens, filled from the clear, cold stream that had carved out the little valley.

"We will stay here until your legs no longer pain you," Renno said.

"I can walk."

"Then let us say that *my* wound needs time to close itself," Renno said, smiling.

The cave was cozy, warmed by the fire. The rosy light danced and glimmered on the walls. Beth sat with her back against rock and relished the meat, tearing it with her white teeth and making contented sounds.

After the meal Renno said, "You will be warm tonight." He took a light blanket from the British pack and handed it to her. He slept on the sandy floor of the cave, waking now and then to put wood on the fire.

They scarcely moved during the next day. Beth's legs tightened up, and Renno rubbed them with the deer fat. The massage created more relief than pain, and she moaned as his hands rubbed her gently. Without the stress of walking, his own wound was closed and good scabs formed. They talked little, dozed, ate rewarmed venison, drank from the canteens, and ventured from the cave only to answer nature's call.

The next day Beth said that she felt a bit of exercise might help her soreness. Renno sat at the mouth of the cave and told her not to walk beyond the limit of his vision. She went to the stream and removed her clothing, even knowing that he could glimpse her through the trees, because she respected his concern for her. The cool water was soothing. The bruises were now yellowing, indicating healing. She reveled in feeling clean, washed her clothing to rid it of the rancid smell of rabbit fat, and went back to the cave refreshed.

"Delicious," she reported. "You should try it."

Renno found the bath to be refreshing too. He rinsed his own clothing and himself, being careful not to wet his leg wound and thus soften the protective scab.

There was more than enough venison for another meal. They sat across the fire from each other, talked with pleasure about the adventures they had shared in the West, spoke of William and his Spanish wife, of El-i-chi and his loss, and then fell silent, each deep in thought. The concerns of the world and their own continuing danger were far from Beth's mind. She was at peace, content like a forest creature with belly filled, warm and safe in a cozy cave. She looked up at Renno and saw that his blue eyes were on her, and an awareness more powerful than anything she had ever known made her feel weak. She dropped her eyes, took a deep breath, looked up to see an expression on his handsome face that made her decision irrevocable.

She rose, picked up the blanket, spread it beside him, and eased herself down on it, leaning on one elbow. He moved toward her so quickly, so eagerly, that she experienced doubt for a moment, but then he was beside her, and his arms were drawing her to him and his mouth was on hers. Just as suddenly he thrust her away and stood, his head near the stone ceiling of the cave.

"Come back," she whispered.

"You are strong in my blood," Renno said in a hushed voice, "but this cannot be."

"Could a Seneca woman have done better than I have in these past days?" she challenged. "Could a Seneca woman have killed, as I have killed, at your side?" She felt so confident, so sure. She laughed. "Other than Ena, I mean."

"There is more to consider."

"Don't you think I've considered all there is to consider?" she asked. "By God above, I have thought and thought and agonized over it all. I decided to abandon my country on the mere chance that you would remember me and someday come to me in Wilmington. Yes, I've thought."

She could see his indecision, the way his eyes came to her, lingered, then forced themselves away.

"We have far to go," he reminded her. "And the land is hostile to us."

"Holani and El-i-chi knew that they rode into danger when we went to the West," she said.

"And Holani died."

"How happy she was, though, before her death."

"If I had only myself to consider . . ." Renno said, then paused, at a loss for words.

"Consider Renna, with your mother-in-law in Knoxville. She needs a mother. She needs to be in the lodge of her father, not with her grandparents, however nice they may be."

"Do you have any conception of what you'd be doing?" Renno asked, speaking so much like a white man that Beth was surprised. "You would be ostracized by many whites who consider the Indian to be an inferior race. We have been pushed back and back, hundreds of miles into the interior, with entire tribes exterminated. This race warfare will not end happily, Beth."

"But you're doing your best to convince your people that the white-man's way is best for them."

"It is the only alternative to endless war and sure defeat by sheer numbers. There are times when I curse my white blood. There are times when I wish I had been born a Seneca in the days long before the coming of the white man."

She read the anguish on his face. "But you are Renno, and you will always do what you think is best. I'm very much in love with you." She smiled. "You are strong in *my* blood, white Indian, and I remember how sweetly Holani and El-i-chi became one before God, under His good, blue, clear skies, and how they were just as married as anyone I'd ever known. I want that, Renno." She paused. "Our path to safety is long and dangerous. If I die, I want it to be at your side, having known how it feels to have been loved by you."

"What about your business? You used all your gold to buy it."

"How much gold do *you* have left? And it was primarily because of you that the gold was taken from the Devil's Mountain."

He spread his hands. The gold held little importance for him, except as it could help his people.

"You see?" she asked. "It doesn't matter, does it? What matters is the way I feel. And, I think, the way you feel about me."

"Woman," Renno said, with a spreading smile, "I am strong, and I like to think of myself as an honorable man, but I am only a man, not a manitou, and I have man's weakness."

"Show me," she said, opening her arms.

He came to her, held her hands to keep her from putting her arms around him. "There is a rite," he said. "Words. Ancient words."

"Teach me, then," she whispered.

He taught her the words, the guttural, now ringing, now soft words that man and woman exchanged. Then, as he loosed the belt on her breeches with intentions other than massaging her bruises or bandaging her wound, she felt faint and whispered, "Darling, my darling, I know nothing of this."

"That, too, I will teach you." And with those words he felt one quick stab of pain, for they were the same words spoken to him by Emily when he was younger and full of want for her and had displayed the wild eagerness of a young man. But then the grief passed. Although she would always occupy a place in his heart and always be the mother of his children, Emily was dead, and there was only this flame-haired one, the flame-haired one of his future.

The coming together of Toshabe and Ha-ace, if a bit less fiery, was for them no less pleasing. They, too, talked and rested, gazed at the lights in the sky and into the flickering fire, exchanged old, once-private thoughts and tales of the past, their childhood, and things they had felt, known, and experienced. When they had blunted their mature but still-fervent desires, when they had talked until they felt that they had shared the same childhood, they made their leisurely way back toward the village.

Ena had organized a wedding feast, and for two days and two nights there was revelry, dancing, and feasting on a variety of meats and the produce of the village garden plots.

To Toshabe's delight and Ena's pride, the shaman El-i-chi, sometimes looking to old Casno for a cue, performed tribal rites to make the union of Toshabe and the panther a part of tribal history. Toshabe's only moment of regret came when she, with the help of her new daughter, Ah-wa-o, moved her personal things out of Ghonkaba's lodge. But Ha-ace's lodge was also large and comfortable, and the blankets and skins were newer. Ah-wa-o's pleasure in showing Toshabe the riches of her new home helped Toshabe to let go of the past.

*   *   *

The past, however, was the subject of the Miami chief Little Turtle as he stood in the medicine lodge of a village in the northwest territory, which was coming more and more to the attention of people in the northern United States. It was officially designated as the Territory Northwest of the Ohio River in many formal documents drawn up by several states.

Little Turtle's audience consisted of many important men—sachems and war chiefs and shamans of many tribes, some now powerful, some once powerful, some mere shadows of their former greatness. They were in Little Turtle's sway, for he was a formidable orator who spoke in favor of a cause supported by most of those gathered: the Miami, Shawnee, Wyandot, Delaware, Erie, Ottawa, Tuscarora, Mingo, and Seneca. Among them—although he did not agree with the main thrust of Little Turtle's thinking—was the part-white Cornplanter of the Seneca. Although Cornplanter spoke English, he was not a student of history and could not read. He had to admit to himself that Little Turtle's oration was impressive, for the man began by recalling past glory as earned by people who were the common ancestors of all.

"From the time that the master spirit of all breathed life into all things that move or crawl or walk or fly, we were here," Little Turtle was saying. "The messages left for the living by the dead tell us that this land is ours. Back to the beginning of time this land was ours. The white man comes in his ships and breeds like rabbits of the field. With his firearms and his greed to own all that exists, that which was ours from the time the water first began to run and the rain to fall, is now his.

"Now he takes our lands here, north of the great river. The white man states his claim in writing in his books. In New York, where whites stole the ancient hunting grounds of Seneca"—he looked directly at Cornplanter—"of Cayuga, and all the others, the white man said again that our land was theirs. In Virginia and Massachusetts—where, my brothers, are the once proud Pennatook, Pocumtuc, Mohegan, and Metoac—again the white claimed our lands, not content with having killed or driven into exile tribes who had dwelt on the shores of the great sea since time began. And now *this* new thing. In the paper that made all the states one, made them the United States, all states agreed that our lands here north of the river belong not to one state but to all—to the United States.

"The white man spreads like the seeds of the thistle, as if blown by the wind. Already his axes ring in our forests, his cabins belch smoke into our skies. His medicine men who worship the god of three heads invade our lands preaching love and peace but prepare the way for the plow, and the ax, and the depletion of our game.

"There are those who say we should adopt the white-man's ways and train ourselves to use his big medicine." Again he looked accusingly at Cornplanter. "Remember the Delaware, who were fooled by the words of those medicine men of the white-man's god, the Delaware who thought to understand this god who can be three. The white men from Pittsbourgh took the Delaware out two by two and killed them in cold blood. Over thirty Delaware children died with their parents and relatives. Such is the peace of the white man! Such is the love of his three-headed god!"

Cornplanter was increasingly concerned. Because of Little Turtle's incitement, he was having more and more trouble keeping his young men in check.

"When one speaks of peace with the white man, remember the Delaware!" Little Turtle finished, and as he took his seat, there was stern, cold silence from the gathered chiefs.

Chapter X

"I have sent runners to our Indian allies who live on the shores of Lake Temiscouata," Caleb Burnhouse said. "They will have men in the field to stop the Indian and Mistress Huntington before they reach Maine."

Striking Snake stood before Burnhouse's desk, his arms crossed. His flesh wound was only a bit sore and not at all painful, but he seethed inside with hatred for the man who had foiled him. "They will not find the Seneca," Striking Snake predicted.

"*You* found him. But you let him get away."

"Save your accusations for the so-called fighting men you sent with me, who now rot on the forest floor, four of them killed by one man and a woman."

Burnhouse fought to control his temper. If he had not needed these naked savages to do the work that should be under way at the hands of good English troops, he would have killed Striking Snake where he stood. "It makes sense that he will take the shortest route to United States territory."

"You are not dealing with an ordinary man," Striking Snake said. "He is Seneca, but he is white. He combines the Seneca's knowledge of the wilderness with the cunning of the white man."

"What else can he do?"

"He will turn to the west. He will know that we would try to ambush him somewhere on the way to the Maine border. He is wounded; I saw the bandage on his leg. And he is encumbered by a white woman. He will travel slowly and carefully until his leg is healed, and he will enter New York State instead of Maine. If I were Renno, I would make for the Richelieu River, steal a canoe, and travel into Lake Champlain by water."

"That's hundreds of miles, without supplies," Burnhouse scoffed.

"The supplies," Striking Snake said, pitying this white man his ignorance, "are all around him."

"I want this man dead!" Burnhouse shouted.

"I, too, have things to settle with him," Striking Snake said through clenched teeth. "I will go to the land of the Iroquois League. He will arrive there, for he has his mission to Cornplanter. If you will arrange water transportation for me to Fort Niagara, I will arrive there before him."

"And then what? You've already had your chance at him."

"I am not foolish enough to walk into the path of a pistol and longbow," Striking Snake said, "for I have things to do before I join my ancestors. I will have allies who will not allow one man and a woman to kill four and remain unscratched."

"Get out of here, damn your red hide!" Burnhouse snarled. "Tell my aide to see to it that you have transportation. And just in case you can't handle the killing of one man again, I'll be behind you with a force of wilderness fighters."

"You will come to Fort Niagara?"

"I will be no more than two weeks behind you."

Striking Snake wasted no time. He was traveling the water southwestward from Quebec before the day had ended. During the trip by small boat and by a sailing sloop across Lake Ontario, he had plenty of time to lay his plans. One aspect, a form of moral support, involved a man for whom he personally had little use, a man who inspired fear in him. He would find that man, a Seneca, in or near Fort Niagara. His name was Hodano.

Even thinking of that medicine man, an ally of Little Turtle, was vaguely disturbing, for Hodano had, by his own admission, made his alliance with the dark forces of evil. The sign of his pact with the great evil spirits was his tongue. He had split it, then had sewn it so that it would not grow together at the tip. Now, when he spoke, his words hissed from his mouth and his tongue flicked like the tongue of a serpent.

Hodano, hungry for the power he had not been able to seize as yet among the Seneca, had recognized his opportunity in Little Turtle's war. For a bribe of British silver, Hodano would use his dark powers to cast an evil curse on Renno the Seneca and assure Striking Snake's victory.

The summer was lush and green, but still there was no word of Renno. Naked children dashed through the Seneca-Cherokee village, yelping in their games of war and the chase, and the creek was always flashing with their naked brown bodies as they enjoyed the warmth. A wide variety of fresh vegetables and the fruits of summer filled every lodge with good cooking smells.

In the midst of peace and plenty, the tall, bronzed warrior El-i-chi was lonely, restless to the point of near desperation. He had dreams and they disturbed him. He had consulted with Casno, and together they had agreed that El-i-chi's dreams portended great danger for Renno.

In his dreams, El-i-chi saw a medicine lodge crowded with chiefs of various tribes. Renno was there. The dream

varied—sometimes there were few men, sometimes many—
but always a dark, cowled figure hovered near Renno. The
dark face was hidden, yet was somehow revealed to be the
ugly head of a great, glassy-eyed serpent, fangs striking
toward Renno.

El-i-chi reminded Casno very much of Renno: They
had the same chisled profile, the look of the white man,
the eyes of the hawk, and the grace of a running stag.
Here, Casno knew, was a true warrior, and now El-i-chi
also had powers usually held only by the old, by the
tribe's chief shaman. Casno had taught all—all the old
lore, all the tribal magic, and because it amused him and
gave El-i-chi pleasure and thus made El-i-chi more interested in his studies, some tricks of the white man that
Casno considered to be cheap and mostly useless.

He saw the restlessness growing in El-i-chi, knew
what was coming. He, too, was concerned about Renno,
although he had devout faith in the sachem's ability to
take care of himself.

"I go," El-i-chi announced one night when the lessons were finished and nothing new had been covered.

"I knew," Casno said.

"Renno can protect himself," El-i-chi added.

"Yes, I know you are not going because you fear that his
own courage and his own abilities are lacking," Casno said.

"I go because of the dreams. You yourself have said
that brothers, sachem and shaman, make a powerful force."

Casno showed amusement. "You go, young warrior,
because your blood stirs and you have not taken a scalp in
many moons."

"I will follow Renno's path to the north."

"Consider this," Casno said. "It is summer, and the
roads in the white-man's lands are good. It is far through
the wilderness by the route Renno took. Cross the mountains from Knoxville by horse. Use the white-man's roads
for horse and coach when you can get passage. You will
cut weeks from the journey."

El-i-chi mused. "Yes," he said. And then, "And I will travel as a white man."

"Good, good," Casno approved.

He left the next morning, with gold from the small family treasury, pausing only briefly in Knoxville to see his niece, Renna, who was crawling now, and to buy a horse. Soon he was in the land of the white man, having crossed the mountains at a pace that he regretted, for they were beautiful in the summer and he would have liked to explore, to swim in the rushing streams, and to hunt the steep mountainsides. He wore the frontier buckskins of the white settler, and although he did not have Renno's gift of languages and accents, he spoke English in the manner of the frontier. Thus, even with his hair very long and tied in back, he attracted no undue attention. He rode by day and into the night, traded one spent horse and gold for a fresh one, and in Virginia found that there were established coach routes that sped him on his way northward. His destination was New York State, the reservation of the Seneca. Unlike Renno, he received no direct message from the manitous, but in his dreams he saw Renno there, in the village of Cornplanter.

Moses Tarpley would never be able to explain why, when the *Seneca Warrior* was safely past the *Assiduous* and headed for the gulf and then the open sea, he lowered sails and let the ship drift on the river. When he heard cannon fire and saw the flashes of the guns in the distance, his every instinct was to run for it, to put distance between him and certain capture if the *Assiduous* came after him. He knew that the crew was frightened, but he continued to let the *Warrior* drift silently long after the last cannon had sounded. With daylight he was just about to give the order to hoist sails. He used his spyglass, however, and saw only the mast tops of the *Assiduous* disappearing back toward the city of Quebec. Then, as if to reward his patience and what he could only describe after-ward as a hunch, he saw rowboats coming and recognized the short, powerful Pequot in one of them. He moved the *Warrior* back to meet the boats, took men and boats aboard, and having been told that Renno and the girl had gone down with the *Apache*, he sadly got under way, running now as fast as he could run.

The *Warrior* carried a lot on her four masts, so that when a sail was spotted low on the horizon—as happened when the *Warrior* was passing the Magdalen Islands and reaching for the open sea to round Nova Scotia—she was able to outdistance what might well have been a British man-of-war. Winds and weather favored the *Warrior*. The crew became more confident and cheerful with each de-gree of latitude toward the south. It was not necessary to put into Boston Harbor for supplies, for the British had stocked the *Warrior* well for their own use.

Ahead was Wilmington and the sad duty of telling Cedric Huntington, the former lord, that his daughter was most probably dead. Moses did not relish that, but he had a ship, a fine ship, and Huntington would need to earn money with that vessel. And Moses would do his best to convince Huntington to give up any idea of trading with the British ports that were off limits to American shipping.

Renno was tempted to stay longer in the cave. His love for the flame-haired one was great, and the days and nights were joy. His leg healed slowly. Beth's own cut, being more shallow, was now a whitening scar. Her bruises were no longer sore, showing only traces of lividity.

When, one night, he told Beth that it was time to go, she sighed and clung to him. "I wish we could stay here forever," she said.

He knew. But they were moving, eating jerky dried in the sun during their days in the cave and drinking water from the British canteens, but they discarded the jackets, keeping only the pack and the light blanket that was their bed at night. They moved much more swiftly now, although Renno still had to favor his leg. The environment seemed to Beth to be a fairyland. Sweet ferns gave off aromatic smells as they were crushed underfoot, a variety of birds serenaded them, and startled animals fled before them and offered easy game to Renno's bow.

They talked in low tones at night by the campfire, never tiring of each other's voice. They spoke of the past and the near future, but both, it seemed, were reluctant to speak of anything past completion of Renno's mission.

Beth often wondered what Renno might have been had he been raised as a white man. She felt that he could have been anything—a great general, a great leader. He had a surprising knowledge of the great battles of the past—not only in the Revolutionary War but in the European wars as well—and could plan battle strategy, she felt, with the best military minds of any nation. He had told her that much of his reading had been at Emily's encouragement. He spoke French because of his part-French mother, who had learned that language in Quebec. He spoke Spanish because Beth herself had taught him. She felt that he understood the challenges facing the new nation as well as any man. But his total loyalty was to his Seneca, and there were times when she feared that his duty to the Seneca would somehow, someday, come between them.

When he talked about the general situation in the United States, his grasp of things pleased and astounded her.

"The British have no intention of complying with the treaty," he told her one night. "And the Spanish have closed the Mississippi to flatboats from the upriver states while encouraging the Indians of the South to make trouble in Georgia and the Carolinas. Meanwhile, the British continue their efforts to starve the new nation by interfering with trading ships. The United States does not have the ships to retaliate. They can trade with ports in England as long as they leave from American ports and make no stops along the way."

"I should have sent the *Seneca Warrior* to England rather than to Canada," Beth said ruefully.

"You showed courage that others lack," Renno commended.

"Do you ever feel that you've become allied with the wrong nation?" Beth asked. "It's said in England that the war was lost only because the politicians were unwilling to admit that the relatively small forces they had in this country couldn't defeat a bunch of backwoodsmen. If England and Spain succeed in splitting the United States into small countries hostile to each other—"

"I feel absolute confidence when I speak with men like General Washington," Renno answered. "If those delegates of wisdom and goodwill in Philadelphia can convince the thirteen states to speak and act as a single nation—"

"And will that happen?" she interrupted.

"Only the manitous or your god with three heads can tell," Renno said.

She punched him playfully in the stomach. "Renno, I've told you time and again that God doesn't have three heads. He is a Trinity—Father, Son, and Holy Ghost."

Renno grinned. He had had the same conversation many times with Emily. "And then there is the mother of God, to whom the Catholics pray."

"Renno . . ." she groaned, feeling helpless to make him understand.

"And the men of some nations worship a god called Allah, others Buddha. In their efforts to protect the place of the birth of your Jesus, I have read that the French, Germans, Italians, and others fought while calling upon God for victory. But their opponents also called upon God for victory, and some claim it was the same God, whether called God or Allah, for both called the prophet Moses their own and traced their ancestry back to the father Abraham."

"Renno, you tease me at times, don't you?" she asked.

"At times," he admitted. "I see no reason to complicate things with labels and words written in books. The Great Spirit created all. He sends wisdom to me through the manitous and the spirits of my ancestors. Is that not God in action? Couldn't it be that God is God, whatever His name?"

"Well, you'd have been burned at the stake in Europe not too long ago for such thoughts," she remarked, "but yes, it makes sense." She felt very close to God there in the pristine wilderness. She felt no guilt for having become this man's wife without benefit of the usual church ceremony. Moreover, she felt so happy, so at peace—even with the daily potential dangers—that she was sure God approved of her actions.

"Let's not dig into so deep a subject," she said, cuddling into his arms. "Tell me, you beautiful man, how you like my hair."

Renno laughed. "Your hair is beautiful. It would have to be, else you would not be Renno's."

"Conceited beggar," she said, punching him again, yelping as he rolled her to the blanket. She struggled playfully, knowing the gentle strength of his arms, and then she went still, her eyes went wide, and her breath became deep.

She watched, pistols at the ready, as Renno crept through riverside growth toward three canoes tied to trees. Beth and he had been traveling mostly at night, for their route led them through the hunting grounds of Indians friendly to the British. Often passing close enough to a village to hear the barking of dogs, they moved directly south for days, forced to hide only once as a hunting party of young warriors passed within feet of them.

Renno's leg was almost back to normal now. The scar was livid and wide, and the damaged muscles sealed themselves. He would not have wanted to try to run for five miles, but he was walking normally and still honed to fighting fitness. He moved with the silence of a hunting cat, loosed the ties of all three canoes, then sent two drifting down the river. He hooted for Beth, and when she joined him, he helped her into the canoe and cast off. A full moon gave the river the luster of silver.

Now they moved only at night, hiding the canoe and sleeping in concealment during the day. Beth insisted on learning to paddle the canoe, to take turns with Renno, although he seemed never to tire. Thus, as the full moon became a lopsided orb and then a half-moon, they traveled distances that would have quailed those who lived in cities like Philadelphia or New York. Then the waterway broadened and seemed to Beth large enough to be the sea, but Renno told her that they had entered Lake Champlain. Now they traveled both day and night, keeping the canoe close to shore, for Renno knew that the small boat would not weather a storm on the open lake. When meat was needed, he hunted. Occasionally they saw other watercraft manned by Indians or white men, and now and then there was a settlement on shore. He pressed ever southward, toward his first objective, Fort Ticonderoga.

The fort, built by the French in 1755—they called it Fort Carillon—had been called "the key to the gateway to the continent," meaning from Canada to the colonies to the south. Renno and Beth had followed part of a water route—water being the swiftest mode of travel in the wilderness—that consisted of the St. Lawrence River, the Richelieu, Lake Champlain, and then the Hudson.

The fort was impressive, with its stone bastions and its star-shaped outer wall. Beth, now dressed in a doeskin skirt and shirt stolen from a hostile Indian camp in the dead of night three weeks past, was not sure of her emotions. Soon they would be back in civilization. Behind her would be her beloved wilderness. The future, so happy, so certain during the long trek, now began to be obscured by reality.

"Did many men die here?" she asked as Renno paddled swiftly toward the fort.

"Enough," Renno answered. "Ethan Allen and Benedict Arnold took the fort from the British in 1775, but it was not a large battle."

"Benedict Arnold, the traitor?" Beth asked.

Renno laughed. "Truly you are my wife, for an Englishwoman would have said, 'Benedict Arnold, the Loyalist?' "

"Yes," she agreed. "I am your wife."

Fort Ticonderoga had lost some of its importance. There was only a small garrison there, and when Renno and Beth drew closer, the fort looked to be the victim of neglect. Renno chose not to complicate matters by contact with military authorities. He did not give Beth time to see the fort or to speak to anyone, but passed the fort and put ashore farther south.

They were back on the water at dawn. Their route now was into Lake George. Time was passing; summer was upon them. Then one morning Renno waked Beth, and instead of heading for the canoe, he gathered their few belongings and started walking.

"We're going to go over those hills?" she asked.

He nodded.

They were in white country now, and Beth got her first taste of something she would, she felt afterward, have to learn to live with. True, she was not the picture of fashion, in worn doeskin and with her hair braided down her back. There in the southernmost extension of the green Adirondacks, they encountered a family of whites driving a wagon. As they approached, the man driving the wagon stopped, and he, a woman, and several children ranging downward in age from adolescence stared openly. As they walked past, one of the older girls said, "Mama, that's a white woman."

"Hush," the older woman said as Beth and Renno passed the rear of the wagon and all heads turned to watch them.

"But she's with a dirty Indian," one of the boys said.

Renno appeared not to notice, but Beth jerked her head around to see that all of the wagon's occupants were still staring, disbelief and disapproval on their faces.

"How rude!" Beth exclaimed.

"When you are in the land of the whites—" Renno said, then clamped his lips closed.

"Never mind," she told him. "It doesn't matter." She took his hand and looked back, winked at the staring whites, and in sheer perversity, wiggled her rump at them.

El-i-chi, on horseback again, was entering New York State after having crossed central Pennsylvania. A heat wave had slowed him, out of respect for the sweating horse. He stopped for the night at an inn on the outskirts of the town of Binghamton. He would have preferred to sleep in the open, but being dressed as a white man, armed with musket, pistols, and knife, he had found that the food was edible in wayside inns and that he saved time by not hunting. In cases where a bed was to be shared with another man, he chose, as Renno had, to sleep on the floor.

He had a meal of roasted beef, potatoes, and tasty dark bread and was preparing to leave the inn's greatroom when, with stomping boots and great shouts for ale, two burly white men entered the room and took a table near him. The larger of the two, a bearded, rank-smelling man

in soiled clothing, glared at El-i-chi. El-i-chi had no wish
for either company or a confrontation. He dropped his
eyes, finished the last of his meal, and rose to leave.

"I ain't seen you around here," the large man remarked as El-i-chi walked past the table toward the door.

"No," he replied simply.

A rough hand seized his wrist and jerked. El-i-chi's
right hand closed on his knife, and he half drew it. But he
was in white-man's land, under white-man's law. Actions
that would have brought swift and deadly battle in the
wilderness had to be overlooked here.

He reached down with his hand, and not showing the
strain of effort, he unclamped the man's strong fingers
from his wrist, then started to move again.

"I ain't used to bein' snubbed," the large man shouted.

"Good evening to you, then," El-i-chi said, taking a
step.

The man leaped from his chair and planted himself
between El-i-chi and the doorway. "We ain't been prop-
erly introduced," he said. His breath reeked of rum. El-i-
chi, white-man's law or no white-man's law, had had enough.

"I see no advantage in that," he said, stepping aside
to go around the man.

"Listen to the fancy talker," the man mocked. He
minced out, " 'I see no advantage to that.' "

El-i-chi was half a head shorter than the large man.
"If you insist that I break your head," he said evenly,
showing his teeth in a grim smile, "perhaps we should go
outside so that you won't damage the landlord's furniture
when you fall."

The large man's bloodshot eyes narrowed. He gave so
much notice of his intentions that even before his fist
began to come up in a broad uppercut from his side,
El-i-chi was moving. He would have had no hesitation in
killing the man, but that would cause complications. He
moved out of the path of the big man's large fist and put

both hands on the underside of the upswinging arm, giving power to its motion, so that the man thudded heavily to the floor on his back. He roared and scrambled to rise. El-i-chi kicked him on the chin, using the side of his foot so that he would not break his toes. The man slumped back, unconscious, and El-i-chi was darting to one side as the man's companion lunged toward him, the bottle that was being used as a candle holder for the table raised threateningly. El-i-chi crouched low and butted the rushing man in the stomach with his head, sending him backward. The down-swinging bottle glanced off his shoulder as the man fell. One more kick and the room was quiet, with two men lying on the floor.

The landlord, who had rushed toward the fight that had lasted only seconds, a large club in hand, halted and looked at El-i-chi. "I don't know how you did that, son," he said with a grin, "but I'd advise you to make tracks. These two are no good. They'd as soon gut-shoot you from behind a tree as look at you."

"I came here to sleep," El-i-chi said.

"Better lock your door, then," the landlord warned. "I'll tell 'em, when they wake up, that you went off, but they might get wise."

El-i-chi pushed the latch on the door inside his room, washed in a tin basin, lay on the soft bed—a ticking filled with cornshucks—and closed his eyes. He was asleep immediately, his hand on the butt of a pistol.

He breakfasted on oatmeal porridge with sugar, heavy cream, and fresh strawberries, then paid the landlord and was on his way with the sun. The road soon left the town behind, passed near a few farmsteads, then entered a woods. The two men whom he had bested in the inn were lying in wait for him not a mile into the forest. They jerked their horses out into the narrow road and blocked his path. El-i-chi had heard the blowing of the horses before he had seen the movement, and he was ready. Each of the men held a thick, long club.

"We're gonna try again, fancy man," the large one challenged. "Get off your horse."

With a swift flow of motion El-i-chi drew his pistols from his belt, leveled, and as he saw two pairs of eyes go wide, fired. His aim was perfect. Both men fell, and their startled horses bolted. El-i-chi got off his horse and dragged the bodies into the woods. Their horses had run toward the north, away from the flash and roar of El-i-chi's pistols. He soon found them grazing in a glade. He removed saddles and harness, spooked the horses into the woods, and hid the gear. He wanted no trouble with the white-man's law, but it seemed to be the same, here in the State of New York, in white-man's country, as it was in the lands of hostile Indians.

He would have felt better had he not shot the men, who had clubs, and he might even have enjoyed the fight if he had had the time. But weeks were passing. And his dreams were the same—there was something inside him that seemed to urge him onward, to tell him that time was growing short.

The proud Seneca had once roamed New York State from Albany toward the west. Now they were confined by treaty to what was, to those who could remember, a shamefully restricted area in the west-central part of the state. The change was evident to Beth as they left farming country and entered the Seneca lands. Paths now were not much more than game trails. She was back in the wilderness that she loved. They traveled in the heat of July. Renno made no effort to avoid hunting parties, and Beth was pleased at her ability to keep up with him. She had lost weight and was as slim as an adolescent girl, her muscles flexible, strong, and tireless.

Renno halted before entering the first Seneca village they encountered, and they bathed in a stream. Using pigments from the lush summer vegetation, he applied paint to his face in a new pattern, explaining to her that it was the paint of a messenger. They attracted a crowd as they entered the village, and soon they were standing before the centrally placed lodge of the village sachem.

Renno, in the language of the Seneca—Beth was becoming more and more proficient in it—stated his business and asked to be directed to the village of Cornplanter, great sachem.

They were welcomed and treated with honor. Beth was put into the care of two women, taken to a lodge, given new doeskin clothing, and allowed the use of a comb and a mirror. She hardly recognized herself. Her flawless complexion was bronzed by the sun. She looked quite thin, but she thought, amused, that she would gain back much of the weight by eating the single meal served by the women who showed great interest as she told them of her travels with her husband.

Husband, she thought. *My husband*.

Renno was eating in the council house while surrounded by several older, courteous warriors and the sachem of the village, who waited for him to finish. When he had eaten his fill and expressed his pleasure with a large burp for the benefit of the women who had served him, he washed his hands in a ceramic bowl and said, "Good."

The Seneca warriors were gazing at him with interest. The sachem lit the pipe, and it was passed. Most of this was done in silence. Passing the pipe along, seeing it back in the hands of the sachem at his left, Renno said, "Brothers, there is much trouble in the land."

"That is true," the sachem agreed.

"We hear of the trouble in the south," Renno said, "where my father, Ghonkaba of the Seneca, led us."

"I hear," the sachem said, "the name of a great war chief. Is Ghonkaba well?"

"He has gone to the West," Renno said. "I, son of Ghonkaba, have come to council with my brothers."

"You have traveled far. . . ." a warrior said expectantly.

Renno knew that there was nothing a warrior liked better than to hear a rousing tale. Having expected such a development, he launched into a shortened version of his travels. He did not recount that he had gone to Canada to rescue Beth and her ships, saying only that he had parleyed with the sachem of the British in Quebec.

"You have indeed traveled far," the sachem remarked. "It will pleasure us for you and your woman to rest with us."

"For one night only, my brother," Renno said, "for my council with Cornplanter is of importance to us all."

He learned that Cornplanter's village was three days' journey to the west and, although he did not show reaction, was concerned when he was told that the talking drums had related that Cornplanter had made a journey to the west, into the lands north of the Ohio. By going to Canada, Renno had allowed Cornplanter to parley with Little Turtle and the others who were in favor of war against the United States. That, however, had been the will of the manitous.

He realized, as a feast was given in his honor—with young men and maidens dancing, the drums speaking, and the old ones chanting and nodding approval—how much his own people had changed, for these Seneca ceremonies had elements that were no longer included in ceremonies among the southern tribe, whereas Cherokee influences had crept into the rites of his own people. Once more he was forced to confront the old, old question of whether to bring his people north to rejoin their brothers.

Renno, too, had been provided new clothing. This was, he knew, a great honor, and he regretted his lack of resources to return such a valuable gift, for deer were not as plentiful as they had once been. So as not to insult his hosts, however, he accepted the gift with thanks.

Beth, at his side, smelled cleanly of fresh doeskins,

and her hair gleamed. She was entranced by the dancing and chanting. Renno had to tell her the meaning of some of the chants—old words, blurred by time and repetition.

They slept in a guest lodge. With the morning Beth was once again taken in hand by the women and Renno went for his obligatory farewell to the sachem and his senior warriors.

"Your council," the sachem said, "is with Cornplanter, and we honor him as a great leader. We would ask, however, the sentiments of your people in this matter."

"We fought with the Americans in the white-man's war," Renno said.

"So it is told."

"With our Cherokee brothers we honor our agreements with the United States," Renno added.

"Did they give you great lands?" a warrior asked.

"We share hunting grounds with the Cherokee," Renno answered.

"They give us a tiny part of what is ours," a warrior said.

"Brothers," Renno said, "the change began when the first white men came to our lands. It will not cease, this change, for in the countries of the European whites, they teem like ants, and their great ships bring more of them each year. You have seen the power of their weapons. You have seen their hunger for land. I would, had I the power, send all white men back to Europe, but I do not have the power." He paused and looked around. "Nor do we, as a people, have the power to resist them. No man can say that Renno avoids a fight, for I have taken my scalps. But to fight means certain death for our warriors, our women, and our children. The Cherokee build log houses, like the white man. A wise man among them works even now to capture the white-man's magic, the art of writing and reading, for his own people. They plow their fields with the iron plow and grow food to supplement the hunting kill."

"To become white, is that the way?" the sachem asked angrily.

"To take from him the things we can use and use them in peace at his side," Renno said, waiting for reaction.

"So says Cornplanter," the sachem said.

"So says Renno of the Seneca," the white Indian said. "The advice of the Miami chief, Little Turtle, will lead only to death."

"The redcoats are powerful," a warrior pointed out.

"The redcoats look to their own interests," Renno said, "and speak with crooked tongues, wanting us and the white Americans to kill each other so the British might step in and take our lands for themselves."

"They are different," said a warrior. "They promise weapons, land, and peace."

Renno shook his head. "If we fight, we are the losers in the long run."

"But what will happen to us if we side with the United States and then the British beat them in war?" the sachem asked.

"The British will not win, not in the end," Renno assured him, "for each British soldier and each British gun must travel many moons over the great waters."

The sachem grunted agreement.

Chapter XI

Travelers converged on the village of Cornplanter from three directions: Renno and Beth moved from the east; El-i-chi, unknown of course to either of the other parties of travelers, rode from the southeast; Striking Snake the Cayuga came from the west, from Fort Niagara, with a silent companion who wore a cowl of wolverine fur over his head, his face always lost in shadows. The manitous had decreed that Striking Snake and Hodano, born Seneca but claiming now only the spirits of dark evil as his tribe, arrived first.

Cornplanter did not receive the visitors immediately. He already knew the purpose of Striking Snake's visit. Since his return from his council with Little Turtle, he had received or paid visits to the sachems of the Cayuga, the Mohawk, the Onondaga, and the Oneida. Everywhere the situation was the same—vast dissatisfaction at the re-

duction of the league's former greatness and terrible restlessness, especially among the younger warriors. There
was among the wiser sachems and senior warriors a great
concern, for the new and restricted lands of the five tribes
already showed the effects of overhunting, with game
animals becoming more and more scarce. Truly, Cornplanter
knew, change was in the air, and he often prayed to the
ancient manitous of the Seneca to give him guidance. It
was his fervent wish that the league's wise men might
agree on the direction of that change and thus prevent the
league members from going the way of the coastal tribes that
had felt the first impact of the white-man's hunger for land.

Cornplanter sent word to Striking Snake, who was
being cared for in a guest lodge, that he would hold
council the next morning, with all the tribe's leaders and
visiting sachems in attendance.

As Renno traveled through the land of the Seneca, his
emotions were a mixture of pride and sorrow. He took
pride in the greatness of the Seneca, for centuries before,
their leaders had had the wisdom to unite with brother
tribes and form a great peace that extended from the
eastern limits of what was now New York southward through
Pennsylvania and into much of the land now called the
Northwest Territories.

As they traveled he remembered old legends half-
forgotten and related them to Beth—how in ages past the
tribes of the league were one and lived far to the south and
west, how messengers had crisscrossed the lands, carrying
strings of wampum on which, in a code that had since been
lost, the messages were contained. He spoke of orenda, that
Iroquois concept that was so difficult to explain, the im-
personal spirit that pervaded all things and was the sacred
essence that related all living things, including men.

Beth was fascinated, and her questions often prodded
Renno into talking. She laughed when Renno confessed
that descent had been traced in the old days through

women, not men. "That seems sensible," she teased, "since women are far superior to men."

"Perhaps that is true," Renno granted, "and we stray from the wisdom of our ancestors; for once, when a sachem died, the eldest woman in his lineage chose the new chief—from the same family, of course. Women determined who wore the deer horns of the sachem."

"Sensible," Beth said smugly.

The Seneca villages were compact and protected by strong wooden stockades. The intricately and skillfully constructed longhouses had roofs that were curved, not quite a half circle, and covered with elm bark laid down like clapboard. Beth learned that a longhouse often sheltered several families, each with a fire of its own in a line down the middle, each fire with a smoke hole in the roof. For privacy the individual family had a room to the right or left of its fire.

There were also lodges built on stilts, holding the floor as much as six feet above the ground. A notched log leaned against a log porch to give access to such houses.

Beth noted wryly that the work of growing food was left primarily to the women, and Renno explained that such was the case in all Indian societies. The rich fields produced several varieties of corn and many other vegetables, and to her surprise, she saw women dressed for the warm weather with their bodies bare from the waist up, casually indifferent to the exposure of their breasts. Their lower bodies were covered by leggings, a skirt that came just below the knee, and moccasins, all made of deerskin. Although the men dressed in different styles, the older men always wore leggings, breechclout, and kilt to cover that area where leggings and breechclout did not meet. Some men, mostly the younger ones, had taken to a variety of European-type clothing, but most wore a beaded sash atop whatever articles of white-man's clothing they had adopted.

It was a chance remark made by Renno as they walked

through a dark forest that once again brought up the subject of religion.

"We are not alone," he said.

Beth looked around nervously.

Renno laughed. "The ghosts of my ancestors are with us."

In Beth's society ghosts were scary. She told him so.

"To the Seneca a man is three, like your god," Renno explained. "Alive, there is his body. There is also his spirit, what you call the soul. And then there is his ghost."

"And it is the spirit that goes to the happy hunting grounds?" Beth innocently asked.

Renno laughed again. "That's a white-man's phrase, just as the Great Spirit is a white-man's misunderstanding of orenda. When the white man first came, he not only had trouble mastering the various languages of the Indian, but he also had preconceived ideas about gods. So he invented the happy hunting grounds and the Great Spirit, and he has been trying to inflict his lack of understanding of the Indian's spiritual beliefs on tribe after tribe ever since."

"But you do believe in a hereafter."

"There is a place, yes. It's sometimes referred to as the West, sometimes the Place Across the River. Which river? A great, spiritual river. The spirit goes there. The ghost continues to share life with the living, although unseen. It is a great comfort when, for example, we go to war, to know that it is not only the living who march against the enemy but the ghosts of all the great warriors of our clan. In gratitude we have a feast in the cold of winter, and the ghosts share in the food, the dancing, the games, and the warmth of our lodge fires."

"Renno, how did Emily feel about this, this difference in belief? I'd guess that she was reared as I was, with the Bible always at hand and taught to believe that anyone who did not share her Christian tradition was a heathen."

He nodded and smiled wryly. He had at first been reluctant to discuss Emily with Beth, for there was still a raw part of his heart where Emily's memory would always be as green as the grass of the new beginning. He had come to feel, however, that Emily, perhaps looking down from the heaven of the white-man's God, would not disapprove, for Beth had shown herself to be brave and strong—a worthy wife for a warrior.

"We had some heated discussions," he admitted. "In the end I agreed that she would teach our children her belief, as I and my people taught them ours."

"Weren't you afraid they would be confused?"

"No." He did not elaborate, but he had always felt that reason would win out, that his children would see that orenda was all around them, that nature was one, and that to encapsulate God in a place of stone or wood, with brightly colored windows and tortured statues of a man dying on a cross, was somewhat questionable.

"I don't scorn your God," he said. "Far from it. And your Bible can be very useful. I once used a tactic devised by David, who slew Goliath, against the Spanish and the Chickasaw. It worked very well."

"You're hopeless," Beth said.

"He was a warrior, that one," Renno said seriously. "And he was not alone when he went into battle against the giant."

"God was with him," Beth agreed.

"Perhaps it is God who is with me now, in the form of the ghosts of Ghonka, Renno, Ja-gonh, and my father."

"Perhaps," Beth said.

"For your God does not despise war."

"Well . . ." she said.

"Your preachers cry peace, peace, but David thanked God for teaching his hands to make war and said that it was the strength given to him by God that enabled him to run through a troop and leap over a wall."

Beth looked at him. "You're always giving me new

reasons to be surprised at you," she said. "So you're a reader of the Bible too?"

"I have read it," he answered. "And Emily liked to read it aloud to me. There were times when she spoke that peace was God's will, and she was very inventive in ways to explain why, if God so loved peace, he set the Jews on a course that required bloody wars to take a land that belonged to others. When I asked her if God had given this land, our land, to the whites, she had no answer."

"Nor do I," Beth said.

"There are those who want to rain down arrows on our enemies, those who want to take all, as Joshua and David rained down arrows on their enemies and took their lands. Soon I will face them. Shall I say this land is ours, given to us by God?"

Beth felt a chill, in spite of the heat of the day. Was this another thing to come between them?

In the night the shaman Hodano left the guest lodge, gathering his belongings, and walked quietly from the village. He sought a far place, atop a hill. Below him the smokes of the cook fires hung low in the valley over Cornplanter's village. There was a small moon and a sky of lights, so he was able to see well enough to gather dry branches for his own fire. When it blazed and gave more light, he began to unpack his potions and powders of magic. First he sprinkled a dark, odoriferous substance in a circle around the fire, being careful to stay within it. Then he applied black and red paint to his face in bizarre patterns. Finished with this, he stripped to the waist and drew the designs of the evil spirits on his chest.

He sat, head down, hands limply in his lap, his eyes gazing into the embers of the fire. His voice began low, a guttural growl, a chant of malevolence, an invocation of all evil. As his voice rose he threw powders mixed with gunpowder into the fire, and puffs of smoke leaped up. He told the spirit of evil that Hodano was his, that Hodano had love for nothing else, not man, not woman, only him, who would not always be vanquished. He drew strength from the night while a wolf howled from afar and a darkness seemed to engulf the moon.

When he felt the presence in a shuddering of his skin, a cold that came from within, he leaped up and chanted praise and gratitude.

"I serve you," he chanted, gashing his scarred forearm with a sharp knife—not deeply, but deeply enough so that blood ran to his hand and down his fingertips. He flicked the drops into the flames, offering his very essence to the evil one. Out of the corner of his eye he could see hints of movement in the night—the ghosts of those who had died in shame, never to rest—and his skin crawled.

He threw back his wolverine hood and revealed a face of horror: scarred, corpse thin, with one eye ruined in some untold encounter so that it stared blankly, whitely, the other reddened, filled with hatred for the enemy he would bring down.

The power of the evil one was in him and with him, and the ghosts of the unblessed dead seemed to dance and gibber with him as he circled the fire, pounding with his feet, chanting his curses.

"Renno. Renno of the Seneca. Power of evil against him. The animals of the forest against him. All men against him. Death to him."

When he collapsed, exhausted, the fire showed only embers, the moon was high, and once again from the forests to the north there came the call of a great wolf.

The summer day dawned without a hint of cloud, so the heat of the sun was felt early. Cornplanter, his decision made—actually reinforced, for he had decided long ago that it would be folly to war again against white men

well armed with cannon—dressed to give a message to
those who would gather in the great longhouse. Usually
he wore traditional Seneca garb, but that day he placed a
round cap of woven white-man's cloth on his head. From
that there flowed upward, from a central cup, a fountain of
feathers. His leggings were Seneca, but over them he
wore breeches of linen and a tunic of purple silk, also
white-man's cloth. Around his neck was a great choker of
silver, and silver earrings dangled from his lobes. He
entered the longhouse with the feather-fringed ceremonial
pipe in his hand.

There before him were the "pine trees" of his own
clan—the men who, by birth, could never be sachem, but
who could rise by achievement to positions of high honor.
One by one the sachems and war chiefs came in silence to
take their places in the great longhouse of council.

Once such a gathering would have consisted of men
with all but a scalp lock shaved. Now most wore their hair
long and in loose braids. Truly, it was an age of change.

It was not a full league meeting. Things had changed
much since the days when all men of power and honor
gathered in the land of the Onondaga for their summer
council. Cornplanter sat impassively, his face stern. His
eyes did not meet those of the Cayuga Striking Snake,
whose message from Little Turtle demanded this council.
He had even less attention for the cowled, slumped figure
of Hodano, who had once been Seneca.

When it was time, when all were gathered, the pipe
was lit and passed in a long, slow circle around the longhouse. This day, Cornplanter knew, would be a day of
crisis, a turning point. What he had to say would either be
instrumental in keeping peace among the five tribes of the
league or, if he failed, in sending many of the men who sat
in their ceremonial circle into war, perhaps to their deaths,
along with many young warriors from all the nations.

A low chanting began, and men beat a rhythm with their hands upon the packed ground. Four lithe young warriors, full of spirit, resplendent in buckskin decorated brightly with beads in intricate patterns and holding banners of eagle feathers in each hand, danced through the doorway and leaped into the open circle in front of the warriors. The solemn day demanded something equally important, and now the chanting grew in volume as the traditional Seneca dance of the eagle was performed.

Sweat poured down the dancers' faces, running from under their beaded headbands. The single eagle feathers atop their heads waved gracefully to their bowing movements.

Cornplanter rehearsed in his mind what he would say and prayed to the manitous for wisdom.

Renno, not wishing to arrive in Cornplanter's village in the late evening, had camped nearby, close enough to hear the cries of children at play and the barking of dogs. A village sachem passed by and paused courteously, expressed pleasure in finding a brother Seneca well, and glanced only once, without overt question, at the flame-haired, bronzed white woman. From this village chief Renno learned much while revealing little.

Thus, knowing what lay ahead, he was able to wait until he heard the chanting of the eagle dance before entering the village.

Beth longed to be able to see and hear what went on inside the council longhouse, but as a mere woman she was left in the polite care of other women. Renno waited outside the lodge. He had dressed in the new buckskins given to him by his brother Seneca. The clothing was not totally traditional, for his shirt was short, the fringe hanging just past his waist instead of below his knees, but he was unmistakably a Seneca warrior nonetheless. When the chanting reached its loudest and the dance its most strenuous, he checked his weapons, positioned the pistols at his waist, the bow across his shoulders, the quiver in place, and the tomahawk at his side. And as if it were alive, he felt the spirit knife tucked into his sash.

He knew that the visitor Striking Snake would speak first. He waited. The four young warriors who had danced now leaped from the longhouse, drenched in perspiration, eyes excited. In the pause that followed, as all eyes would inevitably turn toward the Cayuga who was Little Turtle's agent, Renno stepped into the dimness of the longhouse and smelled the lingering aroma of the ceremonial pipe, the body scents of many gathered men.

Striking Snake had just risen, stepped to the center of the circle, and was in the act of raising his hand to initiate his speech. His back was to the door as he faced Cornplanter. Renno's silent entry had caught a few pairs of eyes, and one by one all the others turned their eyes toward him. Cornplanter's expression did not change, but he saw before him a white Indian and rejoiced, for he knew that in addition to his own powers of persuasion, he would need all the counsel he could get from those of like mind.

"There is one more," Cornplanter announced just as Striking Snake started to speak. The Cayuga turned, saw the man who had almost killed him, and crouched defensively, reaching for a nonexistent weapon.

"He carries weapons into a house of council," Striking Snake accused, recovering.

"You are, I think, Renno of the Seneca," Cornplanter said.

Renno nodded. "Great Sachem," he said, "I thank thee that thou art well."

"Join us, Sachem," Cornplanter invited, indicating with his hand that Renno would sit by his side. "Or would you prefer to speak first?"

"I have counseled with the chiefs of the British and with the great chief general of the American whites," Renno said. "With your permission, Great Sachem, I will speak."

A hiss came from under the cowl of Hodano. He leaped to his feet, his ruined face hidden. "You would listen to this white man?"

Those who were near Hodano felt their blood chill at the sound of his hissing voice. Renno stood firmly, arms crossed, but as light touched the hooded man's mouth, he saw the forked tongue of a snake, flashing redly as Hodano spoke.

Beware of the one who speaks with the tongue of the serpent. The words of the spirit of Ghonka came to Renno, alerted him, sending his blood rushing.

Sounds of protest came from a few of the warriors seated around the walls of the longhouse. Renno was silent.

"See his eyes," Hodano hissed. "Blue. The color of the treacherous eyes of the white man. See his skin. Not even the sun can give it the color of the Indian."

An old pine tree rose and pointed at Hodano. "You speak evil, as you are the evil one," he said. "This sachem is in the line of the great sachem Ghonka, by Ghonka's adopted son, who also had this one's name."

"A line of traitors," Hodano hissed. "Does anyone forget that Ghonkaba, a sachem of the Seneca, stole warriors from the tribe by evil means to fight with the very whites who now take our land?"

There were those who said that Hodano was mad, that the manitous had taken his senses. But there were those who feared him, too, for it was no trifling matter to invite the curse of one conversant with the spirit of evil.

For the majority, this was the council house, and they were gathered to consider weighty matters. The evil cowled one was a guest—not a sachem, not even a pine tree, but a shaman, a man of great medicine and magic. He shared credentials with Little Turtle's official emissary, Striking Snake, and was therefore to be heard.

"Already the white one who calls himself Seneca is doomed," Hodano foretold, "doomed by the spirits, for they see through his deceit to his purpose—to enslave all of us, the Seneca, the Cayuga, the Onondaga, the Oneida, and the Mohawk, so that they then might move their breeding cows of white women into the lands of others who would fight. He is dead, a walking ghost, for the curse is upon him. Heed him not."

Renno was just enough Seneca to shiver inwardly.

"This is a house of council!" shouted the old pine-tree warrior who had spoken in Renno's favor. "You dishonor it, shaman!"

"See the fate of the traitor to his own people," Hodano hissed, his forked tongue flicking from his lips as he struggled to form words. He held out his right hand, drew it slowly upward behind his ear, and from the very air there seemed to materialize a glinting blade, a blade of steel that flashed as Hodano's arm flew forward.

A moan of shock came from the warriors and sachems, for to use weapons in a house of council was unthinkable, but that moan soon turned to a shout of surprise.

Renno was not even aware of his arm and hand moving. But they moved so swiftly that, as the steel blade flew toward his chest, he grasped the warm, almost living haft of the spirit knife and brought it up to meet the force of the steel in front of his heart.

There was a clang, a ringing sound that filled the longhouse, as steel collided with flint. Great sparks flew in a shower, forming a perfect circle of light, with the spirit knife at its center. The sparks did not die quickly, as sparks struck from flint with metal usually do, but floated slowly, slowly, to the packed earth, smoldering there for long moments as the sound of the clash and the surprised shouts died away.

"Exile Hodano," someone cried out, "for he has dishonored the house of council."

"Let the forked-tongue stay," Renno said expansively. "His magic has the weakness of evil. It will not harm us. His weapons have the strength of an old woman."

A sibilance of pure hatred came from Hodano. Once more he raised his arm, and with a hiss as malevolent as his own, there appeared in his hand a rattlesnake, whose thick, writhing body had emerged from Hodano's sleeve.

"My magic is weak?" Hodano challenged. He laughed wildly, the sound chilling. "*Here* is my magic. No ordinary snake, but a spirit snake. A brother who strikes only against an enemy of our people, with a power that cannot be resisted. Evil to evil." He had been moving, flowing it seemed, toward Renno. Renno stood, spirit knife in hand, impressed by the skill of Hodano's magic but not at all impressed by his words. The snake's tongue, forked like Hodano's, flicked out as if searching, but Renno held the spirit knife ready, knowing that one swift slice would end the threat of the rattlesnake.

"Evil to evil," Hodano chanted, and with surprising swiftness threw the snake at Renno's face.

Renno was prepared, the spirit knife warm in his hand, tensed to behead the snake even as it flew through the air toward him. But there was a whirr of sound, a beating of powerful wings, and a shrieking cry of the hunting hawk as a flash of brown shot in front of his face. Cruel talons lanced the snake's scaled hide just in back of the neck, and snake and hawk fell to the packed earth floor where, with one snip of its curved beak, the hawk broke the snake's back. Then the hawk calmly looked around, gave one harsh cry, and began to pluck at the exposed flesh of the snake.

"Hodano's magic is weak and comes from evil," declared a tall, bronzed, white warrior from just behind Renno's shoulder.

There was just enough white man in Renno for him to lose, for a moment, his stoic expressionlessness. He looked into the blue eyes of his brother, and a wide smile flashed on his face before he regained his impassiveness.

Hodano screamed in fury.

"Would the evil one care to match more magic?" El-i-chi asked.

The hawk, perhaps bothered by all the talk, strutted arrogantly to the door, dragging the dead rattlesnake. He brought the snake a few paces into the central compound of the village and began his meal, much to the astonishment of the women and children.

El-i-chi had been watching from the doorway, unseen because of the intense concentration of everyone on the confrontation between Renno and the shaman. He had seen that Renno was ready to cut the snake out of the air with his knife—an odd knife for a warrior in this day and time, he thought, but he was young and had learned much from Casno, and he had seen an opportunity to pit his medicine against another shaman. He had reasoned, too, that the presence of a powerful shaman who agreed with Renno might go far toward helping Renno accomplish his purpose.

It was by sheer accident—or was it, El-i-chi wondered later; it could have been the intervention of the manitous—that he had traded a bit of silver to a Seneca lad for a trained hawk not five miles from Cornplanter's village as he rode in, having made camp some miles away the previous evening.

"I think," El-i-chi said, "that the cowled one has exhausted his magic, having taken a knife from one sleeve and a snake from the other."

El-i-chi raised his own arm, and a bit of white-man's

pyrotechnic magic, touched off by a match held secretly in his hand, shot a ball of fire at Hodano. The fireball struck the evil shaman in the stomach and lodged there, so he had to beat it with his hand. It fell to the floor and burned for a moment longer, then gave one final puff of smoke.

Hodano screamed in anger, "Now the dark forces of evil will come." He raised his arms and howled a chant, the words not recognizable. A hush fell. Renno stood with his arms crossed. El-i-chi widened his eyes until they seemed to be lances of blue fire aimed at the chanting shaman.

From far off, on a day that had been cloudless when those in the lodge had entered, there came a great boom of thunder. Someone grunted in fear or surprise. In the midst of Hodano's screamed curses, El-i-chi moved forward, right hand in front of him, and a knife seemed to materialize in it. He, too, had been taught some sleight of hand, and the knife slashed so swiftly that Hodano could not move. El-i-chi's attack did not draw blood but cut the ties of Hodano's wolverine fur cowl so that it fell to the shaman's shoulders, exposing his terribly scarred face and his dead, white eye.

A moan escaped from several warriors. El-i-chi's knife moved swiftly to Hodano's throat, where it drew a fine line of blood.

"Where is your magic now, evil man?" El-i-chi asked.

With a hiss of despair Hodano backed away from the knife blade, twisted past El-i-chi, and trailing the wolverine cowl behind him, darted out of the council longhouse.

"I am El-i-chi. Brother to the sachem Renno and shaman of the Seneca."

There was a chorus of approving grunts. Many were relieved that the evil shaman was gone.

"Now, my brothers," Renno said, "we will speak of the troubles that are in our land."

*   *   *

Beth had eaten well, been given water to freshen herself, and promising to tell the curious women of her travels at a later time, gone into the central compound of the village to stand gazing at the council house, burning with curiosity about what was happening. She saw El-i-chi, started to run to him, but he raised one hand and told her by motions to be silent. Gladness filled her, for she was aware, although Renno had not said as much, that there was danger for him here. Now he had El-i-chi. She had seen the brothers in action, and she would have chosen them for help over any twenty other men she had ever known. She blew El-i-chi a happy kiss, and he winked at her, then stood in the longhouse door for a few minutes before stepping inside. Beth could hear voices but not distinctly enough to understand what was being said. Then she, like the other women in the compound, gasped in surprise when the great hawk came strutting purposefully from the longhouse, dragging a snake.

She edged toward the door, hoping to overhear, but the women cautioned her, motioning her away. Frustrated, she walked away. A boom of distant thunder came to her, and on the western horizon she saw a dark band of clouds. She was turning to walk back across the compound when a man with a horribly deformed face burst out of the longhouse as if chased by demons and ran directly toward her. She halted, startled.

Hodano, cursing his evil spirits for having abandoned him, at first thought only of escape from his humiliation. When he saw the flame-haired woman, he easily put two and two together. He knew that there had been no white woman in Cornplanter's village prior to the arrival of Renno and his brother; therefore, the white woman was probably with and of Renno. He would strike a blow, after all.

No magic this time. Hodano carried an ancient

weapon—a tomahawk of oak, carved from a single log. It had a long handle curved elegantly to form almost a right angle, at the end of which was a carved and polished ball of oak. With a hiss he drew the ceremonial weapon from his belt, and even as Beth realized her danger and started to run, he leaped at her, swinging the oaken tomahawk.

Beth opened her lips to scream, but no sound came. The ball of the tomahawk struck her on the left rear of her head and glanced off with a solid crack of sound to deliver the remainder of the power of the blow to the base of her neck. She fell as limply as a heart-shot doe and lay unmoving in the dust.

Colonel Roy Johnson, in Knoxville, had company. The governor of the would-be state of Franklin, John Sevier, had ridden down from Nashborough with a small number of armed men and had immediately made his way to Johnson's house. The two men sat on the porch, each with a mug of that finest of frontier products, corn liquor. At first the talk was of weather, crops, and the where-abouts of mutual friends or the memories of men they had known who were now dead. Of course Renno's name came up. Both men knew that the white Indian was a key figure in that always perplexing problem of how best to live, work, and exist with the large population of Indians in the territory.

"He'll be back," Johnson said.

It was then that Sevier began to edge into talking about the subjects that had brought him to Knoxville. "My term as governor expires in 1788," he said after a deep swallow of liquor.

"I expect you can be reelected, Governor," Johnson remarked.

"Don't know whether I want to be, or if it'd do any good," Sevier confessed. "Roy, I don't think there's going to be a state of Franklin."

Johnson was silent. He, too, feared that opposition from North Carolina was too much to overcome, and ever since the federal Congress had refused to grant statehood to Franklin in 1785, he had felt—although he did not voice his thoughts—that the dream of statehood was withering on the vine. The legislature had met only once. The offices filled by that legislature were offices in name only, and the laws passed by it were not enforced.

"Nevertheless," Sevier continued, "we've got to go through the motions. I've had a messenger riding hard down from Philadelphia."

Johnson knew that Sevier was going to talk about the Constitutional Convention in Philadelphia. Two men had been sent from Nashborough, but since Franklin's status of statehood had not been recognized, they were mere observers and not a part of the deliberating body.

"There's going to be a powerful central government," Sevier said, "in spite of strong opposition. They're not going to try to have the thirteen states ratify whatever document comes out of Philadelphia in the usual way, by submitting it to the state legislatures. They're going to have the people elect delegates to a special convention. That way they feel that they can load the state conventions with men in favor of a strong central government."

"Sounds logical," Johnson said.

"History is going to say," Sevier mused moodily, "that those men up there are statesmen and philosophers, wise men all, with the good of humanity at heart. Some of 'em are—Washington, Jefferson, and Franklin, maybe. But mainly they are lawyers, merchants, manufacturers, and plutocrats. And every one of 'em is out to protect personal property rights as much as personal rights."

"Well, I myself don't see much wrong with that," Johnson commented.

"Thing is," Sevier pointed out, "there's going to be a lot of opposition to it if they put it out like they're presently talking. Now they're squabbling over the slave trade, taxes, and export tariffs. The northern merchants are trying to load it so their ships carry most of the southern goods that are shipped by sea. But that'll all be hammered out, no problem. The real opposition is going to come from those who don't want a powerful federal government in Philadelphia running things. The Virginia delegation probably won't vote to approve any constitution that comes out of the convention. Now our problem is whether to side with Virginia or the Northern states."

"Virginia wouldn't mind seeing us become a state," Johnson remarked. "If all the territory west of the mountains becomes a part of North Carolina, that'll make North Carolina pretty powerful in the future."

"But Virginia stands pretty much alone. They have some support from Rhode Island and, surprisingly, from North Carolina at the moment. The power is with the big Northern states now. What we've got to decide is where our best chance for support is, with Virginia or the others. One state can't convince Congress to grant statehood."

"Well, John," Roy said, sipping thoughtfully, "I am not much good at that sort of thing. I'm a backwoods militia commander. I reckon you and the men in Nashborough will have to settle that question. Whatever you decide, I'm with you."

"Good, good," Sevier said. "You have been chosen by the people—" Sevier laughed. "That is, by you and me— who are, at the moment, all the people we can gather—to be a delegate to the special convention of the state of Franklin to consider the proposed constitution when the time comes."

Johnson nodded.

"We've still got a chance, Roy," Sevier said. He looked into the distance, blue and smoky, with hooded eyes. "There's a lot of country out there, enough to make one of the greatest states in the union, stretching from the mountains to the Mississippi. There's enough land out there to feed all of Europe, could we clear it and farm it."

"The Indians might have something to say about that," Johnson reminded Sevier.

"Well, that's true. They'll have something to say, but a flood of new white settlers with guns talks pretty loud," Sevier said.

Johnson felt a chill of foreboding. He hid it with a sip of liquor.

Chapter XII

Cedric Huntington, once Lord Beaumont, had found a seamstress who worked quite inexpensively. He had scraped up enough money to hire the woman to alter a few items of baggy clothing so that they no longer hung loosely on him. He had been losing weight steadily for some time, for more than one reason: first, his concern for his daughter had had a bad effect on his appetite; secondly, sheer lack of funds had altered his habitual diet of rich foods.

Huntington spent his days and nights in the waterfront office now, having given up the house he had leased with his daughter. He was doing a lot of walking, since there was not any business going on. There were no ships to carry goods, and no goods to be carried.

Being broke was no new experience for the former lord of England. Being poor was. It did not take him long to know that he did not like it.

Beth's father was not an ancient man, even though he had married late and had not been as young as most new fathers when William was born. Although not yet of an age to be called a venerable old man, good food, good drink, and lack of exercise had thickened him. His new life-style, however, was gradually paring away the excess, and he was feeling better physically than he had felt in years. Even this was frustrating, for to have energy and the desire to do something, and then have nothing to do, chafed him.

He walked the wharves, became familiar with all the regular coastal trading ships, and got to know many of the men who worked them. He walked the streets of the town and never failed to tip his hat to those he met and to give a courtly smile to the ladies. More and more citizens of Wilmington were beginning to return his greetings, whereas once they had snubbed him. There was still no love for the English there, but Huntington was a well-spoken, polite man, rather handsome now that he was losing some of that paunch.

But it was the seamen who received most of Huntington's attention. "Any word of the *Apache*?" he would ask a ship just in from some northern port. And each time a ship came up Cape Fear he would be there, straining his eyes until she was near enough to reveal that she was neither the *Apache* nor the *Seneca Warrior*.

He was incapable of thinking that Beth was dead. He believed strongly that she lived and would come back. He had unbounded confidence in that white Indian fellow, for he had heard from both William and Beth of Renno's almost superhuman exploits. So it was just a matter of time, and they might even bring back the ships, and if so, it was going to be up to him to have a shipping company intact so that the ships could be put back to work immediately. The problem was, how? All cash assets had been eaten away. The lease on the warehouse-offices was good only until the first of the year. Hell's bells, he didn't even have any more money for food.

Huntington had come to the New World with only his clothing and a few personal items: a fine watch, three rings of varying value, and a few medals that had been presented to one or another of his ancestors. It was one of the medals that went first, sold for its gold weight, the past glories of British arms not having much value in North Carolina. He ate on that for a while and then sold another medal. He had cash in his pockets, then, when he made his morning rounds, speaking to the usual workers, giving a snappy salute of greeting to the captain of a ship being loaded for the voyage to England.

He stopped, as he often did, to watch the gaming of a group of sailors playing at dice. The stakes were small, for sailors did not earn much money, but emotions often ran high, and there was an intensity to the gaming that always attracted Huntington, although he had learned his lesson about gambling. He had promised himself that never again would he risk money in gambling.

But the days of summer were long, and things seemed to change only for the worse. He had come to know some of the regulars in the game, and a couple of them greeted him when he walked up to observe and always invited him—somewhat facetiously, perhaps, for he was dressed as a gentleman—to join in. Until one day in the heat of summer, with the sun low and the game going on in the shadow of a ship lying alongside the wharf, he paused longer than usual to watch the gamblers, his resolve wavering.

"Take a chance, Master Huntington," one of the men he knew was urging.

Well, it was only pennies. . . . "It does seem to be an oddly interesting game," he commented, easing down on one knee. "Might I try it, just once? If you don't mind, I'll risk two cents, gentlemen."

"He's a big spender, he is," one man said, laughing as Huntington's two cents were matched on the weathered boards of the wharf and Huntington took his throw to see his two cents disappear as the winner gathered them in with a chuckle. At his next turn he risked four cents. He won.

Now he had something to do with his time. At first he lost regularly, but then he began to figure the odds of dicing, and with judicious bettings, sometimes when the dice were his, more often in side bets, he began to win. Some days he left the game with his pocket heavy with pennies. He began to accumulate a nest egg, in spite of the money he took from his winnings to buy food. Then, as the weeks passed—to his amusement and often to his profit—men began to seek him out. He found that in his old age he was beginning to earn a reputation as the most skillful dice player in the port of Wilmington, and those men who prided themselves on their own skill felt a compulsion to match their luck with his.

Slowly the stakes went up. Now he played not just seamen but a mate and a ship's captain in the captain's own cabin aboard a sleek schooner. Now silver and gold were on the table, and Huntington's stash became heavier.

Still there was no word from the north, no news of either of the Huntington ships.

He was playing in the daily game with the workers and a few seamen, the stakes in pennies, when the *Seneca Warrior* came upriver. He was having a streak of luck and was not paying any attention to anything other than the roll of the dice when one of those who knew him said, "Governor, ain't that your ship a-comin'?"

He left his winnings lying on the boards and hurried to the end of the wharf, and sure enough, he recognized the graceful shape of the *Warrior*'s prow, soon read the name on her, saw men on the deck, and searched in vain for a woman. When the *Warrior* was maneuvered to dockside, he scrambled aboard, much more agile than he had been before losing weight, and called out his daughter's name.

Billy the Pequot and Moses Tarpley came to meet him on deck, and he could tell from their solemn faces that the news was not good. Just how bad the news was he could not imagine until, in the captain's cabin, he listened, his face going white with sorrow. The *Apache* was lost, but she was only a ship.

It was Billy who spoke of Beth and Renno. "They were last off," he recounted. "I said I was going to stay, for I was acting captain, but Renno threw me over. The ship went down within minutes after that."

"So my daughter is dead," Huntington said.

"I don't want to give you too much hope," Billy ventured, "but maybe not. Renno was with her."

"But you said you waited until the ship sank, and you didn't see them," Huntington said.

"True. But the visibility was not good. The British ship was sending boats after us, so we had no time to make a search. Knowing Renno, they could very well have gotten to the shore."

That was scant comfort to Huntington, although it was a hope to which he might cling, even if it meant that his daughter was alone with Renno hundreds of miles inside British lands. Suddenly he brightened. "They will return to us," he declared. "Now it is up to us, gentlemen, to give my daughter something worth her return."

He listened as Moses Tarpley told him of the problems with the drunk captain, Jonathan O'Brien. "Well, it seems to me, sir," Huntington said, "that the *Warrior* now has a good captain and a good first officer."

"She's a fine ship," Tarpley said, well pleased, "and with some provisioning, she's ready to carry cargo anywhere in the world."

Huntington smiled smugly. It was as if the gods of chance had smiled on him, for in his gambling hoard he had enough silver and gold to outfit the *Warrior*. Moreover, he had an idea about where he could go to get a cargo of rice and indigo on a speculative basis, for plantation owners had had a bumper crop, and there was a shortage of bottoms to carry it. He told Tarpley to make a list of provisions needed for a voyage to England.

Billy was a bit undecided, but he held his tongue. He had always felt that his rightful place was in the prow of a whaleboat, with a harpoon at the ready, but he had held command of a small ship for a short time, and now he could, if he chose, be first mate of a great sailing schooner. Plus, he had never been to England.

As for Cedric Huntington, constructive activity seemed to reinforce his belief that Beth was alive and would come back to him.

A small group of women quickly gathered around Beth where she had fallen. She lay on her face, her breathing making small puffs in the dust, so that they could see immediately that she was alive. Blood ran down the side of her neck to pool atop the dust. Her fiery hair was matted with blood, which was still oozing. Two women discussed the advisability of notifying the white warrior who had brought the flame-haired one to the village.

"One does not interrupt council," an older woman said. She gave quick orders, and four women lifted Beth's inert body and carried her into a longhouse where the older woman washed the blood from Beth's head wound and nodded in satisfaction. "She will live," she declared. "The skull is not broken." She had seen war and its effects. She had seen young warriors, skulls crushed by tomahawks, live for days without waking, only to die in the end. But this one seemed to be nothing more than a blow strong enough to render the white woman unconscious. She would have splitting headaches upon awakening, but she would recover. Unless, she thought as she cleaned the blood from Beth's hair and skin, the blow had let into the white woman's head that evil spirit of death that sometimes lurked unseen for days and then struck. It might also be the will of the manitous that the woman die.

If that were the case, the strength of the blow would be unimportant. When the manitous willed death, the woman would have died from tripping over a village dog.

Renno held the floor inside the council longhouse. He began his speech by talking of the great distances on the North American continent, describing the land between the northern tip of Maine and the southern boundary of Georgia by the number of days it would take a warrior to travel that distance. He spoke of the great areas of land to the west, and his voice rang with the conviction of experience. He talked, then, of the great white-man's wars, of the role of the League of the Iroquois in the French and Indian wars. There were grunts of approval when he said that it was the league that turned the balance of power in favor of the British settlers.

"My father, Ghonkaba," he said, "was guided by the spirits of our ancestors to cast his lot with the thirteen white colonies that have now become states. In the past I have seen the action of the Spanish, the British, and the French against the United States. I admit there is little choice for us. We face the fact that whites now occupy lands that once belonged to tribes no longer in existence. We face change, my brothers, and we ourselves must change in some way, or we can join our ancestors after a glorious losing battle."

He spoke for almost an hour, telling the gathered leaders that conflict with white Europeans was inevitable— that if it were not the United States, it would be Spain, whose inhuman policies in the name of their God had exterminated entire tribes of Indians in the islands and to the south. If not the Spanish, then the British, who, in Renno's experience, considered all Indians to be racially inferior and thus expendable.

"You say, then," an old pine-tree warrior asked, "that

the white men of the United States are different and can be trusted?"

"In their ambition and greed for land and wealth, they are all about the same," Renno admitted. "There are good men among them. In the lands west of the North Carolina mountains, the Cherokee, Seneca, and white men fought side by side against the Spanish, who would have killed or enslaved the Indian and driven the whites back across the mountains. The greatest man of all, General George Washington, fought with the Indian and, in his own words, wants nothing more than for the league to become a part of the United States."

"To live in log cabins and wear white-men's clothing and dig in the earth like a woman?" a warrior challenged.

"The British offer lands in Canada," another pointed out.

"In exchange for war," Renno said.

"This one speaks as if war is not an honorable thing," another warrior said. "Once our young warriors earned their maturity through battle. It is told how one traveled many moons, around the greatest of lakes and into the far north, where his progress was then blocked by yet another lake, to take scalps from tribes whose names were not even known to us."

"I speak of things as they are," Renno retorted. "There will be fighting enough for all, even the fiercest warriors. The question is whether we ourselves choose the time and place to fight, or allow the British to push us into a conflict with a powerful nation of over three million people who are *here*, with the means and the weapons to make ours a losing cause."

Striking Snake, who had seen much damage done to his cause by the mad Hodano, knew that he had to speak; otherwise all was lost through the persuasiveness of the white Indian.

As he rose, however, El-i-chi spoke: "As we listen to

the Cayuga, let us remember his ally, who tried to bring dishonorable murder into the house of council."

The council continued. Striking Snake said things that many had heard before, and it was evident to both Renno and El-i-chi that the Cayuga had his followers.

Then Cornplanter rose and spoke with great dignity his convictions that Ghonkaba had been wise and had truly had the guidance of the manitous when he fought for the United States. There would be no unanimous decision by this council, that was certain. It became clear that the Seneca would not move as a united tribe to join Little Turtle's war. Most likely the tribes of the old league would follow Cornplanter's and Renno's advice, while some of the young, hot-blooded warriors would cast their lot with Little Turtle and the British.

Renno emerged from the longhouse in the cool of early evening with only one certainty in his mind: the time was not right to suggest that his southern Seneca trek to the north to reunite with the parent tribe.

It was with mixed emotions that he clasped El-i-chi's arm in a warrior's embrace, inquired of his people, his mother, his children. He was startled to hear of Toshabe's marriage; then he laughed, throwing his head back. "Good for her!" he exclaimed. "So she has, at last, followed Ah-wen-ga's example and taken her cookpots into the lodge of a fine warrior."

He could not get enough of El-i-chi's fond descriptions of the antics of Little Hawk. So the smell of cooking food was filling the village before he inquired for Beth's whereabouts, and then he was running toward the lodge where she was being tended by silent women.

She was pale, her face composed. Her hair had been pulled away from the wound. She was breathing slowly and easily. He bent to touch the huge knot on her head, satisfying himself that her skull was not broken. She did not move or make a sound as his fingers probed around the wound.

"When?" he asked.

"When the one with the living false face came rushing from the house of council," a woman said. She launched into a lively account of the incident, going through the motions of Hodano, swinging an imaginary tomahawk strongly, then Beth, falling to the floor. Thus Renno knew that long hours had passed since the attack.

He turned as El-i-chi came into the lodge. He explained quickly, and El-i-chi knelt and examined Beth's wound. El-i-chi had told Renno that he had been studying magic, medicine, and the art of healing with old Casno, and Renno knew that if his brother had learned his lessons well, his opinion of Beth's condition would be valuable.

He moved closer as El-i-chi, having felt down Beth's neck to find a swelling at the base of it, carefully rolled her onto her side.

"It is not good, Brother," El-i-chi said, pressing his finger lightly onto the swelling, which was now becoming livid. "We can only wait."

Renno felt cold fury. His hands went automatically to his weapons, his right hand closing over the haft of the spirit knife. His impulse was to take the trail of Hodano at that very moment, but it was growing dark. The long hours in the council house had given Hodano a good head start, and his trail could not be followed at night. But in the morning . . . There was a bloodlust in him, an anger so consuming that he did not even realize that it was his way of compensating for the pain of loss that he felt. One beloved wife had died. Now this.

Together, after giving their thanks to the women who had tended her, the brothers kept a night vigil. Beth seemed to be merely sleeping, but El-i-chi was concerned. He kept cool cloths on the swelling at the base of her neck. Renno sat, his long legs crossed, elbows on his knees, communing with the manitous, knowing a great desire to be away, to be in the wilderness on the trail of the madman.

She opened her eyes just as the morning light was coming in through the open door of the longhouse. Both brothers heard her moan, and both leaped to her side.

At first she opened her eyes only a slit, and then they opened wide, and Renno's heart rejoiced.

"Ren—" She seemed unable to form his full name.

"Rest," he said, taking her hand. "For you are with us again."

When next she opened her eyes, the sun was an hour high and Renno was burning to be away. This time she said, "My head—"

She turned her face to Renno and tried to smile. "Head . . . hurts," she whispered.

El-i-chi was standing at the foot of the sleep bench on which she lay. Renno saw him pick up a small stick from the fire. He moved the glowing tip, a red ember, to within a finger's width from Beth's bare foot. She continued to look into Renno's eyes. Now the ember was almost touching her foot, but she said nothing and showed no pain. El-i-chi was now touching Beth's foot with the sharp point of his knife, moving it up, denting her skin with the knife point at her ankle, onto her calf. He lifted her leg, and it fell limply. He repeated the same process with her hands and arms. She did not feel the sharp point almost breaking her skin.

"El-i-chi," Beth said. "So happy you—"

El-i-chi opened Beth's shirt to bare her chest between her breasts and pressed there with the knife tip.

"What are you doing?" she asked. "I can't seem to feel—"

"Rest," El-i-chi said, closing her shirt and covering her with a blanket. He walked out of the longhouse.

"I'll be back in a moment," Renno said.

"What is wrong?" Beth asked, her voice quite weak. "I can't move my body."

El-i-chi was chanting an old prayer when Renno joined him outside. He waited until El-i-chi had finished.

"It is not good," El-i-chi said.

"The half death?" Renno asked, although his lips almost refused to form the words.

"The half death," El-i-chi confirmed. "The body is dead and has gone, without spirit, to the West."

Renno had seen the half death. It came to warriors with wounds to the spine or the neck. The spirit remained and the head was alive, but the body was dead, felt nothing. Full death soon followed.

"Yet there is no wound to the spine," he said.

"A great blow, here," El-i-chi said, touching the back of Renno's neck.

"Perhaps—" Renno could not continue. He had seen one wounded warrior live for weeks, unable to move his body.

"Go to her," El-i-chi encouraged.

Renno fingered the spirit knife. There was a comforting feeling of heat. "I will go to her only when I have the scalp of the snake who struck her," he vowed.

"Then I will go with you. The women can tend her," El-i-chi said.

Renno clasped his brother's shoulders. "Do this for me," he requested. "Stay with her. Use all the magic, all the wisdom you learned from Casno."

"The snake has had long to travel, and soon he will join with his friends," El-i-chi warned. "Two of us—"

"For me, stay," Renno asked.

"I hear," El-i-chi said, not so sure now that it had been a wonderful thing to learn all of Casno's knowledge.

For an hour, as he left Cornplanter's village, Hodano ran at a warrior's pace. Then he slowed and began to think about being more careful to cover his tracks. He was still burning inside from his humiliation in the council house. He paused on a ridge and examined his back trail. He saw nothing. He knew that Renno would come after him to avenge his woman's death. The idea of facing Renno did not appeal to Hodano—not with weapons . . . but there were other ways.

Now Hodano moved at a comfortable pace. If he reached the lands of the Miami, he would have hundreds of warriors around him, any one of whom would gladly kill the man who was trying to divide the Indians. But even if he traveled as swiftly as he could, Hodano knew there was always the chance that a warrior in Renno's superb physical condition could catch him.

He halted as the sun went down, gathered wood, and began to make his preparations. What he had to do could only be done in blackness, without a moon. Fortunately there would be no early moon that night. By the time of full darkness he was ready: He had built his small fire and seasoned it with magic powders. With a powder as red as blood he had encircled himself. Now he sat before the small fire and let it burn to embers, so there was only a dull glow.

The great evil could not desert him now. As if the spirits had told him, he felt certain that the day's events had been preordained and that the sole purpose had been to lure this great enemy to his cause into the open. Renno, he knew, would come alone; he was that kind of warrior. And he would find more than he bargained for.

Hodano began his chants, the sound startling a sleeping bird into a burst of movement and a cry of fright. When he had evoked the evil one with prayers, praise, and promises, he lanced his arm with a knife and sent his blood sizzling on the coals. He heard a sound that caused the hair on the back of his neck to bristle, and he turned to see the embers' light reflected by two large yellow orbs.

"You are great, indeed," he whispered to the forces of evil as those eyes were joined by others, until, circling him, sitting silently just outside the red circle he had drawn, ten huge wolves with dripping tongues watched the movements of his hands as he drew signs and spells in the darkness of the air.

"He will come, Brothers," Hodano promised. "To-morrow he will come, and we will be ready for him."

He chanted throughout the night, and his audience of wild beasts sat quietly, their only motions being those of drawing their dripping tongues back into their sharp muz-zles. Hodano felt a flow of ecstasy. Never, in all of his strivings for perfection in his spiritual relationship, had he achieved such results. Around him the great wolves seemed to take on a presence beyond their fleshly beings. Their glowing eyes were unblinking. At times it seemed that their eyes projected an eerie light of their own.

In his transported state, he praised his glorious spirits of evil. He felt as if he were possessed by something larger than himself and as if he were capable of soaring into the darkness.

"Dead," he chanted. "He is dead, and my brothers will eat his flesh and his spirit so that his ghost will be homeless forever."

With the rising of a pale, small moon, the wolves grew restless, and one by one they left the circle. Hodano, still enraptured with his newfound power, dozed. He awoke in the chill dawn, his body dampened by dew and his limbs stiffened. Before the coming of the sun he was moving, his eyes alert for just the right terrain. He found it at midday and made certain that he had left a good trail into a glen between two wooded hills, where a stream had cut through the depression between the ridges. At its western end there was a rocky tor, which gave an excel-lent view of the entire glen. There he sat, ate his dried meat, and watched the slow progress of the afternoon sun as he continued his incantations. Several times during the long afternoon he caught a glimpse of blackish-gray among the trees on the ridges, and once he heard a low, haunting call of a wolf. His brothers were there, waiting with him.

The white one who had caused his humiliation would not escape, for all the power of the great evil one awaited him. Once he entered that grassy glen, his would be a meeting with his death.

Renno was on the move, his moccasined feet flashing, arms swinging, his breath hissing through his clenched teeth. From a near distance one would have heard the slap-slap of his feet, for during the early stage of the chase he was moving swiftly, not overly concerned about making noise. He quickly realized that Hodano was not making a great effort to cover his trail. He would have to be more cautious, he knew, with ambush a possibility.

His thoughts were dark. His heart wanted to be back in the village with Beth, but his outrage pushed him forward. To see Hodano dead was all that mattered at the moment, for in his mind he had already accepted Beth's death. A man afflicted by the half death—or a woman, in this case—was already with the spirits. Yet it would have been sweet to sit with her, to talk with her, to touch her cheek where she could feel his caress. The method of Hodano's death would be up to Renno, who, in his outrage, considered something not as swift as the piercing pain of an arrow, the slash of the spirit knife, or the bashing thunder of a tomahawk.

Torture had not been unknown among the Iroquois. Now, however, that largely abandoned practice was not used as punishment but as a mystical tribute to the bravery of a defeated enemy. A true warrior, as the victim of ritual torture, knew that he was being given a high honor. He was fed and cared for, perhaps even given a woman. Then he was killed slowly, by fire. The brave ones, the old

pine trees said, lasted twelve hours. Their courage was
passed along to the victors, when the victim was dead,
through a ritual bite of the brave warrior's flesh. Ritual
torture was not for Hodano. To give him extended pain
would have dishonored the ceremony. So, Renno finally
decided, his death would be swift, his body left for
scavengers.

Without his overt notice, Renno's rhythm of breathing had changed. He breathed easily now, through his
open mouth. His body no longer felt the strain of his swift
pace, for he had entered that stage in which greater amounts
of air were being pumped to his lungs and his body had
adjusted to the additional demands on it. He seemed to fly
through the forest.

Beth was talking to El-i-chi, asking about Renno. "He
will be back soon," El-i-chi assured her without elaboration.

She started describing Hodano's attack on her, and in
the middle of a sentence she paused, a puzzled look on
her face, and her green eyes rolled up so that only white
was showing. Before El-i-chi could leap from the bench on
which he sat, vomit spewed upward from Beth's mouth.
El-i-chi quickly put his arm around her, lifted her torso,
turning her head to one side so that she would not strangle. His heart was heavy. Thus men died when they had
been given a severe blow to the head.

He called the women, and they cleaned Beth, put her
atop fresh skins, and covered her with a blanket. She was
still unconscious.

Renno had eaten nothing and had drunk little, pausing only when he encountered the stream that now ran
alongside the trail Hodano had taken. The summer sun
was low in the west, so at times the glare interfered with
his vision. He found the spot where Hodano had camped,
noted the dead fire, the circle of red around it, and mused

at multiple wolf tracks. Wolves, he knew, still roamed the forests, but they usually stayed farther away from the haunts of man.

"I pray, Brothers," he said, speaking to the wolves, "that you have not robbed me of my vengeance."

Hodano's trail was quite fresh now, laid down only that morning, and Renno's pace took him over the land with a swiftness that could have been matched only by a warrior with great endurance. As he neared a cluster of small hills, he slowed, for he could almost feel the nearness of his enemy. Occasionally wolf tracks were merged with the marks of Hodano's moccasins. The wolf, totem of the Ohkwaho clan of the Seneca tribe, was not ordinarily dangerous, especially in a time of good hunting, as in the summer, but it was not an animal to be ignored. Renno's eyes scanned before him and on both sides. Once he heard the signal howl of a wolf, but his greatest concern was that a pack had chosen the evil shaman as its prey.

He knew that Hodano was near. The tracks were no more than hours old, and Hodano was not running. He had been walking as if he were merely out for a stroll.

On an upgrade among tall, virgin trees, Renno saw fresh wolf droppings. A feral scent lingered. He knew this was odd, for usually wolves hid their droppings. The sun was behind a western ridge, plunging the forest into dim twilight. There was an odd feeling, and Renno slowed his pace and moved with silence, his bow in hand, an arrow ready to fly. As he walked he silently invoked the manitous, feeling the need, somehow, in a way he could not explain.

He crested the rise and started down among the trees. The trees seemed to part, and there before him, in the twilight, was a natural clearing, a miniature valley between two ridges. Tall grass grew along the stream. It was a lovely, serene spot and under other circumstances could have been quite beautiful. Hodano's tracks led him to the stream, and the grass on the other side was still bent by the shaman's passing.

So, Renno thought, it was to be an ambush. Ahead, on either side of the glen, were excellent places for a man to lie in wait. Renno knew that Hodano had left the council house with a tomahawk. If the shaman also had a musket waiting for him outside the longhouse, then Renno was already within range if Hodano was behind the rocks.

Slowly, carefully, Renno crossed the stream and slipped into the tall grass on the other side. A sound came to him from the trees on the southern slope, and he lowered himself so only his head was above the grass, and waited. The sound came again, and he recognized it, the panting of a wolf or dog. When he saw a flash of blackish-gray among the trees, he rose, nocked his arrow, and advanced down the glen, searching the sides of the ridges for any movement.

He whirled suddenly as something splashed in the stream behind him. Two wolves had crossed, and they stood in the grass, mouths open, red tongues lolling, staring at him. A sound from the front caught his attention. Other wolves were there. And then, in silence so perfect that he had to see, not hear, the wolves came from the rear and the side toward the trees on the south.

There were ten of them—summer fat and powerful. He had heard how a wolf pack worked together to encircle a weakened elk or a deer. Now he was the hunted.

The wolves seemed not to be in any hurry. He decided not to waste any more time. They were obviously well fed. Only hungry wolves would attack a man. He walked forward, but the wolves to his front held their ground, showing their long, yellow teeth and growling low, a threatening sound.

"I have no quarrel with you," Renno said softly.

He made a quick shooing motion with his hand, and

the wolves to his front bristled, then lowered themselves as if ready to attack.

"So be it, Brothers," Renno said, letting loose an arrow at the nearest wolf.

It was a matter of yards, and at that range Renno never missed. But the arrow, which at first flew swift and true, faltered in midair and swerved to one side as if broken in the shooting. Such things happened. He nocked another and fired, and this one flew strong and true, only to drop suddenly onto the grass as it neared the wolf.

From the high ground to his front there came a wolf call, followed by a sound that was obviously human, the cackling of a madman.

Chapter XIII

A new world had opened up for Hodano. He no longer resented the events that had occurred back in the council house in Cornplanter's village, for it was obvious to him that everything had been guided and planned by the great evil spirit to show him that power was his, a power never before known to man. He could control and guide wild beasts. He could multiply his strength by many times with the aid of beasts, such as the wolves who were slowly closing in on his enemy.

The power of the magic he had invoked caused him to cackle aloud, for it no longer mattered if Renno knew that he was nearby. He watched, his one good eye wide, the sounds of shrill laughter echoing back to him from the opposite ridge, as Renno's arrows, shot from a bow more powerful than any Hodano had ever seen, fell short of their targets like toy arrows shot by a five-year-old boy playing at war.

With such power he would be invincible. Visions of glory rose in him. He fell to his knees, raised his hands, and praised his spirits. At long last, after so many agonizing years, he was to be repaid for all the things he had suffered.

"I am yours, great one," he chanted. "I will do your work here in the land of the living."

Now that his magic stopped arrows, he could stand against any warrior, and that warrior's weapons would be useless against him. With power like that, what was there, who was there to stop him from being anything he wanted to be? What was to stop him from becoming the greatest sachem? Cornplanter was only a man, Little Turtle was only a man. He, Hodano, was man enforced by the infinite powers of the evil one. Other men would defer to him and give him honor, and he would have his choice of women.

This thought burned inside him as he watched the slowly developing drama below him. *Women.* He remembered. Oh, by the spirits, he remembered. Always they had either laughed at him or run in fear from his ravaged face. But the girl who was responsible for that face had died screaming, far from her lodge, with his knife twisting in her belly.

Now even that painful memory was a revelation. It had all happened by design! From the very beginning of what he had always thought to be his misfortunes, everything had been planned to bring him to this moment of epiphany, when he saw the first results of a power toward which he had been striving all of his life. It was, he knew now, no accident that his father had died in a minor raid into the land of the Pawnee, that his mother had been taken by winter fever soon after. He now could accept that his thinness, his—yes, he could face it now—his ugliness, had been given to him as a favor by that great spirit now allied with him, to form his character, to prepare him for this day when he had found the key to a power that would make him the greatest sachem in history.

He had first known that he was different, that he had

something in him that was missing in others, when he killed the girl who had pushed him into the fire. It happened when he was thirteen, an unclaimed orphan, living on the not-always-generous charity of the people of his village. The girl had been fourteen, a rogue herself, for she had discovered sensuality and—ah, this was a new revelation—the evil one had entered her for his, Hodano's sake, making her willing to sneak away into the forests with any boy, and many young warriors—anyone but the ugly Hodano. Yes! She had been made into an eager receptacle for any male's seed—any but Hodano's—for one reason: to give Hodano that one last incentive to curse the manitous, to curse his people who laughed at him or scorned him, and to bend his efforts toward the arcane, whispered knowledge of evil.

One night with a longing that was so strong in him that he shivered, he had watched her go into the forest and linger with two different boys of his own age. Afterward he had accosted her, demanding that she bestow her favors on him as well. With a grimace of disgust, she had pushed him away, and his feet becoming entangled, he had fallen face first into a fire.

He had never forgotten the pain. His face was ruined, and one eye was a useless, whitened orb. But that, too, had been for a purpose, for with only one eye he could not become a warrior, and thus his interest in learning all the tricks and medicine of the tribe was reinforced.

The girl? One day she went far, alone, in search of the ripe berries of late spring, and he followed. She screamed nicely with his knife twisted in her belly, and she was still gasping away her life when, for the first time, he knew the inner warmth of a woman's body. He used her twice more after she had stopped moaning.

Yes, all had been planned. He had paid a price in suffering, but now the rewards were his. Down below, a man of the kind he hated so much was going to meet his death at the teeth of *his* tools, tools that he would use to show everyone that Hodano had paid all the suffering he would pay and that now it was time for Hodano to assume the position to which he was entitled.

His wild laughter soared to the sky.

Once more Renno loosed an arrow, giving the bow extra power, pulling it to its limit. The bowstring sang, and the arrow made an audible buzzing sound as it flashed toward the largest wolf, the dominant male of the pack. But once again the arrow slowed, as if traveling through thick molasses, and fell harmlessly to the ground.

The hair on the back of Renno's neck stood. He cast a quick look around, feeling a force but unable to see anything but the ten great wolves, now beginning to close on him in eerie silence, quite unlike wolves.

"Spirits of my ancestors, be with me," Renno whispered, pulling both his pistols. He aimed carefully to take out the two largest wolves, and his pistols flamed with a crash and . . . nothing. He could not, of course, see the shot that burst from the barrels, but he could see that the shot did not strike where he had aimed, in the chests of two wolves, that the wolves were—and this was as puzzling as anything that had happened—not even startled by the blast of two pistols.

Tomahawk.

No, something seemed to tell him. He tucked the tomahawk back into his sash, and his right hand felt the heat of the spirit knife. The stone seemed to glow with a life of its own.

"So," he said, crouching, ready. "Come to me, for you are not wild brothers but spirits."

The spirit knife began to glow, to give forth a greenish, eerie light, and with deep snarling, the nearest of the wolves halted the slow stalk.

"Come, evil ones," Renno taunted, brandishing the glowing knife, "for I, too, have spirits with me."

With low growls, two of the lesser wolves, perhaps

becoming impatient, launched themselves, one from each side, digging into the soft mulch with their claws to accelerate, then leaping at Renno's throat. The green-glowing spirit knife made a short arc, leaving a visible imprint of itself in the air as it moved in Renno's hand and sliced through a throat as if it were butter. Renno whirled to meet the airborne weight of the second wolf even as the first went slack and fell. He stabbed into the wolf's chest and twisted away to avoid the impact of the animal's body, then jerked the knife away as he moved to see three others, this time abreast, charging.

Hodano, witnessing two of his allies die so quickly, screamed in rage.

One of the three charging wolves made the mistake of outdistancing his brothers and met the spirit knife in midair. Blood gushed from the animal's slashed throat. Of the other two, one came in low and the other high, so that the animal that kept all four feet on the ground was slashing at Renno's legs as the white Indian gutted the leaping one with one long stroke. He pushed the airborne body away to fall heavily and lie whimpering as life drained away; then he stabbed downward and broke the back of the wolf that had brought blood from his legs with two quick snaps.

Five were left. They began to circle, growling and snuffling, wary now, for the ground around Renno was reddened with wolves' blood—and his own as the slashes on his legs dripped.

The circle was closing slowly. The remaining five animals—or spirits—had learned from observation. Renno felt that all five would come at once, from all sides. He had felt the power of the muscular bodies and had evidence of the sharpness of the teeth.

As one wolf came quite close—close enough for the white Indian to smell the rank, carnivorous stench of its breath—Renno moved with a swiftness that caught even that agile and quick animal by surprise. He threw himself, extending his body and missing the wolf's death stroke but slashing a long, bloody gash in the beast's side. But now he crashed to the ground, and four snarling wolves with bared fangs were on him, slashing, tearing at his clothing, vying with each other for a place at Renno's throat. Renno's arm worked desperately under the rolling, snarling mass, and the glow of the spirit knife flashed as he felt the effects of the savaging. He knew that he was bleeding from the arms, legs, and torso, and fended off teeth that narrowly missed his throat. The spirit knife sliced through a wolf's throat, and Renno was splashed by a gush of warm blood. He buried the knife deeply into a furry belly and hurled aside a jerking, dying wolf to get at still another.

Renno had been in desperate fights before, but never had he felt a greater threat to his life. On one level it was man against beast, and there he knew that he could compete. On another level, however, he knew that he was battling a force greater than the physical strength of the long-toothed wolves. Not only was it man against beast, it was good against evil—the good represented by the green-glowing spirit knife, gift of the great spirit of Ghonka. There was more being contested than one man's life there in the growing darkness in the secluded glen beside a clear, swiftly flowing stream.

From his perch on high, Hodano watched the white one go down under four blackish-gray bodies and saw only a tangle of man and animal. The wounded wolf leaped into the fray, and the sounds of snarling came to him. He began to chant praise to his protecting spirits, for, with five wolves going for Renno's throat, the white Indian would surely die.

Blood gushed from a slashed throat. There was a sound like ripping cloth as the spirit knife disemboweled a wolf. Renno, with the beasts' weight atop him, surged up to his knees. The spirit knife made a descending arc to break a wolf's spine.

Hodano howled as he saw three more of his creatures writhing out their lives, and then he howled again as one wolf locked its teeth in Renno's left arm.

Renno undercut the throat, kicked the animal even as blood poured out, and then there was only one, the wounded one, backing off slowly, its teeth bared.

"The evil that is in you is not yours," Renno said. "Go in peace."

The yellow eyes took on an unearthly glow, and with a howl the wounded wolf leaped to its death, meeting Renno's blade in midair, trying, even in death, to reach his throat.

Renno let his arms fall to his side. Slowly the green glow faded from the spirit knife. He looked around at the ten crumpled bodies of the wolves and felt a shiver as if spirits were passing near him. Then he began to feel the pain of his wounds. He lifted his head and loosed the roar of a conquering bear, then changed the roar into a name.

"Hodano!" he shouted. "Hodano!"

The shaman had been shocked into silence. The white one had killed all ten of his creatures! He whispered, for now there was fear in him.

"The knife glowed, great one. It was the glow of the enemy who always conquers you. Yet you allowed this. Have you deserted me?"

Hodano looked down at Renno, whose arms were raised now, beckoning, as he called, "Come, Hodano, let us end it one way or the other. Come, killer of women. Stand up and be a man."

A voice inside seemed to whisper to Hodano. *Go,* the voice said. *Go, for he will have to tend his wounds.*

So it was *not* over. He had *not* been deserted! He could not understand why it had not ended here, but in his great wisdom, the evil one had other plans. Now, however, it was time to flee. Soon he would be among allies, and not even a warrior as great as the white Indian with his magic knife could stand against hundreds.

"Hodano," Renno was calling as the shaman moved swiftly away. "I am coming for you, Hodano."

First Renno rinsed the spirit knife in the stream, dried it on grass, and replaced it at his belt with a breathed prayer of thanks to the manitous. Only then did he begin to examine his wounds. He rinsed the deepest bites on his left arm. Then he cleaned his legs and the rest of his body. There were minor scratches on his chest and side, slashes and puncture wounds on his legs, and a bit of torn flesh around deep wounds on his left arm. He did not try to stop the bleeding from the puncture wounds, instead letting them ooze to clean the filth of the animals' teeth out of them.

He gathered wood and built a fire at the edge of the trees. With a torch of deadwood and grass he located medicinal plants along the stream. Only the arm required a poultice. He slept with the spirit knife and tomahawk in hand and woke to find that all his wounds had crusted. He was sore in every limb, but the wounds were not as serious as the one that had taken so long to heal—the one he had received while getting out of the sinking *Apache*. They were sore, but they did not interfere too greatly with movement.

It took him an hour to find where Hodano had watched the great spirit battle in the glen. Now the shaman was being careful, so the tracking was more difficult than it had been previously. At times he could move no faster than a walk. He had to eat. That took time. He roasted a squirrel and ate it on the move.

*   *   *

To El-i-chi's surprise, Beth was still alive with the
dawn of another day. He was not sure that was a blessing,
for all of his knowledge, his experience, and Casno's lore
told him that her body was dead and that her spirit would
soon follow. She had no appetite. This, El-i-chi felt, was
good, for with her body in the half death, all functions had
ceased and to have put any kind of food into her stomach
would probably have caused more vomiting. When she
asked for water he gave it to her, and again to his surprise,
she passed it later in the morning.

Her headaches were less painful now. She slept often
and comfortably. The swelling at the base of her neck was
going down slowly. Her mind, when she was awake, was
alert.

"Something is terribly wrong," Beth said, her voice
sounding almost normal.

"Yes," El-i-chi confirmed. "You have been badly hurt."

"That tells me nothing," she said, her green eyes
holding his. "Have you seen or do you know of something
like this happening before?"

He nodded. "When warriors are wounded in the neck
or spine."

"I am injured in the spine?"

He bent over her and put his fingers on the swelling
on her neck. "Here," he said.

"But there's no pain."

"And for that I grieve," El-i-chi said.

His seriousness scared her. "You must tell me," she
implored. "Tell me all that you know."

"Yes," he agreed. "The truth, so that you can prepare
your spirit."

"I'm going to die?" she whispered, her eyes going
wide.

"It is called the half death. The body is dead. Only
the spirit remains, waiting for the call to go. . . ." He
paused, knowing that her belief was not his.

"I'm breathing. I'm thirsty. I can talk and think."

"Yes," he said, his eyes very sad.

"But you have seen this before, when the body, the arms, the legs are paralyzed, and it leads to death?"

He touched her arm, and she felt nothing. "Yes," he said.

She closed her eyes, and tears squeezed from her long lashes. No more to be free in the wilderness with Renno. No more to know the warmth of his body beside her in the night. No more . . . no more anything.

She opened her eyes, and her mouth took on a firm set. "Well, I won't have it," she said flatly. "I am not ready to die."

She finally fell asleep with her will working fiercely, telling her lazy legs to move, telling one toe to wiggle, angry not at God but at fate, praying to her God as she fell into rest. When she awoke she was hungry and El-i-chi had broth brought by a woman. She drank it eagerly.

"El-i-chi," she said, gazing at him determinedly, "I am not going to die. Moreover, I am going to walk out of this lodge. Do you understand?"

Seeing her determination, El-i-chi almost believed her. "Then let me see you move one finger," he encouraged.

Try as she might, she could not.

Beyond the smaller lakes to the south of Lake Ontario, Renno lost Hodano's trail. For days now he had been seeing signs of hostile Indian activity, and now he was sure that he knew where Hodano was heading. He had expected the shaman to angle south, for Miami territory where he had friends, but the trail had pointed west and a bit north, toward one of the forts that the British still held on American soil, Fort Niagara.

His wounds were healing nicely, with no sign of infection. He could move at a warrior's pace now. Thus he was traveling swiftly when a sixth sense warned him to slow down. Renno melted silently into the forest. He had not been consciously aware of hearing a sound, but soon he did—three men moving cautiously, silently. Although their paint patterns and dress were unfamiliar to him, the paint was in the colors of war, and they carried muskets and had bows slung on their backs.

Renno knew that in the wilderness a man was either a friend or an enemy. But he wanted information. He stepped from the trees with the three strangers only ten feet away. They halted. One uttered a grunt of surprise and started to lift his musket.

"Peace," Renno said, but the musket was still jerking up, and the other two were now following suit. Renno's Spanish stiletto flew, embedding itself in one warrior's throat. Renno leaped aside, and a musket ball passed within inches of his head before his tomahawk flew, cracking the skull of the warrior with the unfired musket. Then he leaped forward, armed with the spirit knife, to meet the tomahawk charge of the man who had fired. He wanted the man alive, so he dodged the first swing of the tomahawk, went in low, threw the warrior to the ground, and dislodged his tomahawk by the simple expedient of cutting the muscles of the man's right arm.

He held the wounded warrior by the throat with his left hand, the spirit knife pointing at the man's right eye.

"I asked for peace," he growled in Seneca.

The warrior grunted in a dialect that was difficult for Renno to understand. "I asked for peace, and I get war," he said in French. The warrior's eyes widened.

"You have killed me," the stranger said, also in French.

"Tell me who I kill," Renno said.

"Still River, of the Potawatomi."

"You are far from home, Potawatomi," Renno said. "I would know the reason."

The warrior was silent.

"I seek one with a living false face," Renno said, "the shaman Hodano, he who has killed my wife."

"So," the Potawatomi said wryly, "we seek you, warrior, and you have found us."

"At Hodano's direction?"

"Send me to my ancestors," Still River implored.

"There is ample time for that," Renno replied. "Would you protect a killer of women?"

"How do I know you do not lie?"

"Because I am Renno of the Seneca, who does not lie to his brother even as he sends his spirit to the West," Renno answered.

"The ugly one is in great favor with the chief of the British from Quebec. By now he is safe within the walls of the fort."

"This British chief. His name," Renno asked.

"The House that Burns," Still River said.

"Burnhouse," Renno said. "He is at the fort?"

"With redcoat soldiers," Still River answered. "I speak no more, Renno of the Seneca."

"So," Renno said.

"But you fight the wrong enemy. Seneca should not fight Potawatomi, they should fight the Americans, who stole their lands."

"I choose my own enemies," Renno said. "I call a man enemy when he lifts his musket to kill me."

"Then send me to the West."

Renno granted Still River's wish. He could not afford to leave the Potawatomi at his rear, even with a useless right arm. Soon, having hidden the three bodies deep in the brush, still with their scalps, he was moving again. And now other thoughts mingled with his burning desire for revenge. Why was Burnhouse at Fort Niagara with redcoat soldiers? And why were Potawatomi warriors so far east?

The Potawatomi's range was to the north and west, between Lake Michigan and Lake Huron. They had fought with the British. Burnhouse's papers had listed many weapons delivered to the Potawatomi. Did the presence of three Potawatomi warriors at the western fringe of league lands indicate some offensive move by the British?

His suspicions grew as he traveled, for he saw other war parties, small, obviously searching. There were Miami and Shawnee warriors in mixed bands. He did not engage any of the parties, for now his mission had two purposes, and both, he felt, would be satisfied at Fort Niagara.

El-i-chi was disturbed. With great sorrow for his brother he had come to accept the inevitable death of the flame-haired Englishwoman. Having lost a wife himself, he knew the pain that would come to Renno and knew that Renno had, in fact, left in pursuit of Hodano with certain knowledge that Beth was as good as dead.

But the woman would not die. She insisted on being fed. She drank her broth greedily, as if seeking strength. She spoke to her limbs, saying, "Leg, move, damn you. Toe, move!" The tendons in her neck would strain with her effort, and El-i-chi was helpless to comfort her when her limbs ignored her commands.

He sought the aid of the manitous, going into the forest for solitude, to build his fire in the prescribed ceremonial manner. He danced the dance of healing and chanted the ancient words taught to him by Casno. He received no direct spirit message, but he returned to the lodge where Beth lay, his spirit cleansed, feeling only a bit guilty for having asked the manitous to do one of two things: either make Beth's passing swift and easy, or reward her determined efforts to return from the half death.

"El-i-chi!" she called when she saw him enter. "Come quickly."

He moved to her side.

"Look," she whispered.

The index finger on her left hand moved. It moved ever so slightly, but it moved.

"I am not going to die," she declared. "I am going to walk, for I have much to do."

In Philadelphia, George Washington, acting as presiding officer over the Constitutional Convention, had not taken an active part in the debates over states' rights, slavery, or a strong-versus-a-weak central government. He had for the most part presided neutrally, only intervening now and again to do away with irrelevant things that some tried to put into the document—for example, to leaven the greed of the Northern commercial interests from creating a definite schism with the Southern states. Now, after sixteen weeks of continuous work in the grueling heat of Philadelphia, it was over and time for a vote. The elegant governor Morris had spent many long hours past midnight in polishing the language of the document. The politicking had been hot and heavy, with Hamilton, Madison, and John Jay trying to overcome the anti-Federalist sentiments of men like Patrick Henry, Samuel Adams, and John Hancock.

Washington himself had had quiet conferences with some of the men who feared a strong central government, and he had told both Sam Adams and John Hancock that good men would be needed in high office. Washington and all the rest knew that it was almost certain that Washington would be the first president under the new constitution, but he would need help. Adams and Hancock moved into the Federalist camp. As predicted, the Virginia delegates did not vote in favor of adopting the document as the law of the land—subject to ratification by the several states—but with the backing of Washington and all those who were with him, everyone in Philadelphia knew that the United States was on the verge of great change and that once that change was begun, there would be no turning back.

The nonparticipating delegates from the would-be state of Franklin labored in their efforts to win support for Franklin statehood, until the voting was over and the "demigods," as the absent Jefferson had called the gathering, began to return to their homes.

A Virginia delegate, gloomy from predicting a reduction of personal freedom under the new constitution that was sure to be ratified, sounded a death knell for the hopes for Franklin's admission to the union.

"North Carolina's ratification of the Constitution is vital," the Virginian explained. "So the other states will not buck her in the matter of Franklin."

And so it was that the Franklin men rode home with unhappy news, but nevertheless were imbued with the spirit of hope and optimism that had pervaded Philadelphia.

It was September, 1787.

The approaches to Fort Niagara were cluttered with temporary encampments. War—or at best, council for war—was the obvious reason for the presence of warriors from several tribes, for no women and children were present. Renno soon realized that to try to gain entry to the fort dressed and painted as a Seneca would draw attention. Furthermore, his light-brown hair and white, although bronzed, skin were also handicaps. He solved two problems easily. First he blackened his hair with charcoal dust, made by crushing dead embers. Then he found a particular berry and crushed handfuls of them, smearing the juice on his face, neck, hands, and arms. His disguise was made complete by the silent and unexpected demise of a Potawatomi warrior who had the misfortune to be near Renno's size and who had ventured alone into the forest to answer a call of nature.

Reluctantly, the white Indian secreted his English longbow in a rocky niche. He substituted for it the well-made but inferior bow of the Potawatomi warrior, and then, walking as if he belonged, he passed through various encampments and paused before the great log palisade of the fort that stood, in violation of treaty, on American soil.

A cross section of warriors from several tribes was watching with varying degrees of interest as redcoats drilled in the compound inside the walls. The troop consisted of thirty men. They were well armed, but there were not enough of them to make a determined invasion of either United States or league territory.

There was no sign of Hodano or Burnhouse. Renno imitated the relaxed attitude of the other warriors and wandered apparently aimlessly, but actually in a manner designed to give him a knowledge of the fort's interior. There were log huts to house soldiers, their families, and traders who lived permanently in the fort. One more-impressive hut, he felt, had to be the headquarters of the commanding officer. There, he suspected, he would find Burnhouse and possibly Hodano. There was nothing he could do about that, however, in the light of day.

He wandered back outside the walls, made himself welcome at a fire where there was plentiful venison, spoke in French to several warriors, and learned that a great council had been called by the chief of the British in Canada. Chiefs and senior warriors were gathering from as far away as the lands of the Huron to the north and the Miami and Potawatomi to the west. Little Turtle of the Miami would be there.

"But I see no sachems of the Seneca," Renno remarked.

"There are warriors of the five nations here," he was told. "Striking Snake, the Cayuga, has come, and he tells of a fever for war among the nations of the league."

"We will be many," Renno agreed. "How can the Americans stand against us?"

"When all warriors have good muskets, shot, and powder, we will push the American whites back into the sea," a young warrior proclaimed proudly, brandishing a new British weapon.

Late in the day Renno saw Striking Snake emerge from the fort and begin to make the rounds of the small groups of warriors, passing the word that the great council would begin next morning. Renno avoided an encounter with the Cayuga; when Striking Snake had passed, he joined a group of young warriors with the paint of the Onondaga, Mohawk, and Seneca. Renno had expected that the council would be held inside the fort, but Striking Snake had stated that Burnhouse would speak to all in the open air outside the walls, so that everyone could hear. That solved one of Renno's problems.

He found a secluded spot for sleeping, checked the state of his disguise, had to retouch a part of his hair with charcoal, and slept in brief naps, always alert throughout the night. He knew that lack of sleep had never killed a warrior but that sleeping soundly in the presence of the enemy had been the death of many. One could sleep, he reasoned, after one was dead.

The morning dawned fair and calm. Renno walked among the encampments and was invited by a group of Seneca to have breakfast. There was a low murmur of talk from the gathering, which had grown. Now and then a warrior would laugh as he boasted about what he would do to the enemies of the Indians.

Shortly after sunup redcoat soldiers came out of the fort and quickly erected a wooden platform in the center of the largest cleared area. Renno joined many others making their way to be near.

With crisply shouted orders from a sergeant, the red-

coat troop marched smartly out the gate and formed behind the platform. Their precision, colorful uniforms, and
the way they handled their muskets at drill impressed
many of the younger warriors.

Renno let his breath out in a sigh when he saw Caleb
Burnhouse, in full dress uniform, stride stiffly from inside
the fort. Walking directly behind him were Striking Snake
and a thin man with a cowl of wolverine fur covering his
face. It could only be Hodano. Burnhouse mounted the
platform so that he could be seen even by the warriors at
the rear of the gathering. Striking Snake and Hodano
stood, arms crossed, to the left of the platform. Renno
moved to be partly hidden behind others but still in a
position to see everything. Burnhouse stood at attention
for long moments, and then from the fort came the Miami
Little Turtle with an entourage of sachems and shamans,
all in council dress. Burnhouse reached down a hand to
help Little Turtle to the platform, but the Miami scorned
the aid and leaped lightly to stand by the colonel's side.

Burnhouse spoke first, and he knew how to deal
effectively with the Indians. He appealed to their manhood, pride, and love of their lands. He said that the
British knew how the Indian felt about land and how it
was difficult for an Indian to understand how any man
could own the land, which was a part of orenda. He spoke
of the generosity of the British, citing lands given to
Indians displaced from the territory taken by the United
States. He cited the Potawatomi, with their vast hunting
grounds, as an example of how the British respected the
rights of the Indians to their traditional lands.

Burnhouse then listed the abuses that many tribes
had suffered, specifically the reduction of the hunting
grounds of the League of the Iroquois, and praised all
those warriors from the league who were there at Fort
Niagara, to council with their brothers from many tribes
and with their good friends the British.

"The time has come," his voice rang out, "when you must say to the whites of the United States, 'No more. We will give you no more of our lands. We will give you no more of our women. You will kill no more of the game that is so vital to our existence.' The time has come when men must stand and fight, and that is why we are here. The wise men among your chiefs are here to hear the words of the great chief Little Turtle."

Little Turtle was a fine orator. Within a very few minutes his fiery call to arms had elicited shouts of agreement from all sides. Now and then a war whoop would ring out from a young warrior inflamed by the Miami's zeal. There was nothing new in Little Turtle's speech. Renno began to look at Hodano, feeling his hatred grow. Around him were hundreds of warriors from many tribes. Before him, standing at ease in splendid display, was a troop of redcoats. But Renno's eyes kept returning to Hodano.

Now Burnhouse spoke again, promising eternal friendship and that the lands to be taken from the upstart United States—and from those tribes who fought on the side of the United States—would become the lands of the victors as long as the sun shone and the rain fell.

"Ally yourselves with Little Turtle," Burnhouse urged, "and we will supply you with arms, ammunition, and supplies with which to drive the white man back toward the sea."

A great shout went up.

"Pledge yourselves to Little Turtle, either face to face or through his deputies, Striking Snake of the Cayuga or the shaman Hodano," Burnhouse said. "The first strike will be from the lands north of the Ohio. The Potawatomi will ally with the Miami to sweep the frontier clean. And then we will all move into what the Americans call Philadelphia."

This was news to Renno, for in the papers that Beth had stolen from Burnhouse in Quebec, there had been no mention of a direct attack on a city.

Little Turtle spoke again, and then a sachem of the Potawatomi, but before Burnhouse climbed from the platform, Renno knew that he had all the current information he would get. Now was time for action. He had a duty to get back to Seneca lands, tell the league of Burnhouse's intentions, and to relay those intentions to the United States. But first he would fulfill the other part of his mission.

Chapter XIV

The fiery oratory had created bloodlust in the assembled warriors. Young men of several tribes were dancing, pounding out the rhythms of their war dances. Burnhouse stood on the platform next to Little Turtle, his mouth close to the Miami's ear so that he could be heard. Hodano, cowl hiding his face, was on Little Turtle's left, with Striking Snake beside him. Burnhouse finished what he had been saying to Little Turtle and turned away.

Renno's every muscle was tense as he struggled to control himself. Since his youth, responsibility had been thrust upon him. Always he had been a man of duty—duty to his people, his allies, and the honor of his line. There had been times in the fire and confidence of youth when he had taken risks and had acted precipitously. Maturity had been forced upon him by the will of the manitous, placing him always in the center of great events. But now every fiber of Renno the man was demanding an action that would most likely end in his death. If his only consideration was allaying some of his pain at losing still another wife, his all-consuming need for revenge would have left no question about his actions.

But the moment for action was not to last, for Burnhouse had left the platform and was walking back toward the fort. The sergeant was shouting orders at the redcoats, who were snapping to attention with a slap of heels. Little Turtle, Striking Snake, and Hodano were looking around, not paying attention to the Miami war chief who was now orating atop the wooden platform. The war chief's voice could be heard only by those close to him, for now many warriors were dancing and chanting the words of war.

Renno knew that he should melt away, run far and fast to the League of the Ho-de-no-sau-nee to carry the word that war faced them, then to show Burnhouse's papers to officials of the United States and pass the message to the government of the state of Pennsylvania that Indian war was to come to their borders again. He knew all that, and still he was a man, and his wife, if not dead by now, was as good as dead.

So it was as a man that he acted and, as most would have said, quite rashly.

All those around him were dancing the dance of war, brandishing weapons, whooping and chanting. No one noticed as he nocked an arrow to the Potawatomi bow and drew it back, the flint arrowhead aimed at the black heart of the shaman Hodano.

He felt something akin to elation as the arrow flew swift and true. Such an unexpected death was too good for Hodano, but it was the only choice Renno had at the moment.

In a split second it would be over. He tensed himself, ready for instant action. But at the last moment, just before impact, the flight of the arrow altered in a way that was not natural, and the thud of impact came not with

Hodano's flesh, but with Striking Snake taking the sharp tip directly into the heart. He was dead before he hit the ground.

Hodano howled like a wolf, and he leaped from the rear of the platform and behind the redcoats. Renno moved quickly toward the shaman, then caught himself and turned, raising a great cry warning of an attack and pointing toward the forest. Pandemonium broke out with warriors rushing this way and that, seizing weapons, and whooping. For a moment Renno thought that his ruse had worked and that no one had seen him fire the arrow, but nearby, a Miami warrior pointed at him and shouted, "It was the tall Potawatomi who fired."

Renno burst through a group of startled warriors trying to organize themselves for a counterattack on what they thought was a force hidden in the trees. Bending low as three arrows zinged past and a musket ball whistled over his head, the white Indian weaved his way through the group, running his swiftest, into the trees.

He had failed to kill Hodano. He had taken a great risk but had failed, not because of his own marksmanship, not because he had had to use the Potawatomi bow instead of his own English longbow, but because of Hodano's spirit power. Renno had calculated the risk and had obeyed his heart, and now he was running not so much for his life as to accomplish his duty.

One warrior was swifter to react than the others, and Renno could hear the sound of feet behind him as he ran. One man, and behind him, hundreds. He came to a full halt by planting both feet, whirled, and drew his bow. The eager pursuer went down. Renno was, for the moment, alone. He knew that the sheer numbers of those who would give chase would slow them. His feet flew as he ran directly east. Then, with the sound of the pursuers perhaps a hundred yards behind him, he swerved, ran along their front, and having flanked the main mass of them, doubled back to recover his longbow from its hiding place.

He knew that the forest would be full of warriors, and he had no illusions about being able to kill or elude so many. He laid a false trail, doubled back, hid his tracks with the utmost care, and leaped to seize the low branch of a conifer. Pulling himself up, he climbed until he was well hidden among the dense branches. He had just become still when four warriors crept by underneath the tree, eyes looking for sign, moving in deadly silence. Many more times that day warriors passed nearby, and he was reassured, for so many moving men would destroy any trace of his own passage to his hiding place.

He passed the long, slow day by thinking about Hodano and of how, once he had accomplished his duty, he would return, to follow the shaman to the ends of the earth, if necessary, to gain revenge.

So still was he among the branches that a feeding squirrel came to within reach of him, moving in that graceful, flowing motion, tail jerking. The squirrel plucked a cone and sat holding the delicacy daintily, nibbling, eyes darting around for danger while Renno sat not three feet away. Finished with his snack, the squirrel dropped the cone. It rattled its way to the ground, startling three warriors, who gazed up into the trees. Renno tensed, ready to take two of them quickly with one arrow in his bow and one held in his teeth, but the squirrel, frightened by the movement below, flowed away, leaped, and made a small branch sway with its weight.

A warrior laughed and pointed at the fleeing squirrel, and then the three of them moved on.

Late in the day groups of warriors began to drift back toward the fort. Renno waited until well after dark. He could hear the drums of those encamped before the fort. When a deer crept slyly by below him, he trusted that animal's senses, for the deer would not have moved had a man been quite near, and climbed carefully down. He stretched himself to loosen his cramped limbs, checked his weapons, and began to move slowly, carefully, to the south. He had traveled about a half mile when he came to a stream and saw, not far away, the glow of a campfire. He had hoped that all of the enemy had gone back to the fort, but there were at least three men beside the fire. Still disappointed about not killing Hodano, he would have welcomed the chance to send three of those who sided with Hodano to their ancestors, but he looped to the south around the fire and thought he was safely past when he heard the unmistakable sound from a point in front of him of a man relieving his bladder.

He froze in place and waited. He heard a sigh of contentment and then movement directly toward him. There was a half-moon filtering through the canopy of the forest, giving spotty light. Lifting the spirit knife, telling himself that he would not attack, he watched the Miami, but the warrior seemed intent on death that night, walking directly toward Renno's place of concealment behind a tree. The man would pass too closely to be allowed to live lest he sense Renno's presence and give an alarm.

Renno waited until the Miami was directly even with the tree, then he snaked around it, shot his arm up to seize the Miami's head, palm on forehead, jerked the head back, and slashed with the spirit knife, catching the man before he could fall and lowering him to the ground. It had been swift and silent, but now there came the eerie, rhythmic sound of the man's dying spasms, his leg jerking to rattle leaves. The talk at the nearby campfire ceased. A warrior called out a name softly. Renno moved so that he could see the fire through the trees. Three warriors were reaching for weapons and leaping to their feet.

The longbow's string sang softly as an arrow lanced between the trees, and there were only two men left, leaping into shadows, becoming a part of the night. Renno moved directly toward the fire, knowing that logically he should try to put distance between himself and the warriors. But in a way defined by the manitous, they had started it, even if it was only by accident that one warrior had answered the call of nature and then walked directly into the sharp blade of the spirit knife.

He knew that the two warriors were moving toward the source of the sound that had alerted them, toward the point of origin of the arrow that had killed one of them. He went to the bank of the stream and waited, heard a faint splash to his left as a warrior crossed, gave them time to find the body of their companion, then moved directly toward a soft owl hoot, the signal that told him and the other enemy that the body had been found.

One warrior squatted beside the body as Renno came near enough to see their dark shadows. The other stood, tomahawk in hand, looking around. Renno leaped, giving the fighting call of a hawk, and the squatting warrior jumped to his feet while the other leaped to meet Renno's tomahawk. The weapon slashed in under the enemy's sweeping blow to expose intestines and send him collapsing to the ground. The second enemy hissed with effort as he aimed a blow for Renno's head. Renno ducked and sent his tomahawk upward to cleave the enemy's chin from beneath. Two more strokes relieved the dying man of pain, and it was once again silent in the forest.

Renno waited, listening to be certain that the battle sounds had not carried to others; then he went to the still-burning campfire, helped himself to the venison roasting there, retrieved his arrow from the dead man, and was once again on his way.

He traveled throughout the night, twice skirting campfires that had burned low and were surrounded by sleeping warriors. With the first light of morning he paused, drank deeply from a stream, ate more of the venison, and then started to run. He felt that the enemy was behind him. He knew that many had returned to the fort. He had seen a few encamped in the forest, but they had not even posted guards, perhaps feeling secure against one warrior.

As he ran effortlessly, limbs moving fluidly, lungs

having that second wind, he had time to grieve for Beth and to burn with his frustration. Perhaps it was his emotional condition that dulled his usually acute senses, or perhaps it was the will of the manitous. Perhaps it was the skill of the ambush and the total unexpectedness of finding redcoats so far from the fort. His first and only warning of danger was a flash of color as a redcoat lifted his musket. That movement saved Renno's life. He darted to one side, and three muskets blasted almost as one. Renno dived into a forward roll, coming to his feet with bow in hand.

He had been running freely in a zone between deep forest and a natural, wide clearing, so the natural cover was small saplings, leaving him very much exposed. Ahead was a dense growth of brush, behind which the redcoats had lain in wait. To both sides and to his rear was clear, open ground. He had counted three muskets; he did not know how many more were there.

A musket blasted, and the ball cut weeds over his head. He was now lying close to the ground, looking around for a way out.

"Hold your fire!" a voice ordered. With some amazement Renno recognized the voice of Colonel Caleb Burnhouse. "Sergeant, take those two to the left. You and you, circle to the right."

That was information for Renno. The sergeant and two, plus "you" and "you" made five. Burnhouse made six. Perhaps others. He was in a desperate position. To escape he would have to run through clearings without cover, in easy range of the British muskets. It took him only a few seconds to make his decision. He voiced his intention with the fighting roar of a great bear and leaped to his feet.

Male pride had placed Caleb Burnhouse in ambush directly in Renno's path. Earlier, when an arrow had buzzed like an angry bee and killed the Cayuga Striking Snake, Burnhouse's back had been to the action. He had whirled to see chaos, but his eyes had been drawn to movement as a strong warrior had moved swiftly into the trees, and that one moment had been enough. Burnhouse had made the army his life. Battle was his joy, and he had always had great admiration for a skilled fighter. For example, he had thoroughly enjoyed the humiliation of the effete Royal Navy officer Horatio Jaynes, not only because it had taught the arrogant officer a lesson but because he had seen a superb fighting man in action—perfect coordination in a well-conditioned body. Burnhouse felt that he could tell by the way a man moved how well he would conduct himself in a battle, and as he had watched a Potawatomi push through a group of other warriors and sprint for the cover of the trees, he knew it was actually Renno, the white Indian. There was no doubt in his mind.

He told himself that he should have obeyed his impulse back in Quebec and tested the man himself. Jaynes's fencing had all the skill of a schoolboy. He doubted that Jaynes had ever killed a man with the foil, either in battle or duel. He had ached to try his own foil against Renno, but the man had been a potential ally . . . or at least so Burnhouse had thought.

He admired the sheer audacity of Renno's attack, even though he did not understand why Striking Snake had been the target. His own death or Little Turtle's would have had greater impact on the successful chances of Renno's plans. He knew that this white Indian could not be allowed to get away again.

During the war Burnhouse, with a select, small group of soldiers, had traveled far into enemy territory to gather information. He considered himself to be the match of any Indian in the wilderness, and his men were only slightly less skilled. He had chosen them for their stubborn pride and had told them that if a Seneca could run for a day without resting, then so could a British soldier.

When his war service had earned him a place as the

military governor of Quebec, he gathered a few members
of his old, handpicked unit to him immediately, told them
they were back in action, and as of old informed them that
they would travel light. He reasoned that Renno, after
some clever maneuvers to hide his trail and escape immediate pursuit, would head directly for the land of the
Seneca. Burnhouse was certain that much damage had
already been done to his plans by Renno from the documents he and the woman had stolen from Quebec. Now it
was time to see that that one man could do no more harm.

There had been no time to discard the clumsy uniforms for buckskins, but each veteran wilderness hand
always carried moccasins in his pack for comfort and silent
movement. Burnhouse set and maintained a punishing
pace. The wilderness was huge, and his chances of inter-
cepting one man were so remote as to be almost nonexistent, but Burnhouse had his pride. He would show this
white Indian that he was not the only man who had daring
and knowledge of the wilderness.

So, while Renno had hidden in a tree, Burnhouse and
his squad of twelve men had moved swiftly toward the
east, pausing only to drink.

He kept his force moving for most of the night, but at
a slower pace. He guessed that Renno would be moving
during the night but would not make good time since he
would have to be on the watch for warriors still searching
for him. With morning Burnhouse increased the pace, at
midday splitting his force, placing six men under his finest
sergeant to cover an area that was a natural passageway to
the east. He himself took six men a half mile to the north
to a point where a second growth of saplings had begun to
fill in after a devastating forest fire. He had a fine field of
view and reasoned, by lay of that land, that a man moving
fast would choose one of the two positions he occupied for
ease of movement.

"When he comes," he told his men, "you will fire in

two teams." He designated three men, his best marksmen, as the number-one unit. Should they miss, three other muskets would be ready to fire while the first unit was reloading.

When Renno came running through the old burn as if he were the only man within a hundred miles, Burnhouse smiled grimly. He had proven to himself many times that he could think like an Indian, but in his prejudice and arrogance, he did not feel that was an accomplishment.

Burnhouse's finest marksman was a member of the first group of three. He shot in the manner of a frontier sharpshooter, bringing his musket up, placing it to his shoulder, and firing almost in the same instant the butt touched. It was this that gave Renno his warning. If the marksman, like the other two men, had had his musket braced and ready, there would have been no movement, no flash of red to warn the enemy.

Renno assessed the situation within seconds. The three men who had fired were in the process of jerking their muskets into position to reload. He was lying on the grassy ground, and then three more shots came, the balls whizzing through the grass over his head. He could not go back, for there was enough open ground to give the musketeers plenty of time to take careful aim. There were at least six guns, and he could not expect all six to miss again. Neither could he run to either side, for there was a good field of fire in both directions.

He did the unexpected. He leaped to his feet, gave the challenging roar of an angry bear, the call itself a call to his manitous, the main totem of his clan, the ghosts of his illustrious ancestors. He ran directly into the teeth of the ambush, weaving from side to side as the distance closed. He heard and saw the muzzle puffs of three muskets and heard one ball pass, with that distinctive clap of sound, within inches of his ear, and felt a flick as another cut fringe from the buckskin at his shoulder. But now the distance was closing quickly, and he loosed an arrow from the longbow and heard a cry of pain, was nocking another, not slowing his pace but weaving wildly.

"You magnificent bastard," Burnhouse whispered as Renno defied all logic and rushed directly toward the ambush. He braced his musket on a limb and timed Renno's weavings, drew a bead on Renno's broad chest, squeezed the trigger, and cursed when there was a click and nothing more. The weapon had misfired. He jerked his pistol from his belt. Renno was loosing another arrow at a flash of red and was now so close that Burnhouse could see that his lips were drawn back in a snarl, exposing his teeth, and then the arrow thudded into the man next to him, his prize sharpshooter, piercing the man's jugular. Three of his men were down, and now Renno was discarding his—by God, of all things—English longbow and literally flying through the air.

"Bayonets," Burnhouse ordered coolly as Renno leaped over the concealing brush and crashed into a man whose bayonet narrowly missed.

Never had the bloodlust been stronger in Renno. Angry at himself for having run directly into an ambush, still tasting his disappointment over having missed killing Hodano, and sorrow for Beth underneath it all, he threw his life at the ambush with something akin to wild joy.

He twisted in midair to avoid the probing point of a British bayonet and crashed heavily into the man wielding it, bearing him to the ground and swinging the tomahawk in his right hand while falling, so that when the two bodies hit the ground, one was dead. A pistol discharged so near him that the sound made his ears ring, but the ball merely burned its way on the surface of his left shoulder, cutting buckskin as it passed, and then he was rolling, slinging his

tomahawk to bury its sharp blade into the forehead of a
soldier.

The surviving redcoat, with a scream that was half
anger, half fear, lunged with his bayonet. Renno rolled on
the ground, and the bayonet plunged into the soft soil,
missing his side by an inch, and with the spirit knife in his
left hand he slashed the soldier's hamstring. The man
came down with a scream, and the spirit knife did its work
with one swift plunge into softness.

Renno rolled again and came to his feet to see
Burnhouse standing alone, pistol in hand. Renno now had
his Spanish stiletto in his right hand, the spirit knife in his
left. He was crouched. Smoke oozed from the muzzle of
Burnhouse's pistol to tell Renno that it had been the one
that fired. Renno glanced around. Five bodies lay limply.
A sixth redcoat sat with his back against a tree, an arrow
lodged deeply in his stomach, his eyes beginning to glaze
with coming death.

Burnhouse dropped the pistol and drew his sword
with a harsh sound of metal on metal.

"Impressive," Burnhouse said calmly. "They were six
of my finest men."

Silently, his face now impassive, Renno replaced spirit
knife and stiletto and drew a pistol, aiming it at Burnhouse's
chest.

"I have only this," Burnhouse said, moving the sword
in a small circle in the air. "It's too bad we don't have
foils. I've longed to test you myself with that weapon since
your demonstration in Quebec. But it might be interesting
to test sword against tomahawk and knife, eh?" He walked
to a fallen redcoat, jerked Renno's tomahawk from the
dead man's forehead and tossed it to spin slowly. Renno
plucked it from the air with his left hand. The blade
dripped blood.

"I have no time for games," Renno said. His trigger

finger tightened. He saw Burnhouse go suddenly pale. And then he released the pressure on his pistol.

"Today you will live," Renno decided. "That is my will. My purpose is this: first, you will tell the shaman Hodano that I live and will come for him. Second, be aware that the documents taken from your quarters will soon be in the hands of General Washington, so that he will be prepared for your war in the lands beyond the Ohio. I would imagine as well that the diplomats of Europe, especially the French, will be interested in knowing that the word of the British, given in solemn treaty, is worth so little, that their governor in Canada conspires to renew the war."

"Come," Burnhouse invited, having recovered from his fear. "Tomahawk and knife against sword."

Renno's hand moved ever so slightly, and the pistol roared, the ball striking Burnhouse's sword near the hilt, knocking it away and numbing his hand. The colonel grabbed his right hand with his left, his eyes wide.

"Go, and consider what I have said," Renno said.

The white Indian had calculated swiftly. True, he had England's prime instigator in his sights. True, he would have had no hesitation in killing Burnhouse, for Burnhouse had tried to kill him. But he knew that when Burnhouse marched back to the fort, alone, the warriors there would know that one man had killed six redcoats. That alone would not convince those who were determined to fight that it was futile, but when the fighting did come, all those who had seen Burnhouse come back alone would remember, and there just might be in the back of their minds a bit of doubt about facing the Seneca.

"I will go," Burnhouse conceded. "First, a drink of water?" He bent, took a canteen from a dead soldier, extended it to Renno. When Renno remained motionless, Burnhouse drank. He was thinking that his sergeant would have heard the firing and would be moving even now

toward his position at a swift pace. If he could stall the
white Indian just a bit longer . . .

"I had to admire the way you took the woman,"
Burnhouse said. "I trust she's safe. It must have been
quite a jaunt for you, with a woman in tow."

The British officer's obvious desire to detain him acted
as a warning. Nature gave a second warning when, at the
far edge of the old burn, a grouse feeding in the grass was
startled into flight. Without a word Renno whirled, recovered his bow, and ran into the forest to the east. Burnhouse
had no way of knowing how close he had been to being
killed by the white Indian.

Renno ran about a hundred yards into the concealing
trees and halted, listening. Then he made his way silently,
diagonally, back to the edge of the clearing. His eyes
narrowed as he saw six redcoats emerge from the woods
where the grouse had been startled and move, weaving
and running, toward Burnhouse.

The sergeant led the men up, halting to stare at the
bodies of his comrades, then to look questioningly at
Burnhouse. Renno could not hear what was being said.
He checked his quiver; he had only five arrows left. He
checked his pistols, felt the comforting warmth of the haft
of the spirit knife, and waited. He saw the eyes of all of
the redcoats turn toward the point where he had entered
the woodlands and watched Burnhouse make motions.
The redcoats spread out and moved toward the woods.
One group of three, spreading out toward the south, would
enter the trees near Renno's position. As they neared, he
could hear them talking in low voices.

"He killed six."

"We'll get him."

"But six?"

Fear, Renno knew, was working against the soldiers.
He looked around, found a suitable spot, and lowered
himself to the ground behind an old deadfall that had

almost rotted into the floor of the forest. He let the three men, walking silently in their moccasins, pass by, two on one side and one on the other, then two arrows flew almost as one, and the third man was opening his mouth to yell when he saw the last sight he would see on earth—a painted face, a demon with a flashing tomahawk.

One arrow broke, for its head was embedded between ribs, but Renno retrieved the other. Four arrows were remaining: one for each of the men, including Burnhouse. Renno moved to the north, flitting from tree to tree, as silent as a wraith. He killed one man with the spirit knife within fifty feet of one of his comrades without the other's knowledge, then winged an arrow. It found its mark, but the dying man's finger pulled the trigger of his musket. The blast shattered the silence of the forest and warned Burnhouse and the sergeant, who converged.

"Smyth . . . Warren . . ." the sergeant called softly. "Who fired?"

Silence.

"Hardings . . . Morrant . . ." the sergeant called.

Renno imitated the chatter of an excited squirrel, and both men tensed. Renno was not more than thirty yards away, bow at the ready. He had given Burnhouse his life once. A man who seemed to value his life so lightly should have time, Renno felt, to fear for it a bit.

"Report your whereabouts, damn you!" Burnhouse roared. There was no need to be silent now. Something had happened. A musket had been fired.

Renno's lips twitched in a grim half smile. He gave the cry of a hunting hawk and saw the sergeant spin, looking in all directions.

"It can't be," the sergeant said. "What in the hell are we fighting here?"

"A man," Burnhouse said. "I would to God that I had a thousand like him. I'd sweep this country clean."

Burnhouse moved, motioning to the sergeant to follow. One by one they found the dead ones. The sergeant was now extremely nervous, twitching at every sound and spinning to try to face all directions at once.

Burnhouse, with his reloaded pistol, was calm.

"Where is he?" the sergeant asked.

"Don't worry. He'll find us," Burnhouse said. "He moves swiftly. He is quite deadly with the bow. Take cover. Expose nothing for him to see. When he comes, hold your fire until you can thrust the muzzle of your musket into his stomach."

Renno gave the coughing call of challenge of a bear, and the sergeant, veteran though he was, paled and leaped to stand behind a large tree.

"You will have to come to us, my friend!" Burnhouse called loudly, not realizing how near Renno was. He knew when, with that angry, buzzing hiss of feathers in flight, an arrow ended the sergeant's fears forever by entering his left ear and piercing the only spot of his body that had been visible to Renno.

Burnhouse, noting the flight of the arrow, yelled in defiance and ran toward the arrow's point of origin. Renno stepped into the open.

"You are a brave man," he commented as Burnhouse quickly shifted his pistol. Renno's pistol roared first, the ball taking Burnhouse in the nose.

"I gave you your life," Renno said, standing with the smoking pistol pointed at the fallen officer. "You should have accepted my gift."

With his stiletto Renno cut a straight, small sapling, trimmed away the limbs, and sharpened its tip. He cut it to a length of about five feet, went back into the clearing, and used the stiletto to scalp the fallen soldiers. He then pierced the bloody scalps with the sharp point of the stick, added to his collection the scalps of the redcoats who had fallen in the forest, topped it with the scalp of Burnhouse, and attached to the hair of Burnhouse's scalp the insignia of his rank.

He arranged the thirteen scalps on the stick to balance as he grasped it in his left hand. Then he was moving again, moving at that mile-covering pace that he could maintain for days. Knowing that fear was a dreadful enemy and a useful tool, Renno had intended sending Burnhouse back to Fort Niagara alone, as a statement. Now none of a thirteen man squad would return, and that in itself would give a message more powerful than he had intended. His scalping of the fallen was also intended to influence the thinking of others, this time the shamans and warriors of the five nations of the league. Those who felt the British to be a powerful enemy would think twice when one warrior came bearing thirteen British scalps.

During the process of scalping, he had helped himself to some British field rations and to extra powder. He was not far from the areas where he would begin to encounter Seneca longhouses and villages. Two of the leaders of his enemies were dead. But Little Turtle still lived, and worse, Hodano lived.

He halted to change his paint from that of a Potawatomi warrior to that of a Seneca messenger. First he cleansed himself in a stream, using clean sand to scrub the charcoal from his hair and the berry dye from his skin. When he first encountered Seneca, a hunting party, there were suspicious looks at his unfamiliar dress, but his Seneca speech soon put the warriors at ease. There was awe when thirteen scalps, the scalps of white men, were counted.

He skirted villages in his path. When he was but one day's travel from the village of Cornplanter, he found that he was slowing his pace. He did not realize why at first. His legs were strong; it was just that he had no desire to run. He walked silently, and then he knew why he had slowed.

He imagined Beth's face and her lovely flame-colored

hair. If she had been alive, he would have moved with all the speed he could muster. But she was dead, and her body, in all probability, now was in the ground, for El-i-chi would have followed her own customs in the burial. He knew it and he felt it, and yet he was not ready to face standing beside her grave.

Beth had loved the wilderness and had often re-marked on the beauty of it during their trip from Canada. Quite often Renno himself would stand with her and feel an upswelling of emotion engendered by nature's sheer beauty—of a glorious day, of a spectacular red sunset, of the grace of a leaping stag. Now he was walking through some of the most beautiful woodlands of the American continent, but all the beauty was lost to him, for in his heart there was the certain knowledge that the living beauty of the woman he loved was lost to him forever.

Chapter XV

The nights were becoming more chilly now. Summer was dying, and the colors of nature were beginning to change. Fat squirrels busied themselves by storing food for the winter. Migrating birds darkened the air at times. Soon the snows would come, and this northern land would be cold and white and silent. As Renno neared Cornplanter's village he seemed to smell the different, balmier air of the southern lands and felt a powerful yearning to hold his son and his daughter.

He timed his entry into the village for effect, just as he had the first time he had come. He entered, walking slowly and stiffly, the pole with its thirteen white men's scalps, a bit odoriferous now, held vertically in front of him. A group of young boys saw him first, let out whoops, and began to dance around him, one or two daring to ask questions. Renno walked on slowly, ceremoniously, and two of the boys raced ahead shouting the news that the Seneca sachem of the South had returned, showing much coup.

Renno saw El-i-chi emerge from a longhouse and continued his ceremonial pace. El-i-chi, realizing immediately that his brother intended to have an effect on the thinking of the Seneca, merely nodded and gave a one-handed greeting.

From the council longhouse Cornplanter emerged in the traditional dress of the Seneca. Behind him came pine trees of his own village and several visiting sachems and senior warriors.

"I thank thee that thou art well," Cornplanter said.

Renno gave an equally traditional reply.

"So you have returned, and not empty-handed," Cornplanter said.

"White men," remarked a warrior, moving closer to examine the scalps.

"It is so," Renno responded. "I have much to relate, Sachem."

"You are welcome to my house of council," Cornplanter invited.

El-i-chi, who had come to stand just behind Renno, followed his brother into the longhouse, where other warriors milled around, waiting. A council had been going on, and Renno guessed that the subject had most probably been the same one under discussion when he left: alliance with the United States . . . or war.

Renno noted that the ceremonial pipe was in its place, having already been passed. He stood beside Cornplanter as the others found seats. Cornplanter turned and nodded, then seated himself. El-i-chi sat near the door. Renno got no message about war or about Beth from his brother's face, for El-i-chi was the stoic Seneca warrior for the moment.

Renno jammed the scalp pole into the ground, crossed his arms, and looked carefully around the circle, meeting each man's eye.

"It is not for my own glory that I state this," Renno began, "for any Seneca warrior, any warrior of the five nations worthy of his name, could have done the same."

"White man's scalps?" an old warrior asked, squinting his eyes to be sure.

"British scalps," Renno confirmed. "They fancy themselves to be skilled in our ways of fighting in the forests."

"So," Cornplanter said solemnly to emphasize the point.

"At a great council at Fort Niagara this one"—Renno pointed to the scalp of Caleb Burnhouse, atop the pole —"said that he and his allies would force the League of the Ho-de-no-sau-nee to fight with him or against him, and if the league was against him, he would exterminate all of us."

A growl of protest came from some.

"What tribes would be against us?" Cornplanter asked.

"The Potawatomi, from beyond Lake Erie. Some Huron, from the north. Miami and a few Shawnee. And the ones from the Seneca, the Cayuga, the Onondaga, the Oneida, and the Mohawk who have deserted their homelands and their tribes."

"Not many," a warrior pointed out, "from the Seneca."

"Seneca too," Renno said. "But Striking Snake, the Cayuga, is dead, with his white master, the British governor of Quebec. There will be another British officer to take the place of the dead one, but Little Turtle will remember, and the British will remember, and all the tribes will remember that one came among them and killed many."

"Hodano?" El-i-chi asked, for he was burning with curiosity.

"Hodano lives, with his evil spirits," Renno answered. He stood, his face grim, for long moments. "He lives *now*," he added, with a clear implication that it was a temporary condition. "So it stands, my brothers, nothing will stop the coming of war in the lands north of the Ohio. The events are foretold, and there will be war, but at first it will be far from these lands. The five nations of the league are in a position to secure the northwest flank of the frontier. When Little Turtle's war becomes evident to them, the United States will take time to act. However, they could react swiftly here. Do you hear me, Brothers?"

"I hear," Cornplanter said. "Before you continue, Sachem, Brother, hear me." He stood. "I, Cornplanter of the Seneca, have pledged before the pine trees of my clan and sachems of other clans of the Seneca to fight no more against the United States."

"It is good," Renno said.

"I speak for the beaver clan of the Cayuga," said a tall old man. "We will fight no more against the United States."

One by one others stood. The entire league was not represented, but there were sachems of clans from all five tribes, and each made the identical pledge.

"If there is indeed a move by the British to punish the league for this stand," Renno said, "it will come from the west, from Fort Niagara, and the Seneca will be in the forefront."

"My blade cries out for the blood of any who would invade our land," a younger warrior of the Seneca growled.

Cornplanter nodded. "We are ready, Sachem."

"The allies of the British will have new muskets, and much powder and shot," Renno informed the gathering. "I will go from here to Philadelphia, where I will tell the great leader of the United States what I have learned, with documents from the home of the British governor of Quebec to back up my assertions. If the need arises, he will match the British weapons with guns in the hands of warriors of the league."

"So," Cornplanter said, nodding. "And will our brothers to the south now rejoin us and make the Seneca whole again?"

Renno gave the question much thought while the circle of warriors waited silently.

"My brother Sachem," Renno said, "the way is far, and soon it will be winter. The Spanish push continually from the south. Once we had to stand, with the Cherokee, against them and their allies." He spread his hands. "I, too, dream of the day when all the Seneca will be one, but, my friend, it is in the hands of the manitous."

After a long silence, a young warrior pointed to the scalp pole. "We would hear of this," he suggested.

Nothing pleased a warrior more than a rousing tale of battle, which was not considered bragging. Renno, well versed in the custom, had no hesitation in telling, move by move and blow by blow, about the swift and deadly battle in and around the great burn in the forest.

"To him I said, you are a brave man," he said, nearing the end of his tale, and when he was finished, he glanced at his brother, who was fierce of eye, caught up in the telling and most probably feeling envious for not having been a part of the grim battle.

A shout of approval broke out, and Cornplanter came to give Renno the warrior's embrace. A young warrior began to pound the dirt floor in rhythm, and someone began to chant the song of war. With a nod of his head, Renno signaled El-i-chi to leave the longhouse, then followed him immediately and stood beside him in the open air, which was touched with the feel of autumn.

"Now we go," he said.

"It is time," El-i-chi agreed, leading the way toward the longhouse from which he had emerged. At the door he halted and put his hand on Renno's chest. "Wait."

Renno, thinking that El-i-chi was being considerate of his feelings by not wanting him to enter the longhouse where Beth had died, turned his back and gazed out over the village compound where the young boys had gone back to their endless games. He heard a sound at his back and turned to see Beth, gaunt, her hair loose, walking jerkily out the door, leaning on two crutches formed of forked boughs, the forks padded with rabbit skins to fit under her arms.

He could not move. She looked at him, her green

eyes smiling. He could not raise his hand. He could not leap to embrace her, for she had been dead to him, yet now she lived! She was not a ghost, for ghosts do not smile, and ghosts do not have happy tears running from huge, green eyes.

"My love," he whispered.

El-i-chi, who had been watching from the shadows inside the door, stepped out and struck a heroic pose. "Big medicine, is it not so? Have you ever known or heard of a greater healer than I?"

Renno moved now, taking her into his arms. "Indeed, I am loved by the manitous," he whispered, ignoring El-i-chi's smile.

"And by others," Beth said, reaching for his lips.

In the early evening the three of them sat around a fire in the longhouse. Women had served food, and Renno had eaten heartily.

El-i-chi recounted the story of Beth's totally unexpected recovery. "She had a great will to live," he finished.

"I had much to live for," Beth explained, leaning to put her shoulder against Renno's.

"She will have to be carried," El-i-chi said.

"I can walk a little," she reminded him. "And every day I get stronger."

"We will have to go before the snows," Renno said.

El-i-chi nodded. "I have made a litter."

"Good." Renno smiled. "It will be a story to tell when we are at home, how my brother the shaman healed the unhealable."

"I think *I* had something to do with it," Beth said.

"There was no cut, no injury to the spine after all," El-i-chi said. "The bruise from the blow is almost gone now. The spine, which carries the life of a man, can, it seems, be harmed in some way without being severed or broken. I cannot take all the credit."

"But you danced and chanted beautifully," Beth commended, smiling fondly. During her days of confinement El-i-chi had been constantly at her side, often using the old, healing words of the Seneca. "And you gave me unflagging encouragement. I for one give *you* much credit."

El-i-chi smiled ruefully. "Truly I would have rather been at my brother's side, fighting the British, than here, being the medicine man." He held up a hand quickly. "But I thank the manitous that I was of some help in healing the woman of my brother."

"I sense the birth of a legend," Beth said. "Two brothers—both mighty warriors—one a sachem, the other a powerful shaman who can throw fire at an evil one, who can materialize a great hawk from midair, who can heal the half death."

El-i-chi shrugged. "Let us not build expectations too greatly by such stories."

Beth laughed. "Whispers. Hints. Can it hurt? The invincible brothers!" She turned her face to Renno, and for a moment her lips seemed to pout. "I saw you put on your show with the scalps. Wasn't that meant to influence the thinking of others?"

"This one is far too incisive," Renno said in English. "Fortunately, she is on our side and will not expose all our little tricks to our enemies."

Beth insisted on leaving the village under her own power, moving slowly with the use of the crutches. She had feeling in her limbs now, and her arms were quite normal. Only her legs seemed lazy, as if the healing had to move slowly, slowly, down from her neck. When they were out of sight, El-i-chi unslung the litter he had made from two strong poles and deerhide, and over Beth's protests, she was placed upon it.

To Renno it was a dear weight, and thus nothing. El-i-chi, young and strong, took the front of the litter. At the rear Renno walked, able to look down and see Beth's green eyes lovingly studying his face. That night, after helping to make camp and gather wood, El-i-chi announced that he would hunt.

"At night?" Beth asked.

"I will hunt for the night-flying grouse," El-i-chi called back as he faded into the darkness.

Renno laughed.

"What is so funny?" Beth asked.

"My considerate younger brother has made an excuse to leave us alone," Renno explained.

As he saw that melting look come to Beth's face, Renno's lips became suddenly heavier, fuller.

"So," she said, in that toneless Indian way.

"He is considerate, but are you . . ." He paused, for she raised one hand quickly.

"There is feeling, my husband, in those parts of me that make me a woman."

He smiled. Quickly he found that she was right.

"I want you to kill Hodano," Beth was saying the next day as she took a turn at walking on the crutches. "Not because he hurt me but because he almost deprived me of you forever. Not because he tried to kill me but because I would have lost you. Do you understand?"

Renno was not sure, but he nodded.

"But you mustn't leave me now," she said.

"No." There were other reasons why he could not follow his inclination to find Hodano, wherever he was.

"Do you really believe that he has the help of the evil spirits?" she asked.

"I saw arrows being deflected, arrows that had always before and have since flown true."

"There is good in the world," El-i-chi remarked, "and there is evil."

"Can you somehow make Renno's arrows fly true next time?" Beth asked El-i-chi.

"If it is the will of the manitous," El-i-chi answered. "Now it is time for you to reclaim your throne." He gestured to the litter.

It was a long trip. They angled to the southeast, making for New York City and its harbor, for Renno had decided that they would take a ship back to Wilmington, then travel by land through North Carolina to the mountains and beyond. That way Beth could see her father and decide with him what they would do with the Huntington shipping business. New York, being near enough to Philadelphia for a fairly quick side trip, would allow Renno to deliver the British documents to the officials of the United States, preferably George Washington.

The first snow came when they were skirting the Catskill Mountains to the south, and Renno was reminded once more of Beth's love for nature. She was thrilled as the big, silent flakes came floating down, one by one at first, from a leaden sky. And she cried out in delight when, the next morning, she pushed back her sleeping skins and looked out on a white world.

The wilderness seemed to be a tonic for her. She was walking now without the aid of the crutches. One night she tossed them onto the fire and watched them burn.

Now that their way was sprinkled by white settlements, towns, and villages, El-i-chi used some of the money he had brought with him to buy clothing, whiteman's style, for the three of them. More money went for supplies, and still more to pay the fare for a fifty-mile ride in a coach into New York City.

Beth, still very thin after her months of wilderness living and her illness, was nonetheless radiant with health and happiness. The only lingering sign of her near brush with death was a tendency to stumble when her right foot did not quite get the message to move, but that was occurring less frequently. When Renno told her that she and El-i-chi would stay in New York City while he made a trip to Philadelphia, she insisted upon going along.

"I want you to consult a white doctor while I'm gone," Renno said.

"Nonsense," she said. "Here is my doctor." She patted El-i-chi on the shoulder, then leaned to kiss Renno. "And this is my tonic."

And so it was that the three traveled together to Philadelphia by coach, taking two rooms in an inn at night, husband and wife disagreeing as to the comfort of the beds, with Renno preferring to sleep on the floor but sleeping in the bed for the luxury and pleasure of being beside his wife.

Through newspapers and conversations along the way the three travelers learned that a constitution had been agreed upon in September by the men gathered in Philadelphia. It was basically the strong instrument that George Washington had sought. Ratification by the states, however, was still in some doubt. In Philadelphia Renno discovered that Washington had expressed the desire to return to private life—although all felt he was destined to be the first president—and had returned to Mount Vernon. Renno inquired of other men and found that the venerable statesman Benjamin Franklin was in the city. Renno's only objective was to hand over the British documents and his information to someone responsible and then to be about his own private business.

In 1787 Franklin was eighty years old, and his face showed the marks of good living. A bit portly, he could still move with relative ease and was extremely curious when he rose to greet two young men who looked quite comfortable in their serviceable clothing and a woman whose beauty pleased him, even at his age. He had always had an eye for feminine beauty.

"It is indeed you, my friend," he enthused, taking Renno's hand. Renno introduced El-i-chi and Beth. Beth, with a polite curtsy, caused Renno to smile. "I have heard so much about you, Dr. Franklin," she said, with her best smile.

"I pray, child, that you were hearing it from discreet folk," Franklin said, returning her smile and then escorting her to a chair, leaving El-i-chi and Renno to find their own seats.

"I have information for General Washington about British intentions," Renno stated, getting right to the point, for he had had enough of riding in closed coaches, of crowded streets—of so-called civilization in general. "I know few men that I would trust with it."

"I am honored," Franklin said, inclining his head.

The account was brief. Franklin was impressed by the young man's terseness, which still allowed for clarity of statement and contained all pertinent information. He asked only a few questions and then, putting on his glasses, glanced through the documents.

"The number of troops in any given British fort is, of course, not constant," he mused. "But interesting. Interesting." He looked up. "So the architect of this devilish little scheme to rouse the Indians on our northwest frontier is dead?"

"He is dead," Renno confirmed.

"There will be another to take his place, I suppose." Franklin sighed.

"Yes," Renno said.

"I will see to it that the general gets this information by trusted messenger," Franklin promised. "If I were a bit younger, I'd take it to him myself. He has good cooks down there in Virginia."

"Thank you," Renno said, starting to rise.

"Please don't hurry," Franklin said. "Aside from the fact that your, uh, wife adds a pleasant decorative touch to these aging premises, I like a good story as well as anyone, and I'd like to hear about your adventures."

Renno mused that even the greatest of white men

shared the urge to hear a rousing tale with a Seneca warrior. It was told, and then a meal was taken, and at the table Renno asked questions.

"Of course, he got what he wanted in Philadelphia," Franklin said, speaking of Washington. "The weight of the war rested on his shoulders, and he carried it. Now the fate of this new nation rests largely with him, even if he is an unwilling king."

"King?" Beth asked.

"Excuse me. A manner of speaking, not intended to be disrespectful." Franklin sipped wine and sighed. "It is no secret that I advised against a single head of government. I spoke in the convention for an executive committee and for a legislature of only one chamber."

"But General Washington is the logical choice for president," Beth said.

"But will there be a man as worthy as Washington in the next generation?" Franklin asked. "Alas, young lady, times of crisis have seemed to generate their own great leaders. In times of peace . . ." He shook his head. "Yes, with George as president we will prosper, and this government—assuming that George has his way and influences the states to ratify this constitution—will be administered well for a course of years. He has already started to work rather quietly on those who opposed the constitution. I overheard him tell Patrick Henry that the alternate to adoption of the constitution is anarchy. Who can fail to heed George when he speaks? He has written that we must either choose the constitution or risk disunion. They'll listen. They'll listen in South Carolina, New York, Georgia, and Massachusetts. We'll have our constitution, and a government of a chief executive, the court, and a bicameral legislature, and the force of George's personality will keep it working well for a long time." Franklin paused and sipped his wine.

"And then?" Beth asked.

"It can only end in despotism, as other forms of government have ended before us, when the people become so corrupted as to need despotic government, being incapable of any other."

"Oh, dear," Beth said. "Is the outlook that gloomy?"

"Young lady," Franklin responded with a sad smile, "I have been a wick cutter in a candle factory, a printer, and I once spent thirty hours in a storm just getting across New York Bay. I have swum the Thames. I have done some writing, and I drew down lightning from the sky. I have been postmaster, politician, and ambassador. I saw the first balloon ascension, which brought the first man into the heavens alive, and I have been a sort of midwife to the birth of a new nation. But nothing I have experienced has convinced me that human nature has changed. Power corrupts. Although you will not see it in your lifetimes, your descendants will find cause to curse all those in Philadelphia and all those who later ratified this strong document, for, except in times of great crisis, government attracts petty men unable to achieve against the competition of their more energetic and ambitious fellows in private fields."

There was a silence.

Franklin finally chuckled. "But I *am* being gloomy. Let us drink one final toast to the great ideal for which we have fought. Let us pray, if that is your personal inclination, that I am wrong." He lifted his glass. "May this great land birth us a George Washington in each future generation."

Bundled against the cold, Renno, El-i-chi, and Beth stood on the deck of a schooner leaving New York Harbor and beating its way into an early winter storm. Beth, snug in the cabin with the man she loved, scarcely noticed when the open sea was reached and the ship began to be tossed and battered.

The storm lasted for three days and three nights, so little progress had been made. Wilmington seemed as far away as ever, but then, with a favoring wind and light seas, the watery miles dissolved behind them while the restless El-i-chi earned the title of champion arm wrestler on board. As for Beth and Renno, there seemed to be an unspoken pact between them to talk of the past, not the future, except when they spoke of Little Hawk and Renna. They had been able to obtain only negative news of the *Seneca Warrior*. The *Warrior* had not been seen in New York Harbor, but that was not unexpected, for she would have sailed directly to Wilmington if she had escaped the Gulf of St. Lawrence and the British men-of-war offshore.

The rest of the voyage was quite pleasant. Winter had not descended to the South, so fair skies and balmy breezes saw them into the Cape Fear River. The first sight that greeted them—after the houses on the bluff in Wilmington—were the top spars of a ship very much like the *Warrior*.

"Oh, Renno!" Beth squealed when they were near enough to identify definitely the graceful lines of the *Warrior's* hull. "We have a ship left, after all."

Beth was the first down the gangplank, and Renno watched her run, skirts flying, toward the *Warrior*, which was berthed in front of the Huntington office. He heard her cry out in pleasure as Cedric Huntington emerged from the office, did a double take at the flying woman, and moved swiftly to take his daughter in his arms.

Billy the Pequot leaped a dangerous distance down from the *Warrior's* deck, shouting a greeting as Renno and El-i-chi neared, and Moses Tarpley ran down the gangplank. Stevedores were off-loading cargo from the ship.

"Farming tools," Billy the Pequot said, noting Renno's gaze. "Guns. A highly profitable cargo. We've been to England and back."

Cedric Huntington, Beth clinging to his arm, was approaching. There were tears on his cheeks as he pumped Renno's hand. "I say," he managed, almost overcome with his emotion. "I say."

"Renno, look!" Beth was beaming. "We're in business. Captain Tarpley took the *Warrior* to England, and he arrived there with rice and indigo prices at their highest in years."

"We must drink to this reunion," Huntington announced. "Everyone, come. Moses and Billy, you too."

Inside, glass in hand, Huntington's toast was brief and heartfelt. "Thank you, my son, for bringing my precious daughter back to me." Renno glanced quickly at Beth. One thing they had discussed was how she would break the news to her father that she was wife to a Seneca warrior without, as the saying went, the benefit of clergy.

El-i-chi chose to sleep in the Huntington offices, using the cot abandoned by Cedric Huntington when his fortunes had turned for the good. Huntington drove them in an elegant surrey drawn by two handsome bays to a fine house on the bluff. He was expansive, looking at both Beth and Renno with pride. Beth quickly informed her father of her new status, so she and Renno were shown to the choice bedroom overlooking the river and told to rest before dinner.

Alone, Beth came to hug Renno. "He took it well, the old darling. He said he couldn't think of a finer man to have for a son-in-law."

"So," Renno said.

"Don't play the Indian," she chided teasingly. "He did request that we quietly and unobtrusively ratify the marriage—as North Carolina is going to ratify the constitution—with a minister."

Renno, having done the same for Emily, had no objection. He nodded.

"Isn't it a beautiful house?" Beth now asked, sweeping away with a swirl of skirts to examine the four-poster bed and to look out the window at the view of the river. "Look, Little Hawk and Renna will have such a wonderful garden in which to play."

Renno was silent.

She turned and saw his face. "Renno? I'm so sorry," she said, coming to put her arms around him and press her face to his chest. "I just got carried away. I'm so pleased that Moses and Billy got the *Warrior* back and that my father got a cargo and did so well with it. You are my husband, of course, and I will go with you, wherever that is."

"It is a fine house," Renno agreed.

"We will leave when you're ready."

"We will speak of it," Renno said, turning to look out the window.

Beth stood, her face solemn. Then she saw a large wardrobe and moved to open it. "He's brought all my clothes."

Renno turned and smiled to see perhaps two dozen dresses hanging in the wardrobe.

"I'm going to have a hot bath," Beth declared. "Steaming hot, with real soap. And then I'm going to put on my prettiest dress and let you escort me down to dinner, where I am going to be a shameless glutton."

She called a maid and ordered a bath to be prepared. Renno stood looking out the window, to the west.

The evening meal was a veritable feast, even though it had been prepared on such short notice. The roasted duck was to El-i-chi's liking. Renno ate little. Cedric Huntington was full of questions, and the only way to answer all of them was to tell, once again, all that had happened. He was not much in the mood for story-telling, so when he left something out, either Beth or El-i-chi filled in.

Huntington was especially intrigued by Hodano and his magic. "Do you actually believe, Renno, that the man deflected arrows?"

"My eyes believed it," Renno replied.

" 'starordinary," Huntington said. "It is said that the island witch doctors in the Caribbean can work magic. I suppose an Indian medicine man could too. . . ." But it was clear that he did not believe in Hodano's mystic powers.

Huntington's face glowered as he heard of his daughter's near brush with death. "You see, young lady," he admonished, "such things happen when one goes to places where one has no business. I should never have let you go to Canada. All my fault."

Renno had said enough. The story of Beth's recovery and the trip back to Wilmington was told by Beth and El-i-chi, speaking in turn. In bed he clung to Beth tightly for a long time, silent, and at last their heated blood found outlet in love. And then Beth slept.

Cedric Huntington had made an arrangement to have a private wedding ceremony performed in three days' time. Meanwhile he planned a fête to introduce his daughter and her fiancé to his new friends in Wilmington. He brought formal clothing to Renno on the day of the affair.

"Hope they fit, my boy," he said. "Probably be all right except, perhaps, in the chest. If it's tight there, we'll have one of the maids let it out a bit."

When Huntington had left the room, Renno picked up the swallowtail coat, examined it, fingered its material, and tossed it onto the bed. He left the house by the back door and found El-i-chi on the wharf, talking with Billy the Pequot.

"Tarpley and Huntington have arranged for another cargo," El-i-chi said. "The ship will be going back to England soon. Billy has asked if I'd like to go along."

"No," Renno said, so sharply that El-i-chi looked at him with some amazement.

"I told him," El-i-chi said easily, "that I would be heading west, before the full cold of winter, I hope."

"Yes," Renno agreed. "Come."

He led the way into the Huntington warehouse, to the spot where their meager belongings had been left. The buckskins were wrinkled and somewhat soiled, but the clothing was his, and of him.

A fiddler was playing lively jigs in the parlor of the Huntington house. Beth, in an emerald-green gown, cut low to show her well-tanned skin in décolletage, was wondering where Renno was. His suit had been lying in a heap on the bed, where he had tossed it. She had straightened it, and it was still there, but Renno was nowhere in sight.

When he appeared, she gasped in surprise, and then laughed as she ran to meet him. He stood, El-i-chi at his side, just inside the parlor. He was dressed in his buckskins, his face painted, as was El-i-chi's.

"Good for you," she whispered, taking his arm. "I don't blame you a bit, although I was curious to see how you'd look in formal wear. You would have been very handsome."

Renno grunted.

"All right," Beth conceded. "Your point is taken. Please forgive me and my father. I for one have no desire to change you. Believe me?"

Renno grunted again.

"Yes, well," Beth said, looking around, her smile genuine as she saw shock and disapproval registering on the guests' faces. "Come along, then, and meet my father's friends."

She led Renno into the room. El-i-chi followed. "Forgive me," she said to the disapproving faces, "if I don't remember all of your names just yet, but this is Renno, and his brother, El-i-chi. Renno is my husband."

Cedric Huntington, obviously embarrassed, stepped forth to give the names of his Wilmington guests. The first extended his hand after some hesitation. Renno, his face expressionless, took it, gave it one shake, and dropped it. The next man nodded his head but did not extend his hand. Beth felt Renno tense. Anger flooded into her.

"My dear Mr. Bellamy," she said evenly to the man who had refused to shake Renno's hand, "not long ago I sat at table with my husband and Dr. Benjamin Franklin. Dr. Franklin shook my husband's hand when we arrived and when we left. George Washington has also taken my husband's hand in his. I can therefore understand why *you* are reluctant to do so, since you must consider yourself inferior and not worthy of taking the hand that has been grasped by the likes of Franklin and Washington."

"I say!" Huntington exploded.

With a wry grin El-i-chi poked out his hand to Bellamy, who had refused to shake Renno's hand. "I, too, have shaken hands with George Washington," he said cheerily. "Moreover, this is the hand I use to scalp my enemies."

"I *say*!" Huntington gasped.

Chapter XVI

There was an air of tension in the Huntington parlor as El-i-chi stood, now unsmiling, his hand thrust out to a portly businessman named Bellamy. The fact that two wild Indians were there in civilized company, their persons heavy with weapons, was beyond Huntington's ability to cope. He looked wildly around for a way to defuse the situation, but it was Nathan Ridley, with his wife, Peggy, at his side, who came to Huntington's rescue.

"And those enemies, Cousin," Nate said, taking El-i-chi's hand warmly, "were our common enemies."

Peggy smiled up at El-i-chi and asked, "Is everyone on Nate's great-aunt Betsy's side of the Ridley family as handsome as these two brothers?"

"We're honored to have you back, Renno," Nate said, grasping his cousin's arm. He turned to face the startled assembly of Wilmington's finest. "Renno's Seneca were among the few tribes that did not fight on the side of the British, and only recently the Seneca and the Cherokee stood against an invasion by Spanish-led Chickasaw."

A pretty woman of middle years pushed forward, extended her hand toward Renno, and spoke in a recognizable French accent. "We are pleased to have you in our city."

"Thank you," Renno answered in French. "The pleasure is mine."

The moment of tension had passed. Bellamy, seeing that he stood alone with his prejudice, grudgingly put out his hand and Renno shook it without a word. Renno's blue eyes bored into Bellamy's.

"Now that the honored couple are together," Huntington shouted, "they shall lead the dance!"

Beth winked at Renno. "You will consent to put aside your weapons, won't you?"

Renno smiled, laid his weapons in the hands of a servant, took his place with Beth on his arm, and treated Wilmington society to the sight of a beautiful, flame-haired lady and a tall, bronzed warrior in full frontier regalia moving gracefully through the movements of a pavane. Known to some as the peacock dance, it seemed at first incongruous for an Indian warrior to perform the steps. Beth herself was pleasantly surprised when Renno danced as nicely as any of the men, strutting and skipping with the best of them.

Her face flushed with exertion and her green eyes shining with happiness, she seized an opportunity to lead Renno out onto the veranda overlooking the river. The night was pleasantly cool. She clung to Renno's arm and sighed with contentment.

"Your eyes look to the west," she noted after a few minutes of silence.

"I am torn as I've never been torn before," he admitted.

"There is no need."

He turned her to face him. She was beautiful in the light of the oil lamps coming through the glass of the

French doors. "This is your place," he said. "Here, or in England. You are to be dressed in fine clothing, to have servants tend your needs, to mix with others of your race."

"No," she contradicted vehemently. "No, no, no! Don't start. Don't *ever* say such things." She took his arms in her hands and shook him. "Are you ready to leave this very minute? If you give the word, I will change from this fine dress into clothing more suited for travel, and then I will be with you."

"The wife of a Seneca warrior, even a sachem, has no servants," Renno reminded her.

"Ena has no servants."

"Ena is Ena."

"Am I not her equal?" she asked, but there was no anger, no accusation in her voice. "I held my own, I was no burden when we traveled so far to the west. Even when I was injured, I recovered quickly and walked my own path. And, like Ena, I fought by your side against the Spanish."

Renno had nothing to say.

"You see me one way tonight, Renno. You see me as a white lady, in velvets, simpering and smiling because that is what is expected of me in this situation. But have I not seen you in white-man's clothing? Have I not heard you imitate William's English accent perfectly? You've played your different roles, Husband, just as I sometimes play mine."

"Life in the wilderness is reality, not a role."

"So," she said. "We will travel into winter as we reach the mountains. We should leave as quickly as possible. A day, maybe two—time to accustom my father to the idea. He'll fare well. The success of the voyage of the *Seneca Warrior* has given him new heart. He has a good ship's captain in Moses Tarpley, and he has Billy."

"Think well," Renno warned.

"Are you trying to wriggle out of marrying me?" she teased, but there was genuine apprehension in her eyes.

"In my heart and in the eyes of my manitous, we are married," he reassured her.

"Don't play at words with me. Damn you, Renno, if you think you can get rid of me . . . if you think you're going to go traipsing off without me . . . if you think I'm going to allow you to go home without me and leave me here to wonder how many pretty little Indian girls are flipping their cute little buckskin-clad rumps at you—"

Renno laughed and pulled her to him.

"We'll stop in Knoxville and get Renna," she said excitedly. "I'll be new at being a mother, but Ena and Toshabe will help me learn. We'll make a real home for your children, Renno, and while you teach them the lore of the Seneca, I can teach them all the things they'll need to know to live in white society."

"You have always been twice too smart for me," Renno said, smiling.

She made a moue. "False modesty. Do you think I love you because of these?" She pinched his bicep muscle. "Don't you realize what a desirable man you are? Where in the world could I find a man who lives on his own resources in a virgin wilderness, is deadly fierce when he is in the right, protects himself and his family against human animals and the animals of the forest, and yet knows more about the affairs of this nation than most politicians—plus be able to dance the pavane?"

"Even a Seneca is pleased by flattery." Renno laughed.

"Truth," she said. "I warn you, however, that I am not going to be content to live forever in a longhouse and cook over an open fire. I won't try to change you, for if you were not the man you are, I wouldn't love you so, but I'm sure you, as well as I, want to better life for Renna and Little Hawk. You have spoken to me of Se-quo-i, who wants a better life for his people, the Cherokee. We can work with him, and with others like him. There is no reason for the Seneca or the Cherokee to join other long-gone Indian tribes on the scrap heap of history. We can work together."

"Yes," Renno agreed.

"So that's settled," Beth said, kissing him warmly. "Shall we go back in and think of something new to shock the gentry?"

Renno noted, with wry amusement, that El-i-chi was holding court for two very pretty young girls in voluminous skirts. Others were dancing the new and energetic American jigs. Cedric Huntington was expounding on something, gesturing emphatically, his face ruddy from good food and good drink. Renno tried to imagine Renna in such a setting, dressed in frills and laces, her face powdered and hair cunningly curled and coiffed. An odd uneasiness came over him, for he could not picture Renna—who, in his mind, looked very much like her mother—taking the arm of any one of the young men in that room, not even a man like Nate Ridley. He recalled being with Emily soon after their marriage, lying on a mossy bank beside a clear stream . . . the sky puffed with white clouds, the air balmy, and a lazy butterfly feeding on late-spring flowers nearby. He looked at Beth and realized the reason for his odd feeling. He was a man caught between two ways of life, just as his own children—and any children he might produce with Beth—would be. He had a sudden longing for limitless spaces and remembered the big skies of the Southwest—the unending plains where a man was as free as his spirit.

A cry of alarm and the sound of something falling brought him out of his thoughts. He turned swiftly to see Cedric Huntington lying on the floor. A woman screamed. Nate Ridley, who had been standing near Huntington, knelt beside the older man and put his finger on the side of Huntington's neck to feel his pulse. Beth went white and rushed to kneel beside Nate. A surgeon who was a guest pushed to the fallen man and began to give crisp orders. Renno and El-i-chi helped Nate and another man carry Huntington to his bed, where the surgeon loosened the old man's clothing and punched and probed. Huntington was breathing with difficulty.

"What is it?" Beth asked anxiously. "Will he be all right?"

The surgeon shrugged and looked grim. "We will know more, Mistress Beth, with the morning."

When Renno went downstairs, the parlor had emptied. Only two couples remained, Nate and Peggy and another couple. Nate expressed his sympathy and gave Renno a warm leave-taking.

Peggy said, "If there's anything we can do, anything at all . . ."

El-i-chi came down the stairs and shook his head. Renno did not have to ask. "They do not want my medicine dances." He grinned awkwardly, trying to lighten the moment. He tapped his chest, over his heart. "His spirit flutters, trying to get out of the body."

With the dawn of a crisp and beautiful late-autumn day, Huntington still lived. Propped on his pillows, his face sallow, his breathing labored, he was able to speak, to assure Beth and Renno that he was fine, just a little weak. Beth, her face still streaked with her tears of the night, patted her father's hand. "You're going to be fine," she promised. "And you'll have to hurry and get well, because there's work to be done. I'll not have you lollygagging around in bed."

"Always the slave driver," Huntington moaned.

The surgeon motioned Beth and Renno from the room. In the hallway, out of Huntington's hearing, the surgeon said, "He needs rest. Keep him absolutely motionless. Soups and liquids only."

"Then you think he will—" Beth couldn't complete the question, which by its nature was a statement of her fears that her father would not live.

"I think he'll pull through if we keep him absolutely still." The surgeon tapped his chest in the manner that El-i-chi had used.

As it happened, the surgeon had received his medical training in France and was familiar with the work of famous French and Italian physicians. "The heart is a strong muscle," he said. "It can, in time, repair itself where there is damage."

"How long?" Beth asked.

"I don't want him to lift a finger for at least two weeks," the surgeon said.

"And then?"

The surgeon shrugged.

"I need to know the truth," Beth said flatly, looking at Renno with desperation in her eyes.

"I have seen men recover from such an incident and live for years," the surgeon said. "But only when they obeyed orders. He can get out of bed in, oh, a month, if he behaves himself and if the good Lord wills it. In three, maybe four months he can take short walks on level ground."

"Thank you," Beth said weakly, her eyes down.

Alone with Renno she looked up, her eyes swimming with tears. "Oh, Renno!"

"I know," he said.

"Oh, damn, damn."

"He is your father."

"I know, and you, too, have your duty. I know you have to go, to see your children and to be with your people."

"As your duty now is to your father," he finished.

"Oh, double damn my duty," she wailed, sobbing her way into his arms. "You will stay, please, long enough to know—to know—"

"I will stay until we're sure that he is on the road to recovery," Renno promised.

And in spite of Beth's supervision of the servants tending Huntington, in spite of rising to check on her father constantly during the night, the nights were sweet and lingering, warm with their love. It was as if both wanted to store the feel, the touch, and the essence of the other.

Then she stood on the front porch with Renno. El-i-chi waited on the brick sidewalk.

"My heart goes with you," she said to her husband.

"Then I will use it as my own, for much of mine stays with you."

"We will merge them, whatever the distance," she said. "And I'll come to you, Renno. I'll come to you if you don't come to me first."

On the small ferry that took them across Cape Fear, El-i-chi remarked, "The old man could live many years."

It was not to Renno's taste, but travel in the mode of the white man made things simpler until they had passed into the foothills of the western mountains. The weather was kind to them. When they had at last passed all but the scattered homesteads of mountain men, they traveled light, now running, now walking, now pausing to hunt. As the mountains rose around them, they began to encounter scattered, isolated Cherokee lodges, where they paused to exchange news and be treated to a meal. Although great events had been happening in the United States, things were unchanged in the wilderness. The brothers topped the mountains, walking in a light covering of snow, and arrived in the growing town of Knoxville, wrapped in skins against the first serious winter cold.

Roy Johnson whooped with delight when he opened his front door to see them and dragged Renno into the house shouting, "Nora, look who's here!"

"I knew you'd be back," he told Renno, pounding him on the back. "And El-i-chi, you're looking good."

Nora came from the baby's room carrying Renna, who had been sleeping. The child was just over a year old, and she had Emily's corn silk hair and Renno's blue eyes.

"This is your father," Nora said. "Your da-da."

"Da-da," Renna echoed, reaching out her arms, if not for Renno himself, perhaps for the fringe of his buckskins. Renna seemed to be equally taken with Uncle El-i-chi.

Johnson went all out in his hospitality. The meal was rich and plentiful. Renna, jabbering in baby talk, put on a see-how-I-can-throw-my-food show. The story-telling began before the meal ended because Johnson was eager to hear all. When El-i-chi took his turn, nothing was lost in the telling. Nora took Renna to put her to bed and came back, her face stern. Johnson was catching Renno and El-i-chi up on news around home.

"Toshabe and Ena came, just a week or so ago, wasn't it, Nora? To see Renna. Toshabe looked as happy as a hog in a watermelon patch." He grinned. "How does it feel to have a stepfather?"

"I am happy for my mother's happiness," El-i-chi replied.

"Things have been pretty quiet otherwise," Johnson reported. "There's talk that comes seeping down of trouble up on the northwest frontier and across even to this frontier, but I reckon you know more about that than those who bring the news, Renno. No problems from the Chickasaw or Choctaw this year. There was a little bit of politicking during the Constitutional Convention, with some of the boys from Nashborough going up to Philadelphia. They didn't get any support up there for Franklin statehood, though. There'll be a state out here beyond the mountains someday, but my guess is it won't be called Franklin. More settlers come down and over the mountains all the time. More clearing. More planting. They must be bringing 'em over by the shipload. It's getting so crowded around here that I've been trying to convince Nora that we ought to make a move, farther west, but she won't hear of it."

"A shack in the woods is no place to rear a child," Nora said sharply.

When Renno spoke, his voice was soft and kind. "Renna goes with me," he said, "to her home."

Nora's face paled. "You can't be serious!"

Renno was silent.

"Renno," Johnson began, "I know how you feel—"

"She is my flesh, my daughter," Renno said softly.

"But the winter's here—" Nora said.

"So," Renno replied.

Nora turned to her husband. "Roy, please! You can't let him—"

Johnson shook his head sadly. "You knew the time would come. Renno is her father, Nora."

"Renno, please," Nora begged. "Not in the winter. Don't take her out there to— Wait until the spring, please."

"I know you love her," Renno soothed. "But I have been with her for mere hours. She must know her father."

"Nora, I'm afraid he's right," Roy said.

Nora leaped from her chair and ran from the room, sobbing.

"It'll be all right," Johnson promised. "It's just that she's become right fond of the child. And with Emily gone . . ."

"I know," Renno said.

Johnson took down a jug and drank alone, both El-i-chi and Renno politely refusing. After a long silence Renno said, "You spoke of moving away from the town. I can understand that. There is a place, within a short walk of the village, that would make a fine site for a cabin."

"Well, Renno, I appreciate the thought," Johnson replied, "and if it was just me, I wouldn't hesitate. 'Course, I'm still a so-called colonel in a militia that exists mostly on paper and in men's minds, but I wouldn't mind leaving Knoxville, have a few acres, do some good hunting. Two things: Nora, and the way the Cherokee and maybe even some of your Seneca would feel about a white man moving into their land and settling in."

"You are a friend," Renno said.

"Yep," Johnson agreed, nodding. "I guess Rusog would say the same, but then there'd come along another white family and see me and Nora living there in the heart of Cherokee lands, and they'd say, well, why not us?"

Nora was weeping as if her heart would break. Renna was prattling and having the time of her life, for she was bundled into furs and tucked into a carrying pack on Renno's back. Nora could see the tiny bit of her face that was exposed until Renno and El-i-chi turned a corner down the dirt street. It was cool, but not cold. Johnson took his wife's hand and led her back inside.

"We'll go out in the spring," he said, "and I'll do some hunting and you can spend a couple of weeks with both of them, with Renna and that wild grandson of ours too."

Hardwood trees still showed signs of lingering color, although the forest's floor was littered with oranges and reds. In a sign that Renno took to be favorable, a hawk kept pace with their journey, appearing often above them, his hunting cry riding down the wind to their ears. Then they were entering the village, to the usual welcome of children and the barking of dogs. The news of their arrival spread rapidly, so that by the time they reached the central compound, adults were gathering.

Toshabe stood outside the longhouse of her husband, Ha-ace the panther, with her arm around Ah-wa-o, until her two sons stood before her. Then, unable to maintain an Indian reserve any longer, she flung herself at them and embraced them quickly before turning her attentions to Renna, who had been sleeping but who awoke in Toshabe's arms and treated her grandmother to a smile.

"See how little attention we get," El-i-chi teased.

Ena came running lithely, Rusog not far behind, and

almost knocked El-i-chi down as she ran to embrace first him and then Renno.

Although Toshabe seemed absorbed in playing with her granddaughter, she was casting a look now and then at Ha-ace and then Renno.

Rusog greeted them with the arm clasp. And then Renno turned and walked to face the man who now shared a lodge with his mother. Ha-ace looked uncomfortable. Toshabe, giving Renna over to Ena, came to stand beside Ha-ace.

"Sachem," Ha-ace said, "it is belated, but I ask your approval and your blessings for that which I have done."

"You have them, and gladly," Renno said. "I have long respected you, Ha-ace." He smiled. "And it takes more than just a strong warrior and a good hunter to put that certain gleam into my mother's eyes."

Toshabe blushed.

Renno clasped Ha-ace's right arm, and beside him, El-i-chi clasped Ha-ace's left.

"Now there are three strong men in this family," Ena said.

"Then I count for nothing?" Rusog demanded.

"You *are* my family," Ena said, "but you are only a Cherokee." She laughed.

"I will show you who is only a Cherokee," Rusog pledged, slapping Ena playfully on her shapely haunch.

Ena laughed again.

"My son is missing," Renno noted, looking around eagerly.

"He will be here soon," Ena said. "He was away on a buffalo hunt."

Renno looked at her, puzzled.

"He's in good hands, with older boys, and only at the creek."

As if to prove her words, a whooping passel of small boys rushed up the slope from the direction of the creek, one small buckskin-and-fur bundle churning his short legs to keep up. Little Hawk burst onto the scene with a keen war cry, tossed aside his small bow, and launched himself at his father.

Now it was complete. His son and his daughter were together. He was with his mother, his sister, his brother, and his people. And yet he knew that if the pain Cedric Huntington had felt in the heart was more severe than his own, it must have been terrible indeed.

As it will now and again, summer seemed reluctant to abandon the area, returning to repel the northern chills that came to frost the browned grass. El-i-chi and a group of other young, unmarried warriors left for an extended hunt. Toshabe had arranged for two widows, both mature, one pleasantly fat, to give Renno's unused lodge a thorough cleaning. The happy, smiling fat widow came early to prepare the morning meal, tend to Renna, irritate Little Hawk with her mothering, and remind Renno by her sassy presence that his lodge was empty of one very important thing.

Toshabe had sensed the emptiness in her elder son and, with some careful questioning before El-i-chi went off into the woods, learned that her son had once again given his heart to a white woman. Of course, she remembered Beth Huntington. She did not judge. She was reminded that in the not-too-distant past, terminally ill old Indians had been allowed freely to give up their spirits and thus end their suffering. To see Renno caught in a situation where a dying old man kept him from the love of his heart was, to her, an injustice and a great sadness. But she was silent.

To most, Renno seemed to be happy and content. He took advantage of the beautiful weather to introduce the toddling Renna to the sweetness of the outdoors. Often he and his children would leave the village early and return late, with Renna asleep in his arms. Little Hawk, pretending that Renno was a horse, clung to his father's back.

Before the weather changed and gave way to the first serious cold in early December, Renno had sent a young warrior to Knoxville with letters: one to the Johnsons to assure them that Renna was adjusting to her new life, one to George Washington, and one very thick packet destined for Wilmington, far across the long, east-west distance of North Carolina.

On those cold nights when the wind howled and sleet pounded the roofs, Toshabe entertained in the lodge of Ha-ace. A few warriors at a time, the Seneca and Cherokee listened to Renno's accounts of the long journey and his analysis of the future. Despite Rusog's lack of love for the white man, he was the first to agree that to support the British attempt by causing trouble on the frontiers of the United States would be disaster.

Both Ena and Rusog were greatly relieved to learn that Renno had decided definitely not to reunite the Seneca by a migration northward at this time. Ena, knowing a bit of her brother's dilemma, had long feared that he would return after his visit to the homelands convinced that the manitous decreed reunion, and she had dared not face the question of how the divided loyalties caused by her being the Seneca wife of a Cherokee would be resolved. Rusog, of course, could not be expected to leave his own responsibilities to his people behind simply because Ena was Seneca and wanted to be with her family and her tribe.

In memory of Emily and out of deference to Beth's beliefs, Renno observed Christmas. His spirit was uneasy. His usual remedy for this condition was solitude. Not a day passed that he did not communicate with the manitous and the spirits of his fathers, but he had not purged himself with fasting and had not sought counsel in the solitude of the wilderness, for a long time.

"You and your sister will stay with your grandmother," he told Little Hawk one morning.

"I hunt with you," Little Hawk said pleadingly.

"Later, when the weather is better," Renno promised.

Toshabe understood and welcomed the active children into her lodge, where Ah-wa-o, having matured one more year, was like the flower of her name—a budding, striking young Seneca maid of fifteen summers. She, too, welcomed the chance to play with the lively children and, Renno was sure, would conspire with Toshabe to spoil them hopelessly.

"Before you go," Toshabe said, "there is the matter of Renna's presentation to the manitous."

"I have thought of that," Renno replied, knowing that the presentation involved, among other things, the ritual immersing of Renna into icy water. "She was not born among us."

"She has adapted well," Toshabe said. "She is Seneca."

"We will present her at a later date."

"Have you no faith in the manitous?" Toshabe asked. "Do you fear that your own daughter is not strong enough to be Seneca?"

Renno, who after all was sachem, gave his mother a stern look. Toshabe knew that she had pushed far enough.

"Nor will you do this thing in my absence," Renno said.

"No," Toshabe promised.

He traveled far before he found a place to his liking. Deep in the forest a small waterfall made its music. The ridge that spawned the cataract gave him shelter from a cold north wind. There was plentiful deadwood for his fire and good water to drink. For warmth he had the great bearskin, for comfort to his emptiness the memory of the laughter of his children and the sweet times with Emily, and the burning desire for Beth.

When he began his meditation, Beth occupied all his thoughts. Then, in the night, as he occasionally placed sticks on the fire and gazed at the night lights of the winter sky, he considered the situation in the far north and relived the time he had spent there. Beth took her place in his memories but did not dominate them as he sought meaning to what had happened there. Had his actions had any effect? Yes, for perhaps he had been instrumental in convincing Cornplanter to stand against the pressures to join cause with the British and Little Turtle. On the other hand, the deaths of Striking Snake, Caleb Burnhouse, and the others who had met their fates at the hands of a lone warrior far from home had had no effect, for they would already be replaced by others.

In the early morning hours he felt the heaviness of his responsibilities and asked the manitous why, *why* was it that he, Renno, always seemed to be called for reason after reason and taken away from his family and his people?

There was no answer, and soon that mood passed.

He fasted through a blustery day, snug inside his bearskin, warmed by his fire. With the night he felt cleansed and emptied. He praised the manitous for that which had been given him. Another night passed and another day, and he could feel the effects of his fasting now.

As another morning dawned, he wondered if there was no need for a spirit contact. Peace was in the land—at least in the land of the Cherokee—and the troubles of the young United States were far away and not his, except that the welfare of his people was inextricably tied to the welfare of the United States.

In the cold, small hours of his fourth night of fasting, he chanted under the brittle harshness of the stars, felt the chill, and sang out his determination to remain there until he had guidance—confirmation that he had been

either right or wrong in his decision not to try to reunite
the Seneca.

"I am blessed," he said, staring into the blackness
beyond the fire as writhing, smoky things emerged and
then coalesced into a tall, bronzed warrior, wearing the
ancient, traditional scalp lock of the Seneca.

"Renno," he breathed, not daring to move lest the
vision of his great-grandfather disappear, for it seemed to
waver and become fainter before it ultimately strengthened.

Strong blue eyes—he knew not how he could see the
color in the faint light of the fire—bored into his own. The
vision of his great-grandfather moved closer, seemed to be
close enough, beyond the small fire, to touch.

"Self-pity," the manitou said.

"Forgive me," Renno said.

"Have you not been told that your son will be a great
chief?"

"So," Renno said.

"Your life has been touched by sadness," the spirit
acknowledged. "But is that not the nature of orenda?"

"Guide me," Renno begged.

"Your lodge is warm and tight. Your children are
there."

"I hear, Great One," Renno said, and experienced an
almost overwhelming desire to rise and run to his son and
his daughter.

"Rest. Enjoy your rewards," the vision said, beginning to fade. "For—"

In the place of the spirit of the original white Indian
was a confused scene of blood and smoke. Renno heard
the boom of cannon, saw the puffs of smoke from their
muzzles, and heard the shriek of a dying man. He leaned
forward tensely for a clearer view, and in the midst of the
smoke and carnage there came a figure, his face hidden
beneath a cowl of wolverine's fur. The figure seemed to
float, disconnected, coming ever nearer. Renno's hand
sought his weapons.

"Hodano," Renno whispered as he felt himself drawn into the vision, becoming a part of it.

His right hand was empty and seemed to burn for contact with the spirit knife, the weapon that had served him so well against the evil shaman, but the knife had disintegrated and was now only dust. He faced the tall, cowled figure, from whose mouth now issued sounds not human. Renno floated strangely to his feet, hands empty of weapons, and moved forward with difficulty, as if he walked through quicksand. As the cowled figure wafted toward him, Renno saw the dull gleam of one dead, white eye and the forked serpent's tongue flicking. In the specter's hand was a tomahawk of fearsome dimensions—gleaming with a light not its own.

"Come, then," Renno challenged, his voice low, threatening. "Come to me, then."

He crouched, poised to sweep under the first blow of the awesome tomahawk, ready to use his pure heart and his strong hands against an evil that caused the hairs on his neck to tingle.

The battle sounds increased and then suddenly faded. All was still. All was blackness. Renno's eyes strained, and he willed the vision to return. He felt a great need to identify this site of such a shedding of blood, but what had been at best indistinct was now only darkness. He heard a sound like rushing water and recognized it as the sound of waves being parted by the prow of a swiftly moving ship. He felt the soft warmth of tropical air on his skin. Then there was nothing.

"Hold, manitous," Renno called in vain. "When is this to be? What will be my part in it? What will be the role of the Seneca?"

With a flutter of wings, a hunting owl swept overhead and broke the spell.

"What of my wife?" Renno whispered desperately.

He felt a warmth, as if summer had come, and his

heart leaped as Emily, in a white-woman's gown, stood across the fire smiling at him.

"My wife," Renno whispered, reaching out his arms.

The spirit's smile faded. Gone. She was gone. And her message was unclear to him.

"Wait, please wait," he whispered.

He felt a warmth at his waist, and his hand went to the spirit knife. He drew it and held it before him, and just as it had glowed when he had faced Hodano in Cornplanter's council longhouse, it glowed now with a greenish light. In the glow he saw the face of Ghonka, who had given the knife to him. Then, with a sharp crack that filled the night, the knife shattered into tiny flakes of flint.

The voice was Ghonka's, deep, growling. "It has done its work, as you, my son, have done yours."

The sun found him awake, sitting huddled under the bearskin, dazed and confused. War would come, but where? And for whom? His son would live to be a man and in the traditions of his fathers, become a great sachem. But the questions were endless. Emily, in white, the white of the white God's heaven? Were they one and the same, the place of eternal peace for white and Indian?

"You tell me something, and yet you tell me little!" he shouted, the echoes reverberating from the sides of the canyon. "I will fight the wars, for that is my duty. I will lead my people, for that, too, is my duty, but what about *me*? What of my *living* wife, for I have had two, and one is dead."

He heard no sound, only something inside his mind—the golden, ringing laugh of Beth. And then something dropped just in front of his knees as he sat, wrapped in the bearskin. The thing fell with a thud, and a freshly killed rabbit in its winter fur, still bleeding from talon marks and ready to be eaten, twitched once and was still, and from above came the cry of a hawk. "Brother," he said, looking up in time to see the great black hawk soar away.

*   *   *

"We will make for you, my young warrior, the most fierce, the most ugly, the most frightening false face ever seen," vowed the Cherokee Se-quo-i as his knife moved skillfully. Little Hawk, entranced, watched with wide eyes. "Soon it will be the feast of the new beginning," Se-quo-i continued, "and the son of a great sachem must contribute his own false face."

"I won't be scared of it," Little Hawk boasted. "But maybe Renna will."

"I think not," Renno said.

Renno's lodge was warm and snug in spite of a snowstorm outside. Renna was sleeping, and Little Hawk's eyes were getting heavy. Se-quo-i had come to eat with his friend Renno and stayed to amuse the boy.

When Little Hawk fell asleep, he did it with a suddenness that made both Renno and Se-quo-i laugh, for he simply toppled over, his head falling on Se-quo-i's leg. Renno put him to bed, tucking him into the warm furs.

Se-quo-i's carving was bearing fruit. A face was emerging from the cedar block he had chosen for his gift to Little Hawk. The twisted face leered at Renno, one eye blank, the other staring, and it seemed, in the rough cut, unfinished cheek, that the face had been badly burned.

Hodano, Renno thought, but he did not voice his surprise.

When Se-quo-i finished the false face, it did not look like Hodano at all.